THE
WATER
OF
AWAKENING

A Tale of the Eternal Dream

By
David Van Dyke Stewart

Cover art by Kerem Beyit

Cover design by David V. Stewart

Interior design, including capital art, by David V. Stewart

Map by David V. Stewart

Author photo by Leah Valentine

Fonts used in this work:

Body: *Adobe Garamond Pro*

Headline: *Cinztel* by Natanael Gama

Chapter headings: *Trajan Pro 3*

"Raven Cap" by David V. Stewart, based on *Erbar Initialen* by Jakob Erbar

For Houkje, for letting me dream, and
For Rone, who is a dream.

CONTENTS

THE WATER
OF AWAKENING

NORTHMARCH
AND THE
PETTY KINGDOMS
IN THE FOURTH DOMINION

The
NORTH Sea

FROSTBACK MOUNTAINS

BERGAN

TWIN DELTA

FISKERHOL

GOLICE

MOON HILLS

SOLBORG

The Half-Sea

SHARDISH RIVER

STRANDAM

SHARDISH RIVER

GREENFELD

Ulfar MOUNTAINS

THRUDDEL

HOSTENT

BLUE RIVER

THE WINDING WATER

KIWALL PASS

The Fay WASTES

The
FAY
LANDS

SKJOLLANDING

HUNTER'S LAKE

ATALTHALD

The ORCISH DRY LANDS

The Fay WASTES

I. The Farmwife and the Volva

HELGA WAS a young woman grown from an impetuous and difficult to satisfy girl. Even into adolescence she was mockingly called "Helga the Lion," on account of her brash and arrogant attitude. She was, as a girl, willing to say anything to anyone (including the Jarl, which got her into trouble more than once) and only slightly less willing to use her fists when words seemed inadequate. The people of the little hold of Greenfeld often blamed these flaws on Helga's grandfather, who had a reputation his entire life for foolhardiness and a quick temper. He was known only as Brick, as he had been a stranger to the hold when he arrived at the age of thirty, and his many flaws were frequently forgiven because he possessed a propensity for heroism that exceeded his propensity to brawl with men who should be his friends. It was said when Helga found herself in trouble that Brick had imparted more than his red hair to her, but as a girl, she did not understand that this was not meant to be an insult to his memory; when people said these things, for she loved her grandfather more than anyone in her life.

Even though she eventually grew out of a great deal of her worst behaviors, the memories remained and the title of "lion" stuck to her like an embarrassing scar, which left many of her relationships strained longer than they otherwise would have been. As a young woman, it would have been accurate to say she was tolerated more than liked, especially after the death of her grandfather, Brick the Brave.

Her parents were, as a result, quite happy to see her wed Erling, a tall and homely man of good standing in the little hold of Greenfeld. Erling was the second son of the second son of a Jarl. He had a good name but little else, and was known to be quiet and reserved, even passive, which was not a well-liked trait among the boastful northmen. Helga's parents were unsure their daughter would agree to marry such a man, for her expectations as a girl were lofty, and they thought her beauty in maidenhood was not so profound (though she was indeed comely - as most northern women are, with straight hair, bright blue eyes and fair skin that blushed easily) as to command the fulfillment of such lofty expectations.

They never knew, however, of the secret love she held in heart for Erling, or of what he had done to earn that love. The knowledge of the trinkets he made, the poems he wrote, and the great task he undertook for her (which would make even a proud man sit quietly for the telling) she held fast within herself and revealed to nobody, for those things humbled the prideful girl that she was, and she also secretly feared that such knowledge would make Erling a man too great for her to possess.

And so it was that her wedding was a moment of great triumph to her heart, though to all who witnessed it, the affair was simple and civil. Such joy, however, was fleeting. Before their first winter as man and wife, Erling was stricken with a profound and unexplainable sickness.

It began as a bad cold, but soon the man was bedridden and could not work his field or tend to his livestock. His voice became so hoarse, and his breathing so labored, he lost the power of speech. The village doctor was at a loss, and his arts of healing, passed down by the gods and his ancestors for so long, did nothing to alleviate Erling's pain or discomfort, or to give him enough strength to walk more than a few paces from the bed. Erling's care fell to Helga, a burden she was more than willing to bear, though it pained her to see a man she considered so great to be bedridden.

Though Helga was not well-loved, the people of Greenfeld were kindhearted and took turns working Erling's fields while his health continued to deteriorate. The women helped Helga with her daily tasks, taking the sheep to pasture and back, when they were not busy with their own flocks. Though they were good-natured, people in small towns have a way of gossiping, and the women in Greenfield were particularly adept at making gossip that was meant to be heard.

"Poor Erling, so quiet. I doubt he has the gall to face the fever."

"Poor Helga. To still be young and saddled with the care of the infirm. I wouldn't trade places."

"It's good she didn't end up with child. There are a few good men who would marry her yet, once Erling passes on."

Some of these things got back to Helga, and she resented the words, though she never said so, as she was thankful for the help in the growing of crops and the tending of the house, and never let a favor pass without giving back some form of thanks. In her spare time, she would work her wheel and loom and make what cloth she could for those who came to help her. Most of the townsfolk would accept these gifts, not wanting to shame the proud woman, but would, without telling Helga, sell them and give the money to Bjorn the trader, who would then give Helga a much better price for her crops when he came around to buy them.

This went on for some time. Erling could eat and drink but do little else, and nothing anybody tried seemed to make him better. Helga loved him, but knew he would die without something being done to help him. Just what that thing was, she had no idea.

*

One day, while Helga was tending to her husband, she inclined her ear to the window and listened to two of the townswomen outside, Runa and Astrid, who had brought their children by to feed and tend to Helga's sheep.

"She fancies herself a volva, then?" Runa said.

"I think so, yes."

"Any god she follows?"

"I don't know. Probably Nostera. She has a marvelous assortment of trinkets," Astrid said.

"All of them enchanted to bring vitality, I suppose."

"Some. Some are just pretty to hold."

"I'm not buying that sort of rubbish."

"They're pretty. Who cares if they don't bring health? I was thinking of hinting to Gunnar to get me something. I have a third on the way, and he'll want to buy me a present. Oh! Don't tell yet."

Helga stood up above Erling's bed and poked her head out of the window.

"Hey there! What did you say?" she said.

"Don't be eavesdropping!" Astrid said. "You forget what you heard. I haven't even told Gunnar yet."

"They're my eaves," Helga said. "And when am I going to tell Gunnar anything? I want to know about the volva."

"She's just some old woman," Runa said. "She's down at Bjorn's if you want to talk to her."

Helga was worried about leaving Erling, but he had fallen asleep and was breathing calmly, and Helga had not seen him turn worse in a long time. She laced up her shoes and closed the door, leaving her husband sleeping on his bed. She rushed past the townswomen and up the lane to where Bjorn's big house was. It was the largest building in the main town of Greenfeld, making up a full side of the town's central square. It had a large, open-roofed area attached to the main building where the trader kept most of his goods and did most of his business, like a sort of open-air market. Bjorn stood leaning against a pillar as Helga approached, scratching his thick black beard and watching a few village women look at dishes and cups on a table. He noticed Helga approaching and waved a big, sun-tanned hand at her.

"Helga the Lion," he said. "Out for a prowl?"

"Where is the volva?" Helga said as she approached.

Bjorn smiled and pointed to a grove near the central well. "Nice enough woman, even if she is a bit harsh on the ears. Met her in Skjallanding a few weeks past. Beware."

"I'm always 'ware."

"She's clever and greedy. Not a good combo."

"You would know."

Bjorn laughed his familiar laugh at her back as she turned away from him. "You'll live up to old Brick yet!"

Helga ignored him. As she passed the town well, she threw in a copper coin and said a small prayer to Denarius and to Nostera, the gods of wealth and health. She paused and went back, then threw in another copper coin, saying one more prayer to Verbus (which most of the townspeople properly called Grim), the god of luck.

"Looking for good health?" a dry voice croaked. Helga saw an old woman with dingy grey hair like ropes about her shoulders, reclining on a rock beneath an oak tree that, though it probably had her beat in terms of age, met the old woman well for gnarled features. She wore a fur over her shoulders, though the new spring weather did not demand quite so warm a garment. Beside her, she had spread out a small array of copper and silver trinkets, along with a few tattered prayer books

"Are you a volva?"

The old woman smiled, wrinkling her face even more. "I'm an old woman with lots of experience in some things. What do you need to know?"

"My husband is sick. Will he live?"

"I'd have to see him."

"It's not far," Helga said, and motioned for the old woman to follow.

"What is your name?" the old woman said, not moving.

"Helga."

The old woman cracked her face in what Helga thought was a smile, though it was very strange and disconcerting, as though a corpse were smiling at her for all its wrinkles. Helga's spine tickled at it. "I am Rafnhild. Now, if I am to follow you, I will lose out on some of my livelihood."

Helga reached into her purse and produced a silver coin, which the old woman picked up and gazed at. "Too much," she said, then put the coin in her own purse. Quickly she swept her trinkets into a tattered black bag and followed Helga down the road to her house.

She asked no questions as they went and answered none of Helga's, saying to each question that the answer was not important. She walked slowly, which was as frustrating to Helga as the bad conversation, and she insisted on stopping to greet each woman and child on the way, plying her wares (and even selling a few). And so it felt ages before they finally reached the house and went inside.

"Oh my," the old woman rasped as she stepped through the bedroom door and saw Erling on the bed, pale as a ghost. She tottered around the bed clicking her tongue and staring at him, sometimes cracking that strange smile. She laid a wrinkled hand on the man's forehead for a long moment. Her eyes narrowed and flicked about.

"What is it?" Helga asked.

Rafnhild turned her eyes back to Helga. "I will need to wait to see more, but I think I know this sickness." The old woman then padded around the house, mumbling to herself. She then walked outside and proceeded to circle the house several times. Helga watched from the doorway, keeping an eye on her sleeping husband.

Finally, the old woman stopped and looked toward the setting sun. "Yes, yes." She nodded to nobody and went around to the pen where the sheep and goats were kept, then carefully climbed up on the low stone wall. With slow, deliberate steps, she walked along the low wall until it met the house, then climbed onto the shake roof. She sat down and seemed to relax.

"Is everything alright?" Helga asked from the ground.

"No," Rafnhild replied flatly. Her eyes stared out at the setting sun.

"Is there something I can do for you?"

"No," the old woman said again.

"Why are you on my roof?"

"To see."

Helga shrugged and went inside to make supper for herself and for Erling, when and if he awoke. As she was cutting vegetables, she heard the old woman call from outside. Helga went outside and found the woman sitting in the same place.

"What is it?" Helga said.

"Do you have any mead?"

"No."

The woman seemed to grumble and croak in response. Then she huffed and said, "Any beer?"

"What would one woman do with a keg of beer?"

"Drink it."

"Well, I don't have any."

Again, Rafnhild croaked.

"I have brandy wine," Helga said.

"Not good enough, I'm afraid."

Helga threw up her hands. "Well, do you want any dinner?"

The old woman snapped her head to look right at Helga. "Don't cook any food, for the sake of the gods!"

"Fine!"

Helga walked back inside, but did as the old woman asked. She found from her cupboard a few stale biscuits and set about trying to chew them beside the bed. Outside, Rafnhild began to chant loudly and then to sing. It was a harsh and unmelodious song, quite badly performed by Helga's reckoning, and was in words she did not understand. Helga crunched her biscuits vigorously, deafening herself to the song.

Finally, dusk fell, darkening the sky to a near violet. At last, the wailing song stopped. Helga stepped back outside and looked up onto the roof.

"Well?"

"I have seen," the old woman said, still staring west.

"So you *are* a volva," Helga said, not hiding the sarcasm in her voice.

Rafnhild's voice suddenly jumped up in pitch and rang out in a clear timbre, "I have seen. Much I have seen a second time. Your husband is called to the dark realm, the mist realm, the dead realm, but he clings to this world. He is not called by illness, but by name, and by blood. There is a path to break the spell, but a price must be paid." With that, the volva relaxed her head and stared down. Then, without a word, she stood up and ambled back to the low wall, shuffled down it until it fell back close to the earth, then hopped back down onto the soil.

"You owe me three copper," the old woman croaked, then walked inside. "I'm starving."

Helga walked back inside and put her hands on her hips. "I charge three copper for dinner."

"Too much," the old woman said. "One copper for dinner."

"You said earlier that the silver was too much for the visit."

"Too much for the visit, but not too much for the seeing. For the seeing, I require additional payment. I must pay my way, you know, and the seeing is an exhausting experience."

"You're an old woman."

"Very astute. Now let's have dinner. You owe me two copper."

Not really knowing what else to do, Helga set about making dinner. She cut up a duck that had been killed earlier that day and roasted it in a pan with the vegetables she had been cutting. While she worked, Rafnhild talked to her, or to herself, almost absent-mindedly.

"Smells too good. Would have frightened them away."

"Who?" Helga said.

"The spirits. Music calms them, you know. Food drives them away. Reminds them that they are still dead."

"I didn't know that, but I shall remember," Helga said, not quite able to hide her annoyance.

"No, you won't."

When she was finished cooking supper, Helga placed a serving in front of the old woman, who wolfed the meal down greedily, as if she had not eaten in days.

"Where is the extra bed?" she said after swallowing the last bite.

"There is none," Helga said. She noticed that Erling was awake and rushed over to feed him food and water.

"Don't lie, or I shan't forgive you," Rafnhild said. "You're not a mother yet, so there must be an extra bed. Or two."

Helga's fear of sorcery was starting to wane with the increase in annoyance she was experiencing with the volva, but there was still enough there for her to answer honestly. "There, down that hall."

"Very good. Warm walls." Rafnhild then sighed and leaned back in her chair.

"Are you going to bed?"

"All in good time. For now, I'm going to enjoy the satisfaction of a good, if overpriced, meal. I haven't eaten in a very long time, so even your bad cooking is satisfying." With that, the old woman closed her eyes.

Helga tended to the weak Erling for a few minutes. Just when she thought she could hear the old woman snoring, Rafnhild stood up, picked up her bag, and walked to the extra room without saying another word.

Helga grumbled to herself, but not so loudly that her guest would hear her. Erling went back into a fitful sleep, and Helga undressed and got into bed with him. She lay awake, angry, for a long time, then went to sleep, where she dreamed of angry trees with the faces of old women, snarling at her and scratching her with thin twig fingers.

She was awakened by a long, bony finger poking her. She sat up with a start and scowled at Rafnhild.

"Don't you have any decency?" she said.

"Yes," Rafnhild replied, then walked to the door of the bedchamber. Without turning back to face Helga, she said, "Sun is up, and breakfast should be on the table."

Rafnhild disappeared into the dark hall. Helga gazed around at the room. It was half-dawn at best. "Threepence for breakfast!"

"One!" The old seeress called back.

Helga quickly got up and put on a simple dress, checked on her husband, then hurried into the kitchen. Rafnhild was sitting at the table, calmly looking at her. "I like my eggs over easy and my bacon crispy."

"I haven't got any bacon."

"What have you got?"

"Salted ham."

Rafnhild shrugged. "Not worth a penny, but... I'm a kind woman."

Helga fixed the breakfast hurriedly, dropped Rafnhild's plate down on the table, then shot back to check on Erling. She could hear the old woman smacking even as she walked away.

"Have you considered opening a kitchen?" the old woman said through a full mouth.

"No."

"That is good. I am finished with my breakfast. Now I will tell you what I have seen."

Helga rushed back into the kitchen and sat down, though she scarcely believed at this point the old woman would tell her anything of value.

"Your husband is very sick, girl."

Helga bit her lip and took a deep breath. She said through her teeth, "I know that."

"His affliction is a spiritual one, born of a curse. It's colloquially called the Moss Rot. Really, its proper name is the death bell, or mist blight, but since you are a simple woman, you should call it Moss Rot. Yes, a bad type of curse."

"How did he...contract this?"

Rafnhild shrugged. "Probably an old lover who knows sorcery."

"No. Not possible."

The crone laughed. "You are young and naive. I forgive you. It could also be a lingering from... communion within the dead realm, but of course, that is out of the question."

Helga stared at her.

Rafnhild laughed again. "So that is what it is! Good. No, bad. Well... good that I am here. You are very fortunate to have one as kind and knowledgeable as me on hand. I did well trusting to my reading, that I should come hither."

"How exactly am I fortunate? My husband has gone from sick to cursed. I pity to see what you consider unlucky."

Rafnhild picked at her teeth and said, "Do you want to cure him?"

"Of course."

"Then you are fortunate, for I know of a way to cure him. In fact, I know all the points of ritual, all the runes to cut. It is a very complicated ritual. Few know it."

Helga stood up. "If he can be cured, then let us do it!"

Rafnhild laughed at her. "Surely, child, you know that nothing is free."

Helga narrowed her eyes but held her tongue. "How much do you want? We are young, and my dowry is light, but I can pay well if I must."

"Money? Money is the concern of the young and narrow-sighted. No, I require something more than money."

"What is it?"

"I need you to fetch something for me."

"Name it."

"Eager, are we? Well, perhaps you should not be. In order for me to cure your husband, I will need the Water of Awakening. As full a vial as you can safely hide."

"What is the Water of Awakening?" Helga asked. She was leaning on the table now, almost standing over the volva, but Rafnhild didn't seem to notice.

"What is it?" Rafnhild said almost casually. "That is a great question. It is a substance of power, but only for those who have great knowledge of the spirit realm and the fay, such as myself. It will not be useful to you, I think. A better question is where you shall find it."

"Can you cure him?" Helga said. "Can he really get better?"

"I am not a liar," Rafnhild said. "I will cure him, body and soul, but first I must have the Water."

"How will it cure him?" Helga said.

"I must remember that the young are not usually wise." Rafnhild cracked her knuckles as she talked to herself, then looked up at Helga. "It won't. It is merely payment for my work. I can gather what materials I will need for the ritual here. Of course, if you are thinking of finding another volva who can dispel the Moss Rot, your luck will run dry. I alone in this part of the world still know the runes. I alone have the skill and the mercy, and the courage, to see it done. Yes, it is very perilous, and you are very fortunate that the spirits called me here."

Helga sighed. "Very well. Where do I find this *Water of Awakening?*"

Rafnhild rubbed her hands together and smiled, and the light in her eyes was chilling cold. Her voice, rising in pitch, was like a rattle. "Well, the heart of the Fay is where it is, though of course, you cannot go the Fay, not without losing your mind and probably your body as well. Lucky for you, I know another way. Far east and south of here, there is a great forest that the wise, such as myself, know to be a borderland with the remains of the Prim, and a gateway to the oldest and most powerful parts of the Fay."

"But you said I cannot go there," Helga said.

"You do not have to. There is a tribe of people there, if people are what you wish to call them. They can travel through the Prim safely, and do so. They are called the *Watchers,* or the *Dim Watchers,* though you should not call them that to their faces... Oh, and what strange faces they have. They, I am sure, can fetch you some of the water, for in the Fay it is plentiful, even infinite. It may even be worthless to them. Yes, you are lucky."

"Why must I be the one to fetch this thing for you?" Helga said. "And moreover, what do you intend to do with it?"

"One question at a time."

"Why me?"

"Don't be so foolish as to walk away from a deal by suggesting I find a competitor to do this task for me," Rafnhild said.

"That didn't answer my question. Why me?"

The crone laughed her dry laugh again. "Clever. It must be you because you have something you want from me much more than you would want the Water of Awakening for yourself. If I were to hire some warrior, he would seek to sell this thing at a profit after I told him where to get it. Not that I need a warrior. It is not a particularly perilous journey, though a bit long under the feet. Certainly less dangerous than what I shall do here."

"If it's so safe, then why don't you go get it yourself?"

"I am old."

"That didn't stop you from climbing onto my roof."

"Not the same as climbing mountains, child. Besides, the spirits told me it would be a woman to fetch me this prize. And here you are, a woman, at least in form."

Helga sat back down. "But I still want to know what you intend to do with this talisman. If I am go fetching magic artifacts, I would be responsible for how they are used."

"We all get old," Rafnhild said. "Some foolish men seek to live forever on this earth, but wise women, such as myself, know that the true path to immortality lies in traveling between the worlds. I have, in my long travels, pieced together a mighty ritual that will allow me to depart and return, and to hold the knowledge in my head of both this realm and the timeless before. Know that I speak the truth, child. You cannot easily do evil with the Water of Awakening, but with great effort, you can bring a good life, such as my own, into a more timeless state. Only a volva would understand this path, so do not feel too stupid that you do not understand."

Helga did not catch the insult in this, and though she was hesitant, she felt a strong desire born of concern for her husband to do as the crone bid. She told herself that she would inquire of Bjorn and her mother, or perhaps even the Jarl, when time allowed, as to whether Rafnhild was a true volva and could be trusted, but she could not allow a chance to save Erling to walk out her front door.

"Do we have a deal?" Rafnhild said.

Helga gave herself one last thought. In her heart, she had begun to despair in recent days, and she was desperate to save Erling. "Yes. I will have to make preparations and ensure Erling is cared for while I am away, but I will do this deed for you."

"Good, child," Rafnhild said.

"I will require a bond," Helga said.

"Of course," Rafnhild said. "I will cut the runes in my blood and yours."

"If I fail?"

"You get no cure. I will not bind any other curse. I understand your plight, and I am very merciful, of course, if the task proves too much for a fickle girl's heart."

Still slightly reluctant, Helga shook the old woman's gnarled hand. Later that day, the oath was written on a piece of yew, and each woman signed with a bloody thumbprint with a few of the townswomen as witness, a gesture all present knew to bind the volva to her word. After this, Rafnhild slowly and carefully drew a map on a piece of parchment she pulled from her bag. She sketched out a rough path, noting some mountains and rivers, and drew a road, then slid it across the table to Helga.

"The spirits are not mapmakers, alas," she said. "But I'm sure you will reach what you seek."

The next day Helga went to town to see who might be willing to help her on her journey, for though the Volva said that the road was easy, Helga knew that there were still some dangers in the world.

First, she went to Bjorn, who had two strong sons near Helga's age, though a bit younger. She found him at his post, moving barrels of seed wheat with one of his sons.

"My sons are their own men," Bjorn said. He flashed a hard eye to Snorre, his younger son, as he sniggered.

"You don't usually call us men," Snorre said.

Bjorn narrowed his eyes, but did not chastise him. He turned back to Helga and said, "But I will caution them not to follow you, and I will tell you to stay right here. There's no reason for that old woman to send you off on some wild goose chase, looking for some magic water."

"He's just mad that you didn't marry Stein," Snorre said. "Always thought you'd be good for him, since he doesn't listen to mother."

"Quiet, boy," Bjorn said.

"That's more like it."

"Will you come with me, Snorre?" Helga said.

"Sorry, Helga, but spring is here, and there is lots of work to do," Snorre said, shrugging. "Maybe I can walk you part of the way down to Thruddel, but that's it."

"Good boy," Bjorn said.

"I'm not a dog, dad."

"Well, you smell like one." Bjorn frowned at Helga. "The place to be is right here. Brick didn't stay here for no reason."

"Always my grandfather," Helga said.

Bjorn nodded. "He was a brave man. Foolhardy, but he still didn't take on anything truly pointless."

Svanhild, Bjorn's wife, appeared from the house, her face all smiles in a way that told Helga she had been eavesdropping. "Dear, why don't we send for a priestess of Nostera, a real healer, to help? I hear they travel willingly in the summer."

"Expensive," Bjorn said.

"More expensive than feeding a lame man?" Svanhild asked.

Bjorn grumbled. "You stay here, Helga. I'll pay the way for a real healer from the divine strand come summer. Alright?"

Helga shook her head. "I have to do this. Healing didn't work."

"Mathias is a doctor, not a healer," Svanhild said. "He has no access to magic."

Helga shook her head again. "Summer is too far away. I'll ask someone else."

As she walked away, Bjorn shouted, "Stay here, Helga!"

Next, Helga went to Erling's older brother, who had a farm just outside of town. He likewise said he would be too busy with the spring sowing. She went to cousins, and they also were too busy. She asked all her relations within a day of travel and all of Erling's relatives. After two days of trying to persuade all the men of the town to go with her, and failing, she decided to ask the Jarl for help.

The Jarl did not live in a castle, but in a multi-level hall on a hill, surrounded by stone fortifications designed to repel the occasional raiding party. A low parapet topped the wall, and an ironbound gate marked the threshold to the courtyard. As Greenfeld was a small hold and currently at peace, the gates were open and guarded by a single man at arms named Bradley, who had known Helga from girlhood.

"What's the lion hunting for today?" He asked as she walked through the gate. He was eating an apple and leaning against a tree lazily, his spear in the crook of his elbow.

"A man brave enough to venture beyond Greenfeld," Helga said.

Bradley shrugged as Helga walked past and said to her back, "Good luck."

Helga walked freely into the building and found Jarl Rolfagar at rest in the main hall, reading a book by the light of an ornate stained glass window depicting the god Ferral at his forge. The red flames of the window cast an eerie light on the normally good-natured Jarl, setting his grey hair to red and shadowing his lined face. He looked up and recognized Helga, but did not stand.

"And what does Helga, daughter of Hrolfi, desire of the Jarl of Greenfeld?" he said calmly, flipping a page in his heavy tome.

"I need to make a journey to save my husband from his fate. It is safer for two to go than one, so I need a companion for the road. I thought you might help me."

"You are expecting trouble, then," Rolfagar said.

"No, merely wanting to be prepared," Helga said.

"Have you asked your kin?"

"They are busy with the sowing."

"What about the other men of the village?"

"They will not come. They are all busy as well."

"I see," the jarl said. "Have you asked the younger men? I know you are already married, but they are always eager to impress other women with acts of kindness or heroics."

"They... They will not come, sire."

"Just where are you going, anyway?" The jarl looked up at her with a dark frown.

"To..." Helga hesitated to say. "A volva wants me to fetch something for her, in exchange for the cure for my husband."

"That is not the question I asked, is it?"

Helga hesitated again. "I'm going to see a tribe called the Watchers on the edge of the fay."

The jarl nodded. "How do you know she is really a volva?"

"She had a vision?"

"How do you know?"

"She told me," Helga said.

"I see. What if I told you I was really a reindeer?"

"Sire?"

"Just a rhetorical question, my dear." The jarl sighed and closed his book. "Have you thought much on the reluctance of your kin and clan to help you on this journey?"

Helga paused and thought about it a moment. "Sire, I am not well-liked."

"Who in my hold treats a woman of my kin badly?"

Helga hesitated. "Nobody sire, but-"

Rolfagar held up his hand to silence Helga. He looked at her with sad eyes. "I think you should consider whether going on this errand is a good idea. Well," the jarl hesitated in thought. "I think it is not a good idea. And as much as I love you, I will not reward bad decisions."

"I must go," Helga said. "I already gave an oath."

"That was not wise, Helga. Not wise at all." The jarl sighed. "Are you really so determined to go, Helga the Lion?"

"I am. I must save Erling; this might be my only chance to do so."

"Very well. Tell Bradley he has my permission to escort you to the borderlands, but no further."

"Thank you, sire." Helga bowed.

"My prayers that you return."

*

The next day Helga sent a message to Erling's parents, and to her own, and each woman agreed to set aside time to care for Erling in Helga's absence. Rafnhild had decided on her own to stay in Helga's home, in the room she had occupied, as a "favor" to the family. Neither mother had the temerity to object, for it was long the tradition in that part of the world to accept a volva's stay in a home without thought to cost.

Helga assembled what she thought she might need for a long journey. She loaded a large bag with what foodstuffs she knew would not spoil quickly, which was mostly dried meat, nuts, berries, and hard biscuits. She belted Erling's sword, a blade that was large but nimble, well-crafted in "days of yore" (as Erling's father liked to say), and cared for by the family. Its appearance was mundane, but betrayed a hidden temper, much like Erling himself. She loaded Erling's horse (a fine colt named Raggle) with water skins and other provisions, including warmer clothes for the mountains. On the outside of the saddle, she hung her brother's crossbow, along with a quiver of bolts and spare strings. She dressed herself in simple trousers and a warm tunic over her blouse, along with a tightly woven woolen cloak. Inside her tunic, she kept what money she had saved through the illness of her husband.

Helga's neighbors and family were less critical of her leaving than she thought they might be. She attributed this to the words of the volva, which nobody in Greenfeld seemed willing to rebut. Helga left quietly and without fanfare, and the only residents of the village that seemed reluctant to see her go were her sheep and goats, which bleated their complaints as she led the horse past.

Passing by Bjorn's house, Helga met Bradley, who was dressed in his armor, and, to her surprise, Snorre.

"Stein went up to Skjallanding and Hostent last week," Snorre said as Helga neared. "They say they've never heard of any Rafnhild."

"So why are you dressed for the road?" Helga said.

"I figured if you were still dense enough in the skull to leave, I could at least make sure you had your bearings on the road. I camp quite a bit. Very used to adventures."

Bradley laughed, and Snorre turned a shade of Crimson.

"Well, I'm still going," Helga said.

When Helga and the others reached the edge of the wide road, she found Rafnhild sitting upon a rock, as she had met her.

"Gods preserve you," she croaked.

"Thank you. I did not expect you to see me off," Helga said.

"You still owe me a penny."

Helga drew out a copper piece and threw it to the old woman, who fingered it suspiciously.

"A little light on the pressing, and heavy on the iron," Rafnhild said. "But it'll do. I am a generous woman, after all."

"Hey," Snorre said. "How do we know you're a seeress and not some old daft woman pretending?"

Rafnhild narrowed her eyes at the boy. She snapped her fingers but, instead of it being a quiet sound, it was ear-splittingly loud, louder than anything any of them had ever heard before. The horses bolted immediately, and the crone fell off the rock laughing.

II. Thruddel

THE FIRST NIGHT away from Greenfeld on the eastern road did not even bring them past from the hold's outer farms. All of them stayed at a relative of Snorre's (for he did, despite Bradley's laughs, travel often and had many known stops) who fed them well and gave Helga her own bedroom to sleep in. Snorre somehow found a welcoming home the second night as well. By the third day, they had left settled lands and were entering sparse forest. They made camp in a small clearing and slept beneath the stars, only to wake up soaked by a sudden rainstorm; they struggled to find shelter.

Eventually, they were able to get slightly drier beneath the drooping boughs of an ancient oak, but by morning they and the horses were soaked, for Snorre had trouble lighting a fire. The next day was almost as dreary, but the sprinkling rain gave up by nightfall. They were able to find a dry patch of ground, and there they were able to get a fire lit at last and get truly dry.

"We need to be careful in these hills," Snorre said. "There are all sorts of nasty beasts lurking about."

"Bah," Bradley said. "Nothing to worry about with the fire. Wolves are afraid of fire."

"True enough," Snorre said. They took turns tending the fire during the night, but saw or heard of no sign of wolves or bears. The next day they did catch sight of a beast in the form of a loping black bear, who seemed more afraid of the beating of the horse hooves than he seemed a fearsome beast. On that day, the fourth since setting out, Bradley turned back.

"I've stayed on as I can. You're safely on the road, which is good enough, I suppose," he said. "And my wife will already be mad at me spending time on the road with a younger woman. Best not test her wrath."

That night it got colder and windier, for they were moving higher into the mountains. Snorre made a fire, and they were able to get quite comfortable near the flames. With one less person, they drew lots to see who would tend the fire and the night watch first. Helga drew and so had to stay up and watch the waning moon slowly peek above the horizon. She stared into the flames of the fire and had many small dosing dreams, shaking herself awake and adding fuel each time she found herself imagining dragons or frightening bear-like beasts.

In the end, Helga fell asleep without realizing it. She had a pleasant dream of warm sun and grass-lit fields, but soon in that dream, the sun was replaced by darkness, and she was surrounded by shadowy monsters that moved along on all fours.

"Wake up, you bloody fool woman!"

Helga shook her head and opened her eyes to darkness. She saw in the dim light of the moon and the dying embers of the fire Snorre was standing, his ax at the ready. The horses were whinnying, pulling their halters, and stamping at the wet earth.

"What?"

"It's wolves," Snorre said. "Get up, quickly."

Helga could see shapes moving in the shadows, sniffing and circling with their hackles raised, not attacking the horses only because they were backed up against a large boulder.

Helga got up as quick as she could, feeling stiff, and searched about for her sword, for she did not remember where she placed it. While that happened, a wolf jumped forward. Snorre knocked it away with the haft of his long ax and then chopped at it, wounding it and sending it crying back into the shadows.

Helga felt frantic as she looked for her sword. She stumbled and fell on the pile of wood, but felt as she did so the scabbard for her sword. Frantically she threw the wood off to get to it.

"Where is your crossbow?" Snorre said.

"What? I don't know."

Snorre growled as two wolves moved closer. He swung his ax in wide sweeps, trying to fend them off. Helga picked up her sword and drew it, then lunged at one of the wolves. She never made it to the wolf, for as she moved forward, she was hit squarely in the forehead with the back of Snorre's ax during the wind-up for his own attack. She collapsed to the dirt, dropping her sword and reaching for the pain in her head. She saw by moonlight Snorre slam his axhead into a wolf's shoulder, killing it.

Her face aching and her head still spinning from the accidental blow, Helga sat up and realized she was sitting on her crossbow.

"I found it!" she said. "I found the crossbow!"

"Shoot something!" Snorre said, slamming his ax handle into a wolf that snapped at his feet.

Helga picked up the crossbow and suddenly remembered that she had not loaded it. She got to her feet, feeling the night swim again, but did her best to focus on spanning the bow. She bent down and fit the string into her belt hook. With a hard press upward, she spanned it and threw in a bolt from her quiver. She raised the crossbow and picked a shadow. Her ears were ringing. She steadied herself and shot at one of the shadows. She heard the bolt crunch into bone and watched the shadow collapse. Snorre moved forward, slashing wildly. The wolves scattered, moving off into the trees while barking and whining at each other. Helga could hear their howls just outside the moonlight.

"Quickly, relight the fire!" Snorre said.

Helga did as he ordered and began to prod the hot coals with a stick, trying to find a glowing ember within. She found one and coaxed new flame onto a small twig, then a larger piece of firewood. The howls died down, and the barking stopped. The sounds of crickets returned as the ringing died in Helga's ears.

Snorre, who had stood on the edge of the camp, came back and staggered down beside the fire.

"Damn, that was a close one," he said. His voice turned harsh. "Dreamer! You have *got* to learn a thing or two about being on the road. First, never sleep without your weapon within reach. Never put your crossbow down unloaded unless you absolutely expect no trouble. Third, never fall asleep on your watch!"

"I'm sorry," Helga said, and meant it. "I was just… tired."

"Tired!" he sighed. "Tired? Tired enough to lay down and die?" He sighed and lowered his voice. "Doesn't matter. We're fine, and I guess that's what counts."

Neither of them slept the rest of the night.

*

The next day, Snorre attempted to persuade Helga one last time to return to Greenfeld.

"I can't afford to spend who knows how long trying to find a way on that terrible map of yours to this *Watchers* tribe. Come back with me now, and my father will still pay for the cleric of Nostera to come. Hell, I'll pay. Bloody wolves."

"I can't go back," Helga said. "I have to try."

Snorre sighed. "Listen. I *have* to go back. If you're determined to go on, I can't stop you, but you should have learned last night what I knew from the start. This is a fool's errand if I've ever seen one."

"And eighteen-year-old boys are known for having seen much of the world," Helga retorted.

"I've damn sure seen more of it than you."

"You're just being a coward, like everyone else."

"Alright, be that way. I'll wait on the road tonight, in case you change your mind." With that, Snorre lead his horse away, back west toward Greenfeld.

Helga felt bitter about being abandoned and for what she had said, even tearful, but these tears she choked back, if for no audience but herself.

"Stupid Snorre. Stupid Helga!" she said to herself. She patted Raggle on the neck. "We don't need him. We're two on the road - just you and me. We'll be fine."

*

After making it over a low pass, Helga journeyed south into farm-land nestled among old hardwoods. She got so tired the first night try-ing to tend a fire that she made herself stop at noon the following day and sleep for a few hours. She spent three days and nights through forest and field coming down from the pass, meeting few folks along the way besides farmers and goodwives. On the third day, she rode over a hill and came upon a large walled city. Helga had never been to a city, and could not match the sprawling grandeur she saw to any memory of any description she had heard in Greenfeld. She supposed the city was Thruddel, the only real city-state within any manageable distance from her home. She checked her map and failed to see the city marked on it and so made up her mind to inquire within, in case she had already become lost and happened upon some other city.

The outskirts held the hamlets that were typical of cities that had overgrown their bounds, filled with mismatched and hastily construct-ed houses and shops as well as poorly aligned avenues that wandered and ended abruptly. Helga rode through muddy streets and by all sorts of rough-looking folk to reach the front gate, a massive stone fortifi-cation with great round towers encasing a double portcullis and a drawbridge that was bound in iron. The gate was open, but guarded by hard-looking men. She found herself wishing she had cocked the crossbow and consciously laid a hand on her sword. A guard in dingy mail stopped her on the threshold of the city.

"What city is this?" she asked the guard.

"What's your business?" he said.

"I'm looking for directions," Helga said.

"To where?"

"I don't know."

"Best ask in the hamlets, then."

"I don't trust the people out here," she said.

The guard gave a laugh. "You definitely aren't from here. Try the market, up the lane straight ahead. Plenty of traveling merchants will tell you where you need to go, in the city or out. And welcome to Thruddel. Watch yourself, because others will be watching you."

Helga nodded and rode past him, slowly up the cobblestone street, which was filled with well-built houses of brick and stone with tile roofs. Eventually, the avenue opened and she reached a crowded marketplace. It contained more people than she had ever seen in one place, of more variety than she thought existed. She saw men of all colors and sizes, and even saw a group of short, hairy dwarves (which were a common sight in Greenfeld, coming down from the Half-Moon Hills frequently to trade). Men of clear Orcish ancestry stood in circles talking to each other, their grey skin and high pates drawing the eye in the colorful crowd. She thought she saw one elf, but it was hard to focus on any one person in the mass of moving, yelling people. She dismounted and led Raggle through the throng of people buying and selling from countless carts. She noticed a tall man selling silk – a rare and wondrous cloth she had only seen a few times, and only on the Jarl's wife. She pushed her way over to him and stood up straight before him, doing her best to look impressive and confident.

"Excuse me, sir."

"You're excused," the man said.

"I am looking for directions."

"The castle's up that way. The sewer's down that way." The man turned his back and began unrolling a bolt of cloth.

Helga withdrew the map the volva had given her and laid it before the merchant. "Do you know where this city is on this map?"

"That's a terrible-looking map."

"Sir?"

The man sighed and looked at the parchment. "It isn't marked."

"I know, hence why I asked."

"Why do you think I know?"

"You're selling silk, which only comes from…" Helga heisted when she realized that she no idea where silk actually came from. "From far away. You must know your way or know many traveling merchants. At least, I expect a man like you to be wise in such things."

The merchant stopped what he was doing, scratched his chin, and looked more closely at the map. "These mountains could be the Frostbacks, but I think they're really the Ulfar Mountains. And that must be the Fay Waste. You should really spring for a better map, you know. You're looking for the Dim Watchers?"

"Maybe."

The tall man smiled. "Of course you are. Well, let me tell you that the tales of magic trinkets from that lot are greatly exaggerated. They sell mostly junk, but occasionally a trinket of some trifling power passes through their hands. Frankly, it's probably not worth the journey. A few men here in town have Fay remnants, if you have a bit of coin. Like I said, they aren't worth much since they don't do much."

"All the same, directions would be helpful. I can pay you something for your time."

The merchant waved the suggestion away. "If you want to do something, just give me a first look at what you bring back – if you bring back something you don't have a use for." He pointed at the map again. "Thruddel is up here somewhere. You'll need to go south to the Winding Water. That's probably this line. Then head due east." The merchant narrowed his eyes at the map. "Say, I've got a friend who is a bit better at this than me. He could probably be more specific. What time is it?" The merchant looked at the sky for a moment. "Good timing. Thorvald will be sober still, but over his hangover and back at the pub. It's up this way, then turn right and head toward the castle. Tell him Arnar sent you."

Helga thanked the merchant and found the pub, as he had said, at the end of a narrow street in the shadow of the castle. It was a squat stone structure, two stories tall with grime-caked windows and shudders that hung askew. The doors stood open, but the interior was still dark. Helga tied Raggle to a wood rail (as that seemed the best place to do so) and went inside. After her eyes adjusted, she saw that the pub itself was a large living space from what was once likely a home. The entire great room was deserted, except for one table by an unlit open hearth, where a middle-aged man, shaggy and with a bushy red and grey beard, sat with a clay stein.

"Thorvald?" Helga said as she approached.

"A fine name," the man replied.

Helga took a look around at the quiet place, then pulled back a chair and sat down, loosening her sword as she did so.

"I have a map that I was hoping you could help me find the use of. Arnar told me you were wise in such things." She drew out the map and laid it on the table.

"Aye, I was a very well respected trapper, tracker, and even spy, back when I was well respected." He looked at the map, shifting so he could catch some daylight from the open doors. While he examined it, a man Helga presumed was the pub keeper appeared from a back room, rolling a keg. "Surprisingly accurate, considering."

"Considering what?"

"No points of interest or bearing. Where did you get this?"

"A volva drew it for me."

"She's been there?"

"No. She said the spirits showed her."

Thorvald laughed. "If only they could tell you a name or two. Do you mind if I write on this?"

Helga shrugged. "I suppose it wouldn't make it *less* usable."

Thorvald got up and went to the other side of the hearth. Two men, who she had not noticed when she first entered, sat in a corner, reclining and smoking. Thorvald got from one of the men a pen and an inkwell. He sat back down and spread the map out again. With a slightly shaking hand, he dipped the pen into the inkwell and wrote a few words.

"This here is the Winding Water, but this line here will be a tributary called the Long Line, on account of its long straight stretch here. We're up here." Thorvald drew a thin "X." "Looks like this intends for you to cross the mountains. Where are you making for?"

"A tribe called the Dim Watchers."

Thorvald raised a hairy eyebrow. "What do you want with that lot? You're not trying to walk into the Fay, are you? You'll never walk out, you know."

"No, I am told they can fetch something from the Fay for me."

Thorvald chewed his lip for a long moment, then said. "What is it?"

Helga considered lying, but there was something in the red face of the big man that seemed beyond honest, despite his surroundings. "Something called the Water of Awakening."

Thorvald shrugged. "Never heard of it."

"The volva wants it for some reason. It's payment for a favor."

"Steep favor."

"My hu-" Helga stopped herself and feigned a cough. "A relative of mine has the Moss Rot. She can cure it. I believe."

"Well, I suppose I can at least give you some directions." He scratched his beard as he stared at the map.

"What do you want in return?"

"A pint of the finest ale in the world, and if that is of short supply, a prayer for my wife's spirit."

Helga nodded in understanding.

Thorvald dipped the pen back in the inkwell, then drew a dotted line from the X over some mountains, and toward the tributary. "You'll have to walk down through a low pass here to a valley. It's hard to miss as it's the only road, but on the other side, you are going to bear south until you hit the river. There's an old path I cut there that should still be usable if the weather is good. Follow it on up, and you'll find the old pass over the mountains to the lee side. It's a long journey. And watch yourself when you get close to the woods of the Fay. Strange things happen there."

"I will, thank you," Helga said.

"Who are you traveling with?" Thorvald said.

Helga paused as she looked at the man's narrowed eyes. She suddenly felt eyed suspiciously. "I am traveling with my husband, a knight, and one of his retainers, as well as his squire."

29

"Good," Thorvald said, straight-faced. "You will need strong companions to make it through the Fay waste."

She stood up and rolled up the map, then walked over to the bar-keep. "How much for an ale?"

The keeper cast a dark eye at her. "Twopence."

Helga reached into her purse and gave him two pieces of copper. "For Thorvald."

Helga left the pub and led her horse back towards the market-place. Her purse still felt heavy, and she had a mind to buy some fresh food, if she could find it, and refresh her other provisions. Her dried fruit had dwindled already due to her sweet tooth, and she had managed to choke down only a single chunk of tack, making her saddle-bags heavy in all the wrong ways. She managed to find some small apples and cheap loaves of bread, which she ate right away before stuffing the remnants into her saddlebag.

As she ate, sitting on a small brick half-wall, she decided that a stay in a bed would do her well. Luckily, in the market square, there were two small inns, and Helga chose the more run-down of two, wishing to keep her purse heavy.

The next morning, while she was seeing to the packing of her horse, a man in colorful livery approached her. He stuck his chin out and cleared his throat. Helga laughed before she thought of her manners.

"My lord Magnus, court wizard to King Ivar the Long, requests a swift counsel with you," the man said, doing his best to look important.

"To what end, exactly?" Helga said.

"Mutual benefit in your hour of need," said the stranger.

Helga took the reply (as such sayings were in her hometown) to be the sort of semi-polite introduction that precedes a threat.

She reached for her sword, but before she could draw it, Thorvald stepped into the stable.

"Get out of here, Liegar."

The servant jumped backward. "You!" He looked at Helga again. "My master knows the healing arts and offers them to you, nothing more!"

Thorvald drew a long dagger from his jacket and flourished it.

The servant shrieked at him, "I will have the guards string you up this time, Thorvald."

"Unlikely," Thorvald said. "But you're welcome to go off and try to convince them of the dangerous drunkard."

Giving a high-pitched cry of frustration, the servant rushed out of the stable, grumbling to himself.

"Decided to leave your knightly retinue outside the city?" Thorvald said after the servant disappeared.

"You," Helga said, narrowing her eyes. "You followed me!"

"Come. I will lead you out of the city. It is time you headed home."

"No. I have tasks to complete."

"Magnus has taken notice of you. That means it is time to leave if you value your freedom or possession of your own mind."

"How so?"

"The king is not…" Thorvald shook his head. "Come. I can put you back on your homeward path." Thorvald stood at the door to the stable and motioned her.

Helga grumbled, then said, "*You* help me. You know the way. I can pay."

"Not enough," Thorvald said. "And I have business in this city."

"What business? Getting drunk all day and trying to forget a dead woman?"

Thorvald smiled at her. "She would have said the same thing, but if you think that is my business…" he laughed softly. "I'll say no more, except that it is time you left Thruddel, and I suggest you do not return."

"Trouble, madam?" Helga turned to see two guards with hard faces and the servant standing behind them.

"No," Helga said. "Merely scolding a stable-boy for being too zealous in his attempt to protect a woman." Thorvald gave her a hard look as she stepped away from him.

She eyed the guards. "Very well. You may take me to your master."

The servant bowed low. "Right this way, my lady!"

Helga followed the men up to the castle gates, which they passed through without a word, and up to the center of the keep that held an iron portcullis. The two men-at-arms waited outside as the servant passed inside. Helga handed her horse's bridle to one of the armed men, then went inside the old stone keep, into a hallway that seemed surprisingly bright. It was lit, Helga saw, by rows of glowing globes of what looked like churning water, pulsing slowly.

"Do not let the magic frighten you," the servant said. "It is quite harmless. An invention of Lord Magnus."

"You said you master knows healing," Helga said.

"Of course. He brought the king himself back from the brink of death. That is part of how he earned his station."

"How did he know I needed a healer, exactly?" Helga said.

The servant shrugged. "I do what I am bidden to do."

"What does he know about the Moss Rot?"

"I wouldn't know. I'm just a messenger. Here."

They arrived at a great black door, made of some tight-grained wood Helga did not recognize. The servant neither spoke nor knocked, but the doors opened, seemingly of their own accord. The servant gestured for Helga to enter. She stepped across the threshold into a high-ceilinged round room with walls covered in full book-shelves. A circular platform, open to the center, stood some twenty feet above her, and through the hole in the middle, she could see even more bookshelves. The top of the room was a great glass dome filled with wondrous depictions of dragons and the gods.

The door shut behind her, and Helga realized she was alone.

"You may come," a deep voice said. Helga looked around her, but could not find the source of the voice.

"Where are you?" she said. Her hand went to the sword at her side.

"You will not need your sword, nor will it do you any good."

Helga looked up to see a tall, lean, and handsome man with a greying beard coming down the stairs that led to the platform above. In one hand, he held a crooked staff. His face held a slight smile.

"A wizard?" Helga said.

"Yes. I am Magnus."

"Why did you bring me here?" Helga said.

"Bring?" said the wizard. "I told my servants to ask you to come, not to 'bring' you."

"Armed men do not give me the impression that I am a volunteer," Helga said.

"Escorts. The streets are dangerous for a woman, even armed." The wizard motioned to a table with comfortable, red velvet-lined chairs. He sat in one and looked up at Helga, but she remained standing. "You are as I thought you would be."

Helga frowned. "Thought I would be?"

"I understand you have a relative that is ill." The wizard's voice was smooth as honey, almost condescending.

"And how did you come to understand it?" Despite the words of the wizard, or perhaps because of them, she felt for her sword.

Magnus laughed softly. "I overheard it. I keep an eye on Thorvald. He was once a good man, loyal to the crown and to his brothers, but grief has taken him, and now he is content with disgrace. He even plots against the king, you know, when he drinks. Please, have a seat."

Helga hesitated. She looked back at the door before taking in the warm smile of the wizard. Reluctantly, she sat down. "What else do you know?"

The wizard smiled slightly. "I know this relative of yours has what some call the Moss Rot, which is really an ailing from a tie to the underworld. It can be severed with magic if you have a strong enough mage. I know that you seek the Water of Awakening, but you do not know the value of such a talisman, nor do you understand its use."

"Do *you* understand its use?" Helga said. "You certainly make appearances to look wise."

The wizard's smile did not fade. "Appearances which do not deceive, unlike your own." His eyes crept over her. "I also know the peril of the Water of Awakening, and the peril of those you know only as the Watchers."

"And that peril is?"

"For the water, you would not understand. For the watchers..." The wizard smiled and looked away.

"So, do you intend to help me?"

"I do," the wizard said. "But all things have their costs, as I am sure you know. I have the capacity to cure your...?" Maguns raised his eyebrows at Helga.

She squinted for a moment, then said hastily. "Brother. My brother."

Magnus smiled. "Your brother. It not a simple or ordinary matter, even for a wizard, but it can be done using a special item I have and a well-worked spell, of course."

"I already have one promise for a cure. I don't think I need another."

"From whom?"

"A volva."

"Do you trust this volva?"

"What other choice do I have?" Helga said.

"You can trust me, of course, as a matter of choice," Magnus said. "Has this volva ever demonstrated to you her power?"

Helga thought about the strange old woman and her thunderclap snap as she left the village, which in hindsight seemed more planned than in the moment of its execution. While she thought, Magnus waved a hand, and a book flew off a far shelf and landed lightly in his hands. Helga gave a start as he conjured a ball of light above his head, further brightening the room. He flipped the book open to a page with strange, hand-written letters and showed it to Helga.

"It is the cure, though I'm sure you cannot read it."

Helga gazed at the page, filled with strange runes and diagrams that made no sense to her. Magically, the words began to fade and be replaced by other words. The closer she looked, the more confusing it became, to the point that it seemed as if the words were moving around the geometric shapes, switching place. One would pop into focus, almost readable and familiar, before Helga's eyes would wander to something else.

"Fascinating, is it not?" The wizard said. His voice seemed almost too present to Helga, like a whisper in her ear.

"Yes." As she looked over the double page in the tome, her surety of what it contained increased. She thought she could read some of the words. The word *Niflhel* seemed to weave its way around a circle made of other, more alien words.

"You always were good at recognizing real power."

Helga heard the wizard's voice and realized her eyes were hurting from staring at the small words. With an effort, she shut them and shook her head.

With a snap of his fingers, the wizard's light shot up and away from the book, moving through the vast library from shelf to shelf, as if looking for something.

"Very well," Helga said almost quietly. "What is it that you want?"

"The question is, what can *you* give?" Magnus said.

"I have…" Helga's thoughts came in a jumble. She had… a horse. And a sword.

The wizard's voice interrupted her thoughts. "You could give to me the Water of Awakening and be certain of a cure, but that quest perhaps would be best avoided by one such as you. One so…" The wizard's mouth seemed to mime words as he gazed at Helga.

Helga felt the silence, and did not like it. She said the first things she could think of. "What is so perilous about it? The volva said it would not be dangerous."

"Has it been without danger so far?"

Helga hesitated. "No, but-"

"If the volva intended you to go to the borderlands and acquire an item – any item, mind you – from the Dim Watchers, then it is clear to me she is either lying or has never been there to know just how dangerous it is." Magnus scratched his beard as his globe of light returned. It hovered over him and, with a soft plop, dropped a pipe and a bag of tobacco into the wizard's hand. He began to pack a bowl.

"Volvas do not lie," Helga said.

Magnus shrugged. "The mountains have their own perils a seeress might be inclined to dismiss, if she has the knowledge she claims to have, and of course, even the bandits will respect the right of a volva to cross without harassment. A beautiful woman that is not a volva, however, may not find the men in the mountains as merciful, especially if her knightly husband is merely imaginary. But the bandits are not the real danger. The real danger is the Dim Watchers. Do you know what they are, or have you heard any tales?"

"I've heard only that they can go through the Prim and back again."

Magnus nodded. He lit his pipe with a flame that appeared on his fingertip, then took a few quick puffs off the stem. "They are of the Fay, and not, as it were. Or they are fading from the Fay and the memories of the Prim with them. You see, Helga, they are the lost elves. The elves that never became real and in our world. They are spirits of the timeless dream realm, but they grew jealous of the men who stumbled into the Fay, for they could make permanent within the fay the changes they created within their minds. Even in the ever-moving Fay, men could make something last, and so the watchers desire their ability to pass through the Prim into real existence.

"Being of the Fay, of course, they do not understand man at all, and know not what they envy, thinking only of the perceived power of man without the terrible cost, which is death."

"Death," Helga said. "The volva warned me not to go into the Fay."

Magnus chuckled. He stared at his pipe, which gave off thin wisps of blue smoke as he spoke. "I mean death in general. The eventual departing from this world of permanence to… whatever oblivion awaits. These watchers are called dim by some, for as they try to escape the Fay, the light of that first dream of creation begins to fade from their eyes. They still find the world of man frightening and perplexing; man's quests for survival and glory without sense or meaning. They have lost their ability to remember properly their origins in the Fay, and they cannot understand how to be men. So, they wander the edge of the two sides of this coin, impermanent and shifting, but without the peace of impermanence. Of course, there are those who walk away, and they lead a cursed half-life in our realm." The wizard took a draw on his pipe. "Yes, quite cursed. Do you want a smoke? I have an extra pipe."

"No," Helga said.

"Of course not. Of course," the wizard said with a chuckle. His face hardened. "The watchers are dangerous, Helga. They have powers that have the capacity to move beyond my own, when they think to use them. They can kill a man with a thought, if only they can think it. But what makes them truly dangerous is their lack of humanity. They have no empathy, no morals, no honor. They will kill on a whim, or kill for trivial reasons. Or kill because they simply wish to imitate the men they don't understand. You cannot know what they will do with you. Nobody can.

"I can perform this task for you without nearly so much danger – to yourself, perhaps. I can send for your brother to be brought here, where I can give him the full attention of my knowledge and power." The wizard chuckled slightly under his breath – a rasping, dry sort of laugh. "It is of little expense to me, and I have the guard of the city open to my beckoning."

"And the volva? What of her?"

"I will send her the water. Or, something that she will believe to be it. If you truly wish to give her what she asks for. I don't think any woman of such a stature will be able to tell the difference between the water and what I have in mind."

Helga rubbed her temples, which were beginning to hurt. "I didn't make an oath to then deceive."

"She gets what she wants. What is bad about that? Besides, did she not send you needlessly on a quest beyond your capabilities?"

Helga paused to think. The fair voice of the wizard was easy to listen to, and his ideas easy to consider. She found herself seeing the virtue in what he had said. Perhaps the volva was undeserving of the cure. Helga was most definitely out of her comfort zone and likely her abilities as well. And, after all, what mattered was Erling's well-being, not keeping her word to a woman who was either evil or incompetent.

While she thought, the wizard flicked his finger, and the floating light flew off, and then reappeared with a glowing glass orb filled with what looked like churning water, luminous in a pale green, like the magical lights of the entry hall, but filled with wondrous images that caught Helga's eye. "This is a piece of the true Prim, which I don't need to tell you is quite rare. Its uses are limited, but a wise man can reorder alignment with other realms, especially Helheim. Here."

He handed the orb to Helga. Swirling figures filled the crystal, and as Helga gazed into it, she thought she beheld scenes transforming and re-ordering themselves, of dragons and giants and other things she did not recognize flying through an alien land or through strange skies. She saw trees sprouting and moving, shuffling around each other. Helga felt a sudden longing, a tug on some indescribable part of her inner being, to enter into the images she saw, to walk among the trees.

As she directed her mind, she saw more. Mountains as night faded to dawn. Burning red rocks and seas boiling, receding again to reveal rich pastureland. She watched as a great tree grew from the ground, and it turned and stretched as if it was a man, reaching out.

"Magnificent, isn't it?" Magnus said. "You would always have access to it if you were here."

"What?" Helga asked. "What did you say?"

"Remain here, with me," Magnus said. "That is the cost of the cure."

III. THE WILL OF THE WIZARD

HELGA SWALLOWED and looked at the wizard's hard, brown eyes set above a soft smile. He seemed to almost shimmer. "In what capacity?"

"Just as a friend, of course."

"Why me?" Helga said, lowering the orb.

The wizard laughed softly. "You remind me of…" He hesitated, and his eyes intensified. "It is lonely, my position."

"How long?"

"As long as you wish, but not shorter than a year, for I have many tasks that await me and many dangers that approach my doorstep."

"I suppose I could," Helga said, glancing again at the sphere, which was showing a dragon in flight.

"Good," Magnus said. He stood up and pulled a book from a nearby shelf. He opened it and placed it on the table, facing Helga. The page was filled with unreadable letters, drawn by hand in long, strange loops. Signs adorned the middle and edges that looked like drawings of stars intersecting one another. "Your sign, in blood, shall bind you." Helga looked down and saw a short knife she did not remember being placed there.

She set down the glowing talisman and picked up the knife, turning it over in her palm. It was beautifully made, with a shining blade and a hilt of ivory, carved into a figure of a man and a woman entwined.

"It's beautiful," Helga said, staring at the faces of the two figures.

"I knew you would remember it," Magnus said. "I knew you would, Freydis."

Helga felt the edge, which bit her finger even as she slid it across her skin lightly. She saw a drop of blood begin to form on the tip of her index finger. With sudden focus, she looked at the book and at the blank space at the center of the page. Runes swirled in a set of rings, moving, turning, and fading to allow others to show, all in colors of faded brown, like old, dried blood.

"What does it say?" Helga said absentmindedly. She reached her finger forward, ready to press it into the page.

Magnus's voice entered her ear, loud and yet soft like a whisper. "It says nothing of importance. Only that you keep your word. You always were easily tempted. But no more."

Helga shook her head, and the runes seemed to follow her out of the book. They swirled around the room and around the face of the wizard. She felt dizzy and out of sorts, like she just came up from a deep dive or woke from a dream during the dark night.

"What is the matter? Do you not remember?" The voice of the wizard was now rising in pitch and volume. He stood close at hand.

"No," Helga said. "I… I cannot sign lord."

"Why?" Magnus bent forward, his eyes wide and staring, wilting Helga's heart. She felt a weakness in her knees and felt a compulsion to sign the book.

Watching the runes move, crawling now under the eyes of Magnus, she said, "I cannot read it!"

"Sign it, child. I am trying to help you. I do not wish to see a face so divine fall to darkness. To see such a crime visited twice would be a tragedy for all the world!"

Helga had a sudden and violent apprehension to the wizard's last words. His voice sounded harsh and dry, like the wind through dried reeds.

She screamed as she felt his fingers close around her wrist, pulling her bleeding finger toward the table-top. Her hands went numb with cold.

"Sign it, damn you!" Magnus said, his voice now crackling with anger.

Helga felt his other arm wrap around her, pulling her toward him. Her body felt heavy and seemed to be easily guided. Part of her *wanted* to be guided, but the greater part of her mind held on, screaming against everything.

"No!" Helga said.

"Yes! You were meant to be here!"

Helga was sliding along the floor like a defiant child, toward the table. She looked down and saw, still clutched in her numb hand, the knife with the carved ivory hilt. Summoning her will, she thrust it at the wizard.

He saw the motion and quickly twisted, strong hands wrenching Helga's wrists. He was fast, but not quite fast enough, for though Helga's hands were numb, she was able to change direction at the last moment. She felt the knife slide through Magus's fingers, heard the wizard cry out in pain, and felt the blade pierce cloth and hit flesh.

It did not go deep, for it was a small blade, but it did enough. The grip on her wrist and body weakened enough for her to twist out of Magnus's grasp. She leapt backward, reaching for her sword.

"Away from me!" Helga cried as she kicked at the wizard. The crystal on the table rattled as he stumbled into it. The dagger fell to the ground, but Helga did not reach for it. She cursed as she stepped back, trying to free her sword from her scabbard, which seemed to be stuck shut.

"No!" Magnus cried in a high, raspy voice. He threw his hand forward, and the ball of light hurtled toward Helga. With a desperate jerk, she freed the blade.

She held the blade upward, trying to shield herself from the ball of light, now burning with fire. The ball split itself on the edge of the sword, bisecting into two amorphous lumps before exploding into a thousand sparks. The room darkened immediately, and Helga realized she had lost the whole day inside the tall library. Only the palest light of dusk remained filtering through the stained-glass windows, and the after-image of the light left Helga blind with a bright purple circle filling her vision.

"Curse you!" the wizard shouted. Helga could barely make him out, stumbling in the dim light with his hands covering his eyes.

Without further hesitation, Helga ran to the door, or as near as she could guess it to be, knocking over piles of books and bottles that were invisible in the dark room. She kicked at the door, and it burst open into a dark hallway. Helga put out a hand to find the wall, barely feeling it through the cold in her limbs, and began running down a corridor in as near to the direction she came in as she could manage. A few feet into the darkness, she sheathed her sword and put both hands to the task of feeling.

Her heart was pounding hard, and she felt as though she could not breathe in enough air. Her ears were ringing, and her legs felt weak, stumbling on thick carpet.

Eventually, Helga found a winding stairwell and began to feel her way down it, with a tickle of memory that she had walked it before. Feeling was returning quickly to her hands, and they tingled as she felt the rough stone beneath them. A dim light slowly filled her eyes, and she emerged into the grand entrance hall she had seen earlier, though the magical lights were now extinguished. She found the doors and threw them open to find a man at arms lazily leaning against a rail where Raggle remained tied.

"Evening, Lady," he said with a smile, apparently oblivious to the commotion in the upper stories of the tower.

"Good evening, sir," Helga said, trying to calm her voice. She smoothed out her clothes with her hands and held herself still as much as she could beneath her pounded fear as she stepped past the man. She untied her horse and pulled herself into the saddle. "And good evening again." She checked Raggle into a light trot (not wanting to, at the end, draw attention to herself) and nodded to the men at the large castle portcullis as she passed back into the city streets, now almost empty.

Behind her, she heard the shouts of men and, almost magically amplified, the raging voice of the wizard. She reigned in her horse and turned him toward a side street, hoping to wind her way back the front gate, though she could no longer remember in what direction it lay. She kept urging Raggle forward, but the streets did not run true, and soon she was lost. Disheartened, she stopped in the street.

"What is it, lass?" an old man said from the porch of a thatch-roofed house.

Helga straightened up. "In what direction lies the gate?"

The old man laughed. He pointed down to his right. "The Great Gate is that way, bearing always to your right, but you'd best hurry if you don't want to trouble the gatekeepers, whom *I* certainly prefer not to trouble, to let you out. Gates usually close an hour after sundown."

"Thank you," Helga said. "Perhaps someday I shall be able to re-pay you."

Helga turned at the sound of voices and heavy steps in the alley-way behind her. She strained her ears and thought she heard a man say, "This way."

The old man laughed. "Someday might as well be never with my old bones. Take care of yourself, daughter."

Helga nodded and kicked her horse into a full gallop. Its hooves echoed loudly on the cobblestone street. Dusk was fading quickly, and nobody had bothered to light lanterns, nor had the moon risen to give light to the night. The street below the horse was dim and amorphous, gaining life only in puddles that reflected the dark sky. Helga trusted Raggle to carry her as she took fork after fork bearing to her right. Suddenly, the closed streets opened up, and she saw the great iron gate of the city looming before her.

It was, miraculously, not shut. However, in front of it stood a mass of pike-wielding soldiers and two mounted knights, both fully armored. Helga stopped her horse in the street. The soldiers looked only half-alert, roused to action against a threat they didn't care much to think about, and the knights looked proud, more concerned with ordering the men than being on guard themselves. Helga wondered if such men had been amassed simply for her sake and for what she had done in the wizard's tower.

"Is that her?" a soldier said loudly to one of the knights.

"It's got to be," the knight replied. He whistled, and the rest of the men snapped their heads forward and began moving toward Helga. The two knights leapt ahead of them. Helga turned Raggle and galloped back up the street, only to reign in again as she saw two more mounted knights in a wide courtyard. She turned the horse again, this time into an alleyway. The sounds of hooves dulled on the dirt of the alley, then she turned her horse yet again, this time going back toward the gate, hoping that she could draw the men away and make a run for it, as long as they didn't think to drop the portcullis or raise the drawbridge. She leaned down to get her crossbow, but couldn't think of how to crank back the big steel bows from the saddle, so instead, she drew her sword.

She burst forward from between two houses to see many of the soldiers standing guard. The gate still stood ajar, as if the simple closing of it had escaped the thoughts of all the men in her pursuit. She dug her heels into Raggle and galloped as fast as she dared, straight into the armed men.

Spears went up. Helga cried out and flinched.

"Turn your points, you idiots!" someone shouted.

Helga opened her eyes to see half the soldiers leaping out of the way of the charging horse, the other half trying to grab her or the saddle from behind.

"Fools! Fools!" she heard someone shouting.

She was almost to the gate, but Raggle was slowing in the throng, and the horse threatened to buck her in fear.

"Just a bit further!" she cried to the beast, but it did not obey.

A hook on the end of a halberd grabbed at her wrist, and she shook it off, only to feel large gloves wrap around her ankle. Soon she was surrounded, the arch of the gateway right above her head. Another hook grabbed her by the shoulder, and she felt herself falling, tumbling, turning off the horse and into the hands and gropes of a mass of men. She cried out, only to have a hand shut her mouth forcefully.

"Fools! Fools!" the voice said again.

Helga felt her shirt rip at the sleeve, then felt herself being turned upright, her hands being held behind her back. She struggled against her assailants, but was quickly bound fast in rope then thrown back over the saddle of her horse. She turned her head and saw the face of the wizard a few paces away. He wore long robes of blue filled with gold embroidery and was sitting atop a black horse, holding a tall staff of black wood that glowed with its own sickly blue light. His face no longer looked fair and handsome, but great and terrible, with eyes that were hard to hold sight of.

"You are lucky you did not harm her, dragging her down with those hooks," he said to one of the knights. He caught Helga's eyes and said, "I am sorry for the rough treatment, my darling. I could not let you go twice."

Helga was puzzled by this, but could do nothing against her bonds, and so she went limp over the saddle. The soldiers lit torches while talking to each other, and within a few minutes, the horse began to move.

"Ah, Freydis," the wizard said. Helga did not move her head to see him. "I knew you would return, just not when. Divining the infinite is such pain when you cannot tell one time from another. Do not be afraid. Soon things will be as they were always meant to be."

"I am not Freydis," Helga said, raising her head. "I don't know who she is."

"She is you, of course, but you perhaps do not remember yourself."

"You mad bastard!" Helga said. She pushed against her bonds and tried to control her rising fear and anger, knowing that she could not free herself and was at the mercy of the wizard. "Release me, Magnus. I will leave forthwith. You know I am no threat to you."

"All will be made clear soon."

Helga let her head droop again and contented herself to watching the movement of the horses' legs in the flickering torchlight. Her vision began to get hazy from the blood rushing to her head. Despair settled on her heart like a stone: hard, heavy, and immovable.

45

Helga was shocked out of her daze by shouts and the shuffling of feet. A horse whinnied, and she saw an armored body fall from a mount to the street.

"Quickly, you idiots!" Magnus shouted. "They are nothing but bandits."

"Form ranks!" one of the knights shouted. "Shields and shoulders up. What are you doing!"

Helga could see dimly a chaotic mess of soldiers in front of one of the horses. Armored men shuffled about, trying to loose swords and get shields in position while a group of hooded men, armed with light mail, thrust spears and staves at them cautiously. One of the soldiers took a spear in the neck through his coif and collapsed. A hooded man stepped forward with a great two-handed flail, smashing shields and helmets in the gap. Men cried out, and Helga's ears were filled with the din of battle. She watched the gap close, and the hooded men shuffle backward, away from the spears and thrusting swords of the properly ordered soldiers.

"They're already in the rout!" the wizard said. "Make them pay for thinking to waylay the lord himself." Helga could see the wizard's horse move forward into the fight, but she could no longer make out his orders and heard only his crackling laughter amid the din. The lines were scattering, chasing the attackers into the night.

"Lusty fools!" the knight said. "Get back here and form ranks!" The exacerbated knight wheeled his horse around and gave a shout that was cut short by a sudden dismounting strike to his backplate.

A group of men, wearing hoods and face-wraps above light gambesons, leapt into the light of the torches. Helga pulled herself up as high as she could to see. They wielded quarterstaffs and were using them deftly against the men at arms that surrounded her. The light weapons zipped in arcing blurs, and the attackers were knocking heads and bending knees on the soldiers, the tips of the staves moving like busy insects. The men dropped their torches and groped for swords, shields, and spears, but even those who were already armed were quickly put at a disadvantage. The knight rolled on the ground, trying to right himself in his heavy plate armor. A swift crack to the back of his head made him squeal in pain.

Stout oak found its way around shields to break wrists and collarbones. Swords clattered on the ground as men cried in pain. Several of the guards found their heads naked as helms were knocked aside. Two men fell unconscious, and soon the bandits had the guardsmen in a rout. With no reinforcements, the guards fled.

Helga felt herself being pulled off the horse and felt her bonds being loosed. Her head swam again from being flipped right-side-up at last. A man in a dark hood, with a wrapping around his face, coiled up the rope that bound her and stuffed it into one of her saddlebags.

"Let's get out of here," he said to the other bandits. "Before those buffoons manage to turn about. Can you walk, Helga?"

"Yes," Helga said. "I'll walk as far or as fast as you want if it gets me out of here."

The stranger nodded, then looked to two of his companions and pointed. They both ran away. "This way," the stranger motioned for Helga to follow. He led her and Raggle toward the market, then down a gap between houses only just wide enough for the horse, who entered reluctantly. It was very dark, with only a narrow strip of stars above them to give any light at all. Helga had to feel along the walls for balance.

"Where are we going?" Helga said.

"Somewhere safe. For now."

The hooded figure led her across a wide street and into a sump surrounded by wooden houses and gardens. In the sump was a small pond, and beside it was an ivy-covered wooden fence about as tall as a man, the pickets nailed tightly together. Helga watched as the man reached into the ivy and then pushed on the fence, revealing a hidden gate. On the other side was a small, poorly tended lawn in front of a large open wooden structure, like half a barn, dripping with ivy and other creepers.

"We can hide your horse here for a time." The man pulled down his hood and unwrapped his face.

"Thorvald," Helga said, recognizing the grin splitting a bushy beard.

"None other. But of course, tell no other. Come." He took Raggle's reins and tied them to a rope lead beneath an overhang, then lead Helga to a door. He knocked with a strange rhythm, then put a key in the door and opened it to darkness. He motioned for Helga to follow. She stopped outside the threshold.

"What is the matter?" Thorvald said.

"Am I walking into another trap?"

"I already had you trapped. I freed you. You can take your chances in the city if you like. Of course, I am likely to be the only one who knows a way out."

Helga took a deep breath, clenched her fists, then stepped inside.

The interior of the house was totally dark except for the embers of a fire in a brick hearth. A man leaned against a nearby pile of refuse, snoring loudly. Thorvald kicked him as he walked past.

"What?" the man said.

"Get up, Reggy. We have company." Thorvald crossed to a pile of logs near another door and threw one in the fire.

"What?" Reggy said again. He waved his hand and went back to sleep.

"Lazy bastard," Thorvald said. "I could have been part of the guard."

"You gave the knock."

"How would you know? You were sleeping."

"How would you know I didn't hear."

"Bah," Thorvald said. He pulled a chair up to the hearth and motioned for Helga to sit.

"Thank you," Helga said as she sat in the chair. "But what do we do now?"

"I know a way out of Thruddel that mister odd-man wizard has never heard of. That'll put you out south of the city, and you can make your way home from there. I just need to let things die down for a few hours."

"How did you manage this?"

"I have a few skills, and I'm not usually as drunk as I make out. And I can fight drunk. Actually, I'd say I'm a master drunk fighter. No matter. My friends did all the hard fighting anyway." He laughed. "If Magnus only knew."

"He does know," Helga said. "He said he was watching you, listening to you plot against the king."

"Against him, he means, and clearly, he's not listening close enough," Thorvald said. "He's got the good king under a spell. I put together this little rebellion to break it. This is one of our safe houses. Reggy runs a smithy upstairs on the street level."

"A rebellion?" Helga said.

"No successes yet, though we did save you, which is good, and I don't think we'll lose a man tonight, which is also good. We can't afford to lose men. Magnus will have his revenge at the gallows tomorrow, though. Mark me." Thorvald walked back to the door and said. "I'm going to spy on what's going on. Reggy, keep an eye on the woman."

Reggy snorted in response, then turned over and began snoring again. Thorvald closed the door.

Helga watched Reggy, a big man with a long brown beard, sleep for a time, then stared into the fire and considered the day, or where she had lost it. She looked down at her finger and felt the wound there, which still stung.

"Perhaps I really ought to go home," she said to herself. "Obviously, luck is not with me." She laughed sickly to herself. "Who am I kidding? I have no idea what I'm doing. What could the volva do to me, anyway? What do you think, Reggy?"

Reggy snored on.

After a long time feeling sorry for herself, Helga dozed off in the chair. Her dreams were chaotic, filled with a rippling light like from the wizard's ball. She was running through light and dark and heard in her mind the wizard's voice furious at her escape.

*

49

She woke covered in sweat, startling as the door shut and Thorvald entered.

"The search has moved on," he said dryly. "We have a clear path. Collect yourself and keep the hood of your cloak down low. Your face will attract attention now."

Helga nodded and got up. She followed Thorvald to the overhang to find Raggle sleeping on his feet. She gently roused him and unhitched him from the rope lead, then followed Thorvald back out past the pond in the sump. It was still night, but looking up, Helga could see that the constellations had moved, and she estimated it was close to dawn.

Thorvald led her through strange streets in nearly total darkness, never missing a step. At length, they came to a cluster of small buildings made of stacked stone. They all had thatch roofs in various states of disrepair, but the walls hinted that the little houses were once well-made and maintained, in some distant past. Thorvald looked up and down an empty street, then led Helga and her horse between two of the houses, into a garden that was as black as it seemed possible to be, overgrown by old hedges.

The creak of an unoiled gate sounded in the dead night, and Helga felt old wooden pickets as she put her hands out for balance. A few steps into the darkness, it became clear that they were descending. Then the stars went out, choked out by fingers of darkness that could only be tree branches. The falls of the horse's hooves were soft, and the ground underfoot felt damp and springy.

"Almost there. We're under the south wall now. It's the oldest part of the city, and the original keep was here," Thorvald said quietly. "I don't have a torch, so we'll have to feel our way."

"I'm with you," Helga said, reaching out and feeling the sleeve of Thorvald's coat.

The descent continued, and soon the soft soil was replaced by stone underfoot that was flat and very smooth. The darkness was total, and it was cool and dry. The steps of man and beast echoed in the blackness. Raggle whinnied in fear, and Helga soothed him with a touch to his muzzle. Another creak reported a door of some kind, and Helga this time felt old, rusty bars as she passed by. They started turning, always at a slow pace, winding through the blackness. Occasionally Helga would feel an air around them and could find no wall, but eventually, they went back into confined spaces where she could feel rock defining her path forward.

Light slowly grew, and Helga could faintly make out the shape of the cavern through which they traveled. She began to hear the sound of falling water, and suddenly they came to an opening where they could again see the night sky and something of the surroundings. A rusty gate swung open, and they stepped through. They were on a ledge above a grove of oak trees, the tops of which reached to their heads with the trunks lost in darkness below. A shallow trail of water fell across their path and into the basin below. A half-moon was rising, lighting up an entire valley that stretched to the south, full of farmland.

"I will take you a bit further, but then I must leave you," Thorvald said. "I suggest you stay off of the road on your way back home, as Magnus will be looking for you."

"What if I decide not to go home?"

Thorvald chuckled. "Forget it, girl."

"But, Thorvald, what-"

"You are out of your depth in Thruddel, Helga, and your journey will be harder, not easier, before the end. The Ulfar Mountains are full of bandits and beasts, and it is said there are worse things lurking there now. And the Fay Wastes! Helga, you cannot understand what awaits you there! It is not a place you can walk blindly into and out again." Thorvald took a deep breath. "Nobody will fault you for lack of bravery. You have proven your intentions, but you do not know what you attempt to do. Do not refuse my advice again. Go home."

"My husband will die," Helga said softly. "Is that our destiny?"

"Your husband…" Thorvald sighed and shook his head. "All men die," Thorvald said, his voice smoothing out and becoming kind. "But you have a choice to go on living."

"I see that you are right," Helga said. She looked at his hard eyes in the moonlight. "Thorvald, why did you help me? Surely saving me was a tremendous risk, now that I know what you are really doing."

He touched her face lightly and smiled. "Because you remind me of my wife. She was a good woman, and it was good to remember her, even for a few moments, though unlike Magnus, I know she can never come back. I have no other real reason, other than perhaps hatred of the wizard. He wants something, and so he must not have it."

A strange itch dragged itself across Helga's mind, and she could not stop herself from asking, "What was her name, Thorvald?"

"Freydis. She died twenty years ago."

Helga sighed as she felt the weight of the name in her ears. "I'm sorry, Thorvald."

"In time, things may be made close to whole for others, but never for me."

"I understand. I regret that I have nothing to give you in return for what you have given me."

"What is freely given is freely given. Besides, it is nice to see what has been lost. It sharpens the heart for the hard days." Thorvald said. He led her and the horse down to a landing and a path at the entrance to the trees. "Here, we must part. Follow this path south until it forks. Take the right path, which will lead up into the foothills, but stay off the road itself if you can. Eventually, you will get to a small village called Melding. From there you can get directions back to your home. Live well, Helga. Your husband must be a man of great honor to deserve what you have tried to do for him."

"He would do the same," Helga said. "Of that, I have no doubt. Live honorably, Thorvald."

They shook hands like men at arms, and without further words, they parted. Helga led her horse down the path into the trees. She stopped in a moonlit clearing, then strung and loaded her crossbow before proceeding into the valley where she was able to mount up and ride again, putting as much distance as she could between herself and the city of Thruddel before she and Raggle both had to rest.

She finally let the horse stop at a fork in the road. She looked down the long road leading to the right — to the west. She felt a great shame in her heart, wondering what the others would think of her returning empty-handed and defeated. She thought also of Erling, dying slowly. Her confidence was gone, and her pride was a mere thread holding back her decision, but it was a strong thread.

She took a deep breath, summoned her courage, and took the left-hand path.

IV. BLACK FEATHER FRIENDS

HELGA RESTED in a grove of willows and oaks beside a stream when she could no longer keep her eyes open, and woke to find it was midday. She crept out of the grove to look up and down the long road. It was deserted in both directions, but in a distant field, she could see a group of thrall working. She mounted up and rode south, checking her map again and watching the mountains on her left, knowing that eventually, she must cross them.

She kept pushing the horse for the first few hours but then was content to let the beast walk, feeling more at ease with herself. By dusk of that day, she felt much less anxious and no longer worried about an immediate pursuit from the city. She stopped at a freeman farm, hoping to find lodging for the night. The farmer and his wife refused to negotiate a price for her stay, deciding that as a woman alone, she should be put up without cost. Helga, however, was able to buy some fresh food from them to replenish her stores, including a freshly baked loaf of bread, which was a delight to her senses after eating stale bread and biscuits for a week.

Before retiring, Helga dined on a beef stew with the farmer and his family. She told her story freely to them, trusting their good nature toward her as a signifier of good quality in general, and the children were in awe despite Helga's truthfulness as to her own failings. The adults may have misbelieved her (even though she wore a sword and carried a crossbow), but they made no mention of it. Helga retired to a freestanding hut apart from the main house that had apparently once been occupied by a bound man that belonged to the farmer's grandfather. She was both grateful and disappointed, for though she appreciated the courtesy of privacy, she also felt lonely after being on the road and on the run, and the sounds of the children warmed her heart.

The hut was stonewalled and roofed with turf, sticking slightly into a hillock where the sheep were kept. It had no door, but an old hide that failed to cover the opening, and the inside was sparse, containing only a lampstand, a meager table, and a raised palette bedded with straw. Helga relaxed while looking out through a gap in the hide curtain, watching Raggle as he slept lightly on his feet. He stood under a wooden overhang that served as a small stable for the family's donkey, who also slept nearby.

In the morning, it rained. Helga watched the grey rain fall on the house as she worked on her crossbow, waxing the string and oiling the firing mechanism. When the rain didn't lighten, she worked a coat of oil onto her sword and scabbard, making up her mind to endure the weather if she could, for in the back of her mind, she still feared the wizard and what he might do if he knew in what direction she had left.

With a quick thanks to the family, Helga rode away with her crossbow in her lap. Raggle did not seem to mind too greatly the rain, which was soft but cold. Helga stayed mostly dry and warm thanks to her cloak (made by her own hands in a better day, of excellently tight-weaved wool), feeling only slightly annoyed by the steady drips that fell in front of her eyes from her large hood. She rode the whole day at an easy pace. She came only to one more farm late in the day, but the fields there were tended with men and women who looked to be poorly treated thrall, though nobody watched over them. At dusk, she came upon a heavily fortified house, like a little keep with walls and iron gates, and a parapet that defended the points of entry. Not liking the look of it, she passed it by and hoped for a more inviting house.

Without finding a farmstead close to the road by true nightfall, and the open fields fading to darkness around the road, Helga had to shelter in an abandoned barn. The barn, which was clearly not made to endure long, had been taken over by a huge creeper that covered the northern walls and made a roof over many of the fallen parts of the building. Helga thought the whole thing might have collapsed without the vine, so grey was the timber where it showed, but she was grateful for a place to rest. The vines made a fairly watertight ceiling choking the old shake and thatch, and one corner of the structure was quite dry. There she made a small fire and sheltered herself and the horse.

The following days saw a break in the rain, though the mud remained on the old road. The remnants of people began to thin, with farms and holdings become sparser as she went onward, forcing her to spend the next nights out of doors. At last, she reached the small river and the path that Thorvald had marked on her map, which would take her up and over the mountains. The first day on this narrower and slightly overgrown path, she came upon two travelers with a horse pulling a wagon laden with barrels and bags.

"Hail," Helga said as she rode up. The travelers were a man and a woman of young years, and with them were two children in the cart she did not initially notice. They were all road-worn and dirt-stained, wearing woolen clothes that were once fine.

"Who goes there?" the man said, shielding his eyes from the sun.

"Helga, a traveler. I mean you no harm."

"A woman?" The man cast an odd look to the woman next to him. "I'm called Tian, and you're riding the wrong way," the man said. "Thruddel is the other way."

"I'm not going to Thruddel."

"Well, you can't go that way," the man said, pointed back along the road.

"Why?"

"Bandits. A great many of them. And…"

The woman spoke. "There is something wrong with them. Leprous."

"You seem to be still well-provisioned for traveling past bandits," Helga said.

"We aren't," the woman said. "Which is why they didn't bother coming down to pursue us. Our lord was not so lucky."

"Your lord?"

"Suits him right," said Tian. "Bloody proud coward."

The woman said, "Our hold, Strandam, was sacked three weeks ago by an army from the Northmarch. Coladarn the King razed almost everything aside from the castle. We weren't inside, lucky enough for us, but the lord was set free only after surrendering his treasury."

"I see," Helga said. "Well, there is decent enough land about here. What looks to be good soil. I stayed at an abandoned farm a few days past. The barn even now stands if you intend to settle again."

The man shook his head. "I appreciate the information, but we have no seed crop. The best we can hope for now is to indenture ourselves to someone who has fields already sown."

"You were freemen, then," Helga said.

"Were," the man said.

"You could sell your horse for enough," Helga said.

"Too late to start the sowing, and too little to eat till harvest," the man said. "And we would need the horse to do the plowing."

Helga sighed. "In that case, I passed by a small manor further up the large road on the way to Thruddel. Maybe you will find vittles there."

"Thank you," the woman said.

"Before you leave," Helga said. "What can you tell me of the mountains? I trust the passage was not too hard for you to pull a wagon and a horse."

"Not too hard, no," the man said. "It's the people in the pass I would worry about, not the road, especially for a lady like you."

"I will be cautious," Helga said. "Gods favor you."

"And you," the woman said. "But you should probably turn around."

Helga nodded, then left the family and continued up the road.

The plains subsided to a sparse forest of oak as she gained altitude, and the wind began to blow with a harsh chill. The river fell rapidly over rocks, cool and bright. She camped by herself in a rocky alcove above the river, lighting a fire to keep warm until the wind died around midnight. The next two days were filled with quick climbing up into the mountains, for the road there was yet still well-trod and maintained by travel.

She saw no sign of other people until, on the fourth day since meeting the fleeing family, she came upon a stripped body of a man upon which a few ravens feasted. She supposed it was the lord of whom the peasants spoke, for he looked to be well-fed when alive, though death had swelled his body further, and the carrion birds had already eaten much of him.

She paused for a few minutes to look around her for signs of the bandits, but the forest was quiet. A deep fear in her heart compelled her to leave, but looking upon the body of the slain man, she felt another feeling: a mixture of pity, sadness, and disgust. She made up her mind to bury the man, failing to have any other means of disposing of his body, and so dug a narrow trench with her small shovel and then with great effort rolled the dead man in. She covered the body with soil and leaves as three ravens watched and rocked laughingly at her, unwilling to abandon their feast, even to the earth.

"Foolish Helga," Helga said to herself as she looked at the Ravens. "You'll probably find a way to dig down to him and get what you like anyway."

"We already ate the best parts," one of the ravens said back in a thin, croaking voice.

"And he was past his prime," said another.

Helga startled and drew her sword, only to hear the black birds laugh truly, a dark and menacing sound, though even those grim birds had joy in their laughter.

"Who are you?" Helga said.

"We're the Black Feather Friends," one of the ravens said.

"Or the black feather fiends, ha!" said another.

The largest of the ravens hopped down to a low branch by Helga's head, paying little mind to her long sword. "Introductions for the Black Friends are in order. I am Zim, my mate is Zul, and my friend over there, the one with the murder-look, is Zald." At that, all the ravens laughed.

"You would not understand the humor of corvids," Zul said. She was the smallest of the group and had the largest eyes. "Zim just called Zald a crow. How delightfully insulting!"

"I will get my revenge one day, as sure as the Doom of Man," Zald, who appeared to have a band of blue-green feathers on his neck, said. The ravens all laughed again.

Helga, getting slightly over the queerness of talking Ravens, said, "I'm glad somebody here has some mirth. I tend to not waste laughter over murdered men, even cowardly lords."

"Cowardice is not forgotten in the grave," Zald said, "but it is forgotten in the flesh. Ha!"

"Tell me, child," Zul said, hopping down to a low branch to peer at Helga. "Why do men bury and burn their dead?"

"Is this a riddle?" Helga said.

"It just seems like a terrible waste," Zul said. "All those lovely eyes stuck behind shiny coins and stuck in the ground."

Zald puffed up himself and flew down, landing on the grave. "I saw no coins! I would have the eyes *and* the coins!"

"The dead need passage," Helga said.

"They have passage already," Zim said. "Or do you think souls wait around in empty bodies and have need of shiny things?"

"It's tradition. What else would we do with a body?" Helga said.

"Leave it out for good Black Feather Friends to eat," Zald said. He pecked at the leaves on the ground. "Flesh is good for many days and would feed many chicks. And ravens are good friends to have, little girl. Yes, very good friends."

"Better to make friends using an empty vessel," Zim said, "than to waste it by putting it into the ground for worms."

Zul laughed. "I believe you have agreed with Zald."

"I did nothing of the sort," Zim said. "Our sentiments are totally ad-hoc. Now tell me, girl, where are you going?"

"I don't see how it concerns Ravens," Helga said. "Even talking ravens."

"Ah, but you have taken the last bites of our meal," Zim said. "We are not mad, mind you. I was already stuffed, but that does leave a bit in the owing."

"I propose we get the eyes of the next man she kills," Zald said. "I get the first eye!"

"Yes, of course," Zim said. "We will follow you to your next kill and eat the eyes and the other delicacies before you can throw him in the ground. The deal is made!"

"I have made no deal!" Helga said.

"Nonsense, child," Zul said. "Ravens know when a deal is struck, for we are the craftiest of birds. Worry not. We shall accompany you on your way, and we are no burden on the road."

"Yes, we fly!" Zald cried, and flew up around Helga's head before alighting on a branch.

"But I don't intend to kill anyone," Helga said.

"Then why do you have a sword, eh," said Zul. "And your arrow contraption?"

"Because..." Helga felt herself getting frustrated. "Because you must plan for every possibility."

"Plan, yes," Zim said. "Ravens understand plans better than all creatures, save the most expertly diabolical humans, such as kings and farmwives. We will help you plan, and execute your plan!"

All the ravens laughed again in their strange voices, then took to flight above her, calling out for her to hurry back to the road. Helga sighed and mounted up, hoping the ravens would give up on her after a few miles.

The ravens, however, had no intention of abandoning what they saw as a deal, whether or not Helga intended to fulfill that bargain. The Black Feather Friends flew circles above her as she rode, or alighted from branch to branch if the horse walked slowly, cackling at her and talking to themselves (as if Helga was not there), about the strange blindness of humans, or what parts of a corpse each preferred whilst fresh and what parts remained flavorful after a few days in the sun. Helga had felt lonely, but the company of carrion birds who could talk about the savory-ness of human body parts was not what she had prayed for. She groaned as Zald discussed the best way to cut up an eye for swallowing.

As the sun was setting, Zul came down and sat on the horn of Helga's saddle.

"What do you want?" Helga said.

Zul began to absent-mindedly pick at a loose leather thong. "Tell me, Helga, what brings you out to the Talonbranch Mountains?"

"I thought these were the Ulfar Mountains," Helga replied.

"We were here first, so we get the privilege of the naming," Zul said. "You are clever in trying to avoid my question."

"I am on a quest."

"Aren't we all."

"I am going to the Fay."

Zul laughed. "Are you? Men cannot return there, you know."

"I am not a man."

"You know what I mean, clever girl. And I know your next response, which will be to ask me why I want to know. Well, ravens are curious. I also like to know what risk I am bringing my doom into. Also, I might be able to help you."

"For a price, yes?"

"Things usually have prices, but it depends. Unlike Zim, I often prefer to do things simply because I wish to."

"Do you wish to?"

"I don't know yet, silly." The raven flew away at the call of her companions, leaving Helga to ponder her odd words.

With the light finally dying, Helga got off the road to make camp. As she was unpacking her gear, Zald came and landed on her shoulder, startling her.

"We have found a better place to camp, come!" the raven said.

"Why should I trust you, raven?"

Zald hopped onto her packed tent and spread his wings. "Come! Come!"

Grumbling, Helga set her gear on the saddle and led her horse through the trees, following Zald, who hopped along the ground, cackling. Eventually, he led her to a well-sheltered alcove of granite and trees where the high wind outside was broken into a very soft and pleasant breeze. Zim and Zul were already there, sharing the carcass of a rabbit.

"Not fair!" Zald shouted, flying over to the dead animal. "Not fair! You did not tell me you went to find food."

"We saved you an eye," Zul said.

"Yes, an eye for mighty Zald!" The raven began to pick at the skull of the rabbit. Disgusted, Helga looked away and set about making her bed.

"Did you want some, Helga?" Zim said. "We have already had much to eat today, and we are happy to share. Once we have our fill, of course."

"No!" Zald said. "She is not a Black Feather Friend."

"Do not trouble yourself, raven," Helga said. "I do not eat carrion."

Helga started a fire and sat down beside it. She had run out of bread (which had gone stale, though she ate it anyway) a day before, and so set about to wetting a biscuit of hardtack in a cup of bitter tea. As she chewed it and some dried beef, she silently wished the rabbit was fresh, even picked over by ravens, for her stomach ached for fresh meat.

Despite this, and also despite the long and strange conversations of the Ravens, she fell hard asleep.

Helga was woken in the night by a raven picking at her ear. She startled awake and scrambled for her sword before she realized it was Zim, whispering to her in a soft, rocking voice.

"Quiet, girl. Up, away."

"What is it?" Helga whispered back.

"The killer men are coming back near. You must hide, or you will be killed."

Helga quickly got up and packed her gear. Luckily, she had fallen asleep with her boots on and had no dressing to do. She threw the saddle back on Raggle and covered it with her gear, not bothering to securely store anything.

While she did this, Zul quietly landed on the saddle horn. "I have found a hiding spot for you. I can see it from the air, but not the ground. Quickly, this way."

Helga followed the raven as best she could, but it was night in the forest, and ravens are as black as the color can be. All she could do was guess by the movement of moonspots here and there as to where Zul was.

"You must move faster!" Zul said. "Faster!"

"I cannot see you!" Helga said aloud.

"Drat. Very well," Zul said. "Curse my heart, too eager to bind myself to deals." With that, Helga saw, to her immense surprise, a soft red light envelope the raven, and by that light, she could quite clearly see where the bird was. It was a glowing shape of shadow flitting along the ground, illuminating the path they walked.

"Zul, you must put out your light," Zald said. Helga could make out the bird hopping around a great bush.

"The girl's eyes are no good in the dark," Zul said.

"Not our fault! Not our fault!" Zald said. Zul did not put out the red light that surrounded her, but instead guided Helga through a small parting in the bushes and into a vine-encrusted hallow made by two ancient yew trees, their insides long rotted away to create a wall of twisted wood on either side of Helga.

"I will cover the tracks," Zim said, flying past Zul and back out of the hollow.

"Now load your arrow machine," Zald said. "Load it!"

"I'm trying," Helga said, working hard with her legs to pull the string all the way up into the trigger mechanism. It clicked in, and Helga inserted a bolt just as Zul extinguished her light.

Helga sat down and wrapped her cloak around herself, finding the wind suddenly cold even with the bushes to break it. She could see, or thought she could by some trick, small lights through the distant trees moving here and there. She stood up silently and looked.

She saw faces by firelight, and by some other sort of light, glowing like the wizard's magic staff. The faces did not look right. They seemed sallow and flat, nose-less, though they were far away. She wondered if they really did have leprosy. As the lights moved away, Helga sat back down.

After some time, Zim returned and perched himself on Helga's knees.

"The bandits are already moving. They did not even find your camp. It is a wonder they find anything at all."

"You are fortunate to have the Black Feather Friends," Zald said.

"Indeed," Helga said quietly. "But I wonder why you did not let them find and kill me, if that was what they were going to do. Then you would have the eyes I owe you."

"We had a deal," Zim said. "Ravens never turn their backs on a deal."

"Might it be better for you to follow those bandits?" Helga said. "I imagine they will create more eyes for the eating than me."

"We had a deal, and I intend to collect what you owe me," Zald said. "Do not try to shirk us, for you cannot out-run us!"

"I wouldn't dare," Helga said. "And I'm beginning to appreciate the company."

"Appreciate, yes, but what about enjoy?" Zald said.

Zim spoke up. "Zald, do not prod a woman, especially if she has a crossbow."

"I bet she can't hit me with it," Zald said with a croaking laugh.

"Not the sort of bet to make," Helga said. "I didn't grow up in a palace, my grim friend."

Zul and Zim began to laugh, which perturbed Zald, who hopped about on the ground flapping his wings in frustration before saying, "Be that way. I shall go check on these killers. I don't feel like sleeping anyway."

Helga chuckled to herself. In the dark, she felt the fear of the moment give way to tiredness. She packed her blanket into the hollow of a yew tree and leaned up against it. She laid her crossbow across her lap and unsheathed her long sword, then leaned it up against the tree. Content with what defenses she could have at the ready, she laid her head back against the tree to sleep.

She woke up in full morning light to find the ravens missing again. Her buckles and other tack were still coated with dripping morning dew, so she worked quickly to dry off what iron she could. Her sword, too, had gotten wet, so she took out a rag and some honing oil and put a quick coat on the blade before re-sheathing it. She had loaded up the horse and readied herself for the next day of travel before she realized that she didn't know where she was, or in what direction the road lay.

Not knowing what else to do, she ate a light breakfast of her provisions and waited for the Ravens. When she had just about given up and was trying to decide in what direction to set off to find the road, Zald came flitting through the trees.

"There you are," the raven said. "Why are you still sleeping?"

"I'm not," Helga said. "I've been up for ages. Where have you been?"

"Waiting for you at the road, silly girl," Zald said. "Why do you tarry?"

"I don't know in what direction the road lies. I came here in the dead of night, and quite tired, too."

"Silly," Zald said. "This way!" With that, Zald started flitting among the branches. Helga lead Raggle along through the underbrush and between the twisted trees until, just a short distance from the yew grove, she stumbled out upon the road. She saw down the way the other two ravens, busy eating some small piece of game she could no longer recognize.

"Are you going to complain that they are eating without you?" Helga asked Zald.

"No," Zald said. "I killed the squirrel, and I ate first, hence why I was bored enough to go find you."

"I'm glad I make such good company," Helga said.

"I appreciate the company, yes," Zald said. "But enjoy it? Hardly. You don't talk enough. When I find a mate, I intend for her to talk twice as much as me, so that I will never be bored."

"Good luck finding another talking raven," Helga said.

"No, bad luck," Zald said, his voice sounding slightly sad.

Helga mounted up and rode past the other two ravens who flapped their wings in deference to the horse, but did not stop their meal. Zald sat on the pommel of the saddle and looked forward as the horse rode.

After some time, the other two ravens took flight and easily passed Helga by. She saw them flying above her several times before going off in one direction or another. Zald seemed content to rest on the horse, who didn't seem to mind the additional passenger.

The raven talked unceasingly, and Helga quickly realized that ignoring the bird did nothing valuable. He would assume she had not heard him and squawk louder, or would think she had drifted off to sleep and so bite and peck her hand to wake her up. By mid-day, Zald was convinced that Helga was at least partly deaf, which was when Helga began talking to him in earnest.

By supper, Zald had learned every part of the saddle and could name it, every part of a sword and crossbow, knew at least some instructions regarding needlework and weaving, and also knew what to do when a sheep was giving birth (which Zald found was not to eat the lamb, to his surprise). Helga made a rough camp where Zald suggested, and soon Zim and Zul turned up, and Zald left to find his dinner.

While Helga was trying to choke down a dry biscuit, she pulled out the map and examined it. Zim and Zul flew down and landed by the low fire, and Zim, seeing the map, hopped onto Helga's shoulder, unbalancing her with his girth.

"What is this?" he croaked.

"A map," Helga said. "To lead me where I need to go."

"It looks like poor work."

"Yes, I know."

"I have seen much better maps."

"Have you? I'd be surprised to know a raven has seen any at all."

"I am very old and have seen many things," said Zim, and peered at the map. "So, you seek the watchers?"

Helga quickly folded the map and put it in her lap. Zim, surprising her, bit her hand, then snatched the map while she swatted at him.

"Why did you do that?" Helga said, shaking her sore hand.

"To see better," Zim said. With his large, black feet and beak, Zim spread out the map before the fire.

"Ah," Zul said, joining her mate. "She *does* seek the watchers. Does she know what awaits her there?"

"I cannot think she does," Zim said. "Or she would probably not be looking for them, eh?"

"I can hear you, you know," Helga said.

"Hush child," Zul said. "It is unwise to harry a council of corvids. Now, Zim, should we warn her, or turn her away, or help her?"

"I'm right here," Helga said.

Zim ignored her. "I am not in the business of giving help to strange girls."

"What else will you do with your days, then?" Zul said.

Helga spoke up. "What is so dangerous about the watchers? This is not the first warning I have had, but when I set out, I was told they weren't so dangerous."

"Fay folk are always dangerous," Zim said. "Particularly when they are ravens."

Zul said, "The watchers are a cursed folk, Helga. They covet mortals, and all their thoughts are toward that end."

"What are they?" Helga said.

Zul cocked her head. "I cannot say for sure, other than they are from the Fay, but fear a full return to the timeless dream and are never at rest between the two worlds."

"Can they travel to the Fay?" Helga said.

"Yes," Zim said. "They must return often, but they hate and fear it now. So odd."

"What do they look like?" Helga said. "Are they birds like you?"

Zul and Zim rocked a laugh. "No," Zim said. "They are like men, or elves, but not like men. They are like a dream of men yet to be."

"Yes, you should not go there," Zul said. "We can lead you back from the bandits and send you home."

"After she kills a man for us," Zald said, returning with a dead rat in his talons.

"Of course," Zul said.

"I must go to the watchers," Helga said. "I must. I am tired of people saying otherwise."

"We are not people," Zald said with a laugh.

"Must is a strong word, girl," Zim said. "Should you not better say that you choose?"

"I made a bargain with volva," Helga said. "I cannot and dare not fail."

"Ah, yes," Zim said. "Never break a deal, or you will suffer for it, as sure as my beak is black."

"Now, child," Zul said. "What is it you seek from the Watchers? I am sure there is another way to get whatever it is."

Helga considered withholding the information, for talking ravens were not things she was used to trusting. After a moment or two, she decided to tell the truth. "I must get the Water of Awakening from them."

Zald flapped his wings and hopped forward. "A fancy tale. They have no such thing. There *is* no such thing, not anymore."

"If that were true," Zul said, "The fay would have long dried up and given way to the waking world."

"Have you ever seen the Water?" Zald said. "Have you? I thought not!"

"What is it?" Helga asked.

"I don't remember," Zim said.

"I don't understand," Helga said in return.

"We've been too long away," Zul said. "We cannot recall. Our memories are of this world now, not the timeless dream."

Helga sighed. "I cannot turn back. I must at least try."

"I wonder what the watchers' eyes taste like," Zald said.

"Now that is a delightful thought," Zim said. "We may get a mighty bargain yet from this hasty deal."

While the ravens hypothesized the taste and effect of Watcher flesh, Helga made her bed ready. When she finished, she wrapped her cloak around the back of her head to silence the arguing of the birds. Then, she slept.

V. THE BAND OF THE BADGER

HE NEXT DAY, the ravens journeyed with Helga along the road until the path forked.

"Which way would you like to take?" Zim said to her, sitting on the post of a sign that had long ago rotted to a grey stump.

"I didn't see a fork on my map," Helga said.

"They both go to the same place, more or less," Zim said. "The narrow way carries the danger of wolves and the great cat. Oh, and trolls. Have you ever seen one? Quite repulsive. Of course, the wide way carries the danger of men."

"Well, I don't like the sound of wolves," Helga said. "Trolls even less. So, the wide path. Men are more predictable and not always a danger."

"Funny sentiment from a human," Zald said.

Helga took the wide way, and the ravens left her for a time to see to their own machinations. At the midday meal, Zim and Zul found her again and debated who got to rest upon the saddle horn and who was going to rest upon the cantle.

"This idea of having a beast do your walking for you, I have decided," Zim said, "is quite good. I just wish there was a faster beast for ravenkind."

"Perhaps an albatross," Zul said.

"Far too unlucky," Zim said.

Once they had decided who would ride where (with the two ravens, despite being in what Helga assumed to be the avian equivalent of marriage, making some sort of deal), they set off again. Zul sat on the cantle for the day, and Zim sat on the Horn, happy to watch the road and bob his head.

Near the end of the day, Zul and Zim suddenly took to flight from the saddle. Zim cried out, "I knew this was a bad idea!"

Zul said back, "We still had a deal!"

Helga saw ahead of her what had spooked the birds. Two tall orcs, grey-skinned and yellow-toothed, their eyes shining amber, stood in the shadows of a far tree, bows and arrows ready to be drawn in their hands. The expressions on their hard, angular faces were unreadable.

"Peace, friends!" Helga said, and held up her right hand. Her crossbow hung from her saddle, and she knew she would not ready it in time to defend against the first shot of the archers if they provoked to fire.

One of the orcs waived her forward. Slowly, she approached.

"What be your name, woman?" said one of the orcs. He wore dark, tarnished mail and a light helm inscribed with strange symbols.

"Helga, daughter of Hrolfi," said Helga. "I am traveling to the other side of the mountains."

"Wait there," the orc said. The two orcs conversed in their strange tongue, then one of them left.

"What is *your* name?" Helga said to the one who remained. He stayed silent with his arrow nocked. After a tense minute, the second orc returned with, very much to Helga's surprise, a tall blonde-haired elf in well-laundered casual clothes and carrying a polished long-sword. His straight mane was tied back in a high tail, exposing his long ears.

"She is indeed a woman. Your eyes are as fine as always," the elf said to the orcs with a slight sarcasm Helga thought they did not catch.

"She sat with ravens upon her saddle, sir," one of the orcs said.

The elf looked at Helga with searching eyes.

"Odd, but I deem her no threat if she surrenders her weapons while at camp. Come, friend. I am Trindol, commander at arms for the Band of the Badger. Unlucky name, very fine company."

"I am Helga," Helga said. "Thank you for giving me passage." She surrendered to the elf her crossbow and sword, which very much interested Trindol.

"I should like to have a look at it later, if you will permit," he said, but refused to draw the sword himself.

The elf led her into a wide circle of a camp, with the road going right down the middle. Tents spread out to either side between wagons, and fires were in the making. Smoke curled up here and there, and it was clear to Helga dinner was being arranged. Armed men in mail (and many out of their armor) were everywhere. Helga spotted more than a few women, dressed plainly and working on cooking or other tasks. A few of them wore armor, but most seemed put out of that sort of work.

Trindol brought her at last to the makings of a large fire in a clearing, where sat several burly orcs and rough men, along with another elf of fair visage and grey eyes, like Trindol but with a harder expression.

"Ah, Trindol," one of the orcs said in a deep, slightly ragged voice. "We have a visitor, I see."

The orc stood up, revealing a great height and massive bulk. His arms were bare and covered with strange tattoos, and he wore a simple cloth tunic covered with small objects that were sewn on or hung by leather thongs. He held a gnarled staff of wood in his right hand capped with a misshapen crystal that glowed blue of its own light. His face was less harsh than the other orcs, even gentle, and his eyes were a clear light brown, leading Helga to believe he was not a full orc, but some product of a human or elf union, which was not unheard of in the south.

"I am Thokar, leader of the Band of the Badger," he said. "And the master of sorcery for our little army."

"For all three of our sorcerers," the elf at fire said. "I am Peridan, the lone enlisted man of our corps of magic." He smiled, stood up, and bowed to Helga.

"I am Helga. I am pleased to meet you all, but I am just traveling to the other side of the mountains. I did not expect such a greeting."

Thokar laughed a deep and hardy laugh. "Ah, but I was expecting you."

"Ah yes," Peridan said. "You will find that Thokar has quite the talent for divination, such as it is. Don't let him scare you."

"I am not frightened," Helga said. "But you said you were expecting me. To what end?"

"I don't know," Thokar said. "I merely know that a woman of doom was to come, and I rarely am given glimpses by the spirits of fate when fate is not at stake. What doom is laid on you?"

Peridan and Trindol both laughed at this, a light and carefree laugh. The other orcs at the fire grumbled.

"I know not of any doom," Helga said. "But perhaps your spirits knew I could warn you. There is a group of bandits west of here, moving along the road toward the plains beyond. They murdered a nobleman a few days past, and I believe them to be dangerous. I was able to escape their notice through clever hiding, but such a large group will be trouble, for you and them."

"How many were there?" one of the orcs asked. He had an aged and scared face and did not take his eyes off of a puzzlebox in his hands as he spoke.

"That is Baradict," Trindol said. "He is our Sargent Major and chief of enlistment. Baradict Soft-heart, we call him. He won't look you in the eye, perhaps ever, just so you know. He doesn't want to make it hard to kill you."

"Well, that puts me at ease," Helga said, and both the elves laughed. "As to the bandits, I do not know how many. Perhaps twenty or thirty. Actually, there are probably more judging by their fires."

"Easy work, boss," Baradict said. He turned his puzzlebox and smiled, completing one of the images on its face.

"Better to come to work with full numbers and plenty of rest," Thokar said. "But if the conflict is unavoidable, then we will charge ahead, as always."

"I got a few newbies that could use a taste of combat before we get into anything real," Baradict said. "You still seem concerned, though." Baradict continued to stare at the puzzlebox.

"I am. Helga, would you like to stay the night in our camp? It is safer with many than with one. Many of the men here are married, and we travel with our families. There will be other women, and the soldiers here are no threat to you."

"Very well," Helga said. "But I have little to offer in return."

"You have already paid us well with a warning," Thokar said. "Let us pay you with a hot meal. You have the look of road rations eaten overlong."

Helga agreed. She followed Trindol to a small clearing beside a large and brightly colored tent, where she unsaddled Raggle and made a small camp for herself. Trindol returned shortly and beckoned her to dinner, which consisted of roasted boar, potatoes, vegetables, and a tasty flatbread. It was all served in large bowls as there were no tables at hand. She ate sitting around a fire with the elves, Thokar, an elvish maiden (named Faralinda, Trindol's wife), and Thokar's wife (an orc named Mona).

Around other fires, the men joked and talked jovially of things both trivial and grim. Around her own fire, she listened to the assembly talk of past losses and future plans, old places and unrecognizable names, and of food. The Band of the Badger was apparently a mercenary band, a large group of sell-swords that roamed the eastern and southern kingdoms, where men of war or armed security were needed, as they often were. They were mostly orcs, with a reasonable amount of men and elves mixed in and one single dwarf (who was the cook, and the finest the company had ever known). War had kept them all reasonably well provisioned, and the wagons they traveled in were more alike to those of a carnival than a train of war.

Thokar's wife Mona asked Helga bluntly, "What exactly brings a woman out alone to the Ulfar Mountains and beyond? What is it you are looking for, and would it not be better to be looking for a husband?"

"I am married," Helga said. "It is my husband's fate that sends me hither. He is ill with a terrible disease, and to cure it, I must fetch a rare relic for a volva. A very nasty crone of a woman, but I am desperate to save him."

"I see," Mona said. "He married well, then."

"What disease is it?" Faralinda asked. "I have knowledge of the healing arts. I might know a remedy."

"Moss Rot, as it commonly called. A magical ailment," Helga said. "He cannot leave the bed."

"That is not a disease easily acquired or remedied," the elf maiden said. "It will require a spirit severing, and that is hard work, but I am not so sure it is the work of a volva. I would meet this volva who has such power."

Thokar rubbed his chin and spoke. "I know of a remedy for the Moss Rot. It is old magic, but it will work. Our people once would call upon the spirits of the dead for battle, and very often such sorcerers would fall ill with the Moss Rot, or the Mist Blight as it is properly known, as the dead they were in contact with sought to drag the sorcerer back to Hel."

"Necromancy," Trindol said. "Why on earth haven't you taught Peridan?" He gave a wide smile to the other elf.

"Because he knows I never touch the dark arts," Peridan said.

"He knows you're a poor student," said Trindol.

"The art is lost," Thokar said. "Save for but a few who commune with the dead, rather than bind them. It was never considered a dark art to my people, Peridan. That is an elvish disposition toward the dead. To an orc, his ancestors are his allies and belong to him as much as he does to them."

"Then why did the dead want to bind the living, eh?" Trindol said.

"Because to be dead is like being asleep, and the call back to the 'World-That-Is' only makes them hunger for reawakening. They do not know that they call down the living, only that they desire life and the living to return to them, at least for those spirits that have not made the final escape."

"The desire of every dreamer is to make real the dream," Peridan said sadly.

"You said you know of a remedy," Helga said.

"I do," Thokar said. "If he still wakes enough to drink, that is."

"He does. He can eat and drink," Helga said. "Is there a danger he will cease to be able to?"

Peridan nodded grimly and tossed a twig into the fire, where it burned blue. "Eventually, he will fall into a sleep that appears light, but from such a sleep, he will not be able to be roused. Then the sleep will deepen to the point that he will be like one who is dead. No breath, nor beating of heart, but his body will not decay. His flesh will cool, but not grow fully cold. If he gets to that point, only a spirit severing from the underworld will save him, and even then, it is probably best not to try. Who knows what man will return to you from the land of the dead? Even the hooded one did not come back unchanged."

Thokar nodded. "Then do not let it come to that. I can make a potion that will silence the spirit for three days, which will make the dead give up their grasp of him, for they will cease to know his life, and they will weaken as they stop drawing on his life force. After those three days, he will awake and be whole, though weak."

"How much will this remedy cost me?" Helga said.

"Hard to say," Thokar said. "The brewing is a secret to my people, but not one that is beyond me. I am sad to say, however, that I lack the ingredients, and I do not know at what cost you can acquire them. The rarest and most powerful of these is the Luminescent Russula mushroom. If you do find any of them in your travels, I would happily make you the potion in exchange for the remainder of the mushrooms, for I can use them to brew a powerful health potion that will close wounds and instantly restore the vigor of an injured man. We are a good company here, but war never leaves without demanding a pint or two of blood."

"There is always a catch, isn't there?" Helga said. "Well, perhaps you can give me the list. I still have a journey ahead of me. Who knows? I might find them somewhere. It seems, though, that I am stuck relying on the volva."

Thokar shrugged. "I can write down the other ingredients, but they are easily found compared to the Russula. The mushrooms are also easily identified. They glow a luminescent green-blue at all times and even, if you put the caps to your ears, they crackle softly like a fire. They thrive in dark places, but only dark places that are bathed in the old magic – places where the Prim settled in the making of the world. I know rumor of a cave to the north, supposedly once a dragon's lair, but I do not have the time to leave the company to seek it."

"I doubt I will have time either," Helga said. "My errand, as it is, still demands some swiftness. Still, I shall keep my eyes open, Thokar."

Helga leaned back when she was done eating and listened to Thokar and the others discuss the business ahead, and what wars they might find in the west. There was apparently war brewing all across the north. Hviterland was on a path of conquest, creating a mighty army of its allies. Golice had already fallen, and there was wonder in the air of who would be next and whether the army would turn west or south. The riches of the Northern kings were keen in the orcs' ears, and even the elves seemed interested in what would be brought out of the fortresses of the Petty Kingdoms. While she reclined, Helga heard what she could only consider a whisper, though it creaked like twigs snapping in the fire.

"Helga! What are you doing!?" It was Zim, crouching under the leaves of a bush not far from the campfire.

"Camping."

"These men are dangerous," the raven said, bobbing up and down.

"Of course they are. They *are* mercenaries, after all."

Helga shooed the Raven away. He gave Helga the most indignant stare a raven could manage before hopping away into the darkness.

As the fire died down, the others went to their wagons and tents. Helga got up and found her way back to her own camping spot, where

Raggle picked at some oats some kind person had given him to eat. She settled herself down to sleep, looked up at the stars, then closed her eyes. Before she could do much more than that, she was brought back to waking by a large pair of talons on her chest.

"Awake, child! Awake!" Zul said. "We will help you escape, but you must hurry."

"Escape what, raven?" Helga said, tired and not able or willing to tell one black bird from the other. "I'm not being held prisoner." She turned over on her side. Zul hopped on her shoulder and pecked at her ear.

"Not that, silly!" Zul said. "The bandits from yestereve. They are hell-thrall. Half-men. They approach! But I will lead you on a safe path."

Helga bolted upright and sought her sword, which she realized she had turned over to the mercenaries as a guarantee. "Quickly, we must warn the others!"

"The others are coming," Zul said. "They fly now."

"No, stupid, the men here," Helga said. She cupped her hands to her mouth. "To arms! To arms! Wake! To arms!"

"Fool!" Zul said. "Now we shall never escape."

"These people must be warned," Helga said. She dropped to the ground and started hurriedly putting on her boots. Trindol approached with a lamp, looking bewildered.

"Where is the attack?" he said, looking about at the clearing full of calm horses and tents, just beginning to show the light of lanterns and fire as men awoke.

Helga looked around for Zul, but could not see her. "Zul! Where does the attack come from? The West?" She looked back at Trindol. "Likely the west."

"The west road and the trees too," Zul croaked from a bough above.

"Who told you this?" Trindol said.

"A raven," Helga said, without thinking of just how odd that would sound.

"A raven, are you mad woman?" Trindol said.

"No," Helga said. She went quickly to the closest tent and shook the sides of it. "Wake up, you fools, or die in your beds!"

"You'll rouse my wife!" Trindol said.

"Good," Helga said. "She's bound to have more sense than you." Helga continued her shouting, and soon a good crowd of men and orcs were falling out of tents, swords and spears at the ready, while others busied themselves stringing their bows. Trindol held his sword out but seemed so unused to a woman making such a display that he stood dumbfounded, and the tip of his weapon dangled to the ground impotently. Men formed their companies and moved to the west of the camp at the urging of Helga.

"What's the meaning of all this?" It was Baradict, eyes aglow with rage and holding a heavy mace in one hand, with a look to use it.

"There is an attack coming," Helga said. "Bandits I passed by recently. They must have turned back this way."

"Baradict, I must apologize for this woman. She is clearly beset in the mind with-" Trindol was trying to say *with madness,* but was cut short by the sounding of a horn in the west.

"Turn your frustrations on the attackers, knife-ear," the old orc said, and immediately went sprinting to the west.

Thokar appeared among the throng of men, his great staff giving off a warm orange light from the crystal at the top. His wife, as well as several other orc women, were moving beside him. Mona carried Helga's crossbow and sword, along with a staff, and several of the other women carried weapons.

"Helga," he said. "I know not how you predicted this, but time is scarce. We are sending the women to the protected rear with what children we have. There is a circle of binding there that will obscure you from the eyes of men."

Helga quickly gathered up her things, throwing them onto Raggle in a heap. Mona lent a hand, keeping the gear on top of the horse as she led Helga to the eastern end of the camp. There, beneath a few spreading oaks, was a clear patch of earth. Runes in the dirt glowed in a small circle on the ground, giving a light that seemed to be always shifting its color from blue to orange to purple and back again. The face of Faralinda, once fair, looked grim as she kneeled in the dirt, speaking softly to nobody. Around her, more runes appeared, and as Helga stepped lightly into the circle, she realized that the ground was full of them, and they were igniting magically one by one.

"The wards will keep us obscured," Mona said, leading the horse to a nearby wagon, where a few other horses stood stamping the ground.

"There," Faralinda said. She incanted one more word, and a wide circle of pale orange appeared in the dirt, hemming in all the women and a few wagons. After a few seconds, it fell dim, but Helga could see the air above shimmering slightly, like the haze above a roaring fire. Faralinda caught Helga's eye as she stood. "This barrier does not do a good job of blocking sound. Try not to talk too loudly, or the illusion will not matter."

The sound dampening effects of the circle were indeed quite mild. After a few minutes, the women could hear the sounds of battle, slightly muffled and from no discernable direction, like sound traveling through a fog. Steel clashed. Voices were raised and silenced. Screams echoed, orcs growled and cried above the men, and the subtle voices of an elvish battle hymn sounded all the while.

Helga gave a start, and several of the women went for weapons as a Raven dropped out of the sky and perched itself on the side of one of the wagons.

"There you are!" Zim said. "Where is my mate?"

"She flew away when I roused the camp," Helga said, motioning the bird to be quiet. The other women gave her a perplexed look, and Helga noticed it as she looked about. "If you find a talking raven alarming, you'd best steel yourselves, for there are three about the camp. They are friends, so do not harm them."

"We are friends only to Helga," Zim said. "And to each other, but we are merely birds. What can we do against a man? Yes, we are no threat."

"What news of the battle?" Faralinda said.

Zim bobbed his head. "Men are fighting. Orcs are fighting. Elves are fighting. Orcs are hurt. The strange men are dying. Dun-men? Do not ask for more. I cannot see *that* well in the dark, and I cannot tell one side from the other. Now, I must go and find my mate."

"Wait," Faralinda said, but Zim did not heed her. He went straight up into the air and flew off into the night as an invisible shadow.

"Fear not," Mona said. "A few bandits will be of little concern, and my ears still detect the song of your husband."

"Yes, your ears are better than mine tonight, somehow," Faralinda said.

In the dwindling noise, many of the women stood tense, hands on weapons, but many more sat down with their children, which ranged in age from babes to girls nearing maidenhood; most of the lads over ten were missing, presumably assisting the men as either squires or pages, or else joining in the fighting themselves. It seemed to Helga an odd thing to do to a boy, perhaps even cruel, but she did not have her own children yet and so reserved her thoughts to herself in the company of the hard Orcish women.

A baby started crying; the light was too dim for Helga to see where.

"You must quiet that child," a voice croaked. Helga knew it to be Zald, though she could not see him. "Or else they will hear you. They approach!"

"Is that the raven again?" Faralinda whispered.

"It is one of them," Helga said. "Zald, where are you?"

"Above you, silly girl," the raven replied. Helga looked up but could not see the bird in the tree that arched over the clearing. "But it is best you do not talk. There are strange men coming this way. They will hear you."

"From where?" Mona said.

"The east. Can you not see them?" Zald said.

"I see only the shimmering night," Mona said.

Zald croaked. "It is foolish to use magic that hides things from your own eyes. There are many men coming. Quiet that child!"

The babe continued to cry, but Helga did not wait to hope. She knelt down and folded her bowstring into the hook on her belt. With silent strain, she stood up and drew her crossbow, then loaded a bolt. She loosed her sword in her scabbard and knelt down to shoulder the crossbow, facing east.

"I think I hear them," Faralinda whispered. She had knelt down beside Helga and held a sword in one hand. Her other hand was clinched, but glowed red from within.

"Spears," Mona said, and took her spear in her hands. The other women began to move quickly, arming themselves with what they had, which was mostly spears and light shields. They waited, staring into the darkness, hearing faintly the muffled sound of male voices.

"Zald," Helga whispered. There was no reply. "Zald!" Silence. "Zald, you old crow, answer me!"

"I am no crow!" Zald said.

"I cannot see these men, but they are coming, are they not?"

"Yes."

"Then fly over there and give me a bit of light, will you?"

"How shall I do that? Ravens have no need of fire. And do I look like I carry tinder with me?"

"Well, I can't see you to say." Helga talked to the sound above her, but it was all black shadows. "Do what Zul did. Go light yourself up so I can see."

"All ravens are black, but that is where the similarity ends. Why don't you just ask me to change into a dragon?"

"Well, can you?"

"Light myself up or turn myself into a dragon?"

"Either."

"No, silly."

"Drat you, Raven. How shall I fulfill our bargain if I cannot see the enemy?"

"How are your ears?" Zald said. "They are very large and must be useful for something."

"Useful for listening, when you have something useful to say, Zald."

The voices got louder in the darkness. They spoke a strange tongue, but it was clear they were looking for the noisy child, which had only just then begun to be slightly soothed.

Zald clacked his beak. "Zald will risk his feathers, and you return my gesture with sarcasm and insults. I will not forget this, girl."

The tree rustled above as Zald leapt away, though Helga could see virtually nothing but the movement of branches.

"What now?" Faralinda said.

"I don't know," Helga said. In the little camp, there was a collective breath held before a scream came plunging through the hazy magic barrier. It was a man, crying out in pain and agony, though his voice wailed on odd pitches and rasped like a death rattle.

"Foolish girl, use your machine!" Zald's voice said from the darkness.

"What is that?" Faralinda said.

"Quiet!" Helga said. She raised her crossbow and closed her eyes, focusing on the shouts of the man. "Fly you crow!"

She let the crossbow snap and send a bolt hurtling forward. Another, greater cry, but mixed with the sound of choking, came back. It was mingled with the sound of an impact on armor.

"That was their leader," Zald said, flying back over Helga. "I could tell by the fanciness of his helmet. Fool. Unfortunately, you put out one of his eyes, so you will have to kill another man for me." Zald laughed aloud.

"Good show," the croaking voice of Zim said in the darkness.

"Zim?" Helga said.

"Yes, now is the time to attack, girl."

Helga looked out to see the darkness melt as Zul lit herself up, this time in a shade of pale green. The light revealed a much larger group of men than any there thought would be on the east side of the camp

— much larger by triple. There were at least 50 men scattered through the trees as Zim flew here and there above them, and they were closer than the sound indicated. Most were within twenty yards, though they seemed confused still by the magic circle. The eyes of the grim men all seemed to glow slightly, like those of cats. One of the men was on the ground with a bolt through his eye.

"Quite a shot," Faralinda said.

"Spears and bolts," Mona said. "Hurry, while they cannot yet see us!"

Helga worked again at loading her crossbow, standing and straining her legs to bend the heavy steel lathe. The bowstring clicked in, and she put in another bolt.

"How can they see at all?" Helga said.

"They are lost and faded dim-men," Zim said. "Or maybe dun-men. They are cursed, but they retain the ability to feel through the darkness."

"Lost ones," Faralinda said. "This is no mere bandit group."

"Now!" Mona said.

A flurry of bolts and arrows flew through the barrier and struck the attackers. Some fell, and others stood up, bewildered. Many more began lumbering or charging forward. There was no sense of organization, though a few men barked at others in their strange tongues.

"The magic will not hold much longer," Faralinda said. "I can feel the runes losing their power, though I do not know why."

"Zim!" Helga said. "Can you find the men and send a message?"

"I am no messenger," Zim said. "I shall have Zald do it." He did not waste time on banter, but flew into the air immediately. Zul still flitted back and forth among the trees, catching some attention from the dim-men in the form of an errant spear thrust here and there, all of which she easily avoided.

Finally, the magic of the circle seemed to dissipate, and the details of the men jumped into crystal clarity. They leapt forward. Helga let her second bolt fly, which struck a man square in the chest, though that did not seem to slow him at all. She drew her sword, but before she could meet the men, Faralinda let loose a fountain of flame from her hand, lighting up the night and blinding her, but also setting fire to the first group of men.

"Spears!" Mona said. The women who had armed themselves moved forward, covering each other like a company of regular soldiers, stabbing with broad-bladed steel spearheads at men both burning and crawling over the burning bodies. Helga felt the bodies of the women press around her. Hideous men were falling over each other as the spears stabbed, vomiting blood and crying like dying rabbits. Even those on the brink of death pulled themselves forward, reaching for the legs and arms of the women's line. Feeling hands close around her ankle, Helga, at last, was pushed to action. She put her weight into the longsword and hacked at the arm grasping for her and then at the men that found themselves squirming past the deadly spear tips. Faces turned up, and hands reached, but she swung wildly, cutting and smashing with equal measure. Dark, black blood splashed on her arms and chest. Behind them, the other women were fleeing back into the camp.

Helga saw the usefulness of Zim as he swooped by Zul (still flying in circles, shining her light) and emitted a stream of magic from his great beak, which instantly grounded a man, then another, like he was a small fire-breathing dragon. The larger group of dun-men, however, pressed harder toward the camp, seeing the children fleeing.

They did not get far, as they were soon met by an angry mob of orcs, men, and two bloodied elves, who mowed them down with a sickening efficiency. Peridan lit up the night with blue fire, scorching enemy and earth as well. Within minutes, the press on the defenders turned into a rout, and the strange, cat-eyed men went screaming into the forest while their braver brothers were slaughtered.

With the battle at last dissipating and the mass of writhing bodies at her feet at last stilled, Helga began to shake and shiver. The rush and fear of fighting departed and left her with a sickness. The smell of blood filled her nostrils along with loosed bowels from the slain. She leaned against a wagon and retched even as Thokar approached.

"Sorry," Helga gasped, seeing the massive orc standing above her, lit by the swirling light of his staff, now a pale blue.

"Even hardened men may find battle unsettling," Thokar said. He produced something from a pouch at his belt and held it up to Helga. He pressed a few dried leaves into her hand, then wrapped his own large hands around hers and made her crush the leaves. He pressed her hand to her face. "Simpler than magic, but just as effective."

The smell of crushed mint cleared Helga's nostrils, and the queasiness began to diminish. She stood up straight to look at Thokar, and Mona appeared beside him.

She spoke, "You keep interesting company, Helga, daughter of Hrolfi."

"Valuable company," Thokar said. He sighed, and the light from his staff grew brighter, illuminating their surroundings. "Now begins the arduous task of forming new pickets while clearing the camp."

"How did your men fare?" Helga said.

"Well enough," Thokar said. "None have died, which is good, for we shall have none to spare if war comes south. Two men have injuries which I will heal soon, once my head and heart have recovered from the battle. And there is one severe injury." He stared at his hands as he said this last part, his brow wrinkling.

"Will you let the bodies lie?" Helga said.

"We are not cruel people, but we are still sellswords. We will strip the dead of what valuables they hold, as is our right as victors. Then we will burn the bodies."

"The ravens will want to dine," Helga said.

Thokar gave the woman a puzzled look. "Will they be fit to eat, even for carrion, I wonder?"

"Most will not be," Zim said, flying in from the darkness and landing on the top of the Orc's staff, obscuring some of the light. The raven croaked. "Dun-men do not have sustaining flesh, or even stomach-able flesh, but not all are dun-men. Helga, you will be delighted to know that Zald has devoured no less than four pairs of men's eyes."

"It eases my heart as well as it does my stomach," Helga said.

"It is good that you are finally understanding ravens," Zim said.

"I suppose our bargain is now finished," Helga said. "And just when I was starting to enjoy your presence."

"Our presence, but not our company, eh?" Zim said. He rocked a laugh.

VI. The Ulfar Mountains

ONLY THE MOST hardened men of the Band of the Badger were able to sleep after the attack. For most, who were younger or newer to the profession of mercenary soldiery, the dead men were as unnerving as the battle itself. As the men piled the bodies of the enemy (while the ravens feasted on a few choice corpses), a silence settled among them. The bandits were truly not ordinary men, and in the firelight, their features looked strangely flat and amorphous, like the visage of shades passing with the flickering of torches and pyre light.

In the morning, Helga (who had passed the rest of the night conversing with a woman over the best ways to deal with various types of difficult babies – a welcome change of thought from the battle, though Helga still found the wisdom of little interest) finally got a good look at what the sorcerers among them called "Dun-Men." Their flesh was a rotten grey, though the body itself seemed not to rot after death. Their hair, always a colorless thing, was stringy and sprouted from more places than the head or beard. Some of the dun-men had hair on their palms or on the bridge of their noses – if they had much of a nose. Most of the faces of the men (and indeed a few of them were women – a fact revealed when the bodies were stripped) were as featureless as a face could be and still be recognizable as humanoid. Noses were little more than gentle humps above flat cheeks. The heads had a roundness that made them look almost child-like, and their mouths were like slits as there was no clear place where a lip ended and the rest of the face began. Their hands and feet, likewise, were oddly shaped, with their fingers often too fat or too thin, their length all askew, and some even had too many joints.

Helga spent long minutes gazing at one dun-man who had been stripped naked. His bones all seemed slightly off in proportion, and his ribcage was flat. The skin was withered even as it was smooth, like an overripe fruit. Even his genitals seemed misshapen in a way that defied conventions of deformity. Though Helga had seen few samples in her life to judge this one as strange, the unreality of the form was undeniable.

"They all look a little off, even to me," Zald said. He was perched on Raggle's saddle and gazed contentedly at the remains of the battle. "And I am no master of the forms of men, though I do eat them fairly often."

"I've never seen a race like this," Helga said. "Where are they from, and how did they get this way, I wonder?"

"Zald knows, but he does not like to tell."

"Why not?"

"Too sad a tale, and too dark."

"For a raven?" Helga said.

"I prefer to focus on happier things, my friend," Zald said. He flapped over to the body and stood on its chest. "You must look at the eyes to understand."

Helga squatted down and peeled back an eyelid. It stayed open, revealing one of the strangest eyes she had ever seen. It had no iris and no white, but instead had one large pupil of black, though the whole of the eye seemed translucent and hazy, almost opaque.

"This answers nothing," Helga said.

Zald laughed. "You understand why I do not eat them, though, do you not?"

"I see," Helga said. "But could he? His eyes look like they are full of mud."

"The dun-men are remnants of a world that is worse than destroyed." Helga turned to see Peridan approaching, leaning on his staff and looking tired. "It was a world that never was." The elf paused beside her and gazed at the open eye of the naked stranger.

"I don't understand," Helga said.

"As if you ever could," Zald said. He flew up to a low branch in a nearby oak.

"You said you are traveling to meet the watchers, did you not?" Peridan said.

"Yes, they are who I seek," Helga said.

"How much do you know about the Fay and the Prim?"

"Faerie?" Helga said. "I know it's a strange place and not kind to mortals. Beyond that, I would not guess, because all of our tales conflict with one another."

"I think if you were to go there, you would find that your stories don't really contradict each other."

"Have you been there?"

"I have traveled through parts of the Fay. My sister Faralinda and I were born in Alfheim, not here in the mortal realms like most elves. Do you know much about the fay folk?"

"I always thought that elves and fairies were the same thing," Helga said. "Forgive me, but I see elves only rarely as they pass through my own village."

"It is no offense to me. We are of the Fay, in a way, just as you are. But the true beings of the Fay are very different from you and me, disparate though our races might be."

Zim flew down by the corpse and hoped around on the ground. He regarded Peridan, but did not speak.

Peridan went on, a slight smile cracking his face. "There are spirits in the fay that take the shape of our races, on the surface. Some say they are the dead."

"Not true," Zald said.

Peridan chuckled softly and went on. "Some say they are people yet to be born, or people whose births were lost along the way. Others say they are something different entirely. One thing that is important to understand is that they are one with the Fay and one with the Prim.

When they leave that ever-shifting dream, either by mistake or by its slow withdraw from the world, or by their own desire to see the world of time – when they leave, they often lose their immutable self.

"The watchers are Fay spirits, but they persist in our world by drawing strength from the Fay. Eventually, they will be unable to return and must stay here. Then, we say, they become dim – the light of creation begins to fade from them. They become more like men but lack fundamental humanity. Of course, there are tales of some who escape to become truly like us."

"What about the dun-men?" Helga said.

Zald spoke before Peridan could continue. "For them, all light has gone out. They are lost to their own inner spirit. They are severed from the eternal dream and remember only fleeting images of their true selves, but they can never find true permanence of being. Their bodies become an imitation of the men they meet, changing slowly to the forms you see here. Quite disgusting."

Peridan continued, frowning as he gazed at the closest corpse. "They are more like the dead than the living, but being without proper flesh, they also lack proper death. They lack proper form as they lack a proper spirit from the dream."

"Strange indeed," Helga said. "I cannot say now I am looking forward to these watchers."

"They aren't nearly as bad looking as these ones," Zald said.

"The watchers are beautiful, certainly, but they are still quite strange. I will be able to tell you more on the road," Peridan said.

"But my road leads east," Helga said. "To the edge of the Fay. Unless your band is turning about."

"They are not, but I am," Peridan said. "I will accompany you on the way to the watchers."

"Why?"

"Trindol was injured severely last night," Peridan said. "He was touched by the withering magic of the dun-men, for at least one was a shaman of some might. Unfortunately, that shaman has escaped, and with him the means to dispel the withering. Trindol has an infected wound and, more importantly, an infected spirit. It will slowly leak out of him if I do not find a remedy quickly."

"Mist Blight?"

"Very nearly, but the spirit of an elf does not make the same journey as a man's."

"Neither you nor Thokar knows of a cure?"

"Know of, yes. Between us, we know half a dozen cures, but just like the potion Thokar mentioned, we have not the items necessary to execute the remedies. The watchers are known to have a particular artifact that will stop the leaking of the spirit, sunder that which draws him out, and allow him to heal. I must try, for the sake of my friend and for the sake of Faralinda, who is not yet ready to be parted from her husband on this earth."

"I am sorry for your friend," Helga said. "And forgive me, but why should I trust you to travel with me? Just because you are an elf?"

"You can choose not to travel with me," Peridan said. "If that is your wish. It is good to have friends on a dangerous road, and I have nothing to gain from harming you. The company of women is not hard to come by in my line of work, should I desire it."

"I like him," Zald said. "Elves have a fatalism about them that is unpleasant, but they know lots of things. Very interesting to talk to."

Helga sighed. "Very well, sir. I suppose I could do worse than a sorcerer for company on the road." She glanced up at Zald and raised her eyebrow as if posing the same question to him. He was a bird and could not narrow his eyes like a person, but Helga detected an expression of offense on his dark face.

Once the bodies had been burned or buried, and the whole company had eaten a bitter meal out of necessity, the camp was fully struck and made ready to march. Helga burdened Raggle with provisions that were gifts of the company – preserved fruit in mason jars along with flatbread that stayed fresh longer than a loaf but was easier to eat than hardtack. Peridan packed his own horse, a grey destrier several hands taller than Raggle, with his own provisions and an assortment of magical oddities.

Helga went with Peridan to see Trindol, who was laid on a make-shift mattress in one of the wagons. His face looked grey, and his eyes were sunken, but he was awake. Faralinda was at his side. He forced a smile as they stooped under a cloth roof to talk to him.

"Keep hold of the light, friend," Peridan said. "I will return as soon as I am able. Do not give in to the darkness of sleep, or fight against it so hard that you fully wake."

Helga did not understand the meaning of these words, but she nodded along as if she did.

"How long shall my mind remain here?" Trindol said. His clear voice sounded off from the night previous, duller and more human.

"That depends on many things," Peridan said. "Faralinda knows well the sorceries that will fend off the ghosts of mortality, but they cannot be held at bay forever. I wish there was more certainty to give to you."

Faralinda looked into Trindol's eyes. "I would travel to the shore of corpses and sail the endless sea to find you, but if you return to the Prim I cannot follow. You must fight it."

"I shall, my love," Trindol said. "Go, Peridan, and earn my eternal debt. And Helga, do not let Peridan get too confident with himself. Keep your blade well oiled and your crossbow ready. Magic in the Fay Waste is troublesome, and I will not have Peridan die on my account."

"I will watch him," Helga said. "Such as I can. I am only a simple woman. A farmer's wife, not a shield-maiden."

"Simplicity is not a vice," Faralinda said. "And you are more than a farmer's wife, even if you do not see it yet."

"Farewell, my friend," Peridan said.

"Ride with thunder, see with wisdom," Trindol said.

With that, Peridan left the covered wagon with Helga and went to the east end of the column, his head hanging to his armored chest, his smooth face without deeper expression. Thokar and Mona came to send them off, and Peridan lifted his head, putting on a prideful face.

"Peridan, I lay a bond on you," Thokar said, laying his hand on the Elf's shoulder. "To defend this woman as she defends you and to begin no violence between you. I do not bind you to go further than you will."

Peridan nodded.

Thokar laid a hand on Helga's shoulder. "Helga, I lay the same bond on you as I did on Peridan." She felt something indescribable in her shoulder pass between the orc and herself. "Go now, and waste no more time on goodbyes."

Helga nodded and mounted her horse.

"Now there are two saddle-horns!" It was the voice of Zald, who came and perched on Peridan's saddle before he had even pulled himself up.

"What are you doing here, Zald?" Helga said.

Zim answered from a tree-limb. "Zul has taken a liking to you and, lacking anything of particular purpose of greater import, we have decided to accompany you a bit further."

"Do you trust these birds?" Thokar said. "I cannot read them, nor say just what enchantment lies on them."

"Silly orc thinks we are enchanted!" Zald said, and spread his wings. Peridan climbed into the saddle.

"Shoo! Shoo Bird," the elf said. "I want no raven feces on my tack."

"The nerve!" Zald said, puffing himself up and flapping off of the saddle. "As if I cannot choose when and where I go, like a human child. Rest assured, battlemage, when your armor is stained, you will know it was done with precision and intention!"

"I trust them," Helga said. "At least when they are bound by a deal. As for their free will, I do not know, but I do not have the power or the will to restrict them."

Zul flew down and landed on Helga's saddle. "Ravens do not lie, Helga. We will help you find the Watchers, and we will not harm you."

"Speak for yourself," Zald said. "Not for me!"

"I can speak for you if I wish, Zald," Zul said. "You know that."

Zim laughed.

"Looks like excellent company," Peridan said sarcastically. "I do know a few silence spells, in case we encounter any particularly loud foes."

"Good," Helga said.

"Be careful what you threaten, sorcerer," Zim said. "You might find yourself at a disadvantage, to say the least!"

*

Helga and Peridan rode to the top of a ridge and watched the column of mercenaries march west. Smoke hung in the air from the pyres, which blended with a sky growing grey with a threat of rain. With a last look, Peridan and Helga turned and continued down the other side of the ridge into a narrow and dry valley. When they reached the ridge on the other side, the Band of the Badger was no longer visible.

"I could use a rest somewhere," Helga said. "I didn't sleep last night, and now that we are away from it all, I feel almost sick."

"Let us go a bit further," Peridan said. "There are some high places as we go over the pass, and I don't think we shall beat this storm. If we rest now, we will rest until tomorrow, for I do not want to tread through ice and snow at night."

"How much further?" Helga said.

"Not far," Peridan said. "I know of a good camping spot from when we came this way before. Why don't you have a drink of this?"

He handed Helga a small flask. Inside was a liquid tea, very strong and very pungent, that was shockingly hot.

"Thank you," Helga said, almost choking on the hot liquid. "How is it still so hot?"

"The bottle is a little bit of craft to that end," Peridan said. "Dreadfully hard to make, but very convenient. Drink your fill. I can make more as we ride."

Soon Helga felt temporarily re-invigorated. The ravens were off on their own again – Helga would see one of them from time to time fly overhead, and she wondered if they took Peridan's silence threat seriously. The pair of travelers made good time, and soon the sun was on their backs. It would be hot but for the wind that pushed them forward.

Peridan led Helga off the road and to a clearing surrounded by high bushes that was mercifully protected from the howling wind. There, they camped. Helga unrolled her blankets and went promptly to sleep, not bothering even to remove her boots. She left her loaded crossbow next to her. Peridan, however, made a fire, cooked himself a meal, and did not sleep.

When Helga woke again, it was very dark outside. A light snow was falling overhead, but she felt very warm. Peridan sat beside the fire, a book open in his hands. All three ravens sat around the fire too, which Helga noticed was not fueled by wood. It flickered blue-green from a pile of stones with nothing beneath them.

"She has awoken," Zul said, and flapped her wings.

"We have brought you a present," Zim said.

"What is it?" Helga said, pushing herself up.

"It's a coney," Peridan said, not looking up from his book. "And a fresh kill. Rather worth eating, if you like that sort of thing."

"Then why aren't you eating it?"

"I don't like that sort of thing," Peridan replied. "Besides, it would be more polite to share it with the hunters who gave it to you."

Helga found a freshly killed hare by the fire and set about to skin it and prepare it to be cooked. She had packed (thankfully) one of her favorite knives, a wedding gift from her mother-in-law and well-made. It made quick work of the hare.

As she worked, Helga spoke to Peridan. "Is this fire enchanted?"

"A small thing, but well-worked," Peridan said. "Or the snow would be most uncomfortable."

"Can't you just make the snow stop?"

Peridan laughed aloud, the same high and carefree laugh she had heard when she first met the elf, and it rang in the dell like a little bell. Helga smiled in spite of herself.

"My dear goodwife, if I could control the weather, I would be a farmer, not a mercenary."

"Can anyone control the weather? Wizards, I mean."

"A very few of the highest, oldest of my race can, but only to a very limited extent and time frame. Weather is greater than the reach of the mind, containing too many elements with too many interactions. It is almost impossible to distill any bit of weather down to a concept and grasp, and therefore control."

"How does one perform magic? Can you learn?"

"Very few men can. You must have an inborn connection to the Prim and the realm beyond. To create in this world, or control, your mind must be able to reach through your soul's connection to the Prim and find there the encapsulating concept beyond. That idea which is perfectly what you imagine, nothing more and nothing less, must be crystalline in your mind. Only then can you make it real in the World-That-Is."

"How did you learn?"

"I was taught by the scholars of Alfheim, over the course of centuries, a great many words, which I used to develop my talent; to find the hidden paths to the eternal dream and to make them real here. Countless words must be learned, you see, to access the concepts for each spell. They must be memorized, repeated, but above all, understood within." Peridan touched his chest, then his head. "I am strong among elves. Even so, there is only a small fraction of the infinity of the Prim that I can know and bring forth at my whim. This fire is one of them."

"Can I learn?"

"Unlikely. If you had the gift, it would have presented itself by now. Why?"

Helga laid the butchered rabbit out and wiped her hands. She sat cross-legged and put her head down on the back of her hand. "If I could do magic, maybe I could help my husband."

"I could not help my sister's husband," Peridan said. "Hence I am here."

"Then at least I wouldn't be so useless. At least I would have some power to defend myself. Out here, away from home... I don't know what I'm doing." Helga lifted her head. "Hey, if you are so powerful, why are you a mercenary, anyway?" Helga said. "Doesn't seem like it would suit your sister and friend either."

"Would it be too simple to say it was for the money?" Peridan said.

"Elves can be greedy, yes," Zald said. "But not usually for money, eh? For power and pretty things."

"Yes, well, money can buy both of those things, I would say. But the answer is too simple and too complicated. Trindol and I are sellswords because that is what we wished to be, at least for a time. Yes, I get my share of books from our adventures, and there are always things to be learned, but these things do not go hand-in-hand with the work of war. There is no *real* reason other than we thought it would be a lively existence."

"A lively existence, but a dangerous one," Helga said. "I would prefer my sheep and my garden."

"Is that really true, I wonder," Peridan said with a wry smile. "Men are often a mystery to me and seem to be just as much a mystery to themselves. You do not strike me as an easily satisfied woman."

"I'm easily satisfied by what meets my standards," Helga said.

"Of course," Peridan said with a chuckle. "You know, I've learned more of mankind, as well as the other races of the realms, in a mere twenty years with the Band, in conversations like this, than I had in hundreds of years of study in Alfheim. The libraries we have there are very extensive, but somehow the words can never do justice to human nature, since they are always from an elf's perspective. The concept of a man is beyond me."

"Hundreds of years? Elves are indeed immortal, then," Helga said.

"That is a human word," Peridan said. "Just as you would not consider your skin pale until you met a man from the desert reach, we don't usually consider the length of life until we meet a mortal. The growth and decay of the life of an elf is something very different than a man."

"How is it?" Helga asked. "Do you grow old and die?"

"We can die as a man can, if we are slain, but not from old age. At least, not in the same way. For us, we lose interest in the World-That-Is, and fall asleep. We fade away and sometimes return, though we return forgetful. But that takes a very long time."

"Where do you go when you… fall asleep? I mean, where do your soul and spirit go?"

"Back to the eternal dream, to that part of the Fay in which the spark of elvish creation still burns. There, our spirits are renewed, and we re-imagine that part of the dream that is Alfheim, and so is our realm preserved and grown."

"Have you ever been there? The eternal dream, or the Fay?"

"The Fay. Yes, in its more tame areas. The deep parts? Not yet, but I think we shall meet some cousins soon that have a memory of it, however warped their minds might be now."

"The watchers," Helga said, pausing her work with the hare carcass. "They are fay creatures, are they not? So are elves that way too?"

"Yes and no," Peridan said. He flicked a finger at the fire and pulled up a ball of light. "In the timeless realm, which is the fay, everything is in flux. The spirits there dream, and the dream is real even as they think it, like a constant working of magic, which is why faerie is so dangerous to both our kinds. You can look at one part, and see a wide, sweeping field, then find yourself in a dense forest, for one of the creatures there has been inspired to have a forest, and there may be no other spirit to resist the change."

The ball of light above Peridan's hand took on the shape of a tree, then a fox, and continued to shift. "Once sufficiently created, the Dreamer, that is, the Illuminator, makes real the dream. Even we elves do not know how or why he does this, or who the Dreamer truly is."

"We have this myth too, but it is often considered pure metaphor," Helga said. "It is the twelve gods that men worship primarily. The dreamer is viewed as… a usurper, of sorts."

"Men are a race seeking both flux and permanence – a divided race," Peridan said. "It makes sense that your pantheon would reflect that." Peridan looked at the skinned and butchered hare lying on a rock. Zul walked slowly around it as if considering eating it. "I think you'd best begin dinner before your friends change their minds about letting you eat it."

Helga nodded and stood up. She placed the innards and the head of the rabbit at the edge of the camp. Immediately Zald swooped down and began devouring them.

"You humans waste the best parts," the raven said. "The heart is the most nourishing part. And the eyes. And you cast them away."

"Then enjoy them as you please," Helga said. She returned to the fire and set about making a stew from meat.

"You work quickly," Peridan said, watching Helga cook the hare. "I've seen many road-worn men work a kill in twice the time with much worse effect."

"Like any farmwife, I've done it a thousand times before," Helga said. "And I'll probably do it many more than that before I die."

Soon the stew was cooked and seasoned, and the smell refreshed Helga.

"On second thought," Peridan said. "Maybe I will have some of that stew."

They shared the stew as the snow continued to fall outside the warmth of the fire, piling up in drifts against nearby pine trees. The magic fire kept them warm, and the meal was filling and satisfying.

"I'm not looking forward to treading about in that tomorrow," Helga said.

Peridan smiled. "I wouldn't worry too much about it. It's a late snow and bound to go half to melt in the morning."

Helga doubted these words as the snow continued to fall, eventually getting so thick that above and around her, the storm looked like a flickering dome of white encasing the little camp. Wolves howled in the wind, feeling close and far, but Helga's eyes would not stay open and vigilant for them. They slept and found in the morning that the storm had dropped more snow than even Helga thought was possible. Huge drifts covered up low branches of cedars and pines. Fresh leaves on oaks were dropped to the ground, and limbs had broken here and there due to the weight. The storm had thankfully passed, and the day was bright white above and below, but it remained bitter cold and windy.

"Do you have some spell for this?" Helga said. The magic fire had gone out, and Zim was busy inspecting what remained of it. "I have only a small spade."

"I can cast some fire about to melt it, but it will be hard work and long," Peridan said.

"Then I suppose we'd best get to it."

*

Helga felt rather useless watching Peridan conjure up raging fires on the ends of wet logs, then watching as he thrust them into the banks of snow, which would melt immediately, clearing a few feet forward in the icy drifts. The horses did not mind the sudden bursts of heat, for between each spell, they would begin to stamp and shiver. Helga, however, soon felt like a blacksmith's apprentice from the heat hitting her face. She began to feel sunburned despite the clouds and the snow surrounding her.

Helga thought it might have been around midday (it was cloudy and almost timeless) when Peridan needed to stop and rest, the spell-work apparently physically exhausting for him. He sat down and breathed heavily on a rock, then leaned back against a pile of snow and slept.

Not knowing what else to do, Helga began trying to shovel the snow with her small spade. Very quickly, her arms began to ache, especially her shoulders, which burned with their own fire. She sat down beside Peridan, drained by her own exertion as it began to snow again. She did clear a little extra space, but not enough to be worth the effort, she felt.

As she lay on the snowdrift, panting, Zald flew out of the snow and landed on her knee.

"I don't suppose you could persuade Zim to blow a little fire on the snow, eh?" Helga said.

"You don't suppose correctly," Zald said. "Power is to be used at need, not at one's silly whims. Now, we should wake the mage."

Zald hopped onto Peridan's chest and began picking at the elf's long ears and hair. Peridan woke with a start and waved his arms, shooting streams of magic from them that caught on the nearby trees, smoldering.

"No!" he cried aloud. "I will not! Leave me!"

"This is not your dream, mage," Zald said. "I have news. Wake up and hear it."

Forcing his grey eyes wide, Peridan looked around and frowned at the raven.

"What is it, bird?"

"I have soiled your armor mage," Zald said and laughed. Sure enough, there was a large fresh white dropping on the elf's decorated green and silver mail. Peridan shot a spell of purple magic out from his palm, which Zald easily avoided. Laughing, the raven flew up to a branch of a tree. He laughed more.

"Now, mage, we are even for your pithy insults. And now I shall put you in my debt again."

"What is it, you foul fowl?" Peridan said.

"I have espied some things. I have good news and bad news."

"The good?" Helga said.

"There are no more wolves in the pass."

"Good," Helga said. "I do not particularly care for wolves."

"What is the bad news," Peridan said, wiping the dropping from his chest.

"There are no more wolves because a troll is presently devouring the pack," Zald said.

"Trolls?" Helga said.

"Snowy trolls," Zald said. "Very large. Very mean."

"Can you slay a troll?" Helga said to Peridan.

"Most assuredly," Peridan said. "But did you notice the raven's switching to the plural?"

103

"Clever, clever," Zald said. "There is, in fact, a whole family of them. But just one troll is eating the wolves, for now."

Zim flew out of the snow and landed on a rock. Zul followed close behind. "We bring news!"

"We already heard it," Peridan said. He breathed in and out heavily. "Alas, but I did not foresee this storm or trolls coming down out of the high reaches. One troll is easy enough, but a family-"

"An extended family," Zul said. "Quite nasty looking. They are wearing bear bones as clothing and armor."

"How big are they?" Helga said. "I've never seen one."

"Any troll is big enough to chill your blood," Peridan said. "We should probably turn back. One troll I can manage, but probably not more than that, especially snow trolls. They have a natural resistance to magic, especially fire, and of course, they are already quite resistant to cold. Those are the only two elements of magic I have good offensive control over."

Helga stood up and drew her sword as she heard a strange, howling sort of cry. The ravens took wing, and Peridan, even exhausted, was on his feet. Ahead of them, pushing through the neck-deep snow as if it was nothing, was a large creature. Its head was big and square, covered in thick white hair except for its eyes and its long, misshapen nose. Ragged clothing hung off its hunching body, and it held a tree branch in one hand. Seeing them, it jumped up and down in the snow, howling and hooting. To Helga, it looked slightly larger than a man.

"Ravens truly are not liars," Peridan said.

Helga went to Raggle and got out her crossbow. The troll was rumbling through the snow toward them, his head bobbing. Peridan unleashed a wave of fire at it, but the fire dissipated in the snow, melting much of it. Peridan cast another spell, this one of churning blue fire in a ball, and hurled it at the troll. The magic hit the creature and lit the rags on fire, but seemed only to enrage it. Helga took aim and fired her crossbow. The bold hit the troll squarely in the head.

Its face twisted into a frown, and it began (to Helga's shock) to cry and wail, though with its strange voice, the wail was unlike anything

Helga had heard before. The troll stood up, the bolt poking out of its skull, and ran off through the snow.

"Good shot," Peridan said. "Too bad you missed the eye, as the skull is as hard as iron. Of course, had you done that, the troll's parents likely would have been madder at you than they will be at present."

"It's parents?"

"Yes," Peridan said. "That's a young one."

"I would say about two years old," Zim said. "Quite a big baby."

"His mum will just think he poked a twig into his skin," Zald said. "When they see it is an arrow…" Zald began laughing.

"Let's get out of here," Peridan said. "And quick, before the adults come this way."

Helga did not protest, but did ask as she turned the horses about, "Is there another way to the wastes beyond?"

"I know of a way round the pass, to the south of here, if you are willing to walk some extra miles." Peridan mounted up and urged his horse forward.

"I will gladly walk a few extra miles," Helga said, getting into Raggle's saddle. She gestured in front of herself. "You know the way better than I."

Peridan urged his destrier forward, and the horse found his way, trotting over muddy ground. They could hear faintly the howling of trolls, but the howling did not grow louder or clearer. Instead, it faded as they went away from the pass. The way down the mountain was initially easy, as the snow was already melted in most places. Only when they got to their camp did it become a burden.

"Which way?" Helga said, looking out at a field of featureless snow.

"The road lies this way," Peridan said, pointing across to where a post stuck up a few inches above the snow.

"Why do you ignore your best guides, hmn?" Zim said, hopping up on Raggle's saddle. "We know these mountains better than any elf, and we can actually see where we are going."

"How do men get on without wings?" Zald said. "It's a wonder they aren't always lost."

"Then where is the next pass?" Helga said.

"Pass?" Zul said. "No, not a pass."

"Is there another pass to the south or not?" Helga said.

"There is a valley that cuts most of the way through," Zul said. "But you may be better off going over the mountains here, waiting for the trolls to move on. That valley contains some unsavory ruins."

Helga looked at Peridan.

"I have no knowledge of ruins," he said. "But that does make me curious."

"I have learned from cats that it is not always best to give in to curiosity," Helga said. "But if the valley is easier than walking through snow in troll-infested forests, I am willing to try it. Besides, I have a sorcerer and three magic ravens to guard me against anything unsavory."

"Magic ravens!" Zald cried. "Magic! We are not magic."

Peridan said, "Considering that you talk, I would take you to be enchanted."

"Are *you* magic just because *you* talk?"

"Of course I am," Peridan said with a sly smile.

"I don't know," Helga said. "I've never thought about it. Maybe I *am* magic."

"Well, you are certainly unordinary, raven," Peridan said. "I would like to study you sometime, though I can guess by your disposition you would resent it."

"Study with your eyes, mage!" Zald said. "Since your ears are clearly useless."

Helga laughed.

"Enough, Zald," Zul said. "I will find us a short path to the valley while you backtrack." With that, she flew off.

Peridan and Helga led their horses on foot through the snow, guessing as to where the road was. It was clear when they reached it on the other side of the snowfield, as it looked like a river of snow and ice stretching itself through white trees. Slowly and carefully, they worked their way back west, and the snows gave way to mud as they continued to descend.

Zul returned and found them, then led them through a rough patch of forest to arrive at another path, a game trail that had turned into a human road over time. This they followed through a winding course, past a small icy lake, until it joined a larger road that was, Helga was surprised to see, paved with regularly shaped flat cobblestones. Soon they were descending into a verdant valley, cool, but with enough sun that Helga could remove her cloak, and they were both able to ride slowly.

The sun was setting, and the day was spent. Content that the trolls had not followed them, they decided to camp on the downward slopes beside the cobblestone path. It did not snow that night, but remained dark and cloudy. Helga slept. She awoke in the early morning to see that the storm had moved off. Wind had replaced the precipitation, and she felt cold despite Peridan's magic fire. The stars in the dark before dawn seemed brighter than she was used to; the constellations all seemed off as well. The moon was gone, but even by starlight, she could see the valley below them, covered with trees that swayed in the wind.

In the morning, they packed and continued down the cobblestone pathway. Pines gave way to hardwoods and even willows as they reached the bottom of the valley. They rode past a small, clear lake fed by a slow-moving stream that glinted in the sunlight as it ran along its straight course.

"I don't like this place," Zald said, perched on Peridan's saddle (the sorcerer had, apparently, become tired of shoo-ing the birds away).

"Of course a raven would," Helga said. "It's pleasant and not at all filled with rotting corpses."

"No, fool girl," Zald said. "Your ears are as useless as the mage's."

Helga slowed her horse, then stopped, listening. Peridan sighed and also stopped. "I hear nothing but the brook over there," the elf said. "And the breeze in the trees."

"Precisely," Zald said. "What is missing, eh?"

"Birds," Helga said. "I hear no birdsong." She looked around.

"Not just no birdsong," Zald said. "No song of mice, or deer, or…"

"Deer do not make songs, raven," Peridan said.

"Foolish mage!" Zald said. "They make noise. Noise is song."

"That it is *not*."

"You are missing the point!" Zald flapped his wings and flew up above the trees, making all sorts of noises odd to ravens.

"He is right," Zul said. "There are no animals here that I can perceive."

Zald returned and landed on the rear of Helga's saddle. "These trees are empty! There should be many nests here. I should be feasting on robins' eggs."

"Always thinking with your stomach," Zim said from an overhead branch. "But right, despite your vices. Be on your guard."

"No animals doesn't really sound too bad," Helga said. "That means no wolves or bears, or trolls for that matter. I won't complain about that."

"Perhaps you *will* complain about other things," Zim said.

They continued through the valley, which despite the quiet, seemed to have a healthy air to it. Helga noticed that the sun was westering, and she had forgotten to eat a midday meal, even though she didn't feel at all hungry. She shrugged and ate some walnuts along with some dried fruit as she rode. The trees closed in above and around, making a tunnel of light green that Helga thought was quite beautiful.

Zald flew through the trees and called out, "I see it, it is over here. Come!"

Helga and Peridan pushed the pace of their horses until they reached a break in the trees. Across meadows and sparse groves, they saw a mass of buildings coming right out of the rocky wall of the valley.

"Those do not look so ruined to me," Helga said.

"Indeed not," Peridan said. "Still, those are stone buildings and take a long time to fall into disrepair. Shall we have a look?"

"I advise against it," Zul said. "I see now that they are perhaps not ruins."

"Zald?" Zim said. "You are the young and curious one. What do you say?"

"I say it is not a place for a meal," Zald said. "And not a place to make friends, either. Maybe you are interested in human buildings, but I am not."

"Very well, let us trust the ravens," Peridan said. "If a carrion bird has his doubts, so too do I."

They rode on, going back into a canopy of green leaves. A little bridge ran over the brook, made of wood that seemed fresh and new.

"That will go to the city, I'll wager," Peridan said. "In the past, it might have been the water source for those who lived there."

They stayed on the road, which became more enclosed by brush and more tightly packed trees. Finally, the road opened before them, and they saw the ruined city plainly, for the path led right into it. A stone gatehouse stood empty. The gates, made of some ancient wood, were rotted and stood ajar.

To their right, apparently carved into the granite itself, were a great many open doors and windows: homes that stretched up the sheer face of the rock for at least fifty feet. A path wound its way among these open-doored homes, and stairs crossed between different levels. Each house opened onto the roof of the one in front, giving the city a rough terraced look. Pots and planters still held vegetation in the form of weeds and volunteer shrubs.

The left side of the road, which widened into an avenue as it passed the gatehouse, contained larger buildings of masonry and stone, a few of which lacked roofs or had collapsed completely. Strange, flowing letters remained here and there on signs. Helga held her horse back as he suddenly bucked. The air was still and quiet, with only a slight breeze stirring the dust around the horse's feet.

VII. The Shades of the Red Moon

"WELL, HERE WE ARE," said Peridan. He moved around to see the western side of the valley, but could not see around the dense trees.

"What is that writing?" Helga asked, noticing an inscription on a plaque spanning the great gate doors, mostly worn away by time.

"It is some sort of elvish," Peridan said. "But it is not high-elven; that much I know. The letters are similar. This place might have been a dark-elf city, once."

"Yes!" Zim suddenly said, flying up and landing on a high corner of the gatehouse. "I remember this place now. It was very fair, once, but the elves here were Dark Elves and did not care for the light."

"Strange that you did not remember it before," Peridan said.

"Not so strange," Zim said. "Ravens care little for buildings. It is the people I remember more. And there are no people here."

Zald flapped his wings. "No! All gone."

"It doesn't look that long abandoned," Peridan said. His eyes searched the mountainside, and his lip twitched with a slight tick. "Perhaps it is not abandoned. I can imagine people in the dark places, hiding from a pair of strangers."

"I have an uneasy feeling in this place," Helga said. "Now that I look upon it, it doesn't look ruined at all."

Peridan's eyes were locked on something distant in the city. "I suggest we try our best to work around it."

"Yes," Zim said. "You walk around. I will fly over and look for strangers."

Helga and Peridan backed up the path, but found no place where they could breach the dense undergrowth. Close to the walls of the city was a bog, the remnants of a moat that was once fed by the river, and it was impassible, choked with fallen trees and huge rushes. The sun began to dim as it inched closer to the mountains in the west, and so they both decided they would try going through town.

"If we are to go through this place, I would prefer to do it before sundown," Helga said.

They went back to the front gate and approached. One of the two great doors, both made of immense boards and covered with iron re-inforcements, hung loosely ajar while the other was fixed in its place. Before they entered, Helga loaded her crossbow and laid it in her lap.

They passed through the gates and immediately saw an empty guardhouse. Without dismounting, they could see through the open door. Plates remained on a table inside, as if abandoned mid-meal, though they were clean. A chest stood broken open against a far wall, and all the weapon racks were empty of swords and spears.

"Who ate the food?" Helga said. "Or what?"

Peridan grunted softly to the mystery and turned away.

Within the city, the breeze died, and the only sound was the chatter of the ravens and the soft clopping of hooves on a dusty paved thoroughfare. The buildings to either side were marvelously made, care given to every detail. Intricate stone carvings were laid into tall pillars supporting blue-tiled roofs. Small statues sat under eaves, looking out. Houses had designs laid into their doors (where doors remained; many had fallen down) and had highly decorated porches sitting outside glassless windows.

Zim returned and landed on a rail in front of Helga and Peridan, bobbing his head.

"What did you find?" Helga said. "Is there anyone here?"

"No," Zim said. "They are all gone. I peeked inside a house, but it was empty. The gate at the other side is closed."

"It shouldn't be a problem to open it on this side," Peridan said.

Carefully, they moved through the empty street, and even Peridan seemed out of sorts. He clutched his staff, and his head darted around constantly. They passed by a very large masonry building with great

112

columns and stairs. At the top of the stairs, behind the columns, was a portcullis that has fallen askew, failing to cover the entrance to the building. In front of it stood a statue of blackened bronze depicting an elf holding a great sword up over his head.

"That is Atalthal," Peridan said. "A demigod to the dark elves. He guards the gates to Nottheim, the supposed home of the dark elves."

"Why do you say supposed?" Helga said.

"The dark elves are ultimately beings of this mortal realm, but they remain as people were during the sunless years, a time your race has long forgotten," Peridan said. "They are more like men than like the true fair elves. I do not believe Nottheim exists."

"Perhaps that is the palace or the church," Helga said.

"More likely the palace judging by the gate," Peridan said. "Most Dark Elf kings claim Atalthal as an ancestor. If this place had a better air, I would not mind spending a few days exploring what remains in there, if anything."

The sun began to set, and dusk began to settle into the dark corners of the city. It became cold suddenly, and a mist began to gather on the ground. Helga clutched her crossbow tightly and undid the loop of leather that held her sword down. Finally, they came upon the outer gate, now wrapped in blue twilight. It was much like the other gate: tall and menacing, with massive doors and gatehouses that went up to a high parapet.

Helga and Peridan dismounted and worked against the door bar, managing to dislodge the great wood beam. It fell to the ground with a great thud that reverberated in the city like the echo of a drum. Peridan pulled at one of the iron rings on the gate, but it did not budge. Helga joined in, but it did no good.

"I have an idea," Helga said. She unhitched a rope from the horse's gear and tied it over the saddle, then looped it through the ring. She slapped Raggle on the rump, and the horse pulled forward, but the gate did not budge.

"Come!" It was Zul, and she was resting on a stone ledge above them. "There is a machine you must work."

Peridan and Helga went up several flights of stairs to a few rooms above the gate. In one of them stood an immense crank, set into the floor with an iron chain winding around it. They both pushed against one of the great iron bars that worked the crank, but it did not budge.

"Here!" Zald said. He hopped on the ground beside a metal grate set into a hole in the floor. Helga looked through it to see a large iron ball in the middle of the chain, made so it could not pass through the bars of the grate until it was opened. On three sides of the grate were metal covers with locks.

"Drat!" Helga said. "We would need a key."

"Move aside," Peridan said. He clutched his staff in one hand and held the other out to the grate.

Nothing happened. Peridan frowned.

"What were you trying to do?" Helga said.

Peridan tried again. "I was trying to loosen the lock. I have a spell for it, but I cannot seem to conjure it. Nor can I conjure anything." He looked at his right hand suspiciously.

"What do we do now?"

"Silly girl," Zald said. "Find the key!"

"Where?"

"It's bound to be around here somewhere," Zald said. "Humans always have keys on them."

"These were dark elves," Peridan said.

"Now is not the time for splitting feathers!" Zald said. He flapped up and hopped into a nearby room.

"We will need light," Helga said, watching the sun disappear behind the mountains out an arrow slit, which faced west, out of the city. "Can you create that magic fire again?"

"My magic here is suppressed," Peridan said, "or else at this point, I would just try to blast the gate apart. We will need to find something to burn, I'm afraid."

They quickly went to another room in the guardhouse and found there a table and chairs. Peridan easily broke the chairs apart, but they had no kindling, so they both hurried back down to the horses. There

Helga, as quickly as she could manage, produced her tinderbox and tried to light the dry wood of the chairs (Peridan, being a sorcerer, carried no kindling and relied on magic to start his fires). It was slower work than she wanted, and she found her hands shaking profusely before a corner of one of the chair pieces caught fire and started smoking.

She stood up with the wood and carefully blew on it to get the flame to spring to life.

"You might want your sword, rather than the torch," Peridan said, drawing his own blade.

Surrounding them were many areas of mist, aglow in the twilight. They moved here and there. Helga squinted at them and saw that they bore the slightest resemblance of a humanoid, but all the features and the shape of them were blurred. They walked and floated up and down stairs. Helga looked back into the city and saw many places aglow with mist.

"What are they?" Helga asked. The torch came to life in her hand, and she barely noticed.

"I don't know," Peridan said. "I've never seen this. Nor read of it, to my memory."

Zim flew down beside them, Zul and Zald following close behind.

"Do you see them, friends?" Helga said.

"I see them, yes," Zim said. "Where are they, though?"

"Right in front of your eyes, you witless bird," Peridan said, just as one of the shades swept in front of the horses. Peridan swung at it with his sword, but the blade hit nothing.

"Witless?" Zald said. "We could leave you here, you know, attacking nothings that did nothing to you."

"Do you see them or not?" Helga said.

"Yes," Zim said, "But I don't know where they are! And you call *us* witless. We should work on getting you that key. Silly wingless things."

Helga lit another piece of wood and handed it to Peridan. Quickly, they went back into the guardhouse by the gate and set about looking in every corner or open storage bin they could. The place was filled with the shades, and in some rooms, there were enough standing or sitting about that the torches were unnecessary.

"I'm glad they aren't noticing us," Helga said. When she swept past one, she thought she could see, only faintly, eyes and a mouth moving.

"As am I," Peridan said. "But what will draw their attention, I wonder?"

"I think I would prefer not to find out."

They swept through more rooms in the gatehouse, but could find no set of keys. While they did so, the twilight disappeared and was replaced by full night. The moon, near full, was already rising, but its light was negligible in the presence of the specters that floated around the ruined city. Outside the gatehouse, Peridan and Helga ran into Zald, who was perched on an old stair, looking at the moon.

"Did you find anything?" Helga said.

Zald cocked his head. "We found many things. We did not find your keys."

Helga was startled as Peridan dragged her into a darkened corner.

"Quickly," he said. "I think one of them reacted to me. Put out the torches."

Helga complied, dropping what remained of her piece of wood to the ground and stamping it out with her boot.

"They are elves," Peridan said, looking out to a street that was filling with the specters moving in and out of buildings. "Or perhaps they *were* elves. What they are now, I cannot say."

"I just had a thought," Helga said. "Zald said that humans have lots of keys. So would elves, I would think. Maybe one of them has the keys."

"I have a better idea," Zald said. "Let us flee. It is a few days lost time, which is better than lost life, yes?"

"I agree with the bird," Peridan said. "This is not worth our skins. I say we ride out the rear gate, the way we came in."

Helga hesitated a moment in thought. "Alright."

Zald flew off to find the other ravens as Helga and Peridan ran back toward the horses. They hurriedly mounted up and rode through the city toward the east gate, ignoring the specters as much as their mounts would allow them, for though one could pass through them, they appeared solid and were forming more recognizable features by the minute. With coaxing, Raggle obeyed and ran through the ghostly elves, shaking his head in fright. Peridan's mount ran through them as if they didn't exist, his large hooves pounding the earth the way only a warhorse could. Peridan raced ahead, only to pull up short, crying for his horse to stop.

The east gate, which had stood open and decayed, was now shut fast. Not only that, but it was barred and shone in the moonlight like a thing new-made, its iron hinges polished to a dull luster and its reinforcements shiny white.

"How is this possible?" Helga said.

"I wish I knew," Peridan said. "Wait!" Peridan urged his horse forward and put out an arm to touch the gate. "Damn. It's solid. Well, sort of solid. Hard to describe."

Helga rode forward and felt the gate door for herself. It was indeed solid, but it made her hand tingle as she touched it, and it seemed to give a little with her push. She leaned onto the wood, but it did not budge.

"Ravens!" Peridan called out. "Ravens! Do you see a way out?"

Nobody answered.

Helga nearly jumped out of her saddle as she saw a poleaxe being thrust up toward her face. She looked down to see a very surprised elven face. It was one of the shades, but less luminous. She could see every detail of him and even heard his words as he spoke, though she could not comprehend them. The sharp point of the poleax threatened her again, and she put her hands up.

Soon, she and Peridan were surrounded by six or eight elves, all with pale, luminescent skin and various weapons. They were armored in shining mail, with stout functional helms. They spoke strange words to each other. More elves were coming out into the street by the gate, and among them, Helga could make out maidens in fair dresses of many hues, along with well-dressed men in finery and more warriors.

Helga was forced to dismount by hands pulling at her, and her sword was taken away from her. Peridan likewise was forced to dismount, but the elves did not make him relinquish his staff, refusing to touch it. At threat of spear and bow, a cadre of the armed elves walked them through the street, which was soon lined with a multitude of brightly clothed people, all slightly glowing.

The street, Helga noticed, was very well lit for the dead of night, and with a glance up, she realized why. The moon was still in the sky, but in addition to it was a larger moon of full roundness that gave off a slight red light. The stars were brighter, too, and above the city, clouds glowed of their own green radiance. The city had lights coming from windows that looked warm and inviting.

Windows! Glass filled all the windows, and doors hung on all the jams. Roofs of brilliantly colored tiles tilted from the side of the rocky valley, and columns that were fallen in the day were now raised.

"Where are you taking us?" Helga said. The elves did not reply.

"I doubt they speak the common tongue," Peridan said. He spoke to the men in several languages Helga did not understand, but the elves seemed to not understand either. "Well, I'm at a loss," the mage said at last.

They were brought at length to what they had thought to be a palace or temple, which stood now in its new-made glory. Well-armored guards with high helms stood outside the open doors at the top of the stairs, and the bronze statue of Atalthal stood shining in the light like polished gold. The horses were left at the bottom of the stairs next to the statue, which seemed to ill-suit them. Raggle stamped his front feet nervously.

The armed men stopped to talk to each other when Helga and Peridan reached the entrance. Then, they all passed inside. Even as they walked, the glow around the armed men seemed to pull back into their skin, and their luminescence was replaced by a pale glow from their eyes alone. Helga thought she could understand a word or two of what they were saying, but gave up as her eyes beheld the inside of the palace.

The foyer was brightly lit by flames of colorless white in braziers suspended by chains from great pillars that held aloft a ceiling of pure gilt, depicting countless animals and human-like figures. The floor underfoot was a thick, red carpet, and either side of the room was lined by statues and tables, where beautiful elf maidens sat with each other, talking.

They passed through this great entranceway into a smaller hallway and then into a large, square feasting room. Tables were filled with eating utensils but were all empty, save for one, which was occupied by two tall elves in flowing robes.

"Ah, here they are," one of the two elves said, and stood. He was powerfully fair, his features so balanced they looked almost unreal, and his glowing eyes, slightly purple, paused on Helga. His voice flowed freely, strong but also gentle. "That is a strange one."

"Aye, lord, they appeared out of thin air, like mist taking shape," one of the guards said, and Helga realized she could understand him perfectly.

"Might it have been them that scared half the city?" The other elf in finery said. He was shorter than the first and less fair, but only because his features were so strong by comparison.

"I'm sorry, we didn't mean to come here," Helga said.

"She can talk?" said the guard.

"Quiet," Peridan said, and raised his head to the fairer elf.

"If you are thinking of spinning a story, put it out of your mind," the fairer elf said. "I can easily detect a lie."

At a wave of the fair elf's hand, the guards bowed and stepped back toward the wall.

"Who are you?" he said. He came to stand close to Helga and Peridan, and he towered over both of them by a head. His intense eyes regarded them dispassionately.

"I am Helga, daughter of Hrolfi," Helga said, her voice trembling. "I have found myself inside your city by accident and chance."

"I didn't ask for stories just yet," the elf said. Helga looked down under the intensity of his stare. "And you, light-elf?"

Peridan held his chin level and met Atalthal's gaze calmly. "I am Peridan. And I am a fair-elf. I take it that you are a dark-"

"Fair is a matter of perspective. I am Atalthal, lord of Atalthalda. This is my counselor, Balthal."

Helga covered her mouth in surprise, but Peridan merely raised an eyebrow.

"It is not every day you meet a hero of legend," he said.

"It is not every day that an insolent light elf manages to sneak into my sanctuary, nor," his eyes turned to Helga, and his tone lightened, becoming soft and curious, almost sweet, "is it every day that I meet someone as strange as this." He reached forward, and Helga flinched before she realized he was trying to touch her ears. His hands were like ice on her skin, and she shivered as he held her ear. "She looks like…"

"Like who?" Balthal said.

"Nothing," Atalthal said.

"A quick child, we call them in Alfheim," Peridan said. "But they call themselves men. Have you never seen one before?"

"Yes, I think so, but it has been a long time," Atalthal said, frowning slightly. "You turn from my question, how did you arrive in my realm?"

"It was not intentional," Peridan said, maintaining his calm demeanor. "We found the city in a valley, and to us, it looked abandoned. There was nobody to be seen. It was only after the sunset that we began to see you."

"What a yarn," Balthal said, slapping his leg. "The sun!"

Helga was puzzled. "We only wished to pass through," Helga said.

"And what do you seek in Niflheim?" Atalthal said. "It is not a realm that is kind to either of your kinds."

"We seek nothing in your realm," Peridan said. "We did not intend to come here. We were in Midgard-"

"Midgard?" said Balthal. "What lies, lord. I dare say they would be good sport for the court with such stories."

"Indeed," Atalthal said. "Guards, you may take them the dungeons. Separate cells."

"What?" Helga cried. A guard reached forward and gripped her arm tightly, restraining her. She cried out again, her voice cracking and warbling. "We are travelers, nothing more. You mustn't lock us up!"

"I do not have the goodwill to let spies walk free within my walls," Atalthal said. "Though I think you will find my goodwill to be sufficient as prisoners."

"Please, Lord!" Helga said. "I cannot tarry here. Every day lost is-"

"Quiet!" Peridan snapped.

"Interesting. A time-bound errand," Atalthal said. "Take them away, and maybe some time will loosen their tongues as to why they are here."

"And take the mage's staff," Balthal said. "It's like you were all born yestereve."

Helga hung her head as the guards pushed on her back, leading her out of the dining hall. She cast a glance back to see Atalthal looking strangely at her, his eyes narrowed but shining of their own light. The guards lead them through several halls, less grand than the entrance and dining hall only in their relative lack of gilding.

The walls were filled with paintings of remembrance that Helga gazed at as they walked by. They depicted elf men and women, battles with strange creatures, and many other things that Helga could only guess to be elven cities. None of the events or places portrayed were familiar to her, and she was filled with wonder even as she was frightened of the future.

The dungeon was not what Helga had expected. Rather than a dark, damp, stonewalled pit like those in the castles of men, the dark elven dungeons were reinforced rooms with small, barred windows, but brightly lit by the moons and full of fine furnishings. They had carpets and tables and beds with fine linens.

A pair of guards led her into one of these cells and then asked her to remove her boots. She did so reluctantly, though both of the elves seemed totally disinterested in her as a woman. When she had removed the heavy leather things, the guards looked inside them, then left the boots sitting by the bed, noticeably off the carpet.

They closed the door and left her sitting on the bed, shoeless. The door lock slid loudly into the wall. Helga looked up and saw that the cell was lit by a glowing ball the size of her head suspended from the ceiling, much like those she had seen in Thruddel. She reached up and touched it and found it to be warm. It reacted to her fingers by forming colorful trails wherever she touched, mostly in shades of purple. While she touched the orb, or slightly after touching it, the room was bathed in whatever color light had been left under her fingers.

Feeling quite miserable despite her pretty surroundings, Helga lay back on the bed. She hadn't slept in a real bed in quite some time, and the feather mattress and pillows were almost too comfortable to bear. Despite her full effort at keeping her eyes open so as to think about her situation, she fell quickly asleep.

*

The fire was blazing hot, hovering in the sky above Helga's head. Who had put it there? She put her hand up to block it out. It relieved her eyes, but she still felt hot. Frustrated, she turned away from the light and looked out upon the fields. They were bright and green, rolling and stretching away. The grass grew and swayed. She felt suddenly very alone.

An animal came scurrying over the ground and paused before Helga. It curled up and lay down in the dark beneath her. Her shadow. This gave her a thought, and an idea: *Shade.*

The ground vibrated as the turf underfoot lifted, sending the animal fleeing to the other side of Helga. Up, up, the grass went, along with the ground, which fell away from it in clouds of dust. Soon the grass was high above her head, held aloft by a firm pillar of earth in the center of the misshapen platform of green. Helga stepped forward, and the pillar twisted and firmed. She ran her hand along the outside,

122

finding it smooth and cool. Above her, the pillar split into thousands of smaller versions of itself, holding aloft the grass.

The light continued to peek through the gaps, and Helga watched the grass flatten and grow, capturing all the sun and leaving Helga a space of cool, dark shade. The animal (*Ratatask,* Helga thought) ran to the new creation and climbed it swiftly.

Tree.

Helga breathed the cool air, and then the tree began to flower and drop nuts. Some of these nuts found purchase in the soil beneath the grass, and she watched new trees spread out from her, creating a vast sheet of blessed shade. She picked one of the nuts up and opened it. A glow resided inside, and she ate it.

*

Helga woke from her dream to find talons digging into her arm. The room was dark, but she recognized the soft roc-roc of the bird and knew it was Zim.

"Where am I?"

"Niflheim," Zim said. "Or a piece of it. Do not grow too tired! Or you will slow like the spirits beyond the walls."

Helga sat up, putting aside the dream and taking in the prison cell with its rich furnishings. Her memory returned.

"It's still night. How long have I been sleeping?"

"It's always night here. The sun does not travel this realm. I think you have been sleeping not too long. It took us a few hours to find you in here. The elf is in another room. Not far."

Helga sat up and went to the small, barred window. Outside, the stars were shining brightly, and she could see the edge of the larger, redder moon above. As she looked closely, she realized that the stars were somewhat unfamiliar. Some of the constellations looked to be present, though slightly off, but others that she was more familiar with were absent entirely. Only the Old Man's cane remained clear and bright on the horizon, where she had always looked to find north.

"Now we are here," Helga said, "But how shall we leave?"

123

"Leave the same way you came in, silly," Zim said. "Someone is coming."

Zim flapped up to the window and squeezed his large body between the bars, then flew off.

Helga turned to see an armored elf step up to the iron-barred door, holding a tray of food. He slipped it through an opening in the door and laid it on the ground.

"The master trusts you will tell him the truth soon."

"Tell him he has already heard it," Helga said.

The elf left without responding, his mail clinking in the stone hallway. Helga knelt down and picked up the tray, then put it on a wooden table in the cell. The food seemed almost familiar, consisting of cooked meat, some lettuce-like greens, and what looked like sliced apples. It had no smell to her, however, and she felt strangely that she did not want to eat it.

A few minutes passed by, and Helga, knowing she hadn't eaten in some time, picked up one of the apple slices and took a bite. It had a very mild, almost bland flavor, of sour and bitter, but was full of moisture. She forced it down and ate another slice.

"Don't eat the food, child!" It was Zul, who had just landed on the window. "Spit it out!"

Helga complied and spat out her last bite of food. Zul hopped through the window and over to the table. She began pushing through the food with her beak curiously.

"What is wrong with it?" Helga asked.

"Good that you did not each much," the raven said. "And that you only ate the fruit. Ravens are hungry too, but we can smell that this food is not right for beings of the mortal world. If you eat it, you will be drawn into the mist realm to stay, perhaps forever. To eat an animal of Niflheim would surely draw you further into this realm."

"How shall we leave this world, then?" Helga said.

"The mage is concocting a plan," Zul said. "First, we will wait to see if the sun rises or rises no longer. If it rises, then you will pass back into the mortal realm. If not, you may end up being a permanent resident here, and then our friendship will have to end."

"Will you not be trapped as well?"

"We are cleverer than you give us credit for," Zul said. "Do you think the mortal realm is the only one to put air under our wings? We will find a way out, yes, but of course, *we* are not prisoners."

Helga stood, not wanting to retreat to the unexpected comfort of the bed. She looked out the window and saw the Old Man's cane starting to touch the northwest Horizon. Dawn would be coming soon, if it could come in the realm of Atalthal. Nervously, she paced the room, thinking of how she would be able to get out of the cell, recover her horse, and make it outside the city - but if she left, would she be able to return to her own world? She considered inferring to the guards that she would talk to the lord of the city, then making a run for it, but she knew that would be of no use, no matter where she started running. She thought about taking a sword from a guard, but she had never practiced with a sword, and she was certain the soldiers of the city had, perhaps for much longer than she had lived.

Her heart leapt into her throat as the door to her cell swung open - she had been lost in her own world of thought and had not heard the approach of heavy greaves, the clinking of mail, or the turning of a key in the lock of her cell, nor had she noticed Zul's escape through the window.

It was Atalthal, who closed the cell door behind himself and nodded to a guard, who turned away out of view.

"You are awake again, I see," Atalthal said coolly. He leaned against the wall. "So tell me, Helga, what is your true aim here?"

"I have no aim here," Helga said. "Truly."

"I have a mind to make your accommodations rougher, though it is not to our liking to treat prisoners harshly."

"It will change nothing, except make me more likely to lie, I think," Helga said. She met his stare. "Did you create this place?"

"This is Niflheim. It has always been. It always shall be. But surely you knew this. How did you enter? What were your methods? It would do much to earn my goodwill to teach me such things. And my goodwill can be great."

"I came here through the mountains. Some call them the Ulfar Mountains, others the Talonbranch Mountains."

"I do not know these names," Atalthal said.

Helga heard a raven call from outside. She looked to the window and saw a hint of strange light.

"How are you doing this?" Atalthal said, suddenly angry. He stepped forward and gripped Helga's arm. She cried out as he pulled her close and grabbed her face. "How do you know the secret of the dark mist?"

She looked down at his arms to see they were beginning to glow softly. The edges of them looked blurry and hazy. She struggled against him, but his strength was very great, and no matter how she shook, his grip tightened.

"Tell me!" Atalthal said. Even as he pulled her closer, close enough that she could feel his ice-cold breath on her face, she began to feel his grip begin to soften, in a way.

Looking down, she saw a dagger in the folds of Atalthal's robes. She reached for it, but the elf was too quick. He swung about and threw her to the ground.

She looked up to see him draw the dagger. He looked at it for a moment and then returned it to its sheath.

"Guards, to me!" he said to the door. "Bring chains!" Two armored elves, glowing softly, appeared after a few moments and stepped into the cell. One held a set of shackles. With the best energy she could muster, Helga leapt up and charged the first guard. He was thrown slightly off-balance, enough for Helga to push past without him being able to get a grip on her. She ran for the door. Atalthal held forward a hand and without being touched, the door shut with a muted clang. Helga grabbed the door and shook it.

"Peridan! Quickly! Help!" she called down the corridor. The strong hands of the guards pulled her away from the door, and within seconds, she was in shackles and lying on the bed.

"Not a wise way to repay my hospitality," Atalthal shouted at her. He glowed more brightly now, and the edges of his body looked indistinct, like her eyes were out of focus. His voice, too, sounded blurry. He spoke a few words to the guards that Helga did not understand.

Atalthal rushed to the bed but was, to Helga, beginning to look like mist. His hand closed on Helga's arm, but she felt only slight pressure. She stood up, pushing Atalthal easily. One of the guards swung a sword at her. She screamed and put up her arm and felt the blow lightly land on her forearm. With a push, she turned the blade that had touched her away. Atalthal was furious with the guard, but she could no longer understand any of them. She stood up and shrank to a corner. She looked at the window and saw that the light had grown. The door started to get hazy, and she could see it turning to a rust-red. The shackles on her wrists, however, remained steadfast and strong.

The elves in the room continued fading until they became somewhat amorphous, like when the shades had first appeared at twilight, but the shades did not approach her. Their voices sounded distant and unclear, their language strange and foreign, but they seemed to be debating amongst each other, and though their faces were blurry, Helga could feel their cold eyes move across her.

Helga took a deep breath and walked forward toward the shade she thought was Atalthal. She could see faintly the outline of his face. He moved toward her, his arm outstretched. She felt it contact her, but also felt it slide through and past her, like a cold wind finding a gap in warm clothes. She tried to lock eyes with him, but his eyes were now two glowing halos of yellow light, and she could not see life in them as before.

She gazed around the room and realized it looked quite different. The bed was gone, replaced by a pile of rotting wood, and the carpets were gone too, though the floor was covered with the ancient remains of the warp lying like ghostly grey rags. She walked through Atalthal, feeling both cold ice and soft touch as she passed through him and laid her hands on the door. The wood sections of the door were split and eroded, but the iron frame stood solid. Helga shook the door, hoping the rusty hinges would give, or the lock mechanism would be out of repair, but the whole thing held fast.

"Ah, you have returned!" It was Zim, who had just flown through the window. "The mage is on his way here. His door was in much worse shape than yours – the ceiling of his stone cage fell in many years ago." Zim hopped to the door, then pushed himself between two of the iron bars. "Yes, it appears he was right. Very good. I was not looking forward to a journey out of Niflheim. I don't know if you've walked that path, or talked to anyone who has done it, but it is unpleasant if you can find the way out at all. Most men are forced to make unsavory deals with the powerful dead to escape – also unpleasant. It is a dead land that has nothing to eat, and hunger is most certainly always unpleasant for ravens. Ah, here comes the mage."

Footsteps sounded down the stone passageway, getting louder and faster.

"Ha Ha!" Peridan shouted. He appeared around a corner smiling broadly. "Huzzah! You are alive."

"That I am," Helga said. "But I don't think I can get out of here."

"Yes, that is a pickle," Peridan said. "Perhaps if I can retrieve my staff, my magic will return with the sun. Then I can open the lock and the one at the gate. And the one on your wrists."

"Let us hope," Helga said. "And hurry, the shades in here are unsettling."

"What shades?" Peridan said. "It is morning. We have been brought out of Atalthal's realm."

Helga turned and saw the shades, still in the room, still quietly regarding her, though they were now little more than vaguely person-like clouds of light.

"I see three elves, still in this cell." She pointed at the tallest shape. "There is Atalthal himself, do you not see him?"

"I see nothing but the inside of an ancient cell," Peridan said. "How curious."

"She ate some of the food," Zul said. She had apparently flown through the window without any of the others noticing.

"That was unwise," Peridan said, "But it could have been worse. You are clearly in the mortal world, whatever you might see of Atalthal's realm."

"Zald has found the horses," Zul said. "Soon, you will be able to eat real, living food again, rather than the death poison of the mist world."

"If you can get me out of here," Helga said. "Do you have any tools in your pack? Something with which we could force the lock?"

"No," Peridan said. "I must say I have always relied on my magic to do such things for me. This is a lesson I will remember, if I remain on Earth to remember it." Peridan took a breath and looked down the hallway. Helga followed his gaze to see that a part of the wall and ceiling had fallen in; sunlight streamed in through sparse motes, and dust lay heavy on the ancient, colorless roof tiles that lay amid the stone heap. "Perhaps there are some tools remaining in the city from before Atalthal drew the people here into his part of Niflheim – into *his* dream. We can go search for them, assuming the ravens will help us."

"Ah, clever mage. Why would you assume?" Zim said. "But we will help you, if only because we appreciate your companion. And we are hungry."

"Appreciate, but not like," Helga said. She found herself laughing despite the shades she could see in the corners of her eyes.

"We expect food," Zim said, and flew through the break in the ceiling.

"I'll be back as soon as I can," Peridan said. "Try not to eat any more of the food, eh?"

"It would be nothing but cold mist if I tried," Helga said.

Peridan nodded to her and ran down the hallway. Helga listened to his footsteps echo to a swimming, quiet reverberation that was eventually drowned out by the sound of the shades in the room. The shades, which were extremely pale in the morning sun, so pale that she reckoned if they were to stand in the light, they would be invisible, were emitting soft, strange sounds. It almost sounded like words, or the imagining of words when the wind blows through the eaves of an old house.

She walked toward the shade she thought might be Atalthal (they had moved around and were all three unrecognizable) and passed her hand through it. Icy cold shot up her arm, but she could not feel anything more than if she had passed her hand through mist, or something watery yet much less substantial than water.

With a sigh, she walked toward the corner of the cell, leaned against the wall, and collapsed down to the floor. She watched the shades move for a few moments, then closed her eyes, wondering if only she could focus she could hear the words. Though she made great efforts to hear what sounded like words, she could not make herself understand. With her eyes closed, her mind began to drift.

She shook her head with a sudden realization that she was falling asleep. When she looked up, she noticed the shades were gone from the room. One of them stood outside the door.

"Damn it, I wonder if I had been paying attention, I could have walked out the door when they opened it," she said aloud.

"Not likely," Zald said. He was perched on the windowsill, rocking back and forth from leg to leg.

"Watching me sleep?"

"Wondering if you had died and if I could eat your eyes."

"Sorry to disappoint you."

"I like you better alive, but I am very hungry."

Helga rubbed her eyes. "Find my horse and tell Peridan to give you some food from my pack. Dreamer knows I could use some."

"Your road rations are disgusting, girl," Zald said. "But I will hold you to your promise of food later."

"I made no promise."

"Of course you did. Do not try to deceive a raven in such matters."

Helga yawned.

"Sleepy, are we?"

"Yes," Helga said. "I haven't gotten much of it in the last few days."

"This is not a good place to sleep," the raven said. "I will go looking for your pack. For food. Not for me. For you, and you will give me good food later."

"Fine."

"The bargain is struck!" Zald said, and flew out of the window.

Helga knew it was not a good place to sleep, but often telling a person she mustn't sleep is an excellent way to make her tired, and Helga felt this truth assaulting her dried eyes. She had in her mind to stand up and pace, but before she could conjure the will to stand, she drifted off.

VIII. Waking Dreams

HELGA OPENED her eyes to see swaying branches and a rolling plain of grass that spread out in every direction. The tree (for the word and idea came quickly to her) was the only one in sight. She stood and noticed a squirrel looking at her from a large branch that hung almost to the ground.

"How did you get here?"

"I was always here, of course," the squirrel said back. Its words were quick and articulate, but held a pleasing timbre. It held in its small hand-like paws a large nut.

"You know words."

"You assumed as much when you spoke to me, did you not?" the squirrel said. "Why should it be so alarming? You speak. I speak."

Helga shrugged. She looked out past the tree to the endless plains.

"I was lonely," she said to the squirrel. "That is why I made you talk."

"I am not lonely. Would you like a nut?"

Helga took a nut from the squirrel, who ran up into the tree to fetch another one. The one Helga held now had a broken shell. She split it all the way open and found the meat of the nut. She put it in her mouth and chewed it, enjoying the texture.

"What if I leave?" Helga said. "Will you be lonely, Ratatask?"

"Probably."

"I remember a forest."

"So do I."

"Where is it?"

"I don't know."

Helga looked across the plains. "I'm going to go that direction and see if I find it. Do you want to come with me?"

"I think I like it here."

Helga nodded to the squirrel and set off across the plain. She looked back, and the tree was quite distant. Searching the empty sky, she found the sun and felt hot again. The sun hid itself even as she blocked it out with her hand. Vapors and mists coalesced into clouds, and suddenly the sky was a cool grey. She imagined touching the clouds, but they were too far away.

Above her, she heard something call out, then saw something fly toward the tree, and alight at the top. It was a bird, a dark robin, and the squirrel found it and was talking to it, or looked like he was.

Helga turned back to the plains and walked. Water began to fall from the sky.

*

"Wake up! Wake up!"

It was Zald, and he was sitting on Helga's knees, pecking her on the forehead. "The mage is returning."

Helga pushed herself up, trying to shake the dream from her eyes. She approached the cell door and realized she could no longer see a shade outside.

"Helga!" Peridan called down the hall. He appeared outside the door, but carried no tools or metal.

"No luck with the tools?" Helga said. She pushed against her shackles again, but they were as real as the door.

"Unfortunately, there is nothing in this city of use," Peridan said. "I went to everything that looked like a shop, and even the ravens began going door-to-door, but the best we could find was the rusted head of a hammer with no shaft. But I did find the horses, and it seems our tack has come back to the mortal realm with us, which is splendid."

"I understand," Helga said. She took a deep breath. "I would saddle them both and leave the way we came in. You have my permission. I don't think I'll be getting out of this."

"Yes, well, your ravens-"

"We are not *her* ravens!" Zald said. "Any more than she is *our* human." The bird paused and clacked his beak. "Though perhaps she is our human. Regardless, mage, she does not own us!"

"Of course," Peridan said. "Anyway, the ravens-"

"We came up with a plan," Zim said. He and Zul had just flown in through the cell window. "When it became obvious there was nothing able to break a lock left in the city, which was some time ago, mind you, but we continued our fruitless search because we felt like indulging the mage – Once reality was obvious, we decided to pass the time making more clever plans than breaking down doors."

"What is this clever plan?" Helga said. "Because personally, I find the breaking down of doors to be quite excellent in this scenario."

"Always so impatient and indignant!" Zim said.

"And insulting. You are a crow!" Zald said.

"Not very clever, Zald," Zul said. "And leave the child alone. She is young and hasn't had the benefit of the Black Feather Friends to help her think."

"Indeed," Helga said. "Now, what is your plan?"

"You will pass back into the mist realm," Zim said. "And you will get the king of the city to release you."

"You would imagine if I could convince him to do that, I would have already done so."

"No, silly," Zim said. "You just need him to get you out of your cell. To anywhere, really, and once out, you will fade back into the true realm and be free."

"Atalthal is no fool," Helga said. "Actually, I don't know him well enough to say he isn't a fool, but I think it would be foolish to assume that anyone you don't know well *is* a fool. He will not free me from the cell if he watched me disappear at dawn."

"Ah," Peridan said. "But there is no dawn in the land of the red moon, for there is no sun. Time slips by differently there, and it is unlikely they would reckon the count of hours between our appearance and our disappearance to be of note."

"Do not believe his presentation of expertise, child," Zul said. "It is we who understand the passage of time in Niflheim, since only we have traversed it in its vastness."

"Yes, well," Peridan said. "I am not unfamiliar with Niflheim, being a scholar, but it may not be that realm at all, but one of Atalthal's making himself."

"Preposterous," Zim said. "It is too fixed to be of a Fay power."

Peridan shrugged. "This is your best chance, Helga."

"And how shall I get out of my cell there? Because I would prefer to be out of the cell here more," Helga said.

"Gain an audience with Atalthal," Peridan said.

"And how shall I do that?"

"Use your womanly wiles," Peridan said. "Atalthal is not so great as to refuse the attentions of a young woman, especially one who is exotic. You saw his fascination with you."

"I'm married, Peridan."

"You're in a cell, too. The ravens and I will be in hiding in the city, preparing for your escape. We will need our horses and tack, for the way to the watchers is long yet."

"Very well," Helga said. "I guess I'll have to try, but if I don't make it out, try not to waste another day. Move on."

"You still owe me food," Zald said.

"I lay that burden on Peridan in my stead. May he honor the debts of the dead."

"Of course," Peridan said with a sarcastic drawl. "But I don't intend to pick up those debts."

*

Helga waited patiently for the sun to set, the hours drawing out. She ate a little food and drank a little water that Peridan had retrieved from her pack. The birds kept her company, as best they could between their bickering, and Peridan went off into the city to find a hiding place.

At last, the rays of the sun began to dim, and, clearly and subtly, Helga saw a pale glowing shade pass by the door. The edges of the objects in the room began to get blurry, and soon, the room was as it had been the previous night. She waited for things inside to get clear and real, then approached the door.

"Hello?" She tried to look down the corridor, which was harder with the wood paneling of the door back in place between the iron bars. She tried calling out again, this time as loud as she could. "Hello! Have you forgotten to guard me?"

Steps began to sound: echoing dull thuds that slowly got louder and clearer. A young elf stepped in front of the door, his eyes wide and blazing.

"You're here?" he said.

"I never left," Helga said. "Or are you always so surprised when prisoners don't escape?"

"We watched you disappear," the guard said. "I'll... have to fetch the captain." The elf went running down the hall and returned shortly with another elf, this one having a more experienced look to his eyes and face, though he didn't show much in the way of age.

"What are you doing in there?" he said to Helga.

"Being a prisoner. I need to see Atalthal."

The captain laughed. "Lots of people do. What makes you think he would see you?"

"I'm a spy."

"Then you'll lose your head."

Helga clenched her fists in her shackles. "I can teach him how the city was breached. I want to. You... ah," Helga searched her head. "Are in danger. Yes, an attack is imminent, and I can tell you how your walls will be breached."

"You're lying, or you wouldn't bother telling us about it," the captain said.

Helga felt sweat burst on her brow. "They're... my enemies too. The enemy of your enemy is your friend."

"Not always." The captain looked at the younger guard, then back at Helga. "How about I let you sit in that cell for the next few turns, then I tell the master? I don't think he'd reprimand me, given that we didn't know you were in here. Maybe we still do not know."

Helga gritted her teeth. "Tell Atalthal I came back. To see him."

The captain shrugged.

"You, young one," Helga said to the younger guard.

"Anuldas," the guard said.

"Anuldas. Take this gift to Atalthal." She hurriedly took off one of her rings — not her wedding ring, but one her father had given to her as a present that had delicate filigree all the way around it. She handed it to the elf.

"Captain, I think the master would want to know about this," Anuldas said.

The captain sighed. "Best go inform the master our prisoner has come back."

"Aye, sir," the guard said, and set off down the corridor.

The captain narrowed his eyes and stared at Helga. "I'm going to watch you very carefully."

Helga backed up to the bed and laid herself down.

*

When Helga heard footsteps echoing down the hall, she leapt up from the bed and went to the door, but she did not see the person she was expecting. Instead of Atalthal, it was two elf maidens flanked by two more elves with spears and swords. These guards were clad in mail, and Helga only realized when they got close that they were also female.

A guard opened the door, and two spears were points leveled at Helga around two smiling, youthful, and beautiful elf faces.

"It occurred to us that our guest has not had a bath," the first elf said. She had yellow eyes that glowed slightly and long black hair. Her skin was, as with all the others, alabaster white and without blemish or wrinkle.

"I haven't had a bath," Helga said. "Are you going to give me one?"

138

"Yes, I am Nanaba, an attendant in the household of Atalthal. This is my assistant and apprentice, Marania." The other elf smiled and bowed slightly. Her hair was lighter in color, but her eyes were darker: a shade of yellow-green.

"I hope you do not mind the guards," Marania said. "And I hope you will understand. These are our spear-maidens, and they serve in… sensitive areas."

Helga followed the two elves, flanked by the female guards, down the long hallway and through the palace proper, where the walls were covered with baroque décor, and the carpet underfoot was springy and high. Eventually, they came to a room with a wide door, and they entered. In the corner of the wood-paneled room was a small hearth, already lit with a male elf in plain clothes tending it. He nodded to Nanaba and exited as soon as they were all inside, and Marania began to place a cauldron of water over the fire.

In the center of the room sat a large porcelain bathtub with a ladder to get in and out. Below it were hot coals, which Nanaba raked lightly.

"You may disrobe," Nanaba said.

"I can't," Helga said, and held up her shackles. One of the female guards produced a key from her belt and unlocked the shackles. Helga rubbed her wrists, relieved of the pressure of the irons, and looked around, wondering if she could escape. Both guards now had both hands on their spears — not leveled, but ready. Without anything else to do, Helga took her clothes off, feeling her face flush with embarrassment as she did so.

"My, you are dirty," Nanaba said. "You look like you've been sleeping in stables!"

"I have," Helga said. "But mostly on the ground."

Nanaba helped her into the bath, which Marania topped off with fresh hot water.

"A minute to soak," Nanaba said, "then we shall scrub."

Helga shifted uncomfortably in the hot bath, feeling even the eyes of the women to be crawling over her, evaluating her.

"Stand up," Nanaba said. Helga complied, and the two elf maidens scrubbed her with soapy brushes with long handles. "Back down."

Nanaba took special care to wash Helga's face and hair, then forced Helga (with a push on the top of her head that would not have released its pressure no matter the resistance) to immerse her head in the water. Helga held her breath and squeezed her eyes shut, then gasped as she emerged.

"Much better," Nanaba said. "That dirt was hiding quite a pretty face, though your ears and eyes *are* a bit strange."

"The Master has been known to be eccentric, though," Marania said. "His second wife, if you'll recall-"

"Quiet girl," Nanaba said without a hint of anger. Marania nodded and said no more.

When Helga got out of the bath, she could not find her clothes.

"If you are looking for those rags, we disposed of them. It is ungainly for a maiden to wear trousers, anyway."

Helga suppressed her anger and put on a dress that Marania produced. Normally, she would have thought it was quite pretty, but she was beginning to have a heap of regrets for the "plan" she was attempting to execute (*waiting around, some plan,* she thought), and fear was creeping in, weakening her knees. The dress was a pale shade of amber and was divided in the middle, like those that some women rode for riding horses. The cloth was tight across her bosom (which she noticed was substantially larger than the two elf women) and left bare her arms. It hung from her shoulders by two strips of thin cloth braided into a chord. Her midsection was covered by a laced thing that reminded her of a bodice, and she wore no petticoats or other underclothes (besides a single, very small thing the elves had given her), so the dress ran against her body the whole way down. Helga judged by the dress of the two unarmored elves that this appeared to be the fashion of the city. She wondered, given the immortal nature of elves, if the fashion ever changed.

The two elves led her out of the bathroom, past the feast hall (where she had first met Atalthal), and into a smaller dining area.

There the master sat with several other elves. They wore formal-looking clothes — robes with silk mantles and ornate closures across the chest. All of them still had swords belted.

The smaller dining hall was lined with tapestries and was lit by spheres hanging from the ceiling, much like the one in her cell, though brighter and containing more colors. The tapestries depicted strange scenes: elves fighting great, eyeless monsters; unknown gods giving gifts to supplicant worshipers; dragons and swords; gods in battle; light and magic. She paused on the threshold, and her eyes were drawn to one scene that showed a group of elvish gods, each dressed in strange garb of diverse style, with eyes that were bright white, standing in a circle around a female who was bleeding upon a floor, dying.

"An ancient myth, of the coming of darkness, and the birth of the bright elves," Atalthal said. He was standing beside her, though she hadn't noticed his rising from the table. "The gods were jealous of light and slew her, thinking to take her power, but it cast the world into darkness and mist: Niflhel. Her sight was divested into us, so it is *we* who are the bright ones, not your so-called 'fair' elf."

"The bright elves?" Helga said. "I thought you were dark elves."

"Elves of darkness." It was the gruff voice of Balthal, who had been dining with Atalthal the night previous. "I'm sure you got the idea from that mage friend of yours. Where is he, by the way? And what should we expect him to return with?"

"He will not return to you," Helga said. "I told him to flee. He expected this place to be empty." *True enough,* she thought.

"We should be glad we have armed and trained our soldiers as well as we have," Balthal said. "This forebodes conflict in the future, distant or near; mark my words."

"Perhaps," Atalthal said. "And perhaps that is a good thing. Even the eternal can tire of bliss, can they not?"

Balthal grunted in response.

"There will always be need of heroes, and that is well, for it is conflict and courage that distills the spirit," Atalthal said. "And only a spirit refined can know bliss."

"As you say, lord," Balthal said.

Atalthal looked long at Helga, and she felt cold as his stare held her eyes. "Ready the garrisons," he said at last, then turned to meet Balthal's hard face. "The worst we can say is we stood ready without cause."

"As you command," Balthal said and rose. The other elves, each armored in well-burnished plate and mail, followed him out. The two female guards remained, holding their spears in a relaxed stance near the door.

Atalthal looked back at Helga. "Can I trust you? You have abandoned a friend, or your friend has seen fit to abandon you, which means you are worth abandoning or are bad at choosing your friends."

"I don't know if I would call Peridan a friend."

"Or you are deceiving me?" Atalthal went on. "Either way, I do not have reason to put trust in your words." He tapped his lips with his finger, as if considering some other silent argument in his mind.

Helga lifted her chin, feeling suddenly very angry at the tall, strange elf insinuating she was a liar. She had a memory of being called a liar once when she had seen a black wolf as a girl, and how angry it made her – angry enough to hit the boy who called her a liar. She also felt hot anger in her face toward herself, for she really was trying to deceive him, as much as a prisoner could be blamed for trying to escape.

"I am not a liar," Helga said. "And you insult my honor to call me such."

Atalthal narrowed his eyes and moved to touch Helga's face. Her instinct was to flinch away from the touch as she remembered her hand passing through the man as mist.

"Your face is turning red," he said.

"Just angry," Helga said, which was again *truthful enough.*

"Interesting," Atalthal said. "Like your ears and your eyes."

"Standard where I come from," Helga said. "Have you really never met mortal men before?"

"None like you. The others were dark-skinned and dark-haired. I must admit I find you fascinating. And beautiful. It is an… invigorating feeling after these long years."

Helga looked around the room for something to mark time, but there were no windows, nor any other machines for the telling of time. She looked back at Atalthal. She bit her cheek, but forced out in as sweet a voice as she could muster, "And I find you fascinating as well."

"Come, eat with me, and tell me of your realm," Atalthal said, smiling. He gestured to the now empty table and clapped his hands. Two female servants entered, and he nodded at them. As quickly as they entered, they left. Helga sat down at the table across from Atalthal. Feeling her legs made bare by the divided skirt, she crossed them and held the cloth to her knee. Before she could begin talking, food arrived in the form of fruit and meat.

Atalthal gestured for her to take some, and she did, slicing off a small piece of the roast and taking an apple from a basket.

"Not hungry?"

"I don't think your food suits me that well," Helga said.

"This is much finer than what you had in the dungeon," Atalthal said.

Helga nodded and took a breath. She cut a piece of the meat, not knowing from what animal it had originated, and took a bite. She again thought the food was somehow insubstantial, less rich than what it would be in the normal world, and also less satisfying. This time, however, it carried full flavor. *A little didn't hurt me last night. A little shouldn't hurt me tonight,* she thought.

"Better, yes?" Atalthal said.

"Yes. It reminds me of boar. Is it a form of boar?"

"That is a creature from the sunlit realm, I believe. This is from a lesser dreadtusk, a creature native to Niflheim and quite a bit fiercer and larger, if my long memory is not failing."

"Does an elf's memory fail? It happens to the oldest humans."

"It happens to bright elves as well. I am the eldest in the city. Many elves younger than me have disappeared into the long sleep, though most have avoided it since we have returned to our home realm."

"You were from Midgard, once," Helga said. "Correct?"

"No, we were always from Niflheim," Atalthal said. "Hence why your friend – sorry, your companion – called us dark elves. The sun is a gift, but not to all. We are the eldest race, and for those of us who did not quicken with the rising of the sun, the endless change and destruction of our world became unbearable. That is why I fought to find again our home city. So that we might again enjoy the timeless dark."

"In the Ulfar Mountains?"

"I do not know that name. The mountains that shelter us here we call the snow shoulders."

"But you are aware this city is duplicated in Midgard – the mortal world, yes?"

"I could see how our architecture might be copied. The majority of your most ancient deep places were built by us before the rising of the sun."

Helga was going to correct him, but decided that what he did not realize might yet be an advantage to her. She changed the subject. "Peridan said you were a hero of legend to the… Bright Elves."

Atalthal smiled. "Nothing is gained without struggle, but that was long ago. I was not a hero so much as a man in love, a man desperate, and a fearful man who was forced to do what was necessary."

"So I suppose I could not convince you to brag?"

Atalthal chuckled. "Is that sport among you quick ones? Bragging?"

"It is among men," Helga said. "Women are much more impressed with action than with words. In fact, we could usually do without a man's words if he truly wishes to impress."

"Then I will not brag."

Helga smiled. "Why don't you tell me your most modest story? That will make me question the servants' reports as to your true greatness."

Atalthal laughed. "I once fought a pride dragon. A spirit of the Fay in a wrathful imitation of one of the true timeless dragons, but they are quite deadly. While they are less than an elder dragon, they are still powerfully clever, immune to most attacks, immune to magic, and their blood is poisonous enough to kill a man who *does* wound one."

"Where is the head?" Helga said. "I assume you had it mounted."

"No," Atalthal said. "I gave the head away as a gift, actually. But that's not the story. I first spied the dragon on a balcony of the bedroom of a king's wife, which I had entered into on accident."

"Whose room were you trying to reach?" Helga said, narrowing her eyes into a jealous stare.

Atalthal laughed again, a deep ringing laugh. "Oh woman, how you do ensnare. Anyway, I scared off the beast and saved the king's wife, only to have the king barge in with a greatsword and attempt to lop my head off. I fumbled my own sword, and when I dropped to the ground to retrieve it, the King swung his sword, missing above my ducked head. The sword was magical, of course, and when it hit the bedpost, the entire bed shattered into a thousand splintering pieces, revealing the Queen's true lover."

"I hope he apologized."

"Nothing of the sort. He thought we were both sleeping with his wife at the same time and went into a bigger rage, practically knocking down the walls of the castle trying to chop us both in two. The queen's lover tossed me out a window to a cart of hay he had strategically placed beforehand – apparently, this was not his first risky brush – and followed me down. After we escaped, we fought the dragon together. The king still did not forgive us, but he let us go. We had many more adventures together after that."

"Lord, that was far from a modest story," Helga said. She realized she was smiling unintentionally.

Atalthal grinned back at her and swirled his drink. "You said my most modest, and I gave it to you."

"Sir, a modest story would be a tale of hunting and shooting a boar from the hip by accident."

"Well, I did once shoot a wyvern by accident," Atalthal said. "Though that ended quite un-modestly." Atalthal smiled and raised his glass. Helga raised hers and drank the wine for the first time. The wine, unlike the food, really was substantial and rich of taste, sweeter and more subtle than any she had procured from Bjorn. She held in a gasp as she looked down to find her plate mostly clean. She had eaten most of the meal while listening to Atalthal brag, and her heart leapt with worry.

Let's hope a little more won't hurt me, she thought.

"Helga, I want you to remain in the city a while," Atalthal said. "I haven't laughed like that in… a very long turn, I think. Stay here as my guest, and perhaps you will want to stay."

"One night, and you already want me to stay?" Helga said.

"I am impulsive," Atalthal said with a smile.

"Clearly. But I am not. Do not expect to bed me."

"What I expect I usually get."

"I thought you were married."

"I was," Atalthal said. "Twice. My first wife was slain. The second fell into the long sleep. I remain, and I do not expect to see her again. But I am not asking you to be my wife, of course, but to enliven my city for a time – as a friend."

"Not as a hostage?" Helga said. "Balthal believes that you will soon be under attack from my friends, after all."

Atalthal waved it away. "Outside blood will be good for us, and we don't get visitors. Too many are turning back to the dream. Too few children are born. Perhaps if there is more dreaming in this life, there will be less need to escape back into that greater one."

"The Fay," Helga said.

"The same." Atalthal reached across and touched Helga's hand. "There is much here, for one of the quick mortals. Life eternal, like a bright elf, in bliss under cool moons, without strife."

"That is tempting," Helga said. "If it were spent with the right person, in the right place."

Atalthal nodded with a soft smile. Sadness touched the corners of his eyes, and Helga thought, for a moment while it lasted, that he looked like an actor in a troupe – the sort of troupe she saw pass through Greenfeld every so often. His mouth said the words and expressed a character, but his eyes held his real person, and that person was tired of reciting the lines of his drama.

"Come with me," Atalthal said. Helga, not knowing what else to do, followed him through the main hall and into a throne room. In the center of the room (not the end, but the true center) was a raised dais with a great gilded throne on it, its carvings intricate and abstract. On the ceiling above it were twelve depictions of gods, and though they bore little resemblance to the gods she knew, she thought they might be the same, just made to look more elven. One of the goddesses had her eyes closed, and she recognized it from the tapestry in the small dining hall, but in this one, she was not slain.

The lord led her past this throne and to a spiraling staircase. He held her hand as he drew her up the steps. It grew dark as they ascended until, at last, they emerged on a great platform beneath bright, strange stars and an enormous red moon, all hazy with moisture as if she was near a shore. To her right was a great mountain, the height of which could not be clearly discerned in the darkness. Toward this mountain Atalthal led her, to a door and another staircase that went into the rock itself. This was lit within by torches that were made of steel and carried a soft green flame that consumed nothing.

The stair was long and winding, but Helga realized it did not tire her at all. She felt as if she could climb up the stairs forever and was not even aware of her heart pumping harder or her breathing increasing the slightest.

"Do you feel it?" Atalthal said, as if reading her thoughts. "The endless, tireless energy?"

"I feel like this is as easy as walking," Helga said.

"That energy is from the Prim. Here it still flows over creation like in the mythic ages. It is life, and thought, and purity. Here."

Atalthal turned to a landing off the winding staircase, which continued going up. He opened a steel door and led Helga out onto a stony ledge. Underfoot was solid, rough stone, but beyond the opening, the rocks were covered with ice and snow. She stepped forward to look over the edge and had to immediately step back, feeling almost queasy.

"Are you alright?"

"Yes. I just didn't realize how high up we had climbed. I did not think we were in the stairs that long."

"We travel quickly when the Prim is strong, and it flows with great strength tonight." Atalthal put his arm around Helga's waist, and her immediate reaction, almost a flinch, was to throw it off, but she resisted and allowed him to lead her back to the edge.

Below her, the city was laid out in its entirety, shaped like a small half-moon around mountains that were far taller than what existed in Helga's realm. The trees were lit with their own light and were pale shades of green, amber, and even purple. The forest illuminated the mountains from beneath and even touched a layer of mist just below them that swirled with the same colors. Beyond the valley were additional immense ice-covered mountains, dark to the point of almost non-existence, visible only because they were covered with snow and glaciers.

"How do the trees grow without the sun?" Helga asked.

"This is the source of life here, not the sun," Atalthal said. "The Prim still flows in Niflheim, which is why the dead are drawn to parts of this realm. It feeds us, and it sustains us. It gives life to the dreams that I have designed for my people. To the trees and the animals, and fruit. When you eat the fruit, you eat of the spirit of creation."

Atalthal reached out his hand and whispered something softly. Into his fingers materialized a small plum-like fruit. He handed it to Helga.

"You can do this too," Atalthal said. He took Helga's empty hand and thrust it out past the edge of the alcove. Immediate, freezing pain assaulted Helga's fingertips. "Think of your favorite fruit."

Despite the pain, Helga did as he said, and amid the cold, she saw materialize into her hands a pair of perfect, red cherries.

"You doubt the perfection of this world," Helga said. She bit into one of the cherries, feeling that it could do little harm, and was assailed by the flavor of it. It was richer and purer than any cherry she had eaten, and much more flavorful than the food she had been served earlier. It really was like a perfect version of the fruit.

"When your own thought feeds the growth, it is better, eh?" Atalthal said.

"You didn't answer me."

"Was it a question?" Atalthal said. His gaze lingered on the distant mountains, and he sighed. "Bliss is sometimes not enough."

Helga silently regarded the sky. She could not see the moon — the regular, white moon. Perhaps it was behind the larger red one that lit the land with its grim light, but because she could not see it, she could not tell the time. She knew only that she had to wait long enough for the sun to rise.

"I heard a servant speak of your second wife," Helga said.

Atalthal nodded. "She fell asleep a long time ago. Her body disappeared, which does not usually happen, but can for those who become truly lost in the eternal dream. She was not satisfied with the kingdom I built for her."

"This one, or the one in… the sun realm?" Helga said.

Atalthal ignored her question. "She is gone now."

Helga suddenly realized that the mountain upon which they stood was not in her world. If she were to be pulled back to the real world, would she appear high above the city and find herself falling? The thought did not comfort her.

"Perhaps we should return to the palace," Helga said. She slipped the other cherry and the newly materialized plum-like fruit into a pocket of her dress while Atalthal turned to go back to the great stair.

When they stepped back into the winding stone stairwell, Helga asked, "What lies at the top?"

"Nothing," Atalthal said. "Once it went to Midgard, but the way has been shut for some time."

They descended quickly, and this time Helga could feel clearly an energy infusing her. The cold air felt refreshing when she exited the stairwell and went back into the palace.

Holding her hand, Atalthal led her down a series of hallways that went further into the mountains. Some of these were lit from above with skylights, showing a view of the red moon, but soon the hallways and the rooms that branched off from either side had no windows at all, but were lit by magical torches or glowing orbs of pale green.

A pair of guards flanked a large set of double doors at the end of one of these great hallways, and they opened the doors for Atalthal as he approached. He nodded to each and stepped through into a large, high-ceilinged foyer carved entirely from living rock. The door shut behind them. Helga heard the clang of a lock and cursed herself silently.

"Where is this?" Helga asked.

"The heart of everything I have built," Atalthal said. "This the ancient keep of a fortress gone long ago, destroyed by a dragon during the days of darkness, before the return of the stars and moon, or sun." He grabbed her hand and moved toward another room.

Helga felt a rush of fear, and her hands began to sweat. She had let her guard down too far and become too easy with Atalthal, and now she feared he was taking her to his bed-chamber.

Atalthal smiled at her. "Here is where I keep the things most dear to my people, which you may remember. And here is where I keep myself."

Helga cocked her head at this. *Remember?*

Tentatively, she followed him, but it was not to his bedroom. Rather, it was to an armory that housed swords and spears, arrows and armor on stands and tables in a wide semicircular room. He turned and stood on the threshold, so she could see the contents of the room, but not enter in.

"We have not used these in many ages, but I have kept them well," Atalthal said. "Artifacts from the age of great heroes. Will your friend make me put them to use, I wonder?"

"I do not think you will ever see Peridan again, but elves live long, and I cannot understand their minds easily."

"So you say. The mind of an elf should not be a hard thing for you, of all people to comprehend."

He beckoned her in, and she stepped in carefully, taking in the rows of polished armaments. Most of them had a slightly blued sheen to them, like they had been lacquered with something. Intricate runes of an unrecognizable language crossed the hilts and crossguards and worked their way down many of the naked blades. Scabbards were tooled with geometric patterns with an aesthetic balance that drew the eye. Bows and crossbows made of bone and steel, not wood, hung upon the wall.

Atalthal stopped at an armor stand in the center of the large room. Upon it sat a set of mail, smaller than Helga would have thought useful for an elf of Atalthal's height, along with an inscribed conical helm, matching boots, and shin-guards.

"This I have held long in waiting," Atalthal said. He picked up the helm carefully and handed it to Helga. He then began to carefully remove the mail shirt from the armor stand, inspecting it as he did so. Helga examined the helm, which was made of what looked like steel, though it was darker and with the same sheen as the other armaments. It had runes carved above its brow, and twisting knots of lines ran along every edge, producing an overwhelming amount of detail. The top of the helm held a slot for the placement of feathers as decoration, but those feathers were long gone.

Helga put down the helm on a table as Atalthal held up the shirt of mail. Helga began to examine it.

"Don't just stare at it. Put it on," Atalthal said. "It is yours, after all."

"I don't understand," Helga said.

Atalthal gave her a slightly indulgent smile. "Arms up."

Helga complied, and Atalthal slipped the mail over her head. It jingled as it fell into place on her, fitting her very comfortably, if a bit loose. The coat hung down to her knees and extended to her elbows, and was wondrously light, made of dark ringlets that were riveted together tightly. Her shoulders were reinforced by shifting plates, and the ends of the coat had tooled leather filled with knotted designs.

"Of course," Atalthal said, pulling at the loose parts of the mail. "I forgot the jack, of course." He helped Helga take the armor back off, then helped her put a very light padded jack on over her lovely dress. Erling had had a set of mail armor at home, but his jack was much thicker and heavier, made of linen. The jack she buttoned up under Atalthal's gaze was thinner, breathed easily, was light, and had a slight luster to it. It, like the mail, fit her perfectly.

"It looks like silk," Helga said. She felt the quilted layers of fabric under her hands.

"Of course, it is spider's silk," Atalthal said. "When that jack was made, all garments were spun from the silk of the first spinners, which were spiders. They have become smaller as the years have gone by, very different from the pets of my people. Here." Atalthal helped her put the mail back on, and it hung perfectly, hugging Helga's body as if it were made for her. Atalthal put a belt around her waist and then cinched up the loose mail on her midsection. He belted on a sword whose scabbard had upon it an intricate dragon tooled on strange leather.

"Just as I remember," Atalthal said. "Let's see if the boots fit."

Helga, wishing hard for the sun to rise in the real world, allowed Atalthal to slip boots on her feet, which were tall and made of thick, textured leather that matched nothing she had seen before. The elf smiled as he buckled them over her ankles. They fit well and were well broken-in. Next, he fitted a short pair of plate guards on her shins.

He stood up and handed her the helm. Reluctantly, Helga put it on.

"Yes, it *is* you, after all, isn't it?" Atalthal said softly.

"What?" Helga said.

"Artollanara," Atalthal said. "Returned." His eyes widened, and his jaw was slightly slack.

"What is the point of this dress-up?" Helga said, no longer able to hold back her fear and annoyance.

Atalthal took a breath. "I have kept this armor, the raiment of the greatest hero of all our kindred beings: Artollanara, who was herself sight and light reborn. Long have I held the vigil for your return."

Helga shook her head. "I'm not this Artolla- whatever her name was. I'm not even an elf."

"Born in a different body, but as you can see now, not so different," Atalthal said. "You will remember," he continued, patting her shoulders. "In time, I am sure you will. How you were deceived at the end, and betrayed, to die and bring into the world the sun, cursing those who loved you best, destroying magic-"

"I don't like being mistaken for dead women," Helga said.

"Even your disposition is much the same," Atalthal said with a smile. "I like seeing you in your armor."

Helga clenched her fists, but thought about the sun rising. She had to placate the elf before her, at least for a while longer.

"I apologize," Helga said. "I did not come here expecting this."

"But you were destined to come here. Our restoration draws nearer." Atalthal turned from the room and beckoned Helga to follow. She took a deep breath and *did* follow, feeling out of sorts in the armor. He led her down another hall to a small dining room. A servant was busy cleaning, and bowed her way out as they entered.

Atalthal closed the door and gestured to a nearby table set with a silver ewer and cups. Helga sat down across from him and removed her helmet. He poured a rich red wine into both cups. He held his cup aloft, and Helga returned the gesture, though her hand trembled. She took a tiny sip, and the feeling of nothingness entered her mouth along with a richer flavor as she swallowed. She took another sip as Atalthal did the same

"And now, I think, I will believe you if you say you intended to come back to see me." He did not explain his words, but rose and walked to another door. "Come," he said with a smile.

Helga felt herself rising, not fully of her own will. Her shaky knees carried her closer to the door. He opened it, and inside was a bed. Now, she actively meant to turn, but found that she could not. A compulsion was drawing her toward the chamber, as near as she could describe it in her mind, though she knew not if it was some trick of herself and her will was divided, or if there was something in the food and wine that polluted her mind.

As she entered the chamber, she regained some amount of control, and she clenched her fists. Her feet paused.

"Lord," she said. "I do not know if…"

"This is not such a big thing for elves, or for men, I have heard told. It is what you want, is it not?"

Helga looked down at her hands. They were glowing slightly, with a faint blur around the edges, like her eyes were going out of focus. She felt a temporary wave of relief. The sun was rising, and the plan had worked.

Soon I will be free. Even as she thought this, it occurred to her that the door of the stone keep had been locked behind her. She might end up in an even worse situation than before, if those doors remained locked in her own world.

She felt more in control of herself and walked toward the bed. If Atalthal noticed the change in her form, he did not say anything about it. She moved to him, and he put an arm around her. He leaned down and kissed her; while he did this, Helga slipped her hand over his chest, searching for keys. Neither keys nor dagger were secreted in his clothes, so she wrapped her arms around his waist, looking for a key ring, and found nothing there.

His kiss felt oddly cold on her lips, not revolting at all – rather, it was sweet and enthralling. Most of her revulsion she directed toward herself, and she was keenly aware of it. He pushed her down on the bed, and she continued feeling for the keys to the door; he didn't seem to notice or mind.

"I knew we were the ones always meant to be together," he said, kissing her neck. "How I have dreamt of this moment over the eons…"

As he pulled up her mail coat and parted her skirts, she decided with a sudden and sharp sincerity that she would go no further. She pushed him up and found him strangely able to be lifted, though he was easily twice her size. She kicked at his groin and put a foot on his chest. With a push, she sent him flailing backward into a wooden dresser.

"Not today!" She stood up quickly and raced toward the door.

It was indeed locked. She kicked at it, but the door did little more than rattle on its hinges. She heard a cry from behind her and turned, just in time to see a ball of magical flame hurtling toward her. She threw up her arms as a reflex, knowing it would do no good and bracing for pain.

The pain did not come. Instead, the magic broke around her. Purple and gold flames leapt from her arms and crashed against the ceiling and floor, lighting the carpet on fire.

"Impossible!" Atalthal said. "Guards, to me!" Atalthal grabbed a weapon from the corner – a great poleax with a hammer on one end and a sharp crow's beak on the other. Helga ran to Atalthal and gripped the weapon before he could swing it at her. They struggled against each other, and Helga could hear faintly the sound of boots in the long hallway. Helga pulled with all her strength, and Atalthal tumbled over her onto the carpet, which was still burning. He released the weapon and tried to put out the flames on his legs and arms.

Behind him, the door opened, but before Helga could run out, the space was filled by two grim and tall elven soldiers. Spear points flashed at her, and she fell backward to the ground, trying to dodge them. One of the spear points contacted her on her left wrist, cold, but not any more painful than a scratch from an errant tree branch. She rolled away through the fire on the rug, which did not seem to burn her. Using the poleax to assist her, she pushed herself up and ran away from the guards who still stabbed at her down the hallway, throwing on the helmet as she passed the dining table.

Two more soldiers appeared at the end of the hall, called by the commotion and shouts from Atalthal. Helga turned hastily down a hallway, hoping it came out near the main gates. At the end of the hallway were a few empty storerooms. Cornered, she turned to face her attackers, who spread out with their spears high, aiming downward for killing strokes. Helga swung her hammer at the closest elf, but the soldier defended himself easily. He turned the end of the pole weapon away and stabbed hard into Helga's chest. Helga felt almost nothing of the impact, though it visibly shook the shaft of the offending spear.

Helga pushed forward, letting the point stick in the mail. The attacker fell over as he tried to hold onto the spear. Helga trampled him in an effort to escape, but the other one had stepped into the gap. Helga swung at him, but he stepped back nimbly; the momentum and the weight of the poleax caused Helga to stumble forward. The attacker raised his spear for a strike. Not knowing what else to do, she swung the poleax in reverse. The elf blocked the attack with a vambrace, but the beak of the weapon penetrated the plate, causing blood to pour from the elf's forearm.

The other man was up, and Helga shoved the spiked end of the poleax at him just as he thrust his spear. Helga twisted her body to avoid the spearpoint, which put her own attack off-target. The spike on the poleax hit the man's vambrace, but it slid over the plate easily, bounced over his breastplate, and got lodged in the man's neck, splitting apart mail rings there. Helga pulled back and swung the poleax in earnest, hitting the elf in the head, crushing his helm. His eyes, which had been aglow, suddenly went dim.

The remaining elf staggered back, clutching his arm, locked eyes with Helga, and, with a sudden light of realization she did not understand, he fled.

Helga leaned against the wall, feeling winded and tired. She was startled when a raven appeared out of thin air and landed on the fallen foe. It was Zald.

"More are coming," Zald said. "You must hurry to leave. Zald has explored the ruined palace under the sun very thoroughly, and this place does not exist in it."

"Damn it," Helga said. "Do you know how long until true day?"

"Not long," Zald said. "Alas, that I have not the time to dine. I've never eaten dark elf." He began to impulsively pick at one of the eyes on the corpse.

Helga nodded and began trotting down the hallway.

The raven disappeared.

"Zald!"

"I am here, silly girl. Come!"

Helga growled in frustration. She broke into a run when she reached the first hallway and turned toward the shut gate. Two men with swords were running to meet her. She attacked first. It was difficult to wield the poleax in the narrow hallway and before she could land a definitive blow, one of the swordsmen knocked away the hammerhead and chopped hard at her shoulder with his sword. Helga was surprised to find the blow to be light and not at all painful. A second hit landed on her collarbone, with equal ineffectiveness. She knocked away the man's sword with her hand and choked up on the poleax, pulling at him with the crow's beak. It caught on the swordsman's shoulder, and he stumbled to his knees. Helga, without hesitation, brought the hammer down on his back, which gave a sickening crack.

The other elf was moving back up the hall, calling out in words Helga could only faintly recognize.

She met the rest of the armed elves in the open foyer, standing in a long line with spear and shield at the ready. All of them were aglow, fading now. It would only be a little longer. She paused at a familiar voice.

"There is no chance to escape, my dear," Atalthal said. It seemed to her he spoke strangely, as if with a heavy accent, and yet Helga could understand him. He was standing behind the line of fighters. "You must surrender. The weapons of your past should not be turned on us."

"Some hero you are, Atalthal," Helga said. "Standing behind a shield wall. Was it not you who said you slew dragons?"

"Very well," Atalthal said, and stepped past the other elves. He drew a long thin sword with a baroque basket hilt from his hip (when he had procured it, Helga did not know) as well as his hidden dagger, which he put into his left hand. "I will not hold back simply because of who you were. I may land an errant blow, and we will not cry, for you will return, and you have forfeited my mercy by bringing death to Atalthalda."

Helga held the poleax tightly. Looking at the grim faces of the elves in front of her, she put it down and drew the sword she had belted.

Atalthal attacked with a flurry of timed blows. Helga parried what she could, but Atalthal had unfathomable ages of experience with a blade, and Helga had at best a firm grasp of where to hold it. The blows moved past her feeble guard and rained down on her, striking her arms and chest and ringing off her helm. She felt skin part with cuts and pricks through the mail.

And yet, they were light, almost inconsequential, though each one did bring a small amount of pain. One strike hit her shin and bit, but it was like the stinging of a gnat. Helga pushed Atalthal down with her left hand, and he went sprawling on the floor. She made to strike, but the elf was already back on his feet.

"Damn you, sorceress!" he shouted.

A choir of bird cries brought all eyes searching as the three ravens appeared, spitting magic and clawing at the faces of the men. Peridan was there too, hacking with his sword from the rear.

Helga stepped back and sheathed her sword, then picked up the poleax. She ran into the chaotic throng, trying to push past the line of enemies. They gave fairly easily under a push, and she felt spear blows on her back, knocking her forward as she met Peridan, and they all began charging back up the hall.

"Almost in the clear now," Peridan said, panting. "Soon now. I've recovered our horses, and they wait for us outside. I didn't know you had such strength."

"I don't," Helga said. "I think it is some part of the fading. They are losing their power against me."

"But you have lost none of your own," Peridan said. "If anything, you've gained."

"Let's worry about it later."

Female servants jumped aside as the cadre ran through the halls, shrieking as they saw glowing ghosts and great, strange birds. They arrived at a landing outside the main gate of the palace, where their horses stood tied to a wooden rail. It was sheltered from sight on three sides, having only a view of the street between two great pillars. Two puzzled-looking elves were trying to unhitch the mounts.

"Shoo! Shoo!" Peridan said, waving his arms as he walked through the elves. They leapt back, but cried out again as they saw Helga, who looked grim in her armor and weaponry, bleeding in various places.

Peridan helped Helga mount Raggle as the armor made her somewhat ungainly, light though it felt.

"They are becoming mist again," Peridan said. "Ah, it is good to see the day again."

Helga looked up to see a sky, light blue on the horizon, but it was still dark everywhere else. The red moon shone brightly. The buildings were looking odd too, and in places, she could see things both broken and whole, which boggled her mind and made her squint hard.

"Tell me, Peridan," Helga said. "Do you see the red moon?"

"No. Do you?"

"Yes."

"You have eaten the food again," Zul said. "We told you that was unwise."

"I thought I had no choice. And I did not know how much I ate."

Zald flew up and landed on her helm. "You feel solid to me. Yes, quite solid."

"Perhaps you are between the two worlds," Zim said. "If we leave, you should be able to return to ours, no?"

"Let us hope," Helga said. The sky lightened more, and the sun rose, dim to Helga's eyes as they lay in wait.

"I have recovered tools from the blacksmith's shop. They appear to be remaining corporeal, so long as we have them near us. We can break the lock on the chain of the East gate."

"Might as well try," Helga said. "We're safe now, right?"

"I don't know," Peridan said.

As Helga followed Peridan down the main thoroughfare of the city, she watched elves to the left and right jump out of the way or shrink against the walls. Peridan rode straight through these people, and Helga supposed he must look like the mist wraiths of twilight to the people of Atalthalda. To her, they looked real, or nearly as material as when it was night, though everywhere their features were slightly obscured, especially their eyes, and all of them shimmered or glowed. When they got to the west gate, Helga pulled Raggle up short.

"There the gate is," she said. She watched as armed men formed lines in front of them, blocking the gate and the gatehouse.

"Indeed, and more," Peridan said. "Those shades there, do you see who they are?"

"Soldiers. They mean to block our path."

"Perhaps they can block yours. I can walk through them still," Peridan said.

Helga, feeling bold through her desperation, raised her voice and cried out to the line of soldiers. "Bright elves! If that is what you are, see me and hear me! Open this gate and stand down!" Another thought came to her, and she hoped she could say the name correctly.

"I am Artollanara, and I command you to stand down! Defy me at your peril!"

The men remained where they were, looking shocked. Helga dismounted, having never fought on horseback and not wanting to risk Raggle, however insubstantial the shades of the elves might be.

As she did this, many of the elves, to her great surprise, moved away, raising their spears and standing at attention. Others went to their knees. Only a few men stood in front of the gate, shouting at the others for cowards.

Helga, not knowing what else to do, ran at them, her poleax in front of herself like a pike. One of the men broke ranks. Another ran toward her, stabbing quickly with his spear. She felt the impact of the point on her mail, but she easily turned it aside with the haft of the poleax and struck the man with the hammer head on the shoulder, sending him flying to the side like he weighed the same as a scarecrow.

The last few men stood back.

"Open the gate!" Helga cried. After a tense few moments, the gates began to open, pulled by heavy steel chains. Beyond them, Helga saw the trees, glowing and bright, as they had looked from the mountaintop, and saw also the sun filtering through the many-colored leaves, turning most of them green. Behind them were mountains of immense height, covered with snow and blue ice. It was a powerful and beautiful sight, and though she held it in her eyes for only a moment, she found the image lingering long in her mind. Later, she would find she could easily recall it in all its detail, almost down to the leaf.

Helga ran back to Raggle and quickly mounted, trying her best not to look awkward while doing it and thus breaking whatever illusion the elves had of her power.

Peridan kicked his destrier into a gallop, and Helga followed suit. The Ravens flew alongside them. The elves bowed to her as she rode through into the forest.

Only once the horses began to really fatigue, and once the world started to look more familiar and real to Helga, did they finally slow their pace. Not far through the forest was a winding path that led up and out of the valley. They took this path gently, feeling comforted by the sun on their backs.

They paused to look back in a break of the trees, and Helga could see the city below, wrapped now in haze and mist but looking much more like a ruin. The gates stood open.

"And thus do we escape the realm of the dark elves, and the dreams of Atalthal," Peridan said. "I am richer for the experience, and though there is much to learn, I am glad to be gone."

"I feel the same," Helga said. "There is ancient knowledge there, and goodness, too, but who can retrieve it?"

"Not I," Peridan said. "History fades back into the Prim, I suppose." The elf sighed. "Let us get out of this valley. Your wounds need attending to, warrior."

"Warrior?" Helga said.

Peridan laughed and touched her face, then showed the blood to her. "Come!" With that, he cantered up the hill to the pass out of the valley.

IX. The Wastes

PERIDAN'S POWER returned once they had left the valley, and the mage lit a few bushes on fire just to feel right again. They decided to rest at midday amongst some oak trees, where Peridan fashioned an enchanted fire to break the wind that went swirling over the mountains and amongst the ancient trees. At last, they were able to tell each other what they had seen the final night. Peridan had hidden and moved stealthily among the stables, recovering the horses and most of their equipment after sapping the stable worker with a set of blacksmith tongs. Unfortunately, Helga's sword and crossbow could not be recovered, for Peridan could not discover where the guard had taken them. Peridan's own sword was gone too, but he had replaced it with one taken from the blacksmith. It was sharp and well-forged, but had not yet been polished. He was happy to find with the horses an ornate dagger, ivory hilted and shining brightly, that had been secreted in his tack. Helga watched Peridan smile at the blade as he tucked it into his jacket under his mail coat.

Once settled, Helga removed her armor to find herself covered with bruises and cuts she had barely felt. None of them were particularly deep, but she was upset to find that some spear point or sword had cut her forehead right below the lip of her helm.

"It will scar," Peridan said, applying a stinging salve to Helga's wounds. "If Thokar were here, he could do something for that, but I lack his knowledge of the healing arts, so the standard mending of flesh will have to do. I personally think it will not do much to harm your beauty."

"Thank you," Helga said. "Perhaps I do look like a warrior woman. Maybe that is why the soldiers obeyed me."

"More than likely, they saw a glowing, radiant ghost and were terrified of that. Remember what you looked like," Zim said, pecking through some flatbread Helga had given him. "I would have been frightened of you had I not already known you to be just a girl."

"Come now," Zul said. "Can we really keep calling her a child?"

"I said girl, not child," Zim said.

"Silly girl!" Zald said. He flapped over to Helga's helm and sat on it, slipped off its slick surface, then laughed.

"Atalthal called me Artollanara," Helga said.

"Ah, yes," Peridan said. "I heard you proclaim yourself thus. Did he really think you were the hero of legend?" Peridan pursed his lips. "Of course, he would know what she looked like, considering he was there."

"He…" Helga bit her lip as Peridan found some new wound that needed attention. "He was, um… attracted to me."

Peridan chuckled softly. "It's one of the stories. He and Artollanara, when she was still just a young student named Aphella. She rejected him, despite his glory and grandeur."

"Rejecting him again didn't make him feel any better about it."

"Clearly," Peridan said, looking at another scratch on Helga's leg.

Helga examined her arms and felt some of the light cuts and bruises there. "Still, I wonder why their weapons had so little effect. I took blows that should have split my skull or cracked open my chest."

"I think it had something to do with you being here and there at the same time," Peridan said. He nodded to the mail coat, which sat on a nearby rock. "Though this armor is very fine and surely protected you well. It is perhaps the best work I've seen in terms of detail, and I don't recognize the metal. Keep in mind I have lived a very long time and seen many things."

"It belonged to Artollanara. Or at least, that is what Atalthal told me."

Peridan smiled and sat up on his haunches. "You don't say." He looked over the armor more carefully. "This is why I travel with mortals. An elf can live a very long life indeed, and you quick children have a way of surprising even me." He laughed merrily.

Helga found herself smiling. "There was a whole armory of this stuff, you know. You could be wearing the armor of some hero, too."

Peridan laughed again. "Pity. It is not every century that you come across the pattern work of the dark elves." His smile faded. "I do not think the armor alone was what aided you. The food you ate there held part of you to the mist realm, and I cannot even really speak for the food you were able to conjure from the Prim, if that is what it truly was. It usually takes a powerful will to conjure things in the Fay. More powerful than any mortal."

"Is that where we were?"

"I don't think so, but perhaps some reflection or remnant of it in Niflheim. I will have to spend some time to ponder it." Peridan stood up and walked to the edge of the clearing. "I will set some spells as wards and illusions so that we may rest. I am exhausted."

"I feel quite good, actually," Helga said.

Peridan remained silent. While he walked around the camp, Zald finally found a perch on top of Helga's helm, and he sat staring at her.

"What is it, Zald?"

"You've changed," Zald said.

"I would rather have my old clothes," Helga said, looking down at the amber dress she had been given in the palace. Small cuts dotted it, and it was sweat-stained.

"Not what I meant. Still a bit of a silly girl," Zald said. "Where is my food?"

"You left it on the floor of the keep."

Zald gave an angry roc-roc as reply.

Helga chuckled and got up. As she did, she noticed something in the pocket of the dress. She pulled up the mail skirt to reach it. She withdrew two pieces of fruit: one a perfect cherry, the other a strange mix of gold fading to pink, like a peach, but smooth-skinned and,

Helga noticed, as perfect as the cherry. There were no blemishes on it, and even the shape seemed exceedingly pleasing to the eye.

"Not those," Zald said. "Do I look like a fruit bat?"

"A bit," Helga said. The fruit looked appetizing, but she feared the food from Atalthal's realm now, so she put both back into her pocket.

"How dare you compare me to a flying rat?" Zald said. "It's almost enough to spoil my appetite."

"Almost." Helga laughed and removed from her pack some of the bread and meat she had packed away and laid some out for Zald on a tin plate. He cocked his head and stared at it.

"No, I reject this food," Zald said. "You will find me better food."

"That might take a while."

"Zald is patient, as are all ravens. If only you could have killed one of those elves in the real world. I imagine they would be quite a treat."

Helga laughed.

When Peridan had finished with his spells (Helga now noticed a soft glow around the campsite), he lay down and promptly went to sleep. The Ravens flew to a nearby tree, and Helga was left alone. She thought it odd that she didn't feel tired at all. In fact, she felt restless. After staring into the magical fire for the better part of an hour, she retrieved her sewing kit from her tack and set to work repairing the jack she had worn beneath her mail. Though the garment was light to hold, at least much lighter than her husband's gambeson at home, the layers of cloth were much tougher. She had to up the size of her needle and thread to work at the mending, and twice she had to produce her whetstone to sharpen it. Still, there was a peace to the work of it, and soon the garment was mended completely. Next, she inspected her mail coat. She was surprised to see that none of the links had burst, though there were scratches on a few, and there was a loose rivet or two. Not wanting to remove her clothes completely, she worked on the parts of her dress she could see without removing it.

After doing this a long time, she finally felt sleep call to her. She rolled up the jack and used it as a pillow, then went to sleep beside the fire.

*

Helga walked through a cave. It was cold, almost like ice, and dark, with only a faint light in front of her to show her that her surroundings were, in fact, rock. She put a hand out to steady herself, and felt the rock under her hands, rubbed smooth and polished at different points.

She heard a deep, rasping, but kind voice speak from the walls of the tunnel itself, its tone sliding during words like a mother talking to a baby.

"You are far from where I expected you to be," the voice said. "Far from where I was sure you were."

"Who is it?" Helga made to ask, but a sudden fear made her words catch in her throat.

As if understanding her intent, the voice answered, "Oh, I think soon enough we will meet face to face. Be wary. You will need help before it is over."

"Before what is over?"

"Your life."

"I don't understand."

"You can't until it is time to understand."

Helga tripped and fell.

"It is hard traveling in the dark, is it not? Why not a little light?"

"I have nothing to burn."

"Fire is not light," the voice said, with a deep laugh that shook the sides of the cave. "What you want, you must will to have, Raven-friend."

Helga pushed herself up and sat on her knees. She looked ahead to the light, and as she did so, the light grew, and soon she could see. She stood up and walked more quickly toward it. The light grew brighter, and she moved ahead. Soon she could see light brown around her feet - soil, and then leaves.

She looked up and realized she was in a forest of twisting trees, dense enough to strain the eyes and almost sickening in their angles.

Dead leaves were piled around her ankles, and the foliage remaining on the trees was the red and gold of autumn.

*

Helga woke in the early morning. Peridan was already up, packing the horses.

"Sleep well?" he asked, without turning to look at her.

"Where are the ravens?"

"You know them. Off somewhere. I don't think we'll be rid of them that easily."

"Good," Helga said. She got up and put on the newly mended jack and her new mail coat, laced up her new high boots, and put her helm atop her head.

"Are we going into battle?" Peridan said, pausing to smile at her.

"It's not very heavy, and I somehow I think I'll feel better with it on. Braver."

"Suit yourself," Peridan said. He laughed.

Helga rigged up a leather catch for the spiked bottom of her pole-ax, and when they rode, she let it lean against her body and stand up tall, like the lance of a knight.

"Helga, proud daughter of kings," said Peridan, as he watched her ride out of the campsite and into the wind. Peridan was right about the ravens, and soon they returned, bickering now over who could perch atop the poleax. Zald negotiated his place, but soon wanted to recant on his deal, finding the bobbing and the swaying of the weapon to be not at all relaxing. He ended up settling on Peridan's cantle. The mage, being in a good mood, allowed the bird to remain with only the occasional accidental elbow to the beak.

At midday, they decided to rest the horses and have a meal.

"I wish I had my crossbow," Helga said as she chewed a particularly tough hunk of dried meat. "I miss it, and my husband's sword."

"He's getting a better one in trade, I'd say. I don't think your township makes swords quite like the dark elves of old. The crossbow is useful on the road, 'tis true. Twice I've seen fat rabbits that would make a feast on the road."

"Why did you not kill them? Throw a fireball at them?"

"Why not hammer a nail into the wall with a battering ram is as good a question."

Zim croaked and hopped up and down on a nearby rock. "We can help you catch fresh meat. Come! Bring your long weapon."

Helga sighed and got to her feet. She picked up the poleax and followed Zim, who flew off into the bush. He disappeared from view, and Helga sighed with exasperation. Then she heard one of the worst rackets she could remember assault her ears. It was like a mixture of a crying baby and a dying pig. Before she could react, a rabbit was running out of the bush, pursued by a loudly rocking raven. The rabbit sped past her foot before she could try to poke it with the poleax. Quickly she twisted and threw out a hand, knowing it would find no rabbit. To her surprise, the rabbit rolled over on the ground six feet away, thrashing at the dirt. Zald then flew down and landed on the bird.

"Food!" he cried, and silenced the rabbit with a quick bite to the throat. "Now, you need only repeat that for your own dinner."

Helga laughed despite her hunger. The other two ravens quickly descended on the kill and began feasting.

After the ravens had their fill of the rabbit, Helga and Peridan saddled back up and continued. They found their way up a switch-backing path that was very neglected, its borders made obvious more by its overgrowth of grass than its packed earth. As they went up in elevation, the wind picked up, and Helga felt glad to be wearing the armor, which insulated her well. Near sunset, they reached the pass itself, which was rocky and bereft of trees. They paused and looked back over the hills to the valley of Atalthalda. It was covered with a slight haze, and through that haze, Helga saw trees of many colors glowing in the light of sunset like a paint smear, a remnant of vision from the dark realm, but the city itself was little more than a streak of white stonework. The sun dipped lower, darkening the valley into purple shadows, and the city glowed softly.

"Farewell, Atalthal," Helga said. "May your heart hold your dreams, and not the other way around. May you find the heroism you seek."

"Perhaps one day I shall return," Peridan said. "But for now, I am glad to be rid of the place."

With that, they went over the pass to the leeward side of the mountain. They found a campground in a suitable gully, and Peridan set his wards and built his fire. Helga watched him stand, facing the east in thought until sleep took her.

*

Helga awoke from a dreamless sleep as a great wind passed over the camp, causing the horses to wake and stir and the ravens to rock and chatter. It blew out the magic fire and plunged the camp into darkness. The next moment, the wind passed by, and all was still again. Helga sat up and went to the remnants of the fire. Peridan was, curiously, still asleep, perhaps the only one in the camp who wasn't disturbed by the sudden wind. His face was creased and twitched here and there.

"What was that?" she heard Zim croak in the darkness.

"Didn't get a good look," Zald said. "But I am glad for the trees."

There was no kindling in the makeshift hearth, and Helga felt suddenly cold, so she searched about for some dry wood. Finding a few twigs, she built a small cone and got out her tinderbox. With a few sparks and some shredded wood, the fire caught and grew. Curiously, it turned the flickering blue-green of Peridan's magic fire, as if the rocks had remembered his enchantment at the rekindling of flame.

Helga watched the fire burn the wood for a few minutes, then went back to sleep, listening to the ravens whisper indecipherable things in their croaking, creaking bird tongue.

*

The next day was bright but windy, and high clouds moved fast above the party as they descended through the leeward hills toward the flat lowlands beyond. Pines and cedars gave way to oaks, which

170

thinned out as the old path (where they could find it) leveled out in some dry highlands.

"I am thinking of something," Helga said, watching the clouds change shape.

"Aren't we all?" Peridan said.

"I wonder what I shall be able to trade to the Watchers when, and if, we get there."

"I think getting there will be easy, compared to what we just went through. What they are willing to trade for has sat on my mind, too. I know they envy man for his fixed but changing existence. I have heard they are often willing to trade for things of little value, seeing them as some part of the life of men they can acquire and understand for themselves. I've also heard they ask for exorbitant, impossible things, like the wind, or the throne of a king."

"That wouldn't be impossible for a king. The throne, I mean."

"My point is, it is hard to predict. We must hope that we are carrying something that is valuable enough for them to part with their own treasures."

"What if we do not?"

"Then we either cannot trade, or we must seek to acquire what the watchers desire."

"Damn that volva. She told me this would be an uneventful journey," Helga said.

"Well, she was either lying or not a very knowledgeable volva."

"Yes, I wonder whether she can cure my husband at all."

"Do not be too hard on her," Zul said, cocking her great black head. "Volvas are people, and therefore short-sighted. Besides, the spirits of the dead cannot know the future, whatever you have heard."

"Wait to be hard on her till she breaks the deal, I say," Zald said.

"You might just ask the watchers for a cure directly," Peridan said. "It's what I am doing."

"Perhaps I shall, at that. I wonder, though, if the Water of Awakening is part of her cure," Helga said.

Helga flinched as Peridan reached over and grabbed her arm.

171

"Quickly!" He pointed to an old oak, branching out like a great bush. Helga understood his fear a moment later, as she saw a black shape in the sky, getting larger. The ravens took to wing and flew under the tree as well. Helga dismounted and calmed Raggle, then dared to look out from under the branches at what was in the air above them. It was getting larger and larger and appeared to move faster and faster as it approached.

It dropped its altitude as it flew closer, and the sun caught its great wings, mottled red and made of strange skin.

"A dragon!" Helga said breathily.

She watched as the great wyrm moved its head from side to side, as if seeking something out.

"Get down," Peridan said softly. "A dragon's vision is better than you guess."

Helga did as she was bidden and knelt down, but still kept her eyes on the dragon. It grew larger and finally swooped over the tree with a tremendous wind, sending leaves and other oddments from the tree raining down on them. A moment later, the dragon was going higher and turning north. It let loose a great cry, which was terrifying and mesmerizing to hear, then disappeared around a mountain.

"Dreamer!" Helga said.

"That's not the dreamer," Peridan said. "But it was most definitely a dragon. And a very large, very fierce one at that."

"I've never seen one before. I thought they were just myths."

Zald croaked. "And myths cannot be real?"

"Good point," Helga said. "A dragon is certainly not the first odd thing I have encountered since I left home. But still - what is it doing out here?"

"We're entering the fay wastes now," Peridan said. "This is likely that particular dragon's home range, as they are known to reside near to where the Prim remains intact."

"He appeared to be looking for something," Helga said. "Should we be concerned?"

"Whenever a dragon is involved, you should always be concerned. Whatever he is looking for, I doubt it is us. Still, we must be more careful. Neither of us has anywhere near the power necessary to slay a dragon. Actually, to that end, I've never met or heard firsthand of any person managing to slay a dragon. Except for Atalthal."

Helga swallowed. "What do dragons eat? I mean, do you think he was hunting?"

"Dragons can and will eat anything, from what I have read. There are so many stories it is hard to tell fiction from fact. Some stories say they eat rocks; other stories say they devour virgins. I will say that I haven't heard of a dragon initiating an attack on a person first or second hand. They are quite reclusive. "

"Little of that comforts me," Helga said. "Perhaps the bit about rocks does."

"Dragons do not need to eat, silly," Zald said. "They merely exist."

"Then why the teeth, Raven?" Peridan said.

"I have no teeth, and yet I eat," Zald said.

"That is a fallacy," Peridan said. "The inverse of a statement is not automatically false."

"Foul crow of an elf," Zald said. "Teeth and eating do not have to go together."

"Every animal with teeth uses them to eat."

"Not dragons," Zald said. "Well, they don't use the big nasty ones to eat, only to kill."

"How do you know?"

Zald puffed himself up. "Dare you challenge my experience?" He flew up to a higher branch.

"Another fallacy," Peridan said.

"Leave the young one alone," Zul said.

Peridan waved a dismissive hand at the raven, "We'd best be off. There is nothing for us to do except stay alert. So stay alert!"

*

They camped a night in the highlands. Peridan took special care to obscure the fire from a possible dragon, but none came that they were aware of, and the night passed by in relative peace. The next day, the dragon was absent again, and again they camped, this time on the slope of some rolling, rocky hills that marked the end of the highlands and the beginning of the descent down into the true fay wastes, obscured by mist.

There on the hill in the early evening, they heard the distant sound of voices shouting. Peridan extinguished his fire and readied himself for an attack. Helga had not yet removed her armor. She put her back to a tree and gazed out into the starlit night. Light leapt from the mountainside to the north, far enough away and yet too near.

If it was truly fire, it was magic fire. Colors of blue, green, and purple flashed and died, and trees burst into flame. The fight was too distant to make out clearly any people, but as they both watched the fires burn, they saw the shadow of a much larger and easily recognized form pass in front of the flames.

"The dragon," Zim said. "He comes to feast on the dead."

"Those are dim-men over there," Peridan said. He had produced a telescope from somewhere in his tack and was twisting it furiously, focusing here and there. "I can tell from their magic they are dimed by the Mundus. The magic is much more primal than that of any elf, more chaotic than that of any human. Are they picking a fight with the dragon?"

The question was answered with a mighty breath of fire that lit up all the trees in the fighting area. They watched through the shadows of the flames the dragon land and roar, flap his wings and swing his claws, with tiny shadows fleeing.

"Here," Peridan said, and handed Helga the telescope.

She began to tremble as she put the lens to her eye. She could see the flames leap from the dragon's mouth, and his claws flash against tiny people, and to her horror, he was eating them. She swallowed hard as the dragon turned its head, and its glowing eyes, just for a moment, seemed to stare back at her. She put the telescope down suddenly.

"I guess we know a bit more about the diet of dragons," Helga said hastily, handing back the telescope. "This one has a keen taste for flesh."

"I will set some wards that will obscure us from him."

"Magic does not work on dragons, mage," Zim said. "And that includes illusion magic. Our best hiding will be beneath leaves and without shiny things. Unfortunately, there is nothing we can do for the smell."

"What smell?" Helga said.

"You stink!" Zald said. "You are very smelly, and dragons can smell very well."

"Said by the carrion bird," Peridan said.

"They *are* the experts, Peridan," Helga said.

The ravens laughed.

Helga had to be content spending the night sitting against an oak tree, her poleax across her lap, sleeping only in fits. Every time she went to sleep, she was haunted by great, yellow reptilian eyes and a deep, rasping voice crawling in her head. She saw the dragons of all her imagination pass by as sleep came, then she saw them vanish in fearful cries. Every time she awoke, Peridan was awake as well, watching the stars in deep thought, a hard look on his face of determination and sadness. One time, Helga was certain he was talking softly to himself in an angry, bitter tone.

*

The skies were clear the next day, which was well, for their descent out of the highlands was slow and exposed. Before midday, they had crested a rocky ridge and looked down upon the true wastes of the Fay. The ridge fell steeply down, nearly as sheer as a cliff, with little sign of road or game path. It was rocky and grey and turned the stomach if looked at too long from the heights. Small waterways trickled in many places down the endless slope, creating a spider web of wet miniature streams and dripping waterfalls. These waters, which seemed to

175

spring out of the rock like leaks in a dam, landed in a swamp far below them, which was obscured by strange, moving mists.

The mists continued away for what looked like many miles, fading only in the distance at a long line of bright green trees. Here and there a plume of steam rose, but otherwise, the plain seemed homogenous.

"It looks like the road is lost here," Helga said.

"Here is a threshold, in more than just height," Peridan said. "From here, things will not be as permanent as you are used to. We are still in Midgard, but these lands are still shaped by the wills of the fay. A path would be of little use, for it would shift beneath us. We would have to forge our own anyway."

"Zim?" Helga said, looking to the raven who sat upon Peridan's saddlehorn.

Zim clacked his beak. "I know of no human roads here, and the paths of ravens would be of no use to you or your horses."

Peridan gazed with hard, squinted eyes at Helga. "Do you wish to continue?"

"I have no choice."

"There is always a choice, Helga," Peridan said. "Your peril awaits."

"Then I wouldn't want to keep it waiting," Helga said. She nudged Raggle. Horse and rider went forward over the edge, although slowly. Peridan followed, laughing.

They picked their way down the rocky slopes for the entire day, their eyes often on the skies. The ravens had tired of the descent rather quickly (Zald had called them too sullen, "even for a couple of crows."), and so they had flown down the slope to some shrubs far below. Helga often caught Peridan mumbling to himself, especially when he was looking out to the forest on the edge of vision.

Once, when she noticed a particularly harsh series of strange words, Helga called out loudly, "What?"

"Nothing," Peridan said. "I was… merely trying to remember my incantations."

"Are you in danger of forgetting them?"

"In short, yes," Peridan said. "The Fay itself is dangerous to the mind. There is much to learn, but also much that may be forgotten."

"You need the words to use magic?"

"Yes and no. The words are the way to find the path to the true identity of the magic spell, the true concept of what it is. It is very difficult to find magic only one's mind without the words to guide thought."

"What should I remember, then?"

"I'm not quite sure. If you were a warrior, I would say to ponder your martial lessons." Peridan grumbled. "Pay no mind to me, Helga. I am rambling."

The sun went down behind them, casting a long, jagged shadow they could see on the mists above the wetlands. The way began to get treacherous, and once Peridan's destrier slipped over wet rocks fed by the constant trickles from above. With the shadows deepening, they decided they had no choice but to stop. A small flat area was all they had to make camp, and the horses had to be content to stand.

Here Helga drank deeply and filled her water skins from a nearby trickle. The water was cold but clear and tasteless, refreshing after the dusty, muddy fair of the dry highlands. She sat on a rock and watched the purple shadows stretch across the wet plains to the forest beyond. As the sun vanished, all the land turned shades of blue, and the sky darkened, but the forest remained lit with pale light, as if a shaded sun shone there alone.

Zald landed on a nearby rock and began picking at a silver button on a leather thong on Helga's scabbard.

"You want the shiny?"

"Just looking," Zald said.

"Hmn. You know a great deal," Helga said.

"Thank you for recognizing it," Zald said. "You are getting smarter."

"Why is the forest shining?"

Zald looked at the horizon. "The Fay has its own ideas about time."

"Those trees are bigger than they look." It was Zul, who had flown down beside Helga to look at the silver button. "Much bigger than any trees here in the mortal lands. I do not know how you measure them, but they are much bigger there."

"Good for making raven mansions," Zald said. "If only they would stay in one place!"

*

Helga slept uneasily, dreaming again of the dragon and waking often, fearing it was flying overhead when it was just the wind blowing across the sheer face of the cliff. By midnight, it had gotten deathly cold, but Peridan would not light a fire in fear of the dragon seeing it. They huddled together under a blanket, but it did little good, and the horses were getting cold as well.

After hours of shivering, Helga decided she had had enough. She found a dried shrub clinging to the rocks and ripped it out, then broke all its little dry limbs into kindling. She made a small alcove out of two fairly flat rocks, then put the fire beneath it. It sheltered it from the wind, but only barely. Her tinderbox did little. Her flint sent sparks in her face, and when she got a few embers to catch, they were quickly blown out or off the kindling entirely. She got very frustrated, but did not give up. She tried changing her body position to block the wind. She tried more rocks. She tried more dried shrubs. Nothing worked.

Finally, she got very angry and yelled to the wind, loud enough to make Peridan stumble upright.

"Stop blowing!"

To her amazement, the wind stopped. It didn't just die down; it stopped as if she had stepped indoors. Not wanting to count her blessings before she collected them, she lit the kindling, and soon she had a small, warm fire beneath her little rock tent.

"Clever," Peridan said, and huddled next to her for some warmth. "And lucky."

"You didn't make the wind stop?"

"No. I thought I told you I can't do weather. Air is almost impossible to control."

"Just luck, then," Helga said softly.

She got up and moved the horses closer, which seemed to lift their spirits. The little fire was wondrously warm, and at last, watching the small branches of the thistle curl into little red snails, she slept again.

X. The Shifting Mists

THE NEXT MORNING, Helga and Peridan finished their descent to the misty marshes and plains before the edge of the Fay Lands. It was slow going again, and there was a heaviness to the mood, for though they were both glad to be off of the sheer rock and safely hidden again, the fog-covered lands did not look inviting. When they reached the bottom, they rested a little beneath a half-rotted willow.

Peridan took out a metal device and opened it. Inside, a small, red rock on a metal wheel turned in a dial and pointed away from the cliff.

"What is that?" Helga asked, leaning over to see.

"A special compass. It shows always in what direction the Fay lies. Well, not always. It points off to random directions from time to time, but even if it leads us astray a bit, overall, I think it will point us in the right direction, should we get lost."

Helga pulled her map from her bag, complete with notes by Thorvald, and handed it to Peridan. He pointed to an area near the bottom of the map, where Thorvald had written *Kiwall – lowest pass south of Strandam.*

"The pass is what we avoided by going through the valley," Peridan said, squinting at the poor map. "We're now a bit further south than we ought to be, but if we reach the tree line, finding the watchers should be no problem. As long as we stay out of the trees, that is."

The ravens joined them in their usual places as Helga and Peridan lead their horses on foot through soggy turf and boggy mud, amidst weeping willows that sagged and leaned over water, their roots tangled footholds to the unwary. Above them and around them, fog swirled and moved. The sun was obscured, but sometime around high noon, they saw it shining softly through the mist.

The horses were spooked then by a shadow passing between the sun and the ground. There was a powerful wind around them, and suddenly the mists were moving away, revealing sky and landscape.

"The dragon!" Peridan said, and fought his horse over to a shrubby and sad-looking tree, just big enough to conceal the destrier. Helga found a different tree nearby. She looked out and could see nothing but where the dragon had flown, the mists had parted, and they could see well the trees and waterways in front of them.

Slowly and hesitantly, they both moved back into the mist, away from the cleared area.

"This cannot be coincidence," Helga said. "The dragon is hunting us. He has to be."

"Then why has he not caught you?" Zim said.

"He flew right overhead!"

"Yes," Zim said. "Precisely. If he knew you were here, as he was able to fly overhead, he probably would have just flown down and eaten you. If that is what he wanted."

"And not eat you?" Peridan said.

"Carrion birds are foul eating," Helga said. "They'd probably be fine."

"We'd be fine because we are clever," Zald said. "And because Dragons like us, and those that don't like us cannot catch us. And we are smaller than people. Not a good meal, by comparison."

"Certainly, I would rather eat people than a raven," Zul said.

"Well, ravens," Peridan said, "if he is not hunting us, why pass so close over us, and now so many times?"

"Do I look like the sort of bird to know the mind of a dragon?" Zim said.

"No."

"Then why did you ask me?"

"Rhetoric is lost on you," Peridan said, waving a hand at the bird.

182

"Perhaps he's trying to show us the way," Zul said. "I see a clear path forward. No mists to obscure the vision."

Peridan laughed. "Of course. No, I think we have just been lucky. But Helga is right. He must be searching for us for some reason. Let us not give him the opportunity to find us."

Peridan pulled out his little compass and led them through the mists. Off to their left, Helga could see the strip of clear land, but only dimly. Soon, the white curtains of vapor closed around them again.

*

Evening fell, but they could only tell by the general fading of light. The mist went from white to red and orange, and finally to purple-grey. They stopped beside a tall, arching tree, bigger than any they had seen so far, and of a type Helga did not recognize. Its branches were totally obscured in the fog above them.

"I think I'll go up and have a look," Helga said. She took off her mail coat and helm and climbed up the tree, just like she used to do when she was a girl. At the top, she caught her breath. The marshes still extended in every direction almost endlessly, but she could see the trees more clearly, and they were again lit like the day. They had to each be hundreds of feet high and were all crowned with gold-green leaves and had white bark.

Off in the distance, she watched a dragon circling over the mist, but for what reason she could not grasp. One of the ravens startled her by landing on a nearby branch.

"If you wanted to have a look, you could have just asked one of us," Zim said.

"I wanted to see for myself. There is no substitute for one's own eyes."

"True. Ah. See, the dragon searches for something else. He is not interested in us."

"I hope you are right, but I also hope he is not searching for anything in particular at all. What if he is searching for the watchers?"

"Methinks he would have found them. But who can know the mind of a dragon? Not me."

The raven laughed.

*

That night, Peridan made a fire, for in the mist of the swamp, it was oppressively cold; not the kind of cold that one experiences on a midwinter day, but the wet, dripping, miserable cold that comes with humidity and still, frigid air without ice. The blue and purple fire banished the cold as well as the fog, but it brought other attentions.

Insects, some the size of Helga's thumb, swarmed into the camp, landing in great clumps on horse and human (but not raven – the Black Feather Friends had made their own roost in a tree). The bites were painful, and when the pain subsided, it was replaced by itching. Many of the pests flew with suicidal abandon into the mage fire, only to return from it charred lightly but not flaming.

"Dreamer!" Helga said. "Is there nothing for these foul insects?"

"I don't have spells for it," Peridan said. "Perhaps if you made a true fire, a few of them would fly into it and burn for real, and rid us of at least that small annoyance. If there is something I like less than deerflies, it is half-burned deerflies twice as big as they ought to be."

"Oil and orange used to do it at home," Helga said. "Burned with a wick in a lamp. It at least keeps the bugs off your skin. I don't suppose you have any oranges."

"Alas, no," Peridan said.

"Well, I'm not going to give them much to eat," Helga said. She wrapped herself up in her cloak, so only her face poked out. She covered her mouth with a strip of loose knitted cloth, so only her eyes showed, then laid back down, pulling her hood down as she did so. The insects did not slow their seeking of flesh. They didn't bite Helga, but they crawled over her in writhing waves, and it was sickening.

"I can't take this anymore," Peridan said. "I'm putting out the light."

"Good!" Helga said.

The light went out, and Helga noticed for the first time that the white vapor surrounding them had a soft glow, like the mist in Atalthal's realm. Whether it was lit by bright stars or was truly luminescent

184

itself, she did not know, but she found it oddly comforting. Peridan seemed less soothed and grumbled to himself on the ground.

Helga went to sleep and dreamt of orange trees in bloom, specifically the little trees tended by the Monks of Pastorus in the monastery overlooking Greenfeld. She could smell the sweet blossoms, and as she smelled them, oranges were in her hands. She peeled and ate a dozen before her dreams returned to the dragon and his glowing amber eyes.

*

The next day saw them walking through much of the same country, following Peridan's compass as it moved about. Helga, with the help of the ravens, spotted several small animals - mostly rats or rat-like creatures that lived in trees. These made Zald particularly hungry, but Peridan did not want to stop and hunt, at least while his compass was working.

About midday, they came upon a strange sight, which was a large, bush-like tree covered in small citrus fruits that looked like oranges, only they were a dark yellow rather than orange.

"How curious," Peridan said.

"I'll say," Helga said. "It seems much too cool here for citrus."

Helga plucked one of the fruits from the tree and smelled it. Its scent, to her delight, was exactly like that of an orange.

"Careful, it could be poison," Peridan said.

Helga tore open the peel to reveal reddish flesh, sectioned like an orange. She took a slice out and bit into it, and smiled, for it tasted exactly like an orange should have tasted – sweet and fragrant, with an acidity that made the sweetness all the better. It was actually a better flavor than an orange, yet was still the flavor of an orange, as much as those two ideas could coexist.

"It's an orange," Helga said. "But I'll wait to see how that piece settles before eating more, alright?"

"I suppose," Peridan said. They gathered what oranges they thought they could carry and stuffed them into their bags.

When it was time to leave, Helga found herself strangely reluctant to abandon the tree.

"What's the matter?" Peridan said.

Helga shook her head. "It seems far too perfect. I feel odd leaving it, like I won't see it ever again."

"I dare say you shan't," Peridan said.

She broke off one of the branches and tucked it into a lace on her saddle, then took one more brown-yellow orange and put it in her pocket, where she noticed the cherry and the other fruit again. She pulled out the cherry and looked at it. It looked appetizing, but she decided it would be best not to eat it, and so put it away.

*

Night began closing in again, and before it went dark enough to need a fire, they made camp, this time beneath a healthy-looking willow with long branches reaching over a waxy moss-covered hole. A deep earthy smell suffused the hollow. Helga set about scraping the peel from an orange and mixing it with some lamp oil that Peridan had. When she was done, she had a very fragrant and very chunky pot of oil. They used a bit of loose rope as a wick, and Peridan lit it with a small, snappy bit of magic from his thumb that sent sparks everywhere. The citrus fragrance from the oil was pronounced and (to Helga) comforting.

When the magic fire was lit, the bugs came, but only a few seemed willing to come in and fly about, and even less bothered to land on them or the horses. A few suicidal moths continued their pursuit of the fire, but to Peridan's glad heart, none wanted to then land on him.

"I'm surprised this is working," Peridan said.

"I am, too," Helga said. "Works even better than at home."

*

Days passed, and the terrain changed subtly, though not enough for anyone's tastes, as it remained marshy turf and swamp in most places. Peridan's compass frequently re-directed them, but they never felt like they were going in circles. Each mile brought a deeper sense of travel - that more and more of home was being left behind. The flora changed subtly. The grass blades grew wider. The trees became larger and more twisted. They saw rats and squirrels of odd coloration, spotted and often with exaggerated features. Helga thought she sighted a fox, but it moved too quickly for her to get a good look at it. She often wondered to herself if there were wolves about, but she heard no sound of them and saw no sight.

Peridan grew quieter, and he often repeated strange words to himself. When they rested, he read from his small books and talked little. Frequently he would go stand in the mist and whisper to himself, but the words had a hissing anger to them. Helga contented herself with the ravens, who never had a shortage of advice or questions about the oddity of humans. Zul, in particular, wanted to know more about the strange method of human birth and whether it felt like laying an egg. She was somewhat disappointed to know that Helga had never given birth, though she prodded for details of what Helga had witnessed.

The mist grew heavier with the days, but the insects, thankfully, thinned.

*

Helga woke in the early hours of the morning to a sound she could not place in direction or in memory. It was like a soft scratching or sniffing, or a combination of both. Her mind went first to wolves, then to bears, then to wondering of what beasts actually lived in the bog. She pushed herself up and searched for her crossbow, then remembered it had been lost, and instead drew her sword.

Peridan's fire still burned dimly, and though the citrus candle had gone out, the insects were nowhere to be found. Shadows of grass and trees crawled on the mist itself as it writhed about her. Above, it flowed like a grey river, with the waning moon behind it looking like a shimmering reflection on slow-moving water.

She hunched down as she saw, on the edge of the light, movement. Red eyes that glowed of their own light turned toward her and grew larger, more intent. A slavering mouth opened, revealing a red tongue and teeth of pale yellow-green, with great white tusks protruding from the lower jaw like swords. A shadow above the glowing eyes hinted at a massive head.

"Peridan," Helga whispered, eyes still locked on the beast. It stepped closer, and she could see its large, square head, which was bald and lacked ears. Its neck was covered in a mane of long, quill-like fur that was matted and tangled. Its front paws were large and hairy, and long claws scraped the damp earth as it padded forward.

"Wake up!" Helga said aloud. She slid over to look at the mage, and he was turning fitfully in his blanket.

Helga stared back at the beast, which had moved into the firelight and was looking at the mage, sniffing the air curiously.

"Wake up, for the love of light!" Helga cried, and rushed the bear-like beast, slashing wildly with her sword. The blade bounced and slid over bone and tough hide that covered the beast's head. She dodged a swipe by the claws, then slashed and stabbed at the body of the thing, her sword gripping the beast's strange fur. In a few places, the blade found purchase and slid deeply into flesh.

Blood sprayed on Helga and splashed on her boots. The beast responded by hitting Helga with the back of its paw, sending her sprawling on the ground. It leapt at her, and she rolled away just in time as its large claws slammed to the earth, kicking up a wave of loose soil.

Helga had dropped her sword but saw her poleax leaning against a tree. She made a mad dash to it, only to fall flat on her face as the beast grabbed her shoe, gripping her ankle painfully. Helga reached out for the poleax, but was inches short from its haft. The beast pulled her. She looked at her feet to see that she had injured the thing in her initial attack more severely than she realized. It was dragging itself, bleeding profusely from a hind leg that hung limp.

Desperate, she kicked at the creature. Its hold tightened. Helga reached into the pocket of her dress and found a small orange. She threw it at the burning red eyes, dripping with moisture and quivering with rage. It hit the one on the left and, to Helga's surprise, burst in a spray of juice. The monster howled with pain and released Helga's leg, clutching at its face. Helga did not sit to watch. She stood up and grabbed the poleax. With as much force as she could muster, she slammed the crow's beak down into the skull of the beast. Blood sprayed everywhere, and the thing howled in pain as the spike punctured skin and bone.

Helga planted one boot on the skull and drew her weapon free, dragging with it a snake of grey brain matter. A river of gore poured from the wound on the skull. Helga took a deep breath and steadied herself, for the beast put its claws back into the earth and straightened its hairy, spiked back. It raised its head and stared at her with one eye; the other was burned along with the side of its face into a twisted, blackened mess. It roared – a sound that was both low and high at the same time, like two voices merged into one.

"Dreamer, Peridan, where are you!" Helga shouted. She did not wait for a response, but swung her poleax again, this time hammer first. The beast put a paw up to block the blow, and Helga fell off balance. She leapt back to avoid a claw swipe.

She circled the beast as it eyed her, now cautious but all the angrier for its pain. Helga wished in her heart she had the power she had wielded in Atalthal's realm – the strength and the fearlessness – but her weapon felt immensely heavy, and her arms were tired, her body in a racking pain that hovered outside the fear of the moment, ready to intrude and bring her to earth in tears.

The beast leapt at her, and Helga flinched, throwing up a hand to block swiping claws she lacked the energy to dodge. She felt nothing, but the monster reeled back, as if its paw was swatted by an immense force, and the mist around it swirled like smoke, then turned inward on the beast's body, as if conscious and seeking some prize upon it.

Helga did not waste the moment of respite, but dashed forward, feeling a last burst of hopeful energy. The beast reared up on its hind legs and was cut along its shoulder by the speartip of the poleax. Helga thrust upward into its mottled, semi-hairy chest. The spear buried itself down to the hammer, and then the beast was falling upon her. She thrust a hand out to slow its descent as its paws closed around her, and, somehow, the beast twisted up and away from her, sliding off her spearpoint and landing belly-up a few feet away.

Helga dashed forward and swung the hammer-end of the poleax down into the twisted face of the beast, with all she had left, her mind sharply focused on the blow and the results she wished it to have. The skull and its horrific facial arrangement shattered like a pumpkin. Pieces of bone and sinew and brain flew off in different directions. The arms and legs twitched and then lay still. The jaws split apart, and liquid flesh poured around her ankles, soaking her boots.

Helga watched the living nightmare bleed out for a moment. She collapsed to her knees, exhausted. She looked over at the fire. Peridan was stirring at last.

He sat up suddenly, waving his hands as if irritated by flies. Fireballs shot off into the night, and sparks jumped from his hands as he twisted in his blankets.

"Peridan!" Helga gasped.

He scrambled up, his hands ready to cast a spell, and his face went blank as it fell upon the body of the beast.

"Grim save us," he said.

"What is wrong with you?" Helga said, feeling suddenly hot and angry. "Sleeping through this! I suppose I'll never wonder how my husband can sleep through the sheep bleating in the morning again."

"I…" Peridan searched for his staff as he stammered. "I wasn't asleep. I was here, by the fire. *You* were having a nightmare. I watched you toss and turn, but you would not wake. This thing-" he poked it with the point of his staff. "This thing I have seen in my own dreams, I think, before… but… I cannot say more. How did you slay it?"

"I imagine it was magic," Zul said, flying down and landing on the beast. She pecked at the bear-like thing's remaining eye. "A pity we were not around to watch." Zald flew down and shared it with her.

"Don't hog the tasty bits," he said.

"Magic?" Peridan said.

"Yes," Zul said, swallowing a part of the dead eye. "It had to be. Look at her. You tell me she could do this with her body alone."

190

"I did not know you were a mage. I did not sense the spark in you," Peridan said.

"I'm not," Helga said. "I… merely got lucky."

"Always like a human to blame luck," Zim said. He was tearing open the beast's chest wound, trying to get at the thick muscle beneath. "You crushed its head, and you ought to know how you did it, since when we met, you could barely hold a crossbow or swing a sword."

Peridan looked at the mist around them. "It takes a strong will…" He trailed off and knelt down beside the beast. "I fear now sleep."

Neither of them went back to sleep. Helga, at the request of the ravens, partially skinned the beast, which allowed them to eat their fill and then some. As she eyed the ruined thing over, she was struck by a compulsion to carry some part of it away as a trophy.

"I say you take the claws," Zald said. "The barbarians love to wear bear claws, and these are much bigger and scarier. That will make *you* seem scarier."

"The teeth are more useful," Zul said. "Those big ones. They can be shaped into things, if I remember."

"They do look like walrus tusks," Helga said. "I shall take them. They might make a fine gift or a good drinking horn." Helga shrugged. "I shall take the claws as well. I could do with a more frightening look on the road."

"I can't imagine that you could look more frightening, actually," Peridan said.

Helga looked down and realized how gore-dripped she was.

*

They stopped at midday, feeling exhausted and worn thin. Helga cooked some of the "bear" meat over a real fire, helped along with a bit of magic from Peridan. The meat was far better than she expected, quite rich and filling and another relief from road rations, as they were. She found the meat paired very well with the oranges, and she marinated the meat at the next meal in orange juice to give a sweeter flavor, very pleased with her road cooking skills.

"I would fancy a nap," Peridan said. "But can either of us peacefully go to sleep?"

"I can," Helga said. "Do you really think there are more of those beasts out there? There can't be many, if there are. There's not enough to eat here to sustain something that big."

"Perhaps you're right," Peridan said.

"We can sleep in shifts," Helga said.

"I don't know about that." He opened up his compass and watched it spin in circles before deciding on a direction. "The sooner we get to the watchers, the better."

They pushed on hard through the rest of the day, not stopping until long after sunset. Even then, Peridan was only content to stop because they had reached a slow-moving river that was wide enough he dared not ford it in the dark. Helga took the opportunity to wash herself and her bloody clothes in the river, demanding Peridan stay at camp and not watch her.

The water of the river was cool, not cold, and was refreshing. Overhead, the mist was thin and broken, and she could see bright stars and the moon for the first time in days. She saw, far away downstream, something flying in the sky. It was the dragon, she knew, but naked in the river, she felt, for the first time, unafraid. Fire leapt from his jaws, and in her mind, she imagined the unknowable amber eyes, a cold terror to whomever or whatever the dragon was hunting.

She got out and wrapped a blanket around herself, then returned to the fire, where she laid out her clothes on some branches to dry. Zald came down and picked at them here and there.

"I'll take first watch," Peridan said, staring into the fire with intense eyes.

Helga nodded and went to sleep almost immediately.

*

In the morning, she folded up her amber dress and stacked her armor on Raggle, along with all the gear she wanted to keep dry. She and Peridan forded the wide and shallow river easily, both wearing only their underclothes as they did so. The sky above them was blue, and the sun was shining; the river cut a path through the mists like a knife. They realized about halfway through the river, however, that it flowed in both directions at once. Where they ended, it seemed to be flowing northeast (or what passed for northeast in that tangled land) towards the Fay, but where they had started, it flowed in the opposite direction.

After dressing (Helga put on her full armor – it was light and dry, and she feared another attack by strange creatures), they had a small meal and began following the river, glad to have open sky. Later in the day, they noticed that the river was now flowing back in the first direction. Peridan took a reading with his compass, and they had to turn away from the river and head back into the mist.

The land on the east side of the river was very different than the marshes. It was all turf-covered hills and valleys, with rocks jutting up in many different places, with each cluster of a seemingly different sort. One boulder would be made of pure jade, and another basalt. A granite boulder might be balanced on a sheet of streaked marble. In some places, crystals showed, but neither Helga nor Peridan felt a strong desire to try to remove them, having learned to be wary of the Fay Wastes, which was just as well for they lacked any rock-working tools.

With the harder turf, they were at last able to ride in earnest, though the horses had their own fears that had to be worked against to keep them at a steady pace in the level stretches. The hills grew taller, disappearing into the fog above their heads, and then everything grew darker.

They began to pass hollows in the rocks, which slowly became caves. A few glowed with their own inner light, and others seemed like pits of pure darkness. Peridan was on edge, holding onto his staff constantly with his free hand, the other holding the reigns of his horse. Helga held tightly to her poleax, imagining dark and twisted things residing in the caves. There were few signs of animals. Occasional rodents poked their heads out of dirt burrows, but there was nothing else.

The fall of night was a more subtle change than in previous nights, a dimming and replacement of grey light with warm greens and yellows. They decided to make camp against a rocky wall, far away from any caves or hollows. They needed no fire to see, for a soft glow from the east provided enough light to see by, but Peridan made his fire in a pile of rocks anyway for warmth and comfort.

"We are close. Yes, very close," Zald said. There were no trees in which to perch, so he sat upon Helga's saddle. "Tomorrow, we shall see the Fay and probably the watchers."

"You are lucky to have us," Zul said. "The watchers will be wary if we are about."

"I don't see why," Peridan said.

"Then you are blind," Zul said.

XI: THE WATCHERS

THE NEXT DAY, the mists thinned above their heads. They emerged from a long valley of grass-covered hills to find themselves on the edge of a forest — a forest that began out of nothing, with no area of transition. The plains of grass simply ended, and the trees began, with dark, deep shades of green beneath golden leaves and pale spring shoots.

The trees were indeed as immense as the ravens had suggested, as big around as a good-sized house and towering to the sky, with outstretched branches and leaves larger than any roof. They had a primal look to them; their bark was smooth and pale, but their trunks were twisted in many directions as they climbed up to the sky. Their leaves were of many shades: from pale, almost yellow to a green so dark it was nearly black, with a few reds and purples to be found here and there. Always the leaves were of a profound color — more striking and real than Helga had ever seen a leaf to be.

They followed the tree line north (or what they thought to be north; their sense of direction felt off, and the sun was obscured by the trees). To their left, the mists thinned out more, revealing a long and narrow green plain, endless and flat as it stretched in front of them. Beyond it, and the misty fay wastes, lay the mountains, stark and brown, and looking oddly lifeless.

Helga's spirits were finally lifted. The smell of the trees was overpoweringly earthy, and it invigorated her, as did the hope that her quest would, at last, be at an end. The ravens likewise flew around them, flitting among the trees but never passing far into the forest.

Peridan's mood seemed to darken, however, and he was silent, annoyed constantly by the ravens.

"If I didn't know better, I'd think he was riding to his own trial," Helga said to Zald as Peridan rode ahead to stay in his own silence.

"I like him less as we go," the raven replied. "He's far too dour."

"He's been faithful," Helga said. "I cannot fault him too far."

"He is also at the edge of the Fay, of the dream that is real," Zul said. "That is an unpleasant experience for someone who is used to a world that is static."

"He is a mage, though," Zim said. "He ought to relish the power."

"Elvish power is not like the power of men," Zul said. "Or of ravenkind."

"No doubt," Zald said.

At the end of the day, they approached their final destination. Upon their right stretched a great hedge of living thorns, two dozen feet tall, that writhed like living snakes. Above, they could see glimpses of beings and strange dwellings within the living trees.

At the gate, one of the watchers stood, a lean blue-skinned being with glowing eyes and a fixed, unreadable expression. His appearance drew Helga's eyes, but at the same time, he felt indistinct in his features. His face was smooth and without wrinkles. His eyes glowed of their own light, colorless. He was staring out into the land beyond. He turned to them as they approached. His face still expressed no emotion. His large white eyes searched them over.

"Why have you come?" His voice crackled like dry twigs.

"In trade," Peridan said.

"Enter," the watcher said, and turned his attention back to the plain. The living hedge began to twist and turn in on itself, and before their eyes, pulled apart to reveal a portal inside.

Helga made to follow Peridan in and then noticed the ravens were missing.

"Where have the birds gone?" she said.

"To their doom, hopefully," Peridan said bitterly. His eyes widened when they saw the inside of the great hedge and people within.

Where the watchers lived could be called many things: a camp, a city, a village, a fortress. Within the massive trees, they had hollowed out dwellings, and in the branches of the trees stood platforms and open houses. Stairs of living branches wound their way around the tree trunks to more doorways of a multitude of sizes and shapes. Doors opened downward into the ground below the trees, and strangely shaped windows sat amongst wandering roots in the ground while others shone from holes in the twisting bark. Oddments hung from lines of string stretching through the trees to the high branches. Here, a teacup, there, an arrowhead. There seemed to be no rhyme or reason to the collections.

As odd as the village was, it was the watchers themselves that most shocked Helga. Like the guard outside, they had the look of elves, but their skins were of many different colors, often mottled like the bark of the trees they inhabited. Their eyes shone with an inner light, their pupils obscured by the glow. Their noses were long and pronounced, and they had long pointed ears that put Peridan's to shame. Their limbs were thin, and their fingers equally so. The women were lithe and very slim, with small busts and angular, child-like chins, while the men had a gaunter but wider frame throughout. Both sexes were of a height slightly inferior to Helga.

Their attire could be described as motley at best. Some wore random assortments of armor among more practical clothes. Some of the men wore dresses. Most of them were missing one piece of clothing or another, and many of them were stripped to the waste (including the women). A few walked about naked and shameless.

Peridan and Helga dismounted and walked their horses into the circle of living trees, massive multi-storied houses that stretched to the sky. On the ground, several of the watchers sat in a circle, staring at a small pool that glowed with enchantment. Two of them noticed the pair and stood up. One was a woman and one a man, each with a faint blue-green skin.

"Here for trade?" the man said in a deep, slurring voice. He approached and began running his hands over the flanks of the horse.

197

Helga looked at Raggle, thinking of how she might barter for the Water of Awakening. *I suppose I could part with you, old friend. You'd understand, right?* She thought. The horse looked at her with eyes she could only see as sad.

The woman began to touch Peridan, and he started, withering from the touch. The fay creature looked at him curiously, then went to Helga.

"You are a woman," she said. Her voice lilted and chirped, clear and melodious, like a bird.

"Yes."

"I have not seen a human woman with my eyes. You are different than I thought you were. Larger."

"We are here to trade," Peridan said. "Not be pawed at. What do you desire?"

"You…you must talk to the first ones," the woman said. She pointed at a shorter, squatter, and altogether stranger tree. This one was not just wood, but stone in places — not cut and laid stone like that of a castle, but living rock of marble and granite in the shape of a tree, like it was pulled out of the earth by the growing. From all the branches hung oddments of particular sorts — weapons, tools, and jewelry.

Helga followed Peridan through a gap in a strange vine-covered hedge to the tree. A small, dark-skinned watcher stepped from the dwelling with three others, all taller and with pale skin that matched the trees in color and pattern. They wore fine robes of several colors, and each wore a crown of great wealth, made of filigreed gold and jewels.

"We have waited and watched for you," the dark-skinned man said in a deep, clear voice. "I have been named Ramses, and these are called Eric, David, and Kahn. You are Peridan, of the Golden House, and you are Helga the Lion, warrior-maiden of the north."

He did not phrase it as a question, but Helga almost laughed when the little man called her a warrior-maiden.

"We have watched, and we have waited," David said. "What do you seek?"

"You do not know?" Helga said. "When you know my name?"

"We watch what is interesting," David said.

"I seek the Air of Dreams," Peridan said. The four watchers turned to look at him.

"I see," Ramses said. "What do you seek, Helga the Lion?"

"The Water of Awakening," Helga said.

"These are immense things to ask for," Ramses said. "We will not give them to you without great expense."

"Name your price," Helga said. Peridan remained silent, looking over the strange men.

Kahn spoke. "We must deliberate with each other, and then we will give each of you a price. Go now." He gestured to the open areas where they had entered. When they left, a wall of vines and brambles grew suddenly out of the ground, closing off the odd tree and the kings within. Peridan sat down on a nearby rock.

"What do you think?" Helga said.

"There is nothing to think now," Peridan said.

"Thank you for making the journey with me," Helga said.

"Do not thank me," Peridan said. "Or rather, wait on the thanks."

Sensing Peridan's mood, Helga left him and walked around the trees with her horse. Everywhere, eyes fixed on her from curious faces. None of the watchers smiled, but they had subtle expressions of tension and relaxation as they looked to each other and, very often, into space. She led Raggle to a patch of shrubs beneath the trees and set him to eat.

"Does he eat much?" It was the woman from before, staring at the horse with wide eyes.

"He eats like a horse," Helga said with a chuckle.

The woman frowned slightly. "But is that a great deal?"

"Yes," Helga said. "He's a big animal. He eats a lot. Luckily, he's pretty content on grass and shrubs."

"These are edible?"

"To him."

"But not to you."

"No. I eat things like bread and cheese. What do you eat? For that matter, what is your name? I am Helga."

"I have only eaten a few times. I ate… fruit. It was interesting. I have no name."

"How do you not have a name?" Helga said.

"I do not have a name."

"What do people call you?"

"They don't call me anything."

"I mean, how do your friends address you? How do they get your attention? They must call you something."

"When they want my attention, they have it."

"What about everybody else? Do they have names?"

The woman cocked her head. "Some."

"How do you talk about others? Without a name, how do you say that you saw a particular person doing something?"

"I…" the woman looked confused. "We don't talk about each other."

"What about Ramses and the others? They have names."

"They were named."

"By who?"

"You."

"Not me," Helga said. "I never named them."

"I mean, you humans. Ramses is lucky to have a name."

"Should I give you a name?"

For the first time, Helga saw the hint of a smile on one of the faces of the watchers. "That would be… what do you want in return?"

"You don't have to give me anything."

"We… give back when we give. Trading is the way of humans, is it not?"

"Maybe," Helga said. "But not everyone trades all the time. Sometimes, you give gifts."

"What do you want in return?"

Helga sighed and smiled at the strange, open-eyed woman. "Oh, anything you want."

"What is my name?"

Helga thought for a minute. "How about Freydis? You're pretty. I think it fits."

"I am Freydis." The watcher's mouth opened in a slight smile, then she got up and began walking up a long set of steps on a nearby tree. Each step was made by a branch of the tree, folded over and growing leaves. She disappeared around the trunk, her mouth moving silently.

Helga patted Raggle gently, watching him eat with vigor the shoots of a nearby patch of sprouts, which regrew as soon as the horse finished with each one. Helga knelt down and felt one. She pulled it free of the earth, and as soon as she did, another one sprouted from the ground. Helga nibbled it a little, remembering chewing on milkweed as a girl, and found the sprout to be nutty and flavorful. She shrugged and ate the whole thing, then a few more before she stopped, feeling satisfied.

The newly named Freydis walked back down the steps carrying something in her arms. It was a small box of wood. Freydis sat down next to Helga and opened the box. Inside was a bright, blinding light, shimmering between white, blue, and pale purple. Helga had to shield her eyes.

"What is it?" Helga asked, trying to peer into the box and see just what inside was so bright.

"It is a star. I plucked it from the sky because I thought it was so pretty. Is it enough?"

"Only if you can pluck another if you choose."

"I suppose I could," Freydis said, and handed over the box.

Helga tried again to look inside, and she thought she could detect, by blocking out the light with her thumb, something containing the star.

"Can I hold it?"

"I did."

Helga reached in and felt the star, which was warm and made her hand tingle. Its outside felt crystalline and faceted, but it gave slightly under pressure. It was a little larger than a plum, but as she gripped it, a much greater idea of size seized her mind – a size so immense she could not comprehend it. She removed the star from the box and held it up. It was small, but it brightened the ground around her, even in the bright Fay light.

"Thank you," Helga said. She put the star back into the box and put the box into one of Raggle's saddlebags.

Helga watched Freydis walk around the village, then out to the entrance gate. The fay woman leaned against it and looked out to the sun, which was beginning to set.

"Be careful what deals you make with these creatures." It was Zim, his head poking out of a nearby shrub with purple leaves.

"That deal seemed to favor me," Helga said. "A name for a star."

"You have done something very powerful, giving a name," Zim said. "Very powerful. That has set that creature's fate, whether you know it or not."

"How so?"

"Names have power and meaning. To name someone is to describe them, and with Fay creatures, to give them a name is to write for them a nature upon their inner being. What name did you give?"

"Freydis."

"Interesting. She will command hearts, you know."

"I can see why," Helga said. "She is very pretty."

"You still do not understand the nature of this place," Zim said. "Or of the Fay people."

"What do you mean?"

"She is pretty because you have made her so," Zim said.

"She was pretty before I named her."

"No," Zim said. "You still are seeing with mortal eyes. But what is done is done, probably for good and ill both. I am here to warn you about these kings you have asked to treat with."

"What warnings do I need?"

"Many, it seems. The watchers have changed much since we have seen them last, and these 'kings' are most disturbing. Zald is watching them, hidden as he can be. He will report to me. But before that, you should know that these Fay creatures do not desire the same things that mortals desire. Though they desire to *be* mortals, they are not bound by the moral sensibilities of mortals, or their ethics, having not acquired those sensibilities for themselves… yet. I will return."

Zim flew away, and Helga was left with her thoughts. She watched Freydis gaze at the setting sun. The last rays of light slipped away, but darkness did not set in. The trees themselves were luminescent, sending down soft golden-green rays on the forest floor that shifted underfoot like rippling water. Helga took out her star and cupped it in her hands, shining it on the ground to see that it really was moving; it was not just a trick of the tree light. Grass was growing and glowed green as it did so. Sprouts shot up and fell down. Outside of the dwelling places of the watchers, lamps sprang to life in hues of pink and purple, bright but lit by swirling waters that had their own life. Everywhere, people began to emerge, and under the light of the trees and the lamps, they looked less strange and fairer.

Their eyes glowed in the night shadows, and their bodies were more consistent shades of pale white, soft pink, and iridescent blue. Their gowns and sparse clothes seemed normal, and even nakedness did not seem to be nakedness. Helga watched as they formed a circle around a fire, not burning with wood but with something else, and danced. Music began to be played, not by any crafted instrument, but with voices alone. These voices were inhuman and ethereal; some sounded like lilting violins, others like booming drums. Still, other voices were crystalline and beyond description, playing timbres of sound that Helga had never before heard.

The music wandered from consonance to dissonance and back, from calm, sustained tones to wild scales, and all the elements mixed together. It was discordant and out of time, then would transform into unisons of simple clarity. Fugues emerged amid the counterpoint, only to be lost in more cacophony. Nothing repeated, and nothing stayed the same for long, and no theme or rhythm remained in her mind, but somehow the music was beautiful in its primacy. Helga did not resist when Freydis, with a man in tow, approached and pulled her to her feet. Helga pocketed the star and allowed herself to be dragged into the dance, which matched the music as it changed – chaotic and tumbling like storm clouds in fast-motion.

Her armor felt like nothing as she danced. As she looked to the faces in the circle, she saw a flurry of emotions that she herself felt: sadness and despair, joy, fury, desire, fear, excitement, and quiescence.

She was pulled back from the dance by a strong arm that she realized belonged to Peridan.

"That is unwise, Lionheart," he said.

"What is the harm?"

"Too long in this place, or with the watchers, and you will dream the way they do, and forget what it is to have purpose and meaning. It has happened before. These people might have once been like you."

"I don't believe that," Helga said. "I know quite well who I am, and I know that these people know who they are."

"Do not ignore me on this, at the end of our struggle," Peridan said. "Besides, it is time to hear the demands of the kings."

"Very well," Helga said.

She followed Peridan back to the meeting place of Ramses and the others. They were standing in a semicircle, looking far more radiant and majestic than when she had met them, and they seemed taller as well. Their crowns glowed with their own shining golden light. Each gem set in them gave off its own fire, and their garb glittered with golden threads and pearls. Each one wore a different colored gem around his neck: Ramses wore amber, David blue, Eric red, Kahn green. Their faces were stern, but calm.

"Helga the Lion will hear her price by herself," Ramses said.

Peridan nodded, and a curtain of ivy and brambles grew quickly to separate them.

"You seek the Water of Awakening," David said.

"Yes," Helga replied.

"It is a precious substance in the Fay," Eric said. "It comes only from a river deep within, whose course shifts. It is hard enough for us to find it."

"Say no more," Ramses said. The two exchanged a calm glance.

"The Price for the Water of Awakening," Kahn said, "is your hopes, your desires, and your love."

Helga stood mute. "I cannot give these things."

"The price is what it is," Ramses said.

"No, I mean," Helga stammered, "I literally cannot give you my hopes, desires, and love. I can give you my sword, but not my thoughts or my emotions."

"I think I understand," David said, frowning. "Because they are not corporeal. These things we have the means to take from you if you choose to give them up. They are as real here as your sword. More so."

Helga was at a loss for words and gazed into the face of each of the kings, wondering what was in their hearts as far as desire and emotion.

"Why do you want my desires?" Helga asked. "You clearly have your own."

"To have the power of mortals, you must understand the mortal striving," Ramses said. "We try, for we see the power and the satisfaction of desire fulfilled. Here there is no struggle."

"Walk out," Helga said. "You want struggle? The world will give it to you."

"We cannot," David said. "We have not yet the defined characteristics of beings like you to walk away from the fay and the Prim that feeds us. We have not yet the power of the fixed."

"You look fixed enough," Helga said.

"You only say that because mortals see only the corporeal," David said. "One day, we will be like you."

"But better," Kahn said, "For we have the light of dreams in us still. We will take the existence promised to us at creation."

"Have any of your tribe walked away?" Helga said.

"Some have, yes," Eric said. "When they could no longer abide the mortal world on our doorstep."

"I think I have met them," Helga said. "The dun-men. They are mad, Eric."

"They lack what we still assemble," Eric said.

Helga clenched her fists. "What would my desire serve you? My desire is for my own life. It would make no sense to you."

"You think in specifics, not in the nature of a thing," David said. "Will you give it up or not?"

"Shall I lose it in the taking?"

"Of course."

"I..." Helga took a deep breath. She felt her wedding ring on her finger and visualized her husband Erling, with his long hair and yellow beard, his generous smile and sparkling blue eyes. She remembered him chopping wood, a simple, mundane memory, but one that sent her heart racing, as it was the moment she first felt desire for him. She remembered Erling's labors to earn her heart when she first refused him, for reasons she herself could not recall. She saw herself greeting him on his return from the underworld, the foolish demands of a girl met with ease. She saw him on their wedding day and remembered their first intimate embrace as husband and wife. She remembered feeding him tenderly when he fell ill.

All she desired at that moment was to be back home, with Erling whole and strong, and she knew that she could now never have that. She foresaw that with the loss of her desire, her love for her husband, and her hope to succeed, those feelings which had driven her on her long quest, that she would lose the quest itself. There would be no happy return, for she would wander aimlessly; become one of the dun men or the watchers. Erling would die, and so would she.

She began to weep.

"Tears of a Lion," David said. His face rested on her with a curious expression.

"You ask for a thing I will not give you," Helga said. "I would rather suffer all the loss in the world from the failure of love and hope, than to lose love and hope themselves. Is there nothing else?"

"Nothing," Ramses said.

Feeling weak, Helga hung her head and turned away. The hedge parted for her, and Peridan was there. He gave her a solemn nod and then walked past her. The hedge closed, leaving her outside and him inside. Helga wandered for a few minutes out to the entrance gate, which was now covered in silver and purple blossoms. She stepped through and sat down on the soft turf. The stars in the west were bright, and on the plains of the fay waste, which sat below the forest only a little bit, the mists swirled in blues and greens. The mountains behind it were black shadows, but the snow on them stood out white.

"Ah, here you are." It was Zul, and next to her was Zim, who flew down and landed on the turf. "You appear to be yourself."

"This quest was doomed from the start, and I will wager the old woman knew it," Helga said.

"I doubt that," Zim said. "Why would she send you for something so precious? Something she wanted? No, I think she was not evil so much as stupid and ignorant of the Fay and its creatures."

"Perhaps you're right."

"And you were right to refuse," Zul said. "We were watching over you. What the kings ask for was what makes you human — that is what they covet, you understand."

"Perhaps I could still make the deal," Helga said.

"What?" Zim said. "No. No deal!"

"I could have you take the water back to the old volva, or get Peridan to do it."

"That is a far journey, even for a raven," Zim said. "And we have other business."

"I doubt that," Helga said. "Considering you are here."

Zul hopped onto Helga's knee and pecked at her lightly. "I would do this thing for you. I would carry back the Water of Awakening for you, but you must not make this deal."

"Why not?" Helga said. "It would save Erling."

"But you would be as good as dead," Zim said. "What is a human without her will?"

"I don't know. I just know I want Erling to live. Maybe he would find someone else, and yet have a happy life and marriage."

"No," Zul said. "That is not a trade that is valuable to anyone. Not anyone!"

"It is valuable to me."

"One lives. One is lost. Each is sad. You gain nothing."

"It isn't always about gaining something. Sometimes it is about saving something."

"Think of this," Zim said. "What would Erling have you do?"

"Come home."

"Then do as he wills," Zim said.

Helga hung her head in her lap and began weeping again. She covered her face, and tears streamed through her fingertips. The stars blurred with her vision; she could not stop the tears from flowing. At last, she looked down to see a small puddle of tears on her hand, reflecting the stars.

"There has got to be another way," Helga said. "I will steal the Water."

"You assume they have it." It was Zald, and he was working on cracking open a nut nearby.

"I do," Helga said. "Why else would they barter with it?"

"We told you they are faithless," Zald said. "They are more likely to steal your desires and leave you wandering without giving away anything, for after your desire is gone, why would you want the Water of Awakening? You really are naïve. It is good you are a member of the Black Feather Friends."

Helga smiled through her tears. "I'm a member now, am I?"

"I guess that is up to Zim, but I consider you a sister, for what it is worth."

"Thank you, Zald. I will do my best to honor you."

"Bah," Zald said, still working the nut.

"Let me help you," Helga said. "No deals, since I am family now, eh?"

Zald flapped his wings as Helga picked up the nut. She stood up and found a rock, then smashed the nut against it with her boot, breaking it apart. She handed the meat to Zald.

"At least you are good for something," he said. He ate the meat greedily.

Helga took a deep breath. "So those are my options. Steal the water, if they have it, or trust one of you to collect my debt."

"Peridan must," Zim said. "There is a reason we are out of sight here. The watchers are dreadfully hateful of us."

"Why is that?"

"We… have stolen things from them before."

"Our voices," Zald said.

"Your voices?" Helga said.

"And some gold trinkets. And some silver trinkets. Some other things too."

"No wonder you knew so much," Helga said.

"I do not feel bad," Zald said. "They are faithless. The kings, I have decided, are the worst of the lot. Perhaps too human, they are."

"Perhaps there is another way?" Zul said.

Helga thought for a moment, looking at the stars. "I could get the water of awakening myself. I could go. You all said once that has to exist, or the fay would have dried up."

"True, but finding it and remaining yourself is another matter," Zim said.

"One of the watchers said it was a river, but its course was always shifting," Helga said. "I could chance it. I could try to find it." Helga stood up. "That is what I will do. Perhaps I can convince one of the watchers to guide me."

"If they can find their own way," Zald said. "I told you they are liars."

Helga went back into the tree city, passing more watchers, who eyed her with different expressions than during the day - warmer and more concerned than curious. She found Freydis sitting on some steps looking out upon a few of the men, who moved in and out of dance and music with equal ease. Some would wander off and go inside, and others would come to replace them, so always there was a motion and a music.

Helga noticed the look on Freydis's face as she watched, which struck her as a sort of loneliness.

"What is the matter?" Helga asked.

"Nothing is the matter," Freydis said, but Helga watched the woman's eyes.

"I was wondering if you could help me."

"You already did."

"Well," Helga said. "I need someone to guide me into the heart of the Fay. Somebody who can find something that shifts its location."

Freydis kept staring at the dancers, especially the men. "I cannot hold their attention."

Helga sighed. "If they were human men, I could easily help you."

"They don't have names. That's the problem."

"I could name one," Helga said. "Whichever one you fancy, I'll name him. I just need a guide."

"I can find one that wants a name," Freydis said.

"Good," Helga said. "Now, can you guide me to the Water of Awakening?"

Freydis frowned. "I... don't remember."

Helga sighed again.

"He might, though." Freydis stood and walked away. She returned a minute or two later with a male, whose bright eyes seemed to stare at the trees. He noticed Helga. "What is his name?"

"You can give me a name?" the man said.

"Sure," Helga said. "Easiest thing in the world."

"What is my name?" the man asked.

"Can you find the Water of Awakening?" Helga said.

The man paused and looked off. "No."

"What the Hel," Helga said, clenching her fists. She sighed. "I'll give you a name anyway, if you like."

"I have a limb I plucked from a thirsty tree. It always points to water." The man still looked away.

"But does it point to the Water of Awakening?"

"I know no other."

"Very well, go fetch it," Helga said.

"What is my name?"

Helga gave him a good look. He had an angular face and a proud nose, pale white skin, and shoulder-length hair so blonde it was nearly white. She decided he was more pretty than handsome, but a good fit for Freydis.

"Balthur," Helga said. "You're Balthur."

The man's open face split into a slight smile, and he wandered off. Halfway to one of the trees, he turned back to look at Freydis, with a look of curiosity on his face.

"Good," Freydis said. "I like his name."

"I think he fancies you," Helga said. "Let's hope he isn't a liar."

A few minutes more and the man returned, holding in his hand a small bent limb of wood absent leaves or cracks. He handed it to Helga.

"What is this supposed to do?" she asked.

"Point to water."

Helga held the stick in one hand, waiting for the bent end to turn. It stayed still.

"I think it's broken," she said.

"You must power it with the Primus."

"Primus? The Prim?" Helga said. "Like, with magic?"

Balthur frowned slightly. "Yes, with magic."

"I'm not a mage."

"Are you not?" Freydis asked. "How did you name us, then?"

"It's the easiest thing in the world, like I said."

"Then the divining rod should work for you," Freydis said.

"Thanks anyway," Helga said, and sighed. She stood up and twirled the twig around, but it did nothing.

"What a waste of a name," Zald said. Helga looked around, but could not see him. "I'm invisible."

"It's just a name."

"You still resist the learning. No matter. It is time to leave. Now."

"Why now?"

"You will be in danger, I think," Zald said. "The fay is affecting me. I have forgotten what was so important to tell you, but I know it has to do with danger. We need to leave now. We can try to find the water later."

"You're acting funny."

"Leave now!" Zald hissed. "The sense of it is strong."

Helga tucked the rod into her belt as she saw Peridan approaching. Zald immediately stopped talking, but Helga could imagine he was flapping his wings at her. Peridan was smiling, but it seemed forced.

"Have you made your trade and acquired your cure?" she said.

"Almost," Peridan said. He looked away and watched the dancers. "I have spoken with the kings, and I believe we have come to a new agreement for you."

"Really!?" Helga said, suddenly overjoyed. "What is it? Do I have to give up a hand, or a sense?"

Peridan cleared his throat. "Yes, in a way."

"Yes? To which one?"

"Just follow me," Peridan said. "We must treat with them within the night."

Helga did as she was bidden and followed Peridan back down to the twisting hedge of thorns that ringed in the inner tree, where the four kings sat upon four carved chairs. After Helga entered, the hedge closed.

"Here, Helga, hold this for me," Peridan said. He handed her a clay vessel that was full of holes and emanated light. Helga looked in the holes but could see no substance inside. Meanwhile, Peridan bowed before the kings.

"Let our bargain be fulfilled."

"So let it be done," Ramses said.

Peridan snapped around. Helga felt a jolt to her arms. As she startled, she thought she would drop the little clay object, but she did not. She *could* not. It was stuck to her fingers. She tried to pry her fingers away, but it was impossible. She wanted to turn and run, but found her feet immovable.

"I am sorry, Helga," Peridan said. "But the price was steep, and as an elf, it was a price that was impossible for me to pay."

XII. The Heart of Faerie

ELGA TWISTED her body, but it felt stiff. Her legs began to tingle, and then her feet and arms went numb. She cried out, but her voice was all dry straw and sand. She felt herself falling backward, and then was wrapped in living, growing vines. Some of them had thorns and poked at her face and wrists. The vines carried her forward to lie before Peridan and the four kings.

"You can extract her soul?" David said.

"Yes," Peridan said. "With your help. Without a vessel or phylactery, you will have to consume her soul directly. It will be much like drinking the flows of the Prim once I open the gateway and it begins to pour out."

"Very good," Ramses said. "In one night, we will move so much closer. We were right to reach out to you, Peridan." He put his hand lightly on Helga's forehead, then turned it to her cheek, where he withdrew a single tear and stared at it, wondering.

Eric spoke. "Fortunate too that you could hear our summons through the mist."

"Yes," Peridan said in a soft, almost sickly tone. "Fortunate."

Helga focused her mind through the haze and pain, and willed her lungs to move and her voice to sound. "Don't do... this... Peridan."

Peridan turned to her with a dark look.

"Your spell is breaking?" Kahn said.

"No," Peridan said. He cast his hand at Helga and her mouth shut tightly.

"Let us prepare ourselves," David said. Helga watched them move away, her eyes seemingly the only thing over which she could exert her will.

Peridan looked at her with sad eyes. "I am truly sorry for this, Helga," he said, "but the soul and the flesh of an Elf are one, and cannot be separated. Only you can pay my price. But I give you a gift with this as well, though you do not realize it yet."

"What gift?" Helga said through her teeth, once again willing herself to speak.

"You have grown strong. Thankfully not strong enough," Peridan said. "I give you the gift of lichdom, long sought by your most powerful sorcerers, though only a few have found the secret. We have catalogued it in the great library in Alfheim, and I remember the spell well, for a human colleague of mine, in a time long gone by human standards, wished for this gift, and traded me great power for it. This gift I give freely to you, which is immortality in the flesh."

"No..." Helga thought of the tales her mother and grandmother had told her of Hel and liches, the soulless men who live on in rotting corpses, hungering only for power and domination.

"Your mind will live on in your body, and your body will be hardened. Without the soul to wither the body, you will live forever. Immortality in the flesh. That is what most men wish for, is it not? One day, we will meet again, and then I think you will thank me." Peridan took the vessel from her hands and placed it upon her chest. He disappeared from view.

She was left there, laying in anguish and weeping — for how long, she could not tell, for nothing in the treetops seemed to change. Soft glow and night surrounded her without pause or alteration. She knew only that the time seemed too long in the dread of her fate and too short in the loss of her life as a mortal woman.

Helga wept fully now, though with her binding, she couldn't so much as sob. There would be no return home to a loving husband. There would be no cure. She would bear no children and love nothing. She would be a corpse, tied to the world in famine and anguish.

The fate seemed horrible to her, though she thought of the minds of many men and knew that Peridan was right: many men *would* wish to live forever, whatever the cost.

Her mind wandered. She saw in the movement of the trees various shapes twisting, slowly forming things other than limbs and leaves. She saw, or thought she saw, a man and a woman intertwining, dancing, and laughing. The leaves rolled about like clouds above her head, and she perceived mountains, and men of arms. She saw war and flags twisting in her mind. Death and birth. She saw a dragon, his eyes fixed on her—unknowable, unreadable eyes. Hungry eyes... and she was afraid, but also not afraid. She saw a vast ocean turn into a vast river, which turned into a stream, then a brook, then a trickle over wet rocks. Then, at last, she saw dried, cracked earth, and watched her tears fall down on it. Plants, green and beautiful, sprang up where her tears landed.

The plants became grasses and a tree, then water flowed on the cracked earth, and more trees grew, tall and menacing, stretching their branches to the sky. Overhead, a bird flew, then grew, then became a dragon. She saw his eyes and trembled.

Helga came back to her senses, aware now of a cacophonous sound. Her eyes darted around, and she saw huge vines growing from the ground and the trees, swirling around each other and twisting themselves into a vast wall of living bark and greenery behind the kings' meeting place.

"What is it?" It was the voice of Peridan.

"The dragon has returned," Ramses said. "We must seal the city and move it."

"To where?" Peridan said.

"Elsewhere in the Fay," Ramses replied. He raised his hands, and Helga saw the trees sprout new branches of charcoal grey. She saw, above her, a sudden flash of red and black and bright flame as an immense dragon tore through the canopy. Flames shot through the newly formed and grown branches, withering leaves. She could feel the heat on her face as the flames crawled down the tree trunks.

Softly, she heard Peridan's voice. "But I must have a way back!"

She heard calls and cries from outside, and the kings were gone.

Out of nothing, Zald appeared.

"Quickly, girl, break your bonds while they are distracted!" Zald landed on Helga's thigh and began picking at the vines.

"I… can't," Helga said.

"You are breaking them already, silly," Zald said. "Just focus. You have the magic in you, and plenty of it, or my eyes are no longer worth using."

Helga focused on her hands, willing them to move, but nothing happened.

"I can't, Zald. You have to find a way to break the spell."

Suddenly the other two birds landed and began picking at the vines wrapping Helga.

"What were you thinking?" Zim said.

"I was thinking we needed a distraction, and I was tired of these listless watchers," Zald said. "Now quickly, girl, use your magic. I didn't spend the better part of a week summoning Garamesh so that you could give up now."

"A week?" Helga said weakly.

"Yes," Zald said. "Now stop being silly and use your magic!"

"How? How do I do it?"

Zim spoke. "You must use the power of your soul. You must feel Peridan's magic and destroy it. Think back to all the things you have willed in your mind. You are in the fay now, and dream and reality are the same. Your thought and the thing you think are not separate, or did you believe this place was made only of the chaos of the watchers? Have you no memory?"

Helga saw more flames pouring above them. The earth trembled. She remembered walking through the mist, she remembered fighting the beast, and when she thought hard, she remembered a feeling, just on the edge of her body and mind, that the wind was at her back, and that the earth was solid under her feet, that the mists would obey her if only she allowed herself to command them. She searched the concept of Peridan's magic in her mind, feeling its limits on her body, feeling its cracks.

She focused harder than ever, then fixed in her mind a vision. Peridan's spell was a misty light, lingering in her flesh. She felt it like a wall, then she pushed. She imagined her body covered in sand, and then a great wind came and blew the sand away.

She could move her arms. Then her legs. She pushed herself up, feeling pain in every joint from being immobilized for so long, but the pain was nothing compared to the joy of freedom. Around her, watchers were moving, casting magic everywhere. Many vines and trees were on fire, and she could hear the roar of the dragon. The trees had lost their light, and the darkness would be profound if it were not for the flames.

"Well done!" Zul said. "Now, let us flee this place before the dragon consumes it all."

Helga looked around and saw her poleax lying on the ground, forgotten. She picked it up just in time to see one of the watchers run by, seemingly unaware of her.

"Where do we go?" Helga said. All around them were thick, flaming brambles. Even as they spoke, the trees shifted. Beyond the brambles, the forest moved, or maybe it was that *they* moved *through* the forest.

Helga turned the other way and saw two of the kings standing, gazing at her. Around them, a cavalcade of watchers ran, holding an eclectic assortment of weapons and crying out in strange tongues. Magic leapt from their fingertips as lightning and water, and fire. The earth exploded beneath Helga's feet. The ravens were cawing loudly.

Helga imagined the earth still beneath her feet, and it was as she remembered, only easier now. With the wind at her back, she swung her poleax through the air, and a great wind blew back the magic. She swung again at the closest man, who held an odd old sword in his hand. He made to block her attack. The sword connected with the head of the poleax, then shattered, but Helga's weapon continued its arc. When her weapon hit the watcher in the chest, he seemed to crumble, then parts of him dissolved and blew away in the wind like dust. He fell to the ground, his eyes the sole remaining part of him that seemed whole and immutable, ineffably staring up in wonder as green shoots wrapped around his incorporeal body. Silently, he disappeared into the earth.

The attackers stopped and stared in wonder. Their hands went limp.

"Back!" Helga cried. "I can do the same to all of you!"

"Helga!" It was the voice of Zul.

Helga turned, too late, to see Peridan channeling a massive ball of magic, churning with green fire and pulsing light. In a terrible moment, she witnessed inside her mind her own death, and undeath, as Peridan unleashed the sickly magic.

But she did not die, for the magic was not released.

The magic was stopped by Zald, who attacked Peridan with his talons, ripping skin and flesh like a demon possessed. The magic, however, was already too strong, and what Peridan lacked, the Fay provided; the spell escaped from his twisting hands. A chaotic green flame struck Zald like an arrow as Peridan shielded his face with his arms, the flames turning on him and lighting up his clothes and armor.

He gave a blood-curdling scream, but Helga's attention was on Zald, who tumbled end over end to lie before her, the magic fire dancing off his black feathers. He gave a final look to Helga, then gasped and lay still. Helga stared at the body of the raven, suddenly stark and mundane in the world of strange color.

Helga leapt over his body, feeling rage push blood to her legs and face. Peridan, though burned, was already recovering. Helga needed no magic; she covered the distance in a heartbeat, dropping her poleax and drawing her sword, feeling her heart calling her to take out the weapon. With a single slash, she cut the mage across his chest, cracking bones and sending blood flying onto the trees and the ground. The mage dropped to the forest floor, and Helga looked into his shocked eyes as she ran him through.

The blood poured forth, and where every drop landed, life sprang up. Insects and beetles crawled over the ground. Grotesque vermin and tiny demonic lizards emerged from the elf's wounds. His body decayed before her eyes, turning to maggots that became flies and disappeared into the Fay. Smoke curled up from the blood as well.

Sickened, Helga turned away and ran back to the body of Zald, sheathing her sword. His wings lay half-opened, as well as his beak. She picked up the raven and clutched him to her chest, aware suddenly that she was crying again. Zul and Zim stood nearby, silent.

"I'm sorry," she said.

They did not answer, but instead flew away, roc-rocing loudly like common birds.

She looked up and saw the watchers staring at her, unknowable and immobile. She kept her eyes on them and then returned to the reeking body of Peridan.

All that was left was the wizard's staff and a dagger with a hilt of carved ivory. Helga picked up the staff and snapped it over her knee, then threw it on the ground. Clouds of mist and magic curled up from the wood. She picked up the dagger and thrust it into her belt, thinking for the first time in a long while of Peridan's friend, who was now doomed to die in a way not reserved for his kind, and Peridan's sister, who would now suffer the loss of her husband and her brother beyond the death and rebirth of creation.

"It is time."

Helga turned to see the four kings standing in front of the row of empty-eyed watchers. They turned their faces toward the ceiling of flame, and it began to rain, though Helga could see no clouds. The flames died and hissed.

Helga felt, at the same time, something pull inside of her.

"I can feel it," David said. He opened his mouth, and the other three followed suit, dropping their jaws like snakes to reveal gaping maws. Lights begin to grow and pulse within their throats, and their eyes became hazy. A droning sound filled the air.

Helga could feel something as their mouths opened. An incomprehensible force was pulling at her in a strange way. It was neither her body nor her mind that felt it, but another sense, and she realized what the watchers were trying to do. Peridan, even though he was gone, must have been able to work whatever he planned with the glowing vessel to enough of a degree, and now with sickening clarity, Helga knew the watchers were seeking to consume her soul.

"Back!" Helga said. She focused her mind on the vision of what she wished, then thrust out her hand and threw air and fire at the watchers, but it washed over them as nothing. She thought again, this time of rocks and churning earth. Again she casted, and the earth beneath the watchers crumbled and shook, but the sense of *pulling* did not cease.

Still clutching the body of Zald, she turned and picked up her poleax, then dashed away. She ran around the large tree; in the dark, it looked like it was a deep purple, and she saw many twisted faces in the bark. Somehow, she suspected that this was not a trick of her mind. A vast barrier of vines, trees, wood, brambles, and living, twisting plants blocked her path. She looked back, and though she could not see them as yet, she could feel the pull and knew the kings were walking toward her.

Holding her wishes in her head and heart, she imagined fire and air again, and the living wall burning. She pointed her poleax at the ineffable wall, and a stream of heat flew into it, withering bark and leaf. Like an animal pricked, the brambles and vines withdrew, and even a tree moved, sliding with writing roots to the side. Beyond the barrier was an endless forest. She had no idea where to go, but knew she must escape, for the terror of the kings of the watchers had gripped her.

She thought about Raggle, who must be frightened now and lost, as she ran out into the endless dark forest. She ran as fast as her feet could carry her, over root and shoot and rock, feeling no sense of time or fatigue.

After what felt like many minutes, she turned back to see, coming out of the dark, four sets of glowing eyes and a storm swirling about them, whipping wind and cracking the air. Helga turned and ran again, this time faster and harder, leaping forward with all her thought. She turned back again and saw the same thing – the watchers approaching in a line, moving all things around them with their magic.

Clutching the body of Zald tighter, she held forth her poleax. She concentrated on the feeling – wind at her back, feet firmly in the earth – and she reached with her thought into the ground, deep into the earth, grasping at the concept of boulders and mountains in the abyss of the Fay around her. She closed her hands and imagined them dipping into a stream like the Prim in Atalthal's realm.

The ground burst asunder, throwing the watchers in every direction. A mountain emerged, smaller than a real mountain, the sort outside the Fay, but of the same essence. Huge rocks cracked and fell down its sides, breaking trees and burying the watchers.

Helga breathed in relief, but even as she did so, the rocks stirred and moved with the will of the watchers. The trees uprooted and disintegrated. Two kings emerged from the wreckage, eyes glowing even brighter in the night.

Helga held her breath and tried once again to shape the world she saw. Trying to remember Atalthal's realm, suddenly, all she could think of was cherries. And with the thought, trees grew up in front of the watchers, startling them. They blossomed and dropped fruit in an instant, and then thousands of birds descended in a flock to eat them, binding the watchers in a living prison.

Helga ran, feeling the wind push her forward. Among the cadence of her feet, she tried once again to find the pathways to make real her thoughts. Some of these sprang into existence around her: an orange tree, a hoard of squirrels, another boulder (which sprang up behind her, thankfully), flocks of birds. With each failed attempt, her thoughts became more focused.

Arrows. She imagined the trees were crossbows, and a flurry of bolts flew past her, only to explode in flame. She toppled the trees, and the watchers raised them up. She threw up the earth, and watchers beat it down. She called birds and beasts, and the watchers destroyed them. She conjured mist and fog, but the watchers could feel her, even if they could not see her, and so the chase continued.

A thought occurred to Helga. She imagined herself, as near herself as she could, and beside her, a woman appeared, looking just like her, or how she remembered herself; the last time she saw into a looking glass was in Atalthal's realm.

The shade of Helga's mind stopped and looked up at the trees, suddenly aimless. Helga did not stop. She raced on, trying her best to conjure everything again – trees and earth, roots and birds. She looked back, and the watchers were gone. She still didn't stop. She ran until she felt actual exhaustion starting to creep in, her body reminding her that she was a real, physical woman, even if her mind could manipulate the Fay.

She slowed and finally fell to her knees. The body of Zald was still tucked in her arm. She laid it down and looked closely at the large bird. She shook it, and talked to it, and finally set her mind to reviving it. She imagined him real and animated. She felt for his life, but it was gone. All she managed to do was make the wings flap. She felt herself crying again.

"I'm so sorry, Zald. I wonder if I should bury you here or carry you out." Looking at the bird, she decided that she could not let him lie in the Fay, so little had he wanted to return here. She took a piece of cloth from her belt bag and wrapped his face in it, so at least she would not have to look at the empty eyes. She wished for something to lash him with, and as she thought, a small creeper grew around the body. She grabbed it and uprooted it, then quickly stripped off the leaves. She gave a start as it became twine in her hands. She wrapped Zald's body with it, then made a small strap. She slung the body over her shoulder.

"Not a dignified way to carry a raven," she said, "but perhaps you will forgive me. Or you would. Perhaps Zim and Zul will, if I ever find them."

She looked around at her surroundings. They looked the same as they had before: Great tall trees stretching off in every direction. She noticed that these trees were different. Above her, they were all in bloom in colors of white and pale pink. A sweet, unknowable fragrance filled her nostrils as she looked around.

"I might as well be dead," she said to Zald's body. "For how shall I ever find my way out again?"

She sat on a nearby rock and watched the blossoms sway. They began to fall down in mass, like snow, but above her, the wall of blossoms was no less for it. New blossoms sprang up everywhere. The snow of flowers increased, narrowing her view. She patted the raven body at her hip and felt something poke her.

Curious, she pulled forth a bent twig.

"The divining rod," she said. As she held it up, she felt it turn and almost pull her in a direction. She felt it do more than turn, in fact. "It's like you're saying something to me," Helga said to the twig. It pulled harder, and concepts absent words came into her mind: *Water. Far.*

Helga did not know what else to do, so she followed the twig as it pointed her. She walked through the forest of raining flowers, watching the twig twitch, using her poleax as a walking stick. Every so often, the twig would point off in another direction, seemingly at random. Remembering the compass Peridan had held, and remembering she was lost anyway, Helga followed the divining rod.

Soon she passed out of the raining blossoms and into a darker, more twisted forest, with low, squat trees like the tree of the watcher kings. Leafless twigs reached for her, growing and stretching in the longing of flesh, and she brushed them away with a thought. Soon, she was walking through a corridor that grew darker and darker, roofed overhead with limbs tangled so thickly it was like walking under a gigantic basket. The incandescent night died away, and she had to pause, for the darkness was total. She also felt, for the first time since entering the Fay, very, very cold.

She thought about lighting a torch, but remembered her tinderbox was with her horse.

"Poor Raggle," she said aloud. "It seems I've lost all my friends." She could still feel the rod pulling her, so she slowly stepped forward. She could feel roots and... squishier things underfoot that she dared not even imagine. "I'll never get anywhere going this slow."

An idea dawned on her. She reached into her pockets and felt around. First, she noticed the fruit, still uneaten (though she knew if she brought out the fruits, they would still look perfect and likely never rot anyway, being what they were). She found what she was looking for in the bottom of one of her dress pockets.

She took it out and held it up, and the star lit up the darkness, revealing that she was now underground, though the walls of the cave she stood in were actually the trunks of twisted trees; its ceiling was dense limbs filled with dead leaves, and the floor was roots that crawled on the ground (in some places, they did this literally, moving and searching like tiny snakes). Without having to touch it, she felt the rod pull her forward, and she followed, letting the star illuminate her path.

She began to see light again after a very long time walking in the tunnel (it felt like days to Helga, and could have actually been days — she could feel time stretching in odd ways since she entered into the city of the watchers). She put the star back in her pocket as the light ahead grew bright enough for her to see. Her eyes almost hurt from the brightness at the end of the tunnel, and she stumbled when she exited onto a vast, green plain.

She looked back and could see the forest stretching out to the horizon in either direction. The plain was rich and smelled fresh, and a cool wind blew across it. It reminded her of spring as a child, running without care after all the snow and frost had given way to moss and fresh grass and wildflowers.

"Did we come to the end? Did I escape Faerie?" Helga said. As if in answer, she looked down and saw a dandelion sprout from the ground, turn into a seed ball, and blow away to her right. She watched more flowers sprout, grow seeds, and then blow away. Within moments, whole acres were covered in yellow dandelions that spread and moved over the plain. It reminded Helga sharply of a ripple in a pond, growing wider and weaker as it spread.

She took out the divining rod and followed it again, this time over the empty plain. The hills rolled on for miles and miles under her feet until the standing forest was small and distant. As she crested a hill, she saw before her a huge, twisted hardwood whose branches bent almost to the ground. The rod wanted to pull her past it, but she stopped. It was so familiar... and then her dreams came back to her. She looked up in the tree and saw the squirrel there.

"Hello?"

"Good day," the squirrel said back, and ran down the trunk to meet her. "You've returned, and with the bird. He doesn't look so good, though."

"No, he's..." Helga felt tears welling in her eyes again, and pushed them back. "No, he's not well at all. Maybe I can make him better."

"I hope so. I haven't seen him in a terrible long stretch of years. It gets boring out here by oneself. I made some other squirrels. I hope you don't mind."

Helga looked up in the tree and saw several other furry squirrels in colors of brown and grey. A few of them were staring at her, dark eyes wide.

"You made them?"

"Yes," said the squirrel. "It took a lot of effort. Less than you used, I think."

"I think it's great you have some friends out here, Ratatask."

"Me too. Are you staying?"

"I can't."

"Oh well. Maybe in another few years?"

"Maybe," Helga said.

"Good. I like you." The squirrel ran back up the tree. "There is somebody following you, just so you know."

"Where?"

"Still in the wood. He'll be here soon, though. He has friends."

"Damn it."

"We can slow them down if you like, but they look like they have power. I don't want to risk ourselves too much."

"No, of course not," Helga said. "I should probably hurry on anyway. I have something to find."

"What is it?"

"The Water of Awakening, though I don't know how I shall leave here with it."

"Drinking the water will awaken you," The squirrel said. He hopped over to the edge of the shadow of the tree. "But I don't recommend you leave that way. It won't be as pleasant as last time."

"Last time?"

The squirrel looked at her with a cocked head. "Of course…" He pointed with a paw out over the plain. "No matter. The water is that way. Or used to be."

"Thank you, friend," Helga said.

"Here, before you go." He dug in the soil nearby and pulled up a nut, still looking fresh. "I saved this one a long time. It will grow where you *will* it to grow."

"Thank you," Helga said, and pocketed the nut. "You will not need it?"

"Another one will drop eventually."

"Farewell."

"Take care of Zald."

"I'll try." Helga turned and walked back out into the sun. She let the divining rod pull her in the direction the squirrel had pointed. She kicked herself into a run, which felt more real and physical than it had in the forest, though she still felt more invigorated and stronger than normal.

Soon the grass began to thin and to change color. Rich greens were replaced by dull yellows. Shrubs swayed in the wind around her, twisted and thorny. Her lungs began to hurt with the running, and she slowed to a walk. Miles went by with little change, except in that the landscape became drier and duller. Yellows faded to muted greys and browns. The shrubs became red bushy weeds. She crested a ridge and saw rocky plateaus and mesas ahead. Large, round bushes rolled in the wind, and she saw dust kicking up here and there.

She wondered if she had left the fay at last, and she knelt down to catch her breath. A bead of sweat fell from her forehead and landed in the dirt. Immediately a dandelion sprang up and grew a yellow flower from where the sweat touched the dusty earth. Within seconds it became a puffy seed ball, then disintegrated. The seeds flew off to her left, growing new flowers wherever they landed, which in turn put out more seeds. The color was refreshing, but as the plants spread, they changed. They became taller and more like a nettle, with spiny leaves and twisted stems. They went from green to grey, and the flowers turned to white, then an ugly brown.

Helga took a breath and continued. Miles rolled by, and the day seemed to pass slowly. Somehow, she knew it had to have been much more than a day since she had fled the watchers, but the sun, when she could tell where it was (most often, she was merely aware of a bright white or blue sky), seemed to wander rather than pass from one side of the earth to the other. When she walked by the mesas, she felt suddenly cool in the shadows. The land became rockier, and she had to pick her feet up high and walk carefully among many awkwardly placed small rocks, many of which were broken and sharp.

After countless steps and miles over the rocks, she looked up and saw the edges of what looked like a river course, the ridges of which were lined with dried rushes. She ran ahead and pushed herself through the weeds to look down into a small canyon. At the bottom was nothing but a dry, cracked bed of dust and limestone. She slid down the sides to stand in the canyon. The divining rod had gone limp.

"There's nothing here. Damn it. There's nothing here!"

She wanted to snap the rod, but held back as she felt the rod tug, not so much in her hand as in that part of her being which she had touched in her fight with the watchers. Silently, she followed the weak pulling, which pointed through the canyon. She walked, and at last, the shadows slowly deepened. Her legs began to ache with tiredness, and her mouth felt dry.

The sun dipped below the horizon. In the dark canyon, Helga's eyes grew wide. The cracks in the hardpan glowed a soft green, creating a spider web of light beneath her feet. The shrubs glowed softly, too, in shades of purple and pink. The dried rushes moved in the breeze, glowing amber. Helga watched them sprout small flowers like lilies, and pollen poured out of them as glowing dust. It stuck to her armor and her boots, where it remained shining softly. Succulents in the cracks of rocks flowered and threw forth their own pollen and seeds.

Helga smiled. *There must be water hidden here somewhere.*

However, as she walked on, she saw no water. Slowly, she began to despair again, even though she could still sense the divining rod carrying her onward. She looked up at the sky and saw that not one moon, but several, had risen. One of them was the pale red from Atalthal's realm, but smaller and dimmer. One was the moon she knew. Two were unfamiliar and shone brightly, though they were small.

While distracted, Helga slipped and fell – into mud.

XIII. The Desert of the Soul

HE REACHED with her hands and felt the mud squish in her fingers. She sat up, feeling suddenly joyful. *Where there is mud, there is water.* Looking around, she could see no water, but in the mud, pickleweed grew, and it was brighter than the other plants, sending off motes of pale pink from its light green and red shoots. Helga bent down and picked some from the ground. She ate it, and it was sweet rather than salty. There was some power in the plant, for as she ate it, she felt again the touch and presence of power between her body and mind – a tickle on her soul that she could reach out and grab if she felt for it.

Despite the mud, she could find no stream. There wasn't so much as a puddle. She trudged through the pickleweed, thinking that it looked like a tiny forest in autumn from above, though lit with its own light. Tiny trees swayed in the breeze. As they bent, pushed by Helga's legs, they sent off motes of life, like birds taking wing. Tiny creatures – insects and worms – moved underfoot like the fauna of the forest.

The moons had moved in random directions in the sky when Helga had to stop. The ravine ended with a pile of round rocks and a sheer cliff going up that might once have been a waterfall. The rocks were wet, and as Helga spied among them, she saw that from a dark opening in the rock came the tiniest bit of moisture. A luminescent stalactite hung from this fissure, and a single drop was slowly building on its tip, lit like a dim star.

"It's all gone," Helga said. She looked at the drop. *Maybe if I stay long enough, I can collect those drops. I can collect enough to satisfy the old hag.*

The moons moved across the sky, and light began to grow on every point of the horizon, very slowly at first. The drop on the stalactite had grown no larger.

In final despair, Helga collapsed onto a rock. She hung her head in her hands and wept, harder now than when she was held by the Watchers, and harder than when she had realized Zald was dead. She reached back and felt his body, wrapped in cloth, cold.

She sat and thought about where she was, recalling hazily the dreams she had dreamt on her way to the land beyond lands, the dreams she had crossed – one of a man wishing to be a king, one of a king wishing to be a god, and one of the gods wishing to be men. There was something timeless about the land. She felt with her soul the land's living breath. A part of her, that part which she had grown to know so well on her journey, from which flowed her will and the magic that went with it, spoke wordlessly a strange truth: that in the Eternal Eream, she would not pass like a mortal. She had been changed on the road, and staying here, she would change her still, to be that dream-self she always was, like the Watchers, but with a cruel memory of mortality.

Everything was in vain, and here in this desolate dream, I will be lost forever. Erling will die and depart to the next world, but I will never join him. Like Ratatask, I will be here forever, won't I?

She heard a sound above her and looked up. A shape flew across one moon, then another. It moved through the stars, glowing faintly even with the threat of dawn in the fay.

It was unmistakably the dragon, and she could see its head turning toward her, as if regarding her from a distance. She crouched down, knowing that it would do nothing, but feeling too afraid to stand. The Dragon circled again, coming closer to earth and closer to Helga, making for a landing.

Her fear was snapped by the crashing of magic near her head, shattering the rocks and the fissure that issued forth the single drop of water, now gone. Helga scrambled to her feet and saw, coming down the ravine, all four of the Watcher kings. She glanced away to see the

Dragon land on the mountain near her. Flame leaked from his nostrils, and there was no doubt his strange eyes were fixed on her. More magic was flung her way by the watchers: flames of green and blue burst around her, singeing her hair and clothes.

"If you are here to kill me," Helga shouted to the dragon, "then I don't care. Just let me kill these vile watchers so I can die at least a half-satisfied woman."

The dragon tilted its head and then laughed. It was deep and unfathomably loud. It was as if the earth was quaking, and the pickleweed at Helga's feet shrank into the ground like anemones. Rocks went loose and fell down the mountain in dusty streams.

"Go then," the dragon said in his deep, booming voice, which held in it no echo as if he were speaking into her ear. "Though it is not a fair fight." His amber eyes locked with hers, and she imagined that he smiled, as much as a dragon could.

Helga turned away from the dragon, feeling hotter in her cheeks from being mocked than by her impending doom. At least she would give the watchers a last, good fight.

She felt to that edge of her soul — that magical thing she could command and sense with, indescribable and beyond even her own comprehension, like trying to grasp touch itself. Power of thought and the infinite dreams of life coursed through her, and she felt the wind at her back and her feet firmly in the ground. Light and heat she felt for, and found, primal and raging, eager to leap forth, contained in her mind in concept and reality.

She raced forward toward the watchers. As she raced, vines and tendrils of living thorns burst from the ground to twist around her legs and arms. As they touched her, the heat inside her was unleashed and withered all. Next, trees were cast up. They, too, burned under her feet even as they grew.

The watchers spread out, their eyes burning bright like tiny suns, but Helga was closing the distance quickly. They chanted something Helga could not understand, but from their words, the earth burst asunder. Helga leapt over the fissures. Even as she did so, twisted beasts broke free from the earth. Helga stumbled and fell as the ground under her feet rose suddenly and threw her backward.

A great eyeless beast emerged, twice as tall as a horse with two great bleached tusks protruding from its gaping mouth. Its sickly pale skin was drawn tight over bone shields where its eyes should have been. It apparently did not need its eyes, for it pointed its mouth at Helga and leapt, its slobbering mouth growling.

Too desperate and filled with power to feel fear, Helga put her left foot forward and swung her poleax to meet the mighty beast, feeling strength and speed moving in her body. The tusks each brushed her sides as she brought the weapon down. It landed where the eyes should have been with a deafening crack. The head split asunder as the poleax continued its arc into the ground, splitting the rocky riverbed and creating a great crack in the earth that disrupted the chanting of the Watchers.

The beast gave a dreadful cry and gurgle as it died. Helga jumped over it, a greater leap than she had ever thought she could do, and thrust a hand toward the closest watcher, who she saw was David.

He raised his hands to create a shield of vines, but they were already being blown away like dust. He put up his hands over his face as a final defense. Helga struck at him with the crow's beak. It connected with David's arms and pierced through, then slammed into his chest. They both went tumbling forward.

When David died, it was not like the watcher Helga had killed earlier. He did not recede into the earth with open eyes. He died like a man, gasping and rattling and trying to cry in pain, though his lungs were filling with blood and his ribcage was crushed. His eyes, burning like stars, dulled to a soft, human brown, then went dim, withering into his own head.

Helga twisted the poleax to dislodge it, but it would not budge. She raised her arm just in time to deflect a ball of fire cast by Kahn. The spell split apart on her vambrace and raced over her armor, singeing but not burning. Helga left the poleax and drew her sword. She rushed Kahn, but in the space it took to slay David, the watchers had grown more cautious. Kahn stepped quickly back, away from Helga's swings. He conjured bamboo from the earth to build a wall. Helga's sword cut through it like it was nothing, and the plants disintegrated into motes of light as she jumped through to hack at Kahn.

The other two hurled spells at her as she attacked Kahn. Some of these she felt land like heavy rocks; others missed or only glanced along her armor. None budged her feet or burned her, and her focus on her enemy was total.

She reached out to the fire in herself again and unleashed everything she could feel and think of into Kahn, whose clothes burst into flame. His flesh seared and blackened. It wrinkled and withdrew to bone, but the king would not die. He drew from his scabbard a sword, but Helga could see him do it weakly. She attacked his legs and cut them. He collapsed, screaming in pain. She ran him through without mercy, already stepping past him to focus on the remaining two kings.

She pulled her sword free, feeling the fire oddly sated and withdrawn from her, to see Eric and Ramses drawing their own swords, which were lit with a pale magic fire. They attacked in tandem, their swords flinging magic from them as they continued their chanting.

She felt suddenly devoid of anger and of fear, feeling cool and thoughtful as if time had slowed. Helga felt with her deeper senses the magic they were using and let that guide her movements. She could feel earth tearing, and she leapt away. Wind rushed, and she would push air from the other direction. Fire she ignored, for it seemed to have no effect on her. She swung her sword as swiftly as she could, for she had never been trained in the use of a blade, and hoped that her speed might make up for lack of skill.

The watchers were not unskilled, however, and deftly parried Helga's wild attacks. Helga pushed harder and harder, but the watchers matched her and seemed to be in cool control all the while. Time seemed to slow even more as she focused, and she could see their attacks almost before they were happening. Ramses or Eric would step back, and Helga could see what way he was swinging his sword. She attacked at the weaknesses she could see, but both of them adapted quickly, parrying each sword swing, though they were always backpedaling.

Finally, a thought occurred to Helga. She dug her toe into the dirt and kicked up a wet clod of soil and weeds into Eric's face. Blinded, he swung his sword wildly. Helga rushed in, knocked his sword away, and cut him across his ribcage. Her sword, though ancient, was deadly sharp. It sliced Eric nearly to his spine. He collapsed. Helga did not wait to see his death throws.

She rounded on Ramses, who wielded a long sword much like her own. Something changed in the strange king, for his eyes went from a bright white to a shade of cool blue, and his mouth twisted into a grimace, the first emotion Helga had seen from him.

He went on the attack, hacking and slashing at Helga. She did not have the skill to parry the attacks, but her armor was strong. The watcher's cuts did little, and she felt more pain from the force of the blows than from the bite of the blade. She swung back as much as she could, but found herself desperately trying to protect her vitals from the well-aimed swings of the watcher where she was not armored.

She started to feel tiredness in her lungs and pain in her side. Her feet felt uneven, and she felt hot, trying desperately to repel the attack of the shorter Ramses. The magic seemed out of her mind's reach, either exhausted or sated (as she felt the heat was).

In a last effort, she sprang forward and met Ramses, turning the blade aimed for her neck with her left vambrace. Her arm sprang alive in pain. She felt her bones breaking, but she already had a hold of Ramses. He fell backward with her on top, and she drew Peridan's dagger. Ramses crossed his arms to block the dagger coming down from above. Their arms collided, but not far enough away from Ramses's neck, and the tip of the dagger met his flesh. Ramses screamed in surprise, weakening slightly. Helga put her left arm (which radiated pain from being broken) on top of her right and pushed down with all her weight and strength.

It was enough, and the dagger went through Ramses's neck, all the way into the dirt. His eyes fixed on Helga with deep sadness, turning truly to blue human's eyes before withering away. His body, like a human's, remained on the ground, but it looked hollow and empty – more like a clay vessel than a man.

Helga fell back, panting. She suddenly remembered the dragon, but was too weak to stand. She searched for her magic, but it was beyond reach. Before she could turn to look upon her doom, she heard a new sound: many feet running over hard earth. She lifted her head weakly. In front of her, cresting a hill above the dried riverbed, was a horde of watchers, holding weapons or conjuring magic in their eyes and hands. They sang a strange, haunting song that fell dead on the muddy earth.

Tears flowed again, unbidden. None of it was enough. She had spent everything she had, and there was none left even to flee the watchers for one last race, or to turn and run from the dragon. She struggled to pull the dagger free of Ramses's body, thinking that in the end, she could kill herself rather than losing her soul, but she felt like a weak child, and the dagger would not budge.

Helga got to her knees and then her feet, though the effort was immense. She spread her hands out and turned back to the ruined rocks and the lost fissure, hoping the dragon would kill her swiftly.

It did not. It was no longer there.

Helga snapped her head to the sky to see the wyrm flying in from above. It landed with a mighty crash among the watchers sending rock and dirt everywhere. Those in the vanguard had not the time to consider the new threat, and the dragon, in swift bites, swallowed them. He was even bigger than Helga realized. His head alone had to have been eight feet tall, and the rest of him was proportionally large, so he stood towering above them.

His claws, like gigantic scythes, swung through the watchers, sending them flying or cutting them to pieces. He breathed fire and burned down others, which he then ate with speed and vigor. They turned to fight him, conjuring magic that did nothing to the dragon. He lashed them down with his great tail, or burned them with his fire, or ate them whole, one by one. Many turned to flee. The dragon took flight and scooped some of these up in his hands, then ate them. A few were left to escape, and Helga knew that they were surviving by the dragon's choice rather than their own effort. That, as much as her exhaustion, let her know flight was futile.

Those that were dead the dragon returned to eat, one at a time and usually whole, grumbling with satisfaction as he did so.

Helga watched as the dragon took flight again, circling around the battlefield as if looking for stragglers. He landed in front of Helga and sat up. A great red tongue came out of his mouth, and he licked his lips.

"I have not the strength to fight you," she said.

"Which is good, because you would not stand a chance," the dragon replied. His deep voice rumbled and stirred the dust, but seemed softer than before.

"Are you going to eat the kings, too?" Helga said, wondering if she could at least delay her death a few minutes longer.

"No. They have become too mortal now," the dragon said. "Eternal beings must eat eternal things, you see."

"What?" Helga said.

"Gather your things, my lion. You have been here far too long. Far longer than any mortal I know, and that means far too long, considering the great heroes and sages who have lost themselves in the eternal dream before you."

"I don't understand." Helga shook her head.

"Your weapons. You will need them soon, but of course not for me," the dragon said. "For other things. Important things. I need a few minutes to let my meal settle, so don't take what I said to mean you ought to rush. When you are ready, I will take you from this place."

"You will? You won't eat me?"

"As I said, eternal beings must eat eternal things. And your body is not eternal. Not yet. Perhaps if you remained here, continuing to change yourself, but no, not yet."

Helga pushed herself to her feet, her knees knocking and shaking. She stepped on the body of Ramses, which seemed to be withering by the minute, and withdrew Peridan's ivory hilted dagger. She wiped it on Ramses's shirt and re-sheathed it. The simple effort seemed immense, and she sat down again. After slowing her breathing, she stood up and retrieved her sword from the ground, then worked the poleax out of the body of David. She sighed and leaned on it, feeling fresh pain in her broken left arm.

"All this, for nothing," she said.

"Not nothing," the dragon said.

"I have not gained what I sought. In the end, the object of my quest did not even exist."

"But you did gain many other things, did you not?" the dragon stood up and walked toward Helga on his huge legs, shaking the earth. Helga could not help but feel afraid that he might be toying with her and decide to kill her anyway. "No man looks back on the dreams of his childhood and considers himself a failure for not fulfilling them."

"I am not a man."

"An excellent point, Helga Ravenfriend," the dragon said.

"How do you know my name?"

"I know lots of things. My name is Garamesh, by the way. Don't misuse it."

The dragon picked up Helga with one of his hands, far more gently than Helga had thought possible, and closed his claws around her. He held her up high.

"This was the heart of the eternal dream, once, when the Prim flowed freely and in greater quantity than it does now. Take a good look, for you may need to find it again one day."

The dragon leapt into the air. The beating of his wings was almost deafening, as was the sudden pressure on Helga's ears. She looked down to see a vast desert, though filled with the life of strange plants and creatures that stretched out to grasslands, and finally the forest in a vast ring. A riverbed cut through everything, and as she rose, her mind reeled with the scope.

"It's so big," Helga shouted over the rushing of air.

"The heart of dreams is tiny compared to what it once was. At one time, the World-That-Is was the strange place, and the Fay was the familiar and normal. Now, it is dying."

"Why?"

"Because the dreamers have made real their dreams. The world is as you have imagined it, Helga Ravenfriend. You and all your kind, including the elves."

Helga saw one last glimpse of the land of Faerie, and the dry heart of dreams before the dragon flew into clouds, and all became white. He emerged on top of the clouds, which spread out beneath them like a rolling sea. Billowing waves swept across the white ocean as the wind whipped about. Far in the distance, Helga could see great peaks of snowy white with rocks protruding from glaciers.

"Where are you taking me?" she said.

"To my resting place, for you need rest gravely."

"I don't feel tired. Come to think of it, I don't remember the last time I slept."

"You are more grievously injured than you realize, and you will feel it, now that we are leaving the fay. You have spent a long time in waking dreams, but your body will remember reality soon, changed though it is."

"What about Raggle? What about my horse?"

"Do not fret over Raggle," Garamesh said. "He is wild and free now and has his own tasks."

The mountains grew larger and more defined. Helga looked down on the fay waste, wrapped in mist. The scattered willow trees were bare, and the waterways were fallow. Garamesh swooped low, and the wind of his wings swept away the mist, revealing snow and ice among the water. He began flapping his wings and gained altitude again, rushing over pines and rocky crags, going higher into the mountains.

The further and faster they went, the more pain Helga began to feel in her arm. She couldn't see her arms or hands while cradled in the dragon's massive talons, but she knew her fingertips on her left arm were going numb and becoming swollen. Her head began to hurt terribly, too. True to the dragon's word, she felt more and more like she was waking from a dream to find that she was hurt.

Garamesh swept past the first snowy peaks and rushed northward to others, taller and blue with everlasting glaciers. He dropped down into a valley devoid of vegetation and filled with sharp sheer boulders, the rocky white mountains reaching up above them like old men with broken skulls protruding from their white hair and beards. Iced waterfalls lined the rocky walls, and Helga could see the breath of the dragon, like great clouds of steam, rolling over her and back to his huge, swishing tail.

"Everything is frozen," she called out, watching the flows of ice race past her.

"You've been out of this world for a good stretch of months," Garamesh said. "It is winter now."

"Erling must be dead by now," Helga said to herself, quietly beneath the sound of rushing air.

The wings beat again, and the dragon was up and over a ridge, then banking through fog into a lower valley. The fog thinned, and Helga saw a woodland below her, of autumn-colored leaves swaying beneath the wind of the dragon. They circled around, and Garamesh slowed, landing softly on an outcropping of rock extending from a great cave in a sheer cliff. Water dripped over the rocks to either side, collecting in a calm pool on a plateau below.

When the dragon landed, he set Helga down carefully. "Here is a resting place. It is probably not well suited to… a human, but it is what I have. Come."

Garamesh then crawled inside the enormous cave, leaving Helga to look out upon the valley. Other than the pool below the outcropping, it was a sheer drop of hundreds of feet to the trees below. She shivered, and, not knowing what else to do besides trust the dragon (*If he wanted to devour me, he surely would have already,* she thought), she went inside the cave.

241

It was bigger on the inside than even the great entrance would reveal. The rocks were worn smooth and even, and were of many crystalline shades. Pinks and purples merged with pale yellows, and all of them seemed to glow with a soft light of their own. She worked her way over the floor, which was slippery and uneven, full of sharp protrusions, trying to see where the dragon was going. Her arm now pained her terribly, and had she not been clutching at her poleax, she would have clutched the broken limb. As it was, all she could do was let it hang limp.

Passageways girded by great masonry arches seemed to open on either side of the long tunnel going from the entrance, all dark. Eventually, the tunnel opened up into a large room, lit softly by the glow of the dragon's fire and luminescent veins of blue and purple running through the living stone. It felt warm and comfortable despite its strangeness.

Helga put down her poleax and sat. She removed the glove from her left hand with much effort and looked at her fingers, red and swollen. She wondered how she would be able to get her armor off without the use of that arm, but as she sat, new feelings returned to her: drowsiness and a deep emptiness in the pit of her stomach.

She did her best to ignore them, and undid her sword belt, and pulled forth the body of Zald. She looked at the wrapped bird and sighed softly.

"I'm hungry," she said aloud. The dragon, which lay curled at one end of the cavern, picked up his head and turned his glowing eyes on her. "Why am I so hungry?"

"You have not eaten food of physical substance in a long time," Garamesh said.

"All of my provisions were with Raggle."

"Are you sure?"

Helga thought for a moment and remembered the fruit in her pocket. She reached in and withdrew the cherry, a small orange from the fay waste, a strange fruit that Atalthal had given her, and a nut.

"It's better than nothing," she said, looking at her vittles.

"Far better." The cavern shook as the dragon laughed.

Helga tore open the orange and ate it quickly, even swallowing some of the seeds. She immediately felt better. The pain in her arm even seemed to subside slightly. She considered eating Atalthal's fruit, for it was fairly large, but before she could, she felt herself collapsing down to the ground. Her eyes felt heavy. She was nowhere near comfortable wearing her armor and lying on cold stone, but it didn't seem to matter. She fell into a deep sleep.

XIV. Memories of Myth

HELGA WAS DREAMING, and though it felt profoundly real, she knew it was a dream. There was a feeling inside her, in the space between her mind and body that could instinctively understand she was not in the real world. She felt powerful here and felt her instincts were truer than when waking.

She was on a grassy plain, and a familiar tree stood a ways off. She was not wearing her armor, she saw, but a simple dress of linen that was light and breathable. She walked toward the tree and saw the squirrels moving this way and that along the branches.

"We slowed them down for you," Ratatask said as she stepped into the shade.

"I know. Thank you. Did they all die?"

"All that came this way."

"What about those that didn't?"

"I would have to ask around."

Helga nodded. "I set two of the watchers on another path, not knowing what I was doing. I named them. I am curious now what became of them."

"You named me," the squirrel said.

"So I did. This is my realm, isn't it? This little place. Funny that it has remained when so much seems to change all the time."

"It was yours. It is mine now," the squirrel said. "You would make different worlds now, right? You have become so different."

"Yes, but I like this place. It is not a place to stay forever, for me, but it is a place to return to, once."

Helga knelt down and felt for that place that itched in her spirit. She thought of a flower, and one grew before her, orange and yellow.

"Pretty," the squirrel said.

"Something to remember me by. I liked flowers once. I probably still do. I wore orange ones like this on my wedding day."

***

Helga woke to find that she was still in the cave, but she was curiously naked underneath a blanket on a bed of straw. A small fire of wood was burning in the cave, but there was no dragon. Her armor and boots were laid out on a nearby stone, and her padded jack hung on a line strung between other rocks in the cavern.

A large shadow on the wall made Helga start and look about for her sword, but she could not find it. She relaxed slightly as she saw a middle-aged woman emerge from around the fire, carrying Helga's split-skirt dress on her arm. She had greying blonde hair and wore a simple dress of wool. She hummed softly to herself in a high, sweet voice.

"Oh my, you've finally opened your eyes," the woman said. She carefully hung up the dress, which was dripping wet. "I was beginning to think you never would."

Helga tried to speak, to ask who the woman was, but her voice and throat hurt from the effort.

"Would you like some water?"

Helga nodded.

"Just a moment." The woman disappeared behind the fire, casting her great shadow on the glowing walls, and then returned with a waterskin, which she held to Helga's lips. Helga reached up to take it and realized that her arm was wrapped in linen with a wooden splint. Consenting to the help, Helga drank deeply, feeling the water work its way down her throat, icy cold, and relieve some part of her arid voice.

"Thank you," Helga said.

"Nothing at all," the woman said. "Well, not nothing. Quite a bit, actually. You're welcome. How's that?"

Helga nodded. "Who are you?"

246

"Oh yes, you wouldn't know my name, would you? You've been asleep so long. My name is Tisha. Garamesh brought me here to tend to you. He and I have an agreement, of sorts, that frankly I never expected him to collect on."

"How long have I slept?"

"I'm not sure. It's been three days since I came here. I think you might have been sleeping before that, though."

"I know this will sound a bit odd-"

"Not at all," Tisha said. "I'm in a dragon cave caring for a sleeping woman warrior, and a mage too, I would guess. What else could possibly sound odd?"

"When is it?"

"Morning, dear."

"What season?"

"Winter. We're ten days past the new year."

Helga sat up and wrapped her blanket around herself. "Um... what year?"

"Twenty-five eighty-seven. Fourth dominion, if you follow the new ways."

Helga nodded. It was still short of a year since she had set out. She must have spent eight months at least within the Fay. Erling was almost certainly dead, but there was a glimmer of hope in her heart, and though she knew it was foolish, she put that hope forefront in her mind. Maybe there was still a way to save him. That hope felt oddly out of place now, like the memory of enjoyment of a child's game, where when one condescends to the toss of the dice, the nostalgia of the act is more pleasurable than the act itself.

She sighed, and another desperate thought came to her.

"Where is Zald?" Helga said.

"That's not the dragon's name. It's Garamesh."

"No. Zald is a Raven. I had him with me."

"Child," Tisha said sadly. "He was dead."

"I know," Helga said. "Where is he?"

"I... buried it. Was I not supposed to? I saved a few of the quills."

Helga gritted her teeth. The thought of taking Zald's feathers made her think of taking the hair of a dead woman – somehow dishonorable. Helga took a breath.

"I cannot fault you. I likely would have done the same. I just thought…" Helga shook her head. "I just thought that there might be a way to bring him back."

"From the dead?"

"He died helping me. I was hoping… it was a fool's hope, but in the Fay, there is so much power; so much is possible!"

"Not that. Child, nobody has that power. Even a necromancer can only animate the inanimate body, not bring life. When the spirit is severed, it cannot return. Not until the world is broken and all of Hel is unleashed at the last."

Helga lay back down. "How do you know Garamesh?"

"He plucked me from a river when I was a little girl, told me I was to be volva, not a fisherwoman, then told me he would collect on the favor of saving my life in kind."

"Is that what you are? A volva?"

"Oh, I'm lots of things. Mostly I'm mother and wife, but I'm doctor and volva too, when my clan needs it."

"Do you know Rafnhild?"

"Isn't that you?"

"No, I am Helga."

"Sorry, Garamesh called you Ravenfriend. I don't know of any Rafnhild, but we seeresses do not hold a guild. What village?"

"Greenfeld. Well, that's where I am from. I don't know where she was from. I think maybe the next town over."

"Interesting," Tisha said. She knelt down by the fire and hung a cauldron over it, which began to steam. "Why are you so concerned with her?"

"It's her that sent me on this infernal quest. This fruitless, pointless expedition."

Tisha laughed.

"What is so funny?" Helga said.

248

"Just imagining the dragon. He'd tell you your journey was far from fruitless or pointless. Although, she can't have been a very good seer to send you to the watchers, or the heart of the fay."

"I've heard this sentiment."

"But you didn't listen."

"I listened, but I had already made a deal."

"Clearly not one you were intended to survive."

"No," Helga protested. "I think she just didn't understand the danger, having not really been anywhere."

"Still, you continued. Why didn't you have help?"

"I did," Helga said. "I had Thorvald, a good warrior of a man, but he didn't want me to go on with my quest. I had Peridan, for a time, and the Black Feather Friends – they're a group of ravens. Zald was one."

"I see." Tisha poured the contents of the cauldron into a shallow and wide earthen bowl. She placed it near to Helga. It smelled rich and earthy. "For the humours and the pain. Wondrous what even a little pinch of Luminous Russula will do. Now, nobody helped you from your village?"

"What did you say? Luminous Russula?"

"It's a rare mushroom used for healing, don't fret over it. Nobody from your village would help you?"

"Well, two men helped me for a few days, but I harped at them and chased them off," Helga said. "Even they thought I was being foolish, like everybody else, and just thought a few days on the road would send me home."

"Perhaps that would have been a good indicator as to the validity of your errand, eh? I know if I had a way to save my own husband – a credible, real way, that is – no less than twenty men from my clan would lend their shields to my cause."

"Why must you castigate me?" Helga said. "Is it not enough to have failed and to suffer pain?"

"Forgive me," Tisha said, standing and holding up Helga's dress to examine it. "After being a mother so long, you start to view life as just an unending series of hard-learned lessons. Ah, this is a very fine dress. It's too bad it's got so much damage. I bet I could fix it, though."

"Yes, it is a very fine dress. Given to me by a king, of sorts."

"And you say your journey was without profit." Tisha laughed. "Do not be too hard on yourself, Helga Ravenfriend. We take what chances we can for those we love. Now, get some more rest. Your bones have much knitting to do. The vapors will help them on their way."

Tisha bent down and adjusted Helga's pillow, smiling and humming to herself. She got up when she was finished and disappeared around a tall rock. Helga lay on her back. She felt her arm, which hurt much less than she expected. It was still tender and sore, leaping to red pain if she pushed on the skin. She could feel the bones where she knew they ought to be broken, but they were not. At least, they were already mending, and she could not feel the severe breaks she had suffered at the hands of the watchers.

Staring up at the ceiling, with its pulsing, racing veins of magic, she felt like resting, and she closed her eyes to a blessedly dreamless sleep.

*

Helga woke. The fire in the cave had gone out, but everything was still lit by the glowing veins in the rock, softly growing and decaying, slowly changing between hues of green, blue, and purple-red. Helga sat up and felt her arm, which was missing the splint now. She felt down the length of it and detected two subtle knots, one in each bone of her forearm. She flexed her fingers, and they felt stiff but whole. A slight pain lingered when she made a fist.

In the glow, she could see her dress laid on a nearby rock. She got out of the bedroll, feeling her skin tingle and turn to goosebumps, even though the cave was not particularly cold. She picked up the clothing and noticed that it had been mended in many places. The amber dress was an incomparably beautiful thing, though she hadn't taken time to really look at it before. It shimmered under her fingers, and she smiled as she looked at the delicate needlework that adorned the neckline.

A low rumbling sound made her start and cover her naked body with the dress. She turned around quickly, looking for her sword. She saw around a boulder the hulking body of the dragon. He gave a sort of sigh (or as near to a sigh as a dragon can give) and looked over the rock at Helga.

"You are mended, it seems."

Helga continued holding the dress to her body, though she knew it was unlikely a dragon had salacious thoughts about women. "Where is Tisha?"

"Back home. She put you on the path to healing, but I would not compel her to stay longer than a week and a day apart from her family."

"Thank you."

The dragon laughed, and the walls shook. "You are welcome, Helga Ravenfriend."

"I don't think I am a raven friend any longer," Helga said. "Zald is dead. Zim and Zul have abandoned me. They might be dead, too. I don't think they will forgive me."

"For you, once is always. You must get past your permanence," Garamesh said. "They scattered at Zald's death because of the release of his will that bound them to him."

"What do you mean? Zim was the leader."

"Zim was created by Zald, as was Zul. Did you not gather that yourself?"

"No."

The dragon tilted his head. "Yes. Zald was lonely, as you were lonely, so in the heart of dreams, he created the companions he wished to be himself, which is not so uncommon an action for creators in all realms. Zim was powerful, as Zald saw power, and clever, and had a wise mate. With Zald gone, they are free to go their own way now, but they remain as he created them."

"There is no way to bring back Zald?"

"You would not want to," Garamesh said. "Let him go. His own will and choices guided him at the end, and he was freed as a mortal of his own will, having found his creator in the end, as all beings wish."

Helga thought about the tree in the dream and remembered suddenly dark wings in the air. "I created him."

Garamesh said softly. "Yes, but he was freed quickly from your dream."

"He wasn't a raven when I made him."

"He became what he thought he should be." The dragon laughed again. "It's always so interesting to see what some beings make of themselves. Do not trouble your heart, Helga."

"I think I'm going to cry."

"There is nothing wrong with crying. You should dress when you feel ready. You have much to do and far to go, even now. Tisha brought you some better traveling clothes than that dress."

Helga nodded and sat down. She did cry for Zald.

When she felt better, she stood up and found new trousers and a light shirt of linen to wear. She carefully folded the dress and tucked it into a drawstring sack that Tisha had left for her. Nearby, she found, covered with an oilcloth, her weapons and armor, and near the now cold hearth, she found another small, well-sewn bag of red silk. She opened it and had to shut her eyes against the starlight inside. She took out the star and held it up, seeing for the first time the real detail of the cave, which was almost overwhelming.

In the sides of the rock, and in the living ceiling split by many crystals and veins of bright magic, there were carvings, too numerous and too detailed to take in, except when focusing on one at a time. Dragons wheeled among men in arms and armor. Other beasts were there too, ones that were strange and frightening. Some of the crystals, she could see now, made up the carvings: two glowing eyes in one place, and red twisting veins of fire breath from a carved dragon. Figures of gods she thought she could recognize, along with others that were unfamiliar, lined the edges of the massive room.

"Did you carve all of this?" Helga asked.

"I have not the skill," Garamesh said. "They were made long ago by a far-sighted... well, I guess you would call him a man, but 'man' was not so much a thing back then."

"How did he reach so high? The ceiling must be a hundred feet in the air."

"With his mind," Garamesh said with a chuckle.

Helga gaped at the scale. The more she stared, the more detail she saw; trees stretched across the scenes and waters that glowed blue with the magic strands in the rock. She walked toward a far wall of the cavern, seeing there a compelling figure carved in stone. She was a woman, or an elf, with eyes that glowed of their own power, but also seemed to fade to darkness from certain angles. She held a spear and sat on a throne. Above her, in much less relief, as if in the background, there stood an immense dragon. She saw that in the queen's hand was a crystal growing from the living rock, but it was dark. She gazed upon the face and placed it – she had seen it in a complex tapestry in the halls of Atalthalda.

She felt the air move as Garamesh turned his head about to look with her.

"An old memory," he said. "Only the dark elves still hold it dear."

"I remember."

"Do you?"

Helga turned back to look into the dragon's unknowable eyes.

"Where do I go from here?"

"Back to where you started, of course," the dragon said. "I can help you along the way."

"I loathe to return empty-handed," Helga said, "but I suppose I never should have left. I know you are going to tell me I'm not empty-handed while I hold a star, but I do not have what I sought to gain. I was bound by oath to gain it-"

"The water of awakening," Garamesh said. When the dragon spoke, with his deep, rumbling voice, there was no chance of continuing.

"Yes."

"Why did you seek it?"

"My husband is ill," Helga said. "I made an agreement with a vol-va, that she would cure him in return for a sample of the water of awakening."

"Did you? Are you sure?"

"I did."

"Hmn. Perhaps I can help you. I do not make a habit of helping mortals with gifts, but then again…" The dragon sat up on his hind legs, rumbling the earth. He folded his wings and rested his great horned head on his hand and looked to be thinking. "Go find a bottle or two. And keep them small. The second passage on the right, if you are heading out, will have some, as it was once a lab for an alchemist."

"Did you not always live here?"

"Not always. The world changes. I remain. I cannot stay in one place forever. Go."

Helga nodded and walked toward the large open hallway at the far end of the cavern. As she exited the large room, she felt chill and realized how thin her linen shirt was, and also how warm the dragon kept his lair. She raised up the star, which filled the hallway with bright white light, and she saw that it was not a mere cave, but an intricately made stonework palace, with rafters cut from the rock and stone reliefs of men and women, worn down by the centuries. The second passage on the right loomed up before her, and she perceived the remains of great iron hinges, though the wood of the door had been burned or rotted away.

She walked inside to find not one room but several, connected by a foyer. Iron poles were fixed into the stone walls, presumably to hold tapestries, but were now empty. Tables of stone and iron lined the walls, and rotted wood stood in debris piles that were probably once tables and chairs. A thick layer of dust covered everything, but under the dust, she could see glasswork of various sizes, still amazingly intact after the many centuries when all else had turned to nothing.

She picked out several bottles. As she picked them up, she heard the sound of running water in an adjoining room. She walked in to find a fountain of sorts: a steady stream of clear water was running from an opening in the rock into a carved basin, which then drained away; to where, Helga could not guess. She ran the bottles under the water to rinse them off and took a long drink for herself, realizing that she ought to be parched from being so long asleep.

She carried the bottles back to Garamesh's great room and found the dragon still there in thought. He saw her and bent back down, laying his stomach on the ground. He laid out his neck so that his enormous head sat on the floor in front of Helga.

"Come closer."

Helga stepped closer, seeing now the huge overlapping scales that covered Garamesh, mottled black and red and airtight in their fit with one another, shining like glass and steel combined. Horns of metallic ivory sprouted from the Dragon's brows and skull, and from the sides of his head. Each one was as large and tall as Helga. His nostrils breathed brutally hot air, but it was the eyes that frightened her the most. As she approached the eyes of the wyrm, her pulse quickened, and she felt sweat working its way to the surface of her skin. Garamesh's wavering, vertical pupils regarded her with an inner light that was inhuman and fathomless. She held her breath as she saw water collecting in the corner of the dragon's eye.

Not knowing what else to do, she stepped forward and held the bottle up to the edge of the Dragon's eye. Water ran down into the bottle, clear as crystal and yet glowing with its own light.

The dragon raised his head and sat up again.

"Your tears?" Helga said.

"Shed for Helga that was; Helga the Lion; gone now and replaced with Helga Ravenfriend. It is the Water of Awakening, which you have sought wrongly in its utter source. Give that to your volva."

"Thank you."

"It is a more precious substance than you realize."

"No, I understand how precious, now that I have seen the dry-lands."

The dragon nodded his head. "I have one more gift for you." Garamesh took the claw of one hand and reached to his belly. He worked the claw under a scale and then pulled the claw free. Hanging on the tip was a drop of black-green blood that was slightly luminescent and shimmering.

Helga held up the other bottle, and the enormous drop fell in. It did not coat the glass or thin itself, but remained whole in the bottom, like a drop of quicksilver.

"This is a terrible poison, but it is also life. It takes years to create. Use it wisely."

Helga nodded. She set aside the bottles. There were ancient copper lids that went with them, the cork dried and crumbling. She made these watertight by running around the edge a piece of leather thong scavenged from the bag Tisha had left. Carefully, she added the sealed bottles to her bag and nestled them in the folds of her dress.

"It is time to go," Garamesh said.

Helga gathered her things, rolling up her bedroll and tying it tight with a leather thong. She put on her padded jack and armor, which felt just as wondrously light as when she had first donned them. Inside her helm, she found a small leather-bound package and letter. She folded it carefully and put it in her belt pouch to read later. Inside the package were several bottles and small bags of herbs, along with a tiny book with runes she did not recognize across the front. There was also, she was delighted to see, a nut, a cherry, and Atalthal's fruit. Feeling hungry just seeing these, she tore open Atalthal's fruit. It was sweet and sour, like an orange but with crispy flesh like an apple or pear. Inside was one great pit, which she put in her bag, thinking she might try planting it in her garden when she got home.

The fruit set to work on her immediately, suppressing her hunger and making her feel refreshed and energized. *The fruits of the Fay are generous,* she thought.

She put Tisha's package into the bag. She tied her helm to her belt and slung her burden on her shoulder. She followed the dragon out through the great hallway. She held aloft the star and looked again at the great work of masonry and carving that surrounded her. Each face she passed seemed to tell a story, and as they ascended, she began to see remnants of other decorations: broken pots and fallen occasional tables; rusted swords and rotted shields. Rune-covered inscriptions appeared along walls, but the letters were strange to her, and she wondered what they meant.

As if sensing her thoughts, the dragon said, "There is much here that is forgotten. It is a pity, what befell Peridan's heart, for once he would have delighted in this place."

"Part of him delighted in Atalthal's realm," Helga said. "I could see him spending many years here in study."

"A true tragedy, then."

"How did he fall?" Helga asked. She realized she was coming to accept the reach of Garamesh's vision.

"The world of men can be corrupting. He spent too long studying the darker arts of the world. Originally, it was in hopes of understanding and combating the darkness."

Helga allowed silence to fill the space, punctuated by the landing of the dragon's great feet and his dark, heavy breathing. At last, she gave voice to the question in her heart, which filled her with fear. "Why did you eat the watchers?"

Garamesh grumbled. "They are not beings that can exist in Midgard and remain themselves. The dun-men you met were like the watchers once, but they are not by their nature permanent. A life of suffering is the destiny of those who seek to have a nature other than their own. And, more importantly, they willingly became corrupt. They attempted to do something profoundly evil, something that is within my dominion to pass judgment upon. They had to be returned to the Prim to be remade."

"I understand."

"Do you?"

"Well, maybe not," Helga said. "But maybe I don't need to understand."

They emerged in the sunlight, and Helga stepped out onto the outcropping of rock to see that it too was once made of well-cut stone, now worn away. She could see a broken stair leading down to the pool below, and noticed now that the pool ran calmly over the edge of a stone parapet to the autumn-colored forest below. Among the trees, she could make out more ruins, some grand and some mere piles of stone.

Helga felt the dragon's claws wrap around her, and seconds later, her hair was being whipped about by the wind and the beating of Garamesh's wings. He flew south and west, skirting snow-covered peaks and rocky cliffs. After a time, the mountains shrank and became more hill-like. Helga could see off to her left a faint grey line that she knew must be the fay waste, but Garamesh was not taking her there.

Finally, they flew over a mountain, and Helga could see a familiar line of grey stone buildings and a forest that remained oddly-colored yellows and greens.

"Are you taking me back to the ruins of Atalthalda?" she cried out over the wind.

"If you wish it. You could wake Atalthal, if you willed it."

Helga hesitated. "He is where he wishes to be, I think."

"But not necessarily where he needs to be," Garamesh said. "He was a mighty hero, once."

"No," Helga said at last. "Let him stay there."

"Very well," Garamesh said.

He started to fly downward and finally landed in a pristine snow-covered clearing in the mountains. As his wings flapped, the loose snow and ice flew around, biting Helga's face. He gently put her down in the white powder, which was melting as he breathed.

"Here I must leave you," he said.

"What? I was expecting door-side service from my dragon carriage," Helga said.

The dragon laughed. "There you are."

Helga cocked her head in confusion.

The dragon looked westward, but Helga could see only an expanse of trees and snow. "It is not my place to go so far into men's lands or to interfere more than I have. It is man's place to walk the earth, and on the ground will he meet his needs and the needs of the earth."

"And what about a woman?"

"I don't see wings on you," the dragon said and laughed again, this time deep enough to rumble the earth and disrupt a flock of birds in a nearby tree. "Farewell, Helga the Lion, Helga Ravenfriend. May you gain wisdom to go with your power."

"*Gain* wisdom? I daresay you are calling me a crow," she said with a smile. "Farewell, Garamesh, and thank you."

"Until we meet again." The dragon turned and took wing, bending the tree limbs with his wind, and rose flying to the northeast. Helga watched him go, disappearing into a black speck. She was left alone in the clearing, which was probably a meadow in warmer seasons. She leaned over and looked at the massive footprints in the snow, each one as big as a wagon. Where the dragon had stepped, the crushed snow was steaming, and she could see dirt and withered grass beneath. It slowly turned green as the snow melted, and flowers sprang up.

Helga smiled and turned westward.

XV. Out of the Mountains

THOUGH THE DRAGON had dropped Helga far from any forged path or trail, and snow covered all the empty places in the forest, he had also released her at the top of a ridge. Her progress westward, by her standards braving the winter snows of Greenfeld, was quick. Occasionally, she was arrested by a tangle of bushes or deep undergrowth that she had to then work her way around, but these delays were few and not of particular annoyance, for Helga was always heading west.

The sun dipped behind a ridge, and Helga could see, looking backward, how much the loss of Raggle had set her back. Her hunger was returning as well, and she had no food. A memory and an idea came to her mind, and she set down her bedroll and sack in the shelter of a rock, as good a place as she could find to make camp. She left it there and walked out into the woods. She hunched down and relaxed.

She scanned her surroundings and at last saw what she sought: a few dents in the snow. People not acclimated to living in the North would have thought nothing of them, but she had lived long with snow and cold. She quietly ambled over to the disturbed snow and found what she sought. She stepped into some brush and kicked at a bush.

A snowshoe hare, awake and foraging even in the dead of winter, shot out from the bush, making for other cover in a dense cluster of short pines. Helga threw her hand out, feeling for the memory of the wind at her back, and the hare flipped end over end, along with a great pile of snow. Helga leapt forward and killed it with her poleax before it could recover.

Helga carried it back to the sheltered cove where she had dropped her other things. Even here, beneath leaning cedars, the ground was littered with snow. She put out her hand and turned in a circle, blowing all the snow away and melting the ice with a thought of heat. The bare ground greeted her, and she smiled. She found a few rocks and stacked them in a small pile. She didn't really believe that was important, but that is what Peridan had done with his magical fire, and so she replicated it, hoping to capture the concept of it, as he had talked about.

She focused on touching that other part of herself, focused on the memory of lighting Peridan's fire, but this time it did not come easily. She put her thought and effort toward the stones and reached desperately for heat. A few sparks jumped from the pile.

"Light, damn you!" She snapped her fingers at the rocks.

Finally, a tiny blue flame erupted within the stack of stones. Helga focused on growing it, blowing soft puffs of air (which she was finding an easier thing to do) across the stones to feed the flames. At last, she had a good little fire. She set about to preparing and cooking the hare, feeling warmed by the magical fire, and sad too, for with it, she remembered Peridan, not as he was, she found, but as Garamesh had thought of him: a great student of history and of magic.

It was a good meal, and by the light of the fire and the dying day, Helga took out and read the letter from Tisha.

To Helga Ravenfriend,

May you have health and happiness, wealth and warmth. I have enclosed a number of herbs that have good healing properties, should you find yourself again in need of them and without help. I have also enclosed a copy of a manual for creating the correct poultices and potions, handed down by the women of my clan for many generations. Let it be an heirloom for your people when you become a healer yourself.

Helga pulled out the small book and flipped through its unreadable script. "I think this woman assumes too much. A fat lot of good this will do me or Greenfeld." She shrugged and kept reading.

In separate bottles you will find ginger root, thiefleaf, witherbark, aspirin, wort of totality (very useful for the pox), and a leaf called tobacco useful for extraction of mild poisons, such as spider bites (men like to smoke it, but you shouldn't let them, it's a woman's duty to keep a man from such vices-forgive me for the advice, but I can tell you are a newlywed, and new brides need much guidance to manage young men). I have also enclosed a very precious substance called Luminescent Russula, the extract of a mushroom that grows only in Garamesh's lair (or similar dragon lairs, but I've met no other dragons and do not intend to. Only men are foolish enough to wish for dragons). Use it wisely, for it is more valuable than gold, and its powers of healing are remarkable if (and I say **if**) *you understand its preparation.*
    -Tisha

    P.S. I enclosed the raven's feathers. I'm sorry I didn't understand. You can do with them what you will.

Helga did find the feathers among the bottles, which she had overlooked at first glance, but that was not what held her mind.

"Luminescent Russula," she muttered. Here in this small package, casually given, was the cure that she had sought from the beginning, and new hope filled Helga's mind. The deceptive volva need not be trusted now to deliver on her promise. "If she has even remained in Greenfeld this year, which I would wager she has not." She looked through the small vials and bags, but they were labeled with the same runes in the book. "Perhaps Thokar will know what it looks like."

Helga had a sudden surge of anxiety. How would she find again the Band of the Badger? How could she face Trindol and Faralinda after killing Peridan? Surely they would want revenge. Surely Thokar would consider her an oath-breaker for what he had laid on each of them.

"I just won't tell them," she said to herself. "I'll just say he died in the Fay, which is true enough."

She worried about it still, but it was enough to satisfy her.

The sun set, and the temperature dropped, but around the magic fire, it was warm. Helga laid out her bedroll but did not undress, for as the moon rose, she heard a wolf howl in the distance. Sitting there, alone, she felt again, as she did her first night away, afraid and very small. The hare skin was hanging on a nearby tree limb, and she suddenly regretted trying to save it, sure that the smell would attract the wolves. She imagined falling asleep and waking up to fangs around her throat and shuddered.

Frustrated, Helga got up and set herself to making more small campfires, since it was something she knew how to do, and wolves, she remembered, were often afraid of fire. The first fire she built came slowly, but the second and third she made quickly, finding the path of sensation from her imagination to the world well-tread. Snapping helped, and soon she had a small ring of blue fires, burning on their own. She buried the remains of the hare as best she could and covered them with snow.

She lay down. Sleep did not come easily, but it did come. She dreamt of running wolves, but she was not afraid of them.

When Helga awoke, she saw that the fires had died. She sat up and looked around, and her heart skipped a beat when she noticed the disturbed ground where she had buried the bones and skin of the hare. What remained was bone shards and fur. Pawprints surrounded the fire ring, and there were even places where it looked like wolves had come and laid down.

"Well, that could have gone worse than expected," she said. "Helga wolf-friend? Ha!"

She packed her things and continued west, only slightly more afraid than before.

*

By the end of the second day of foot travel, she had come upon landmarks she recognized. She found the wide clearing where the Band of the Badger had fought their battle against the dun-men. It looked serene, covered with fresh white snow. The place still misgave her, so even though the sun was setting, she continued onward to another, smaller gully.

When she was making her fire (finding it frustratingly difficult to conjure up again), she heard a strange howl. It was not a wolf, but sounded like icy winter and dead summer combined and given to sound. She held her poleax close and set her ears to listening. When she closed her eyes, she could hear, not far off, a scratching as of something moving through the trees.

She stood up and held forth her polearm, waiting for something to strike. After a few silent moments, she shouted, "Come on then!"

In the darkness, two glowing eyes slowly grew large. Helga dug her heels in. The eyes were joined by others, but most halted in the ring of snow-laden pines beyond the fire. The first set of eyes continued to approach, and the firelight revealed a sickly face with a smashed-flat nose and a slit for a mouth that was contorted to one side. The being was nearly bald, his pate covered in wispy white and grey hairs that pointed to his shoulders like old twigs. His ears were long and mal-formed, and he wore only torn trousers and half a shirt, even in the biting cold. His feet were buried in the snow. He held up, palm-forward, his long, thin white hands.

"Do not strike," he said in a grating, airy voice, as though his breath were leaking out as he attempted to speak.

"Why are you here, dun-man?"

The dun-man breathed heavily, turning his face so his eyes, all glowing pupil, took in Helga from several angles. "We... felt the pow-er. We thought..." He trailed off and hunched down, looking back at his other companions hidden in the shadows. He looked back. "You are very beautiful."

"So?"

"So beautiful to behold, like one of the children." He stretched out a hand as if he wanted to touch her.

"Back!" Helga said, and raised the back end of the poleaxe for a stabbing strike.

The dun-man recoiled. "Pretty, and perfectly made. How did you find a key to the mortal flesh? Have the watchers succeeded at last?"

"The watchers are dead now."

"Dead? Then they did succeed." The dun man stood up. "But did you?"

"You think I'm one of them," Helga said. "You actually think I am one of the watchers, don't you?"

The dun-man stared at her with a mild, flat surprise around his open mouth, full of teeth growing all the wrong way. "You are not? The power…"

"She is mortal," another one hissed. Helga would call her a woman, but she was a twisted vision of one. Her hair grew in a spiral of grey around her head, and her ears drooped down like a dog's. "She's a mortal wizard," she said, stepping into the light. She wore a blanket over her slight frame and too-smooth grey skin. Her breasts hung like sacs at different levels, and one was bared; it had a strangely deformed nipple – flat, wide, and discolored.

"No, it is not the power of the wizards," the dun-man said. "You can feel it."

"I am mortal," Helga said. "What do you want?"

"Your secret," the dun-man said.

"No, we must take her power while we can," the twisted woman said. She opened her mouth, and a swirling light began to emerge. Helga stared in amazement as it shot out at her. Instinctively, she raised her hand, and the magic burst apart on her palm, imparting heat but little else.

The dun-men burst from the shadows in attack.

Helga was ready.

The first took a flying leap at her, but Helga stepped aside, and he went sprawling. Helga knelt quickly and felt a familiar pathway inside of her. She opened her hand, and a rush of air surrounded her and traveled over her arm to her fingertips, then along the ground to the campfire. The blue fire raged forward in a jet as the dun-men ran, ambled, and crawled toward her. Helga could see now that many crawled along the ground like beasts, eyes upturned and mouths open wide. Fire engulfed several of them, and they stood watching their flesh burn in amazement or rolled up on their backs, staring at their burning arms.

One of the attackers missed the burst of flame and rushed Helga from the side. She threw-out the spike end of her poleax and tripped him. He fell face-first into the snow, and Helga crushed his head swiftly with the hammer end of her weapon. His skull came apart like a pumpkin, and Helga nearly vomited as she pulled her weapon free, so disgusted was she by the sight and sudden smell.

The twisted woman, whose dirty blanket was now on fire, struggled forward on all fours, sending out sparks and streams of odd magic. Helga kicked at her, but had to leap back as the first dun-man to speak swung an old, rusty sword at her. She caught the next clumsy stroke with the haft of the poleax and pushed into him. With a burst of strength, she threw him back. The dun-man flew twenty feet backward to crash into a tree, and only as he was in the air did Helga realize she had used her power to strengthen her limbs.

Feeling suddenly strong, she attacked the remaining dun-men, swinging her poleax wildly. With one sickening, crunching stroke, she caught two of them, and their bodies flew away like rag dolls. One on her flank grabbed her weapon, and she thrust the spiked end into his belly. It burst from his back in a spray of grey-black bile and blood, but it did not kill the man. Instead, his arms flailed at Helga, trying to gain control of the weapon.

Helga threw the polearm forward, along with the impaled dun-man, and drew her sword. It flashed in the night, polished and bright in the light of fire and magic. She circled and slashed, letting the wind power her arms, and more blood flew. Weapons shattered as she struck them, her strength and the wind blowing around her being more than enough to compensate for her lack of practice with the blade.

"I will draw this power from you," hissed the woman, who was standing behind Helga, her legs blackened from the fire. She had staggered to her feet and was trying to work some sort of spell with her hands. Helga could feel the magic paths inside her stuttering, and her blade felt suddenly heavy.

"You don't belong in this world," Helga said and stepped forward. With all her strength, she brought her blade down on the woman's head. It landed slightly off of edge alignment and knocked her skull sideways, which made the woman stagger. Suddenly, Helga felt magic empowering her again. She swung backhand at the woman and watched, surprised, as her body split cleanly apart in a spray of sinewy gore. She turned around to attack the remaining dun-men, but they were gone. She heard rustling in the trees, moving away, then a slow, sickly silence.

"Never thought I'd wish for wolves," Helga said. Her stomach heaved, and she could hold back no longer. She leaned over and vomited.

Feeling better with an empty stomach, she looked about at the dead. Some looked more human; others looked more beastly. The woman, if she could be called that, seemed to be one of the most human on the outside, but her chest cavity was filled mostly with what looked like random tissue. The sight made Helga feel sick again, but as her heart rate slowed, she found it easier to control her stomach. Instead, she felt a sort of low relief – what her grandfather Brick had once called the "void after battle." There was little to loot on the dead, as the dun-men were mostly destitute and had poor weapons. The twisted woman, whom Helga guessed to be some sort of sorcerer – what Thokar had called a shaman – was arrayed in strange fetishes and loose clothes.

She had with her a small stick with a translucent globe at the end, like the sort of staff a child would imagine a wizard carrying, only it was just the final foot and a half of the staff. The sphere at the end was held in place by wood carved to look like the talon of a bird, or perhaps the claw of a dragon, but the claws twisted over the globe in such a way that it could only have been carved from a limb that grew around the sphere. Helga thought it was curious, especially to be in possession of a being so devoid of aesthetic beauty, so she put it in her bag. Once she was done inspecting the dead, she pulled her poleax free and wiped it clean with a tattered piece of clothing from one of the fallen. The old wood of the haft was dark and lustrous, but even it was not impervious to the strange blood of the dun-men, and grey-black stains ran along the grain where it had impaled its last victim.

"Shall I burn the bodies, like the Band of the Badger?" she said aloud. She wondered if she would have the strength to move so many bodies, and whether she could make a pyre in the wet snow, even with magic. She looked up at the dark sky, with bright stars shining as they always had, and thought of the ravens.

She left the bodies open to the air and struck the path again, determined to be well away in case any of the cowards among the dun-men returned for her. She walked all night through heavy snow, which she found was indeed not very easy to melt in large quantities using magic. Light snow showers began to fall after midnight, and Helga missed dearly her cloak. She lit a tree limb as a torch, and though it gave little light as it smoldered, it provided comforting warmth.

At dawn, she crested a ridge and looked down into the valley of Thruddel, empty of movement and buried under the fresh snow. She was now very tired, but she was so relieved to see the valley that she did not stop on the descent except to melt some snow for water. Getting across the valley proved harder, and she felt stalled out by not having a horse. She found a grove of oaks beside a fallow field, with a ruin of a house standing open beneath the branches. There, she made her camp, finding the fire easy to conjure.

Hunger gnawed at her again, so she ate the cherry she had in her pocket. It was incredibly delicious and refreshing, tasting like it had just been picked, though it was not nearly as filling as she had hoped. She saved the pit, like with the other fruit, with the thought of planting it in her own fields when she returned home. Another snowstorm came in, but the fire kept it off of Helga, and she was able to rest at last among the old stone walls.

The next two days went slowly but with little hunger. She was able to catch another hare and saved enough of the meat (now no longer fearing wolves) to last her several hearty meals. The third day, she came upon the abandoned farmstead she remembered from her journey out of Thruddel. The vines and brambles that held up the old barn remained, but were grey now and covered with snow. The interior of the barn was clean and full of personal effects, well-organized. Helga found herself puzzled as she looked at it.

Helga saw movement by a low ruined wall, and she left the road to investigate. Beside the barn, she found a family rebuilding the stone-walled and turf-roofed house that had originally served the land. More than half of the roof beams were already up. She recognized the man.

"Ho there!" Helga said, walking casually toward the man.

He looked up and started. His wife and child got behind him.

"We don't want any trouble."

"You'll get none from me," Helga said. "I just thought I remembered you. We passed on the road. In spring. You were fleeing a military campaign coming from Northmarch, weren't you?"

"Yes, we were, in the spring, but I've never seen you before in my life."

Helga laughed as she got closer. "You're joking, right? I remember you as clear as day. Your name was… Tian, though I don't remember hearing your wife's. You had two children. Where is the other one?"

"You're a cruel woman to ask such a thing," the wife said.

"What?"

"Quiet, Nona," Tian said. "I think I do remember her. Maybe. She told us to seek the manor."

"Nonsense," Tian's wife said. "That's not the same woman at all. This one's an elf or something. Which is good, for I'd give her a good punch on the nose for her advice if she was the same woman."

"What happened?" Helga said. "I only gave the best advice I knew of."

"We found the manor lord, and he took us on, but after the fall harvest, our youngest fell ill, and the lord turned us out into the cold. She…" the man took a deep breath. "We had less than when we started."

"I'm sorry," Helga said.

"Are you?" Nona said.

Helga ignored her. "Are you intending to work this land?"

"What else can we do?" Tian said.

"Move closer to the city," Helga said.

"No good with the army there."

"Army?"

"Yar," Tian said. "Been besieged for the better part of six months. Stubborn kings and generals. Where have you been?"

"Far away," Helga said. "Why did you not flee to the city?"

"The army and its mercenary bands passed us by. This place is just a ruin to a passing army."

"How big is this army?"

"Big as I ever seen, especially with the merc bands."

"That is well, then, that you are here," Helga said. "If I was a betting woman, and I suppose that I am that, I would wager that petty lord up the way is hanging for the crows."

"Don't try to cheer me up," Tian said. "Just makes me angry."

"Very well," Helga said. "Tell me, did you see a mercenary band of mostly orcs?"

"Several."

"What about one called the Band of the Badger?"

"Odd name."

"A good name, if you've ever met a badger."

"I saw a band with a badger on a banner. Figured it was a family crest."

Helga smiled. Thokar and his band might still be employed in the siege, which immediately lifted Helga's spirits. She turned the smile to Tian. "What can I do to ease your struggle? I am becoming a rather good hare hunter if you need a meal."

"How?" the child, a little girl, said. "You have no bow."

"I catch them with the wind," Helga said with a smile.

"With magic?"

Helga shrugged.

"She *is* an elf," the child said to her mother. Nona sniffed in response.

"Feed us a hare, and you just put off dying another few days," she said. "I don't suppose with your magic you can make crops sprout out of frozen ground."

A thought occurred to Helga. "Perhaps..." she said aloud.

"What?" Nona said. "Are you serious?"

Helga smiled. She walked over to the bare end of the ruined barn, the place where it had fallen inward long before. There was a large patch of ground there, open to the sky. Helga knelt down and snapped her fingers, remembering the pathway of fire that was becoming familiar. A small flame emerged on the snow and began melting it until it reached the earth. Helga felt for the wind, which was always behind her, and fanned the flames. They leapt high and melted the snow, turning a small patch of earth into mud.

Helga drew from her pocket the nut Ratatask had given her. It looked much like a walnut, but it was... *perfect* was the only word that came to mind. She bent down and dug a small hole. She placed the nut into it and covered it with new mud.

Nothing happened.

"Great," Nona said. "You buried a nut. I'm sure the squirrels are impressed."

"Oh, they are, goodwife. The squirrels are very much impressed with me." Helga scratched her chin. "I have to will it?" she said to herself.

She tried wishing, praying, and talking, but none of them made the nut grow as she expected. "Perhaps he meant it will eventually grow."

She decided she would try magic. First, she tried pushing wind into the nut, which did nothing. She felt the earth for strength, her feet making deep ruts as she touched that extra sense, and then she "felt" the nut in the ground. She felt its life. She tapped into the recesses of her memory, a thing long forgotten... when she had willed it into existence. She tried touching the nut again and then imagined it in her mind growing, fixing the image of a great tree like the one she had made in her dream. She felt a soft heat in her palms.

A shoot sprouted from the ground and grew, twisting into the air. Helga held onto whatever magic she was doing, slippery and intangible in the paths of thought and truth, and tried to do even more. Soon the shoot was a woody, tiny tree, and then it was a sapling. A few nuts grew on the limbs and fell off. Helga stepped back as the tree reached high into the air. Limbs grew out with fresh green leaves. All of the leaves turned red and dropped, blowing in every direction.

Helga continued pushing the tree with her thoughts, begging and coaxing it to grow. And grow it did. New walnuts grew and fell. New limbs grew and dropped their leaves. It was as if they were watching dozens of seasons pass before their eyes. Soon they were all standing knee-deep in dead leaves mixed with fresh nuts. The tree reached high into the air and stretched over the barn, catching the snow in dark green leaves.

Helga blew away the dead leaves on the ground with the same magic she used to catch the hare. What was left was the nuts and limbs, refuse from countless seasons transpiring in moments. Helga turned to see the man, woman, and child all bent over, gathering up nuts.

"Don't mind if I help myself to some," Helga said. "It's been a lean few days."

"Of course!" Tian said. His shirt was full of nuts.

Helga bent down and picked a few of them up. Feeling for the earth for strength, she cracked open the nut with her hand and ate the meat of it, which, partially because she was so hungry, was the best nut she had ever tasted.

"I told you she was elvish," Nona said to her husband.

"No argument here, but she does look like that other woman, Helga, does she not?"

"No. Maybe a little. What is your name, lady?"

"Ravenfriend will do," Helga said.

She spent the afternoon gathering the hundreds of nuts from the ground with the family, roasting them, and eating them beneath the tree, which sheltered them. She slept there, warmed by a magical fire, with the family around her. The nuts were good, but she had a sadness in her heart, for thoughts came to her of their other little girl. When she dreamt, she dreamt she was looking for her in the forest, trying to call for her, but her name was only the sound of wind.

The next day, she bade farewell to the family, wishing them all good health and wealth; they were already planting more trees.

At sunset the next day, she came upon the fortified manor, which was burned out. Helga did not enter the ruins to find what had happened within. Rather, she walked around the house to see everything, including the thrall's quarters, empty. She was within a day of Thruddel, she knew, but she could not see the city through the perpetual low clouds and light snowstorms. All she could make out was the base of the rising hill that marked the outskirts of the walled city.

She walked on into the night and came to a farmstead she knew, where she had been permitted a small house to herself against the rain. The family was not there, but the house was intact and whole, and the fields were all wintery ice. The door was locked, but the house in the back stood open. Helga decided that the family had made their way to the city ahead of the armies, probably seeing the burning of the manor, and that thought made her glad.

She slept in the little stone house in back, this time watching the snow fall on a magical fire. In the morning, she had a curious itch to do something for the family. She found an empty plot near the house and dug a hole. Into the hole, she put the pit from the cherry she had eaten and saved for planting in her own garden. Doing her best to find the same magical touch as with the walnut, she caused the pit to sprout and grow quickly into a small tree. Like the walnut, it grew cherries and leaves and threw them off as it progressed through its quick seasons. These cherries she gathered up greedily.

Now they'll have at least a small thing to harvest when they return, instead of having to work these empty fields.

She ate the cherries on the road the next day, and though they were very fine, they could not compare to *the* cherry. The cherry she had conjured from the Prim in the realm of Atalthal was still better by far, hunger-seasoned or not.

XVI. THE WINTER SIEGE

THE SNOW had stopped overnight, but the clouds remained, and Helga had a clear view of the hills that rose out of the valley and the swift cataracts of the river that ran by Thruddel, though she could not clearly see the city walls until she began to climb out of the valley. She did her best to tread on the road, holding her course by the occasional dark milestone that stuck out of the shallow snow. It was not long into her climb, however, that she encountered signs of the passage of armies. Refuse piles lay under trees, and the snow on the road became hard-packed and slippery.

When she neared the higher plains that held the city and outskirts of Thruddel, she came upon a few tall and lean soldiers, pale of face and hair, holding guard beneath snow-heavy cedars. One of them leveled a crossbow at her as she approached. She raised her right hand in peace.

"Would you fire on a woman?" she said breathily, tired from the climb out of the valley.

"One who's armed like you, sure," said one of the guards.

"I seek the band of the badger."

"To what end?" the guard said.

"I have business with Thokar."

The guard cracked a slight smile. "Go on, then. You'll find them camped outside the main pickets, should be able to tell them by their banners."

"You're lucky you came when you did," the other guard said. "Another day or two, and I think they'd be packed and gone."

"Why is that?" Helga said.

"Six months of a siege is why. King Coladarn is out of money and food. We regulars will be packed up before the week is through, which is just as well as far as we're concerned. Just don't want to share the march home to Hviterland with them damn Golicians."

"What of the people inside?"

The first guard spoke again, "Starving, I expect, but they have a wizard inside, and he either keeps up their morale, or they're all more afraid of him than us. Either way, Coladarn's grand march is ending here."

"Thank you for the information," Helga said.

She left the guards and continued over the hill. She came upon a large break in the trees that she could see had been felled to make many things for the siege, most of which lay ruined in the battle plain beyond the great gates of Thruddel or in the dense city outgrowth, which was now mostly razed. Burned trebuchets and catapults formed a picket in front of a frozen moat at the great gatehouse of Thruddel.

Helga wandered through the ruins, finding here or there a building that had survived only to become quarters for officers. Half a dozen soldiers stopped her along the way to ask her business or threaten her, which gave her an odd sort of feeling, like the men were afraid of her.

After a short search, she found the banners of the Badger flying over a fallen masonry house and a fallow field full of tents. Several orcs stood outside a well-made barrier of sharpened wooden stakes. They straightened up as she approached.

"Yes, lady," one of the orcs said, bowing and flashing long, yellow teeth. "How may the band be of service?"

"I am here to see Thokar. I have something of great value for him."

"This way."

Helga followed the guards past the house and into the forest of tents. Horses stamped bare earth among the tents, staying near to cooking fires and eating from small, mostly empty troughs. Men and orcs glanced up at them from bowls of sloppy stew as they passed, narrowing their eyes on Helga and eyeing her cautiously.

They arrived at a large, purple-dyed hide tent, and the guard took his spear and tapped on one of the poles.

"A lady here to see you, commander."

"Can it wait?" Thokar said from within.

"She is a high lady, sir. An elf of some status, I think. Or I wouldn't have bothered."

Helga heard an audible snuff. "Very well."

The guard nodded to Helga. She pushed open the leather flap of the tent and stepped inside. It took a moment for her eyes to adjust from the grey daylight. She saw inside a large round table with papers spread out on it and small coins in various odd places, lit by a clearly magical globe hanging from the roof. She recognized immediately Baradict, the hard orc sergeant major, who leaned over the table on his fists. Thokar was raising himself from a folding canvas chair.

"Greetings," said Thokar, bowing slightly. "I am Thokar. Who are you, and how may the Band of the Badger be of service to you?"

Helga narrowed her eyes in confusion. "Perhaps you don't remember me. I am Helga, daughter of Hrolfi. I was with you the night the dun-men attacked your company."

"Naw," Baradict said. "That was some little farmwife. I'd remember you."

Thokar gave Helga a considering look, turning his head this way and that to take her in. "So it is you. I am sorry, Helga, but you look very different."

Helga patted her armor. "You have to dress for danger in dangerous places, eh?"

"It's not your clothes," Thokar said. "It is you, yourself. I look upon your face, and although it looks much the same, now that I gaze hard at it, your face is also quite different. Your body is different. Your being is different, somehow. I feel like I am talking to a stranger."

"Maybe the scar?" Helga said, reaching to touch the scar on her forehead. She had trouble finding it, which surprised her. All she could feel was a thin line below the skin.

"No," Thokar said.

"She doesn't look quite so human," Baradict said. "Which normally I like, but she got prettier, which I don't like."

"You don't like pretty girls?" Helga said.

"I like my women capable of standing next to me."

"What about standing up to you?"

Baradict laughed. "I remember you. Sort of. Yeah, you could stand next to me."

"Are you calling me ugly?"

Baradict laughed aloud again. "It's good to have a bit of humor among this grimness."

"What is so grim?" Helga said. "Besides a six-month-long siege in winter?"

"We are at the end of our capacity here," Thokar said. "We are running out of resources. Our food is running scarce."

"I heard you were hired by a King. Shouldn't he be paying and supplying you?"

"Coladarn," Thokar said.

"Greedy bastard," Baradict said. "We negotiated for full supply, but he gives us the same rations as the regulars."

"I do not resent him that," Thokar said. "It would be unwise to overfeed your irregulars."

"I resent him lots of things." Baradict pointed at the table. Helga inched closer and saw that it was a drawing of the city, complete with a rough sketch of the castle. "We made the mistake of bargaining for plunder rights in lieu of a regular stipend. Thought we'd have cracked this nut in a week and been on our way with all we could carry."

"Alas that we did not take into account the wizard," Thokar said.

"I am sorry I did not warn you," Helga said. "I had dealings with him when I was in Thruddel."

"I don't expect you to see the future."

"Why have you come back?" Baradict said.

"Yes," Thokar said with sudden excitement. "Did you fulfil your quest? It has been on my mind and in my dreams, dark as they are. Where is Peridan?"

Helga remained silent and chewed her tongue. "I'm sorry, Thokar."

Thokar gazed into her eyes. "I see. Did he die honorably?"

Helga looked down. "I cannot say."

"You will not," Thokar said.

"I don't know how to face Faralinda."

"I will face her for you, if you wish," Thokar said.

Helga looked at the sad face of the huge man, leaning on a staff with a collapsed posture. "I do wish it, but since he was my companion at the time, I should be the one to tell... of his fate."

"You need not reveal all the details," Baradict said. "I've talked to enough widows and mothers to know they don't want them."

Helga nodded. "I did fulfil my quest, but not in the way I wanted. Does Trindol still live?"

"He does," Thokar said. "But he is weak. Elves can hold on a long time to spiritual sicknesses, but this one is bad. The dun shaman was more powerful than I realized."

"It is because they still hold in them the power of the fay dream," Helga said. She quickly added, "I have learned much. I have also returned with a possible cure. I have some Luminescent Russula."

Thokar forced a weak smile. "A rare gift, but it is only one ingredient among many."

"Well, look at these." Helga threw her bag down on the floor and began rummaging in it.

"Hold on, what's that?" Baradict said, seeing Helga put aside the globe in the carved tree limb.

"I killed a dun shaman that was carrying it," Helga said. "I thought it was a little odd, so I took it."

"It's called a focus. It's supposedly for some type of elvish magic left over from the old days," Thokar said. "Peridan would have known much more than me. You should bring it to Faralinda, though."

Helga found the satchel of herbs and opened them. "I don't know which is which because the labels are in a language I don't recognize, but one of them is Luminescent Russula. The healer who gave them to me said so."

"This is an old elvish script," Thokar said. "Which I do not know. But, I do know Luminescent Russula when I see it." The orc snapped his fingers, and the lights went out. In his hand was a bottle full of glowing powder. "It is called luminescent for a very good reason, as you can see."

"It makes sense now," Helga said. "It only grows in dragon lairs, you know, and the dragon lair I was in was full of luminescent rocks."

"Egad, woman, you were in a dragon's lair?" Baradict said.

"Aye, and with a dragon," Helga said.

"Forget about standing with me. You'd run me right over."

"The dragon was really quite nice," Helga said. "Other than eating all the watchers."

Baradict laughed. "I'd call you a liar, but your armor says you just might be telling the truth. You and I will have to share a keg of ale when this is over. You can tell me all about it."

"I will," Helga said. Helga snapped her fingers, and the globe lit again.

Thokar gave her a curious look.

"I learned a few tricks from Peridan," Helga said. "But you have the Russula. Now we can cure Trindol."

"Would you not rather have it?" Thokar said.

"I have the water now," Helga said. "I can trade that for my own cure when I return."

"A gamble, but one I will thank you for. One Faralinda will thank you for. However, we still have a problem. I need several more rare ingredients for my potion to work on Trindol. I have no means of gathering these, and our camp followers know nothing of alchemy. Trading is out of the question, or I'd already be stocked."

"Well, keep it," Helga said. "I heard the siege is breaking soon and that the king ran out of money."

"I heard that too," Baradict said. "He'll be out of food, too, which means we'll have to abandon our contract and leave with less than when we got here. I'm not happy about that."

"That is why we are devising one last attempt at infiltration," Thokar said. "If we can get around to the rear of the gatehouse we can take it and break this siege, get our plunder-"

"And come out of this with at least half our asses still intact," Baradict said.

"Speaking like that in front of a high lady," Helga said.

"I ain't got no sense when it comes to you elven types," Baradict said. "So find somebody else to kiss your ass — maybe the poor sod you hire to wipe it, eh?"

They all laughed, even Thokar.

"A thought just entered my mind," Helga said. "I know of a way to infiltrate the city. I escaped Thruddel through a secret tunnel. Have you found it?"

"We haven't found any," Baradict said. "How big is it?"

"Not big enough for any sort of real assault," Helga said. She shook her head. "But the way in is through an old catacomb, and I don't know the way."

"I thought you went out that way," Baradict said.

"I was led out," Helga said. "There is a rebel faction within the city as well. They might be willing to help you break the siege, as long as it deposes the wizard."

"The wizard isn't the king," Baradict said.

"But he has control over the king. He controls his mind... somehow. If we kill the wizard, the king will surely at least negotiate with Coladarn. That's what Thorvald told me, and I believe him."

"You have a man on the inside, too," Baradict said. "Damn, but you should have stayed on."

"Yes, but there is no way to contact him." Helga clenched her fist. "Ah! The wizard! He has a library and all sorts of alchemical devices and ingredients. If anyone has what you need, Thokar, it is him."

"Well, we might still try it," Baradict said. "Even risking getting lost underground might be better than our current idea."

"What's your current plan?"

"Breach the guardhouse via the toilet," Baradict said. "I have a few lads who could do it. But give them the choice, they'll happily get lost."

"The young are not always wise," Thokar said. "I will think on it. Faralinda and Trindol are in a nearby tent. You will recognize the aesthetics of it, no doubt."

Helga nodded and walked to the flap of the tent.

"And watch yourself," Baradict said. "Especially in the main camp."

"I will," Helga said, and exited.

Finding Trindol and Faralinda's tent was not difficult. It stood taller than all those around it and was colored with purple canvas and dark green trim. Embroidered vines covered all the edges, and the tent flaps had an embroidered tree that split in the middle. Helga paused outside to collect her thoughts and also to consider how one asks for entry at a tent, lacking a door for knocking.

"May I enter?" Helga said, not knowing what else to say.

"Yes," came back the voice of Faralinda.

Helga went inside to see Trindol lying with his eyes closed on a cot next to a small folding table. Faralinda was seated nearby, reading a book and taking notes with a garishly plumed pen. Her face lit up when Helga entered.

"Helga? Is it... yes. Helga!" Faralinda stood up. She ran forward, trailing her cloak behind her, and wrapped her arms around Helga. "You have been in my prayers for so long." She pulled back to look at Helga and cocked her head. "You look so beautiful, even in that armor."

"It's good to see you too."

"Where is my brother?" Faralinda's eyes fell as Helga's smile left. Wordlessly, Helga drew forth Peridan's dagger and handed it to Faralinda.

Faralinda gazed at the ivory-hilted weapon with open, calm eyes. Helga burst into tears, partly for the woman before her, who had lost her immortal brother, and partly because she saw in the wondering eyes of the elf all that Peridan was. Understanding beyond vision entered her mind. All his goodness was laid before her, his strength and intelligence, as if she was seeing Faralinda's vast memories for herself.

"Thank you for bringing this to me," Faralinda said. "It belonged to our father, who purified it long ago. It has been stained with blood." She had not withdrawn the sheath.

"I was forced to use it on the watchers. They attempted to... steal my soul."

Faralinda raised her head, and her eyes were wet. "Our father will wait for the return of this blade, but it will not come back to him in the right hands."

Helga sighed. "I have good news, too. I have recovered some Luminescent Russula." Helga looked over at the sleeping Trindol. "We can cure Trindol, even without... whatever Peridan sought from the watchers. It had something to do with dreams. He never talked to me about it."

"A dream. He was supposed to bring back a particular dream. A dream of this world."

"Well, I am working on getting Thokar the other ingredients for his potion. Peridan's quest will be fulfilled. I promise."

Faralinda nodded. "I did not want this. Please leave me with my husband. I will tell him of the loss of his friend when he wakes."

"What about you?"

"I will grieve as I can."

Helga bowed and left, wiping tears from her eyes. *Well, at least that's over,* she thought.

Without any other idea of what to do, she wandered the ruined city, taking in the sights. It occurred to her that she would need someplace to sleep, and she didn't have much money in her belt purse to begin with. *Of course, people might be desperate to sell, and I could get a bargain on a tent.*

She found her way across the main road. She looked down it and saw the city gate looming. A few companies of archers were shooting at each other without any effect, with the attackers hiding behind great portable blinds and the defenders firing from arrow-slits below the great parapets of the gate.

She crossed over and noticed a crowd of soldiers gathering a ways away, surrounding a great old oak tree. She ambled over toward it, but had trouble seeing over the tall soldiers, many of whom were wearing helms or warm hats. She could hear people yelling toward the front, but couldn't make out the words.

"What's happening?" she said to a nearby man at arms who was leaning on a spear. He turned his head to her and blinked as he looked at her.

"Um… Deserters."

"From the regular army or the mercenaries?"

"Mercs can quit when they want. Lousy bastards. Only one band still hanging about hoping to get paid now."

"What's the penalty for desertion?"

"Hanging. 'Course some men might say it's better to hang than to starve, or die on the march home. Some men, but not me, Lady."

"I won't tell on you for being sensible. Any man that would first ask your death to fulfil valor has none himself."

"That's sedition."

"Coladarn is not my king, sir. Or should I say 'some men might say' as a preamble?"

"Who are you, anyway?"

"I'm with the Band of the Badger, for now."

"Bloody merc. Should have known. Well, they're bringing up the prisoners now. You could find a tree to climb into if you like."

"I don't think I have a taste for watching executions. It seems odd to me that any soldier would."

"Technically, everyone in a man's company is required to watch the execution. Sends the message home."

"You know these men, then?"

"Sure, they enlisted after we sacked Golice; most of the bad ones are Golicians anyhow, even though they come from the outlying country. Greedy bastards, not understanding soldiering properly."

"Well, keep your head on," Helga said.

"My goal in life. Walk lightly, lady."

Helga nodded and started walking around the crowd to a row of mostly intact houses that had a mass of wagons amongst them, where she thought she might find some merchants or camp followers. The crowd was wide, however, and she had to pick her way among jeering men. Despite her intentions, she looked back to the oak as the whole assembly of men threw up their right arms in salute and cried aloud, "Sir!" An older man in a formal jacket flanked by two knights held up his hands.

Helga stared as she saw three men be put up on logs; she could clearly see their faces over the crowd. Two of them looked terribly frightened, and the remaining one looked as if he expected his scowl to change the minds of the executioners.

As nooses were put around their neck, carrion birds, mostly crows, landed amongst the branches of the oak and along old parts of a wooden fence that still stood. The men were not hooded, but their hands were bound behind their backs.

The man with the knights shouted out loudly. "Witness the consequences of cowardice and abandonment of your brethren. For the Northmarch!"

"Hail Coladarn! Hail Ragnur!" the assembly said in response.

The logs were knocked out all at once, hanging the prisoners. The men called out a half-cheer, half-wail as the damned fell. Two of the men died instantly; the third seemed to writhe and struggle, not falling far enough to break his neck. He kicked his legs and struggled against his bonds, his face turning a sickening purple. The birds descended on the two dead men. One of the executioners waved a spear at them to shoo them away, then thrust the spear into the man who was struggling. He kicked a few times, then fell limp as blood poured from his chest.

This time, the soldier did not bother scaring away the carrion birds. He threw up his hands and left, following what Helga presumed to be a general or judge.

"As usual, the crows are the only ones getting fat," said a nearby man, suited in dingy mail and other accoutrements.

"Who knows? This week might be the week," said his companion, who wore only a short sleeve mail shirt and was clearly in the archery corpse, if only because he looked better fed.

"The week we head home hungry with our tail between our legs? I'll say…"

Helga walked away from them and toward the camp at the end of the lane, which looked to be full of followers and tradesmen, though as she approached, she noticed many abandoned sites and clearings where tents and wagons had recently sat. Most of the traders were sitting around idle, a few wares left out on leather aprons for perusing. The whores of the camp ("comfort women," the men would call them) stood looking just as bored, wrapped against the cold with only their cleavage showing. The goods (women included) were obviously meant for military men. There were various pieces of rusty armor, parts for crossbows and sword hilts, a great many whetstones, arrows with fletching ranging from poor to very poor, and even a few long-bows.

It was obvious to Helga as she looked at the armaments that most of them had come from the regulars in camp, selling what gear they could for a meal. None of the stands save one sold food, and that one merchant held only rotten apples and salted mystery meat.

Helga saw something laid out that caught her eye — a simple scarf of brilliant amber, almost the same color as her dress.

"How much for that?" Helga said.

The merchant, a middle-aged man with sallow cheeks and wispy hair, spoke back, "For a lady like you? Free, if you have passage to a better town."

"Better is relative," Helga said. "But if you are looking for protection on the road, I have none."

"Surely your bodyguards can afford to look after one follower."

"Alas, but I have no bodyguards," Helga said. "Just myself. How much for the scarf?"

The merchant narrowed his eyes. "Five silver."

"Might as well buy the yarn and weave it myself for that."

"Very well... um, three silver."

"I'm guessing you pulled this off a woman killed here in the outskirts."

"I come by my wares only honestly, hence why I am called Honest Ian."

"You aren't called that, and if you are, it's in jest. You have a dead woman's scarf, and the whores here are so desperate for food even in this cold they wouldn't cover-up."

"You mistake me," the merchant said.

"Don't attempt to cheat a woman on the value of clothing," Helga said. "I'll give you two copper cyprils for the scarf, and I throw in avoiding telling anyone you plundered the dead."

"You're a hypocrite," Ian said.

"What did you just call me?" Helga said.

"You would wear something off a dead woman, and you dare chastise me for taking it off her to begin with?"

"The right of plunder does not belong to you, Honest Ian, but I pity you, and I know that this scarf would be misused." Helga took two copper coins from her bag and tossed them at the man before scooping up the scarf. The man almost stood up, and he eyed a quarterstaff he had sitting next to himself. "Now, are you selling any tents?"

"You're buying?" Ian said, clearly surprised. "Yes, I have several for sale. All well-waxed and oiled, waterproof and snowproof. Just one – two! Aurals each."

"An ounce of gold for a tent you traded for whiskey money and half an hour with a comfort woman? I'm feeling charitable, so I'll give you the four silver you asked for earlier."

"I asked for five."

"Are you trying to insult me?"

"No! I am not; it is just, before-"

"Very well," Helga said with exacerbation. "I'll give you five, but I expect you to give me the best of the lot."

"Of course," the merchant said. He stood up and searched through his things, piled under a canopy. He withdrew one large satchel and a few short poles. "These, uh, screw together, very easy to load on your horse."

Helga snapped her fingers. "A horse! Does anyone have one for sale?"

"What? No, they're worth a fortune right now. Even I sold one of mine. Each time one gets slaughtered, the price goes up."

"I see," Helga said. "Very well. Remain honest, Ian, and I'm sure good things will come to you." Helga leaned forward and put out five silver coins, which the merchant scooped up. She hefted the tent on her shoulder next to her other bag and set off back toward the Band of the Badger's pickets. She wrapped the scarf around her face to keep off the chill, and it did that wonderfully, for it was well made in spite of its simple design.

On her way back, she passed by the tall oak, which still had all three men hanging from it. Helga noticed that most of the carrion birds stayed back, and two large ravens were keeping the corpses to themselves. Helga walked nearby the oak, for it was the shortest distance between where she was and the Band's camp, and saw that the convicted men had already been stripped of all valuables save their breeches. The first man was also missing both his eyes.

"Just so you know, there are four men following you."

Helga looked around and realized that one of the ravens was talking to her.

"Zim? That's you!"

Zim croaked and flapped his wings indignantly. "How do you know my name, mage?"

"Don't you remember me?" Helga said. She pulled the scarf off of her face and smiled.

"No," Zim said. "I would remember someone like you."

"We spent a whole month traveling together. It's me, Helga! How can you not remember? Zald…" Helga cut herself off.

Zul spoke next. "Yes, I see it is you. You look so different. I didn't recognize you." The raven flew down from the body and landed on a fencepost to stare at Helga. "You looked part elvish from afar, and your hair is longer."

"Probably just the armor, but you should remember that."

"No, it is not that," Zul said. "There is more to you than before. Now to your arms, those men are coming."

Helga turned and saw four men approaching, loping around a gate. She could see that they were armed and had a leering look in their eyes.

"They mean you harm," Zul whispered.

"I can see that." Helga set down her things and readied her pole-ax. At the same time, she felt for the magic she knew and made herself ready to unleash it.

"Don't forget the sword is for Ian, or we won't get half a penny," whispered one of the men, and Helga could just make out his voice.

Helga had learned enough in her time in the wild to know that attacking first was generally the best thing to do if you wished to actually survive and win a fight.

She rushed forward, watching the eyes of the lead man, a tall and lanky fellow with drooping long black hair, widen with surprise. She felt magical strength flow into her arms as she swung the poleax. The ruffian held up his shield, a battered round oak armament typical of freeman soldiers. The hammer hit the shield head-on, shattering it to splinters and crushing the left arm of the man. He fell backward, crying in pain as Helga's momentum carried her forward. Helga knocked another man over with a strong gust of wind and then needed to fight no more, for her display was enough.

The men quickly gained their feet and ran off into the nearby trees. The lead man clutched his arm, which hung bloody and limp at his side. Helga did not pursue, but instead watched, a slight smile forming on her face.

"I can honestly say I did not expect to do that when I walked out of my door last year."

"You should have killed them," Zim said.

Helga looked up at the Raven. "You don't look like you're hurting for food."

"What?!" Zim said.

"Besides, I don't want to incur the wrath of the king by killing any soldiers."

"They weren't soldiers," Zim said. "And you know it. But I like it this way, too. Nobody will believe them when they say the man's arm was crushed a woman."

Helga picked her things up.

"Listen," Helga said. "I never got to tell you I was sorry."

"For what?" Zim said. "We were the ones who gave up on you when the dragon attacked. I must admit I assumed you were dead."

"I cannot believe Zald called him down," Zul said.

"It is well that he did," Helga said. "But I am sorry. Zald died because of me."

"Zald died of his own free will, mage," Zim said. "Do not take that from him. He loved you too much for his own good."

Helga buried her face in her hands, feeling fresh tears well up and stream down her cheeks, chilling them bitterly.

"You fat fool. You made her cry," Zul said.

"Fat. Fat!?" Zim said.

"Yes," Zul said. "Quickly! Drat these crows!" Zul flew up and rocked loudly at a group of crows that had descended on the corpses and were pecking at the eyes. They all flew away in terror.

"You cannot trust the lesser corvids," Zim said. "Remember that."

"Oh, we might as well let them have it," Zul said, flying back down to the fence post. "Now that Helga is here, there will be plenty for the eating."

"I'm not sure I would be so confident," Helga said, wiping her tears. "I haven't had the best luck."

"But you *do* have a way of producing corpses," Zim said.

"I suppose," Helga said. A man-at-arms approached with a spear, waving off the carrion birds, including Zim and Zul.

Helga hefted the tent and sighed as she watched the ravens fly off, bickering with each other quietly.

She returned to the camp of the Band of the Badger and was surprised to see the ravens sitting on the ruined house as if waiting for her.

"I'm back in your good graces, then?" Helga said.

"Good company is dreadfully hard to find around here," Zul said. "Everyone is so morose."

"I'd be too," Helga said. "And I suppose I am."

Helga found a clear space in the camp and set about setting up the tent she had bought, which was slow going. As she worked, a thought came to her.

"Zim, would you be willing to do me a favor?"

"That depends on the favor and what you intend to repay me with."

"More dead?" Helga said. "I expect this will generate more bodies than you can happily dine on."

"I have plenty to eat already, as you said. Perhaps I should eat less."

"He'll do it," Zul said.

"Do not speak for me!"

"I have, and I shall," Zul said. "What do you need?"

"I need you to fly into the city and find a very specific man," Helga said.

"Not easy when you all look the same," Zim said.

"You can always ask around," Helga said. Zul laughed. "His name is Thorvald, and he may be in hiding, even within the city, but you may know him by his large beard, height, and drunkenness."

"Might as well try finding a mouse in a hayfield," Zim said.

"He will remember me, and I owe him a favor he will want to collect on. If you can find him, tell him that I have a thought for usurping the wizard and breaking this siege. Can you do that?"

"Can I?" Zim said. "I probably can. Will I be successful? Probably not." Zim took to flight, with Zul following behind him. "We do too much work for her."

"She's a friend, Zim."

"I bet her eyes aren't even that tasty."

Helga couldn't make out the rest of the conversation as the Ravens flew high into the sky and toward the city. She thought she could make them out as they flew over the high wall and parapets to disappear into the low city.

Helga turned herself back to the work of her tent. Several times she tried to get it to stay upright, but each time the support poles would fall down, leaving her with a flat piece of canvas. Exacerbated, she hid her things under the canvas of the tent and set off back toward Thokar's big meeting pavilion.

She nodded to a guard as she entered, and was surprised to see more men there, along with a few scrawny boys, none of whom looked over the age of fourteen, though there was a grimness in their faces that Helga found disconcerting. Mona was there too, and she raised her angular eyebrows as Helga entered.

Thokar, seeing his wife's eyes, turned to glance at Helga and then returned his attention to the boys.

"We'll be hitting the gate hard. I'm going to work out our coordination with the regulars, who still have some covered battering rams. With the fighting heavy at the gate itself, getting to the outlet and climbing up it will be relatively easy. You are also not likely to be in any immediate danger once you emerge-"

"From the toilet," one of the lads said.

"Aye," Thokar said. "I will give each of you a potion that will deaden your sense of smell to the stench and increase your visual awareness. I will also give you a sparker tube. Set it off when you are inside and ready to push the inside of the gate, and I will focus all the defenders' attention on me. From there, you can use a smoke bomb-"

"Best to wrap your faces, if you can," Faralinda said. "The smoke is quite acrid, and may make you retch even if you can't smell anything."

"From there, you will find the bridge release. Tripping it will be no problem. Faralinda and I will tear down the iron gate, so get out as soon as you've dropped the bridge."

"Why not just blow the bridge apart if you can use magic?" one of the boys said.

"You don't think I would have tried that?" Faralinda said. "Or the mage that's in with the regulars? The drawbridge is enchanted to withstand magic, or at least whatever magic we have available."

The tallest boy (though skinnier than the others) spoke up. "I want a triple share of the plunder."

"You get first choice, but a standard share," Thokar said. "Do not forget that once the gates are down, your fathers and brothers will be doing all the hard fighting."

"What if you didn't have to climb up the toilets at all?" Helga said.

"Have you remembered the way in?" Thokar said.

"No," Helga said. "But I'll be in contact with someone who does. The secret rebel on the inside."

"How exactly can you contact him?"

"By raven," Helga said. "Or am I called Ravenfriend for no reason? Zim and Zul are scouring the city as we speak."

"They don't know where he is?" Thokar said.

"Not yet," Helga said. "But they are very resourceful. They will find him."

Thokar shook his head. "I don't think we can wait. We've another five days sitting here at the most, and then the morale will break, and the whole army will desert. We have to crack the city now, even if I would not normally send our sons to do it."

"How many days can you give me?"

Thokar scratched his chin and looked to Baradict, who shrugged. He looked at Faralinda, who said, "Trindol isn't waking anymore."

Thokar looked hard at Helga. "On the third day, we try our plan."

"Plenty of time," Helga said.

Baradict snorted. "Heard those words before, usually before a man dies."

"I'm not a man," Helga said. "And I will find the rebels for you."

XVII. The Gates Open

ELGA HEARD nothing from the Ravens for the rest of the day. Night fell, and she once again could not get her tent to stand up; she was beginning to think that the merchant had sold her one that was missing some critical piece, so she built a fire of magic for herself, knowing it would keep the snow off of her. Her bedroll she set out on the tent itself, for the ground had become quite soggy with the snow.

Baradict wandered by after sundown, carrying a bowl of thinly flavored gruel for her, which according to him, was a better ration than what the regulars got.

"Can't have our men deserting us for a regular position, can we?" he said.

"Would the king take on orcs?"

Baradict shrugged. "Good point, I suppose. Why didn't you pitch the tent?"

"I couldn't get it to stand up," Helga said.

Baradict laughed. "Am I going to pitch a tent for a human?"

After a close inspection, Baradict realized that the posts were driven too far apart and helped Helga fix the tent.

While they were doing this, the ravens returned, flying out of the night like invisible spirits and landing by the fire.

"This food is terrible," Zim said, dipping his beak into the gruel and letting most of it fall back into the bowl.

"Those are precious rations, I'll have you know," Baradict said.

"Go eat a corpse," Helga said. "Those hanged men are still strung up, I imagine."

"Eat after crows?" Zim said. "That is a great humility you ask."

"What did you find?"

"Nothing," Zul said. "We can find no man named Thorvald. We even asked some children."

"They were looking none too good. Skinny by my standards," said Zim.

"Why did you ask children and not somebody who actually knows something?" Baradict asked.

"Children do not think a talking raven is something to be afraid of, or even that extraordinary. It's only after they grow up and lose their imagination that they think a talking raven is odd," Zul said.

"And I did not much feel like dodging arrows," Zim said.

"How well do you see in the dark?" Helga asked.

"Very well," Zim said. "Much better than you, I'm sure."

"Well, try looking about tonight. I would bet that the rebels are moving at night, especially as this siege draws on to the end of food, inside and out. Find the men who are moving and plotting, and you will find Thorvald."

"No rest for the charitable," Zim said. "But plotting humans are often inept. I suppose I shall try tonight once I've had a bite." He dipped his beak into the gruel again and shook his head with a croak, sending opaque liquid everywhere. Zul took to the air, and he followed.

"Useful to have raven friends, even if they are a bit insolent, eh?" Baradict said.

"It's fine. I'm insolent too, so I think the fit is right."

Baradict laughed. "You'd make a good mercenary. I have other duties. Sleep well. If all goes well, we shall have a busy day tomorrow. If it doesn't, then we shall still have a busy day."

"Farewell."

Helga watched the fire for a while after Baradict left. She opened up Tisha's satchel and looked through the contents again. Zald's feathers were there, and they shined with a slight pearl-like sheen in the blue fire. She picked up her helm and began working them into

298

the round ferrule at the top, making a crest of black feathers. She did not notice Faralinda until the elf sat down beside her.

Helga regarded her quietly as she worked.

"You really have been changed," Faralinda said. "How did you learn Peridan's fire spell? That was always a tricky incantation."

"I... just was able to make the fire exist. The more I did it, the easier it got. Now I just think it, and I can make it."

"You just think it? How long did you practice the words?"

"I don't know any words," Helga said. "And there is a bit more to it than that. I can feel the fire wanting to come. I can feel the limits of what it is... It's hard to explain. Another sense, not like touch, but touching on something just beyond reach. Just beyond reality. The *concept*, as Peridan said."

"Really," Faralinda said, her pale eyes growing large. "Truly, you have been changed. That is a gift not seen for a very long time among elves."

"What gift?"

"To weave magic at a thought, rather than through a practiced method. It's-" Faralinda noticed the strange stick Helga had found on the dun shaman. She gestured to it and said, "May I?"

Helga nodded, and Faralinda picked up the talisman.

"What is it?"

Faralinda smiled as she turned it over in her hands. "It's called a focus. Supposedly it was a necessary part of an ancient magic system possessed by the dark elves called 'lightweaving,' from the mythic primal darkness. You would incant, through a focus, magic that was light itself, rather than the natural elements that we are familiar with now. All matter is light, really, but the system was lost long ago. Most, dark elves included, believe the magic was weakened and destroyed with the coming of the sun. Others believe it is still awake, waiting to be rediscovered by the powerful."

"What do you believe?"

"I think it was probably just an earlier system of what mages and wizards use today, which is built around drawing on the true essence of a thing in the Prim. These focuses are often made and traded among the fair elves, and collected by the dark elves, too, mostly as an art piece or a curiosity. It's a bit of a cliché to have a travelling merchant claim that they recovered a true ancient focus from some mythical ruin. This one," Faralinda said as she held the carved bird claw up, "is quite beautiful and well made. If a merchant were to have this one, I might actually believe him."

"It was being used by a dun shaman," Helga said. "She conjured magic out of it."

Faralinda smiled and looked at the focus. "You don't say? Well, perhaps there is some truth to the old stories if one of the fallen folk can still find the lays. It's a nice little trophy either way." The elf handed the talisman back to Helga and stood up. She looked up at the sky, which was dark with clouds. She frowned.

"What is it?" Helga said.

"I never thought time would be as precious as it is. Should I be thankful?"

"I don't know. I guess it depends how the lesson is learned."

Faralinda sighed. "Rest easy, Helga. Dream deeply. Pray for Trindol."

"I shall."

Faralinda walked away into the dark, her golden hair bright in the firelight. Helga looked at the focus in her hands for a long time, tracing the talons over the crystal ball, entwined in what was once a living tree limb.

At last, she became tired and went to sleep.

*

Helga was awakened by a croaking and the sensation of cold. She sat up, smashing her face into the taught canvas of her tent. She looked down toward the flap opening and noticed a very large beak pulling her blanket off, inch by inch.

"What are you doing?" Helga said.

"We found your man," Zim said. "Wake up. It's time to go. He will meet you within the hour."

"Within the hour? But I've no time to plan."

"That is what he said, too, but he also said that now was the only time if you wanted to get men inside."

Helga scrambled out of the tent and found her weapons. "Go find the master sergeant, Baradict," she told Zim and Zul. "I will find Thokar. We need to assemble what we can, quickly."

The birds flew off, and Helga ran through the camp, calling to the tents for commanders to ready. There were a few grumbles and a few upset voices when men staggered out into the night to find they were not under attack. Helga reached Thokar's tent and tore open the flap.

"I can get your men inside the gates, but it must be now, right now!"

"I heard you halfway down the lane," Thokar said. "I'm already dressing, now close my door and meet me at the command table."

Within a few minutes, numerous people stood around the command table. Helga recognized Baradict (looking somewhat more cheerful than usual, which was indeed odd for the early morning hours) and Thokar, as well as several other orcs that wore sergeant's insignias. Mona stood by Thokar, her face grim in the light of the magic globe. Faralinda entered behind Helga.

"Faralinda," Thokar said. "I am surprised to see you gone from your husband's side."

"He's why I'm here. You may have need of my magic."

Thokar nodded. "By your will, then. Helga?"

Eyes turned to her, and she said, "What?"

"What is the plan?"

Helga felt suddenly abashed. "I...uh... the ravens will know. Zim! Where are you?" She called to the tent opening. Zim and Zul appeared outside, cocking their heads curiously. They hopped past Helga and flapped up onto the war table, knocking over coins used as markers. Zim picked up a silver coin and turned it over.

"I don't need any more silver," the raven said.

"What is your plan?" Thokar asked the raven, his inflection flat, as though talking to a raven was nothing out of the ordinary.

"Hmn? Plan?" Zim said. "We had a message, not a plan. The passage will be open within the hour. It will be closed soon."

"What does the man inside intend?" Thokar said.

"How would I know?" Zim said.

"So there is no plan," Baradict said. "Bloody brilliant. Well, might as well get on with it."

"Should we trust this?" one of the orc sergeants said.

"It is better than the alternative," Thokar said. "Keep in mind, one day, you will have a son."

Helga cleared her throat. "I trust Thorvald. He will work with us as long as our goal is the overthrow of the wizard."

"I wouldn't trust him," said Zim. "But of course, I trust very few humans."

"Time is short. Let's go," Faralinda said.

"Very well," Thokar said. "If we are to take the gate from the rear, I want the strongest single men we have. I will go, as will Aarne, Harpa, Nit, and Faralinda. And of course Helga."

"And I will go too," Mona said.

Thokar looked at his wife. "It is unwise to put all our mages behind lines."

"Not if we face the wizard. You will need all the help you can get."

"My idea, unless your man has a different one," Thokar said, glancing to Helga, "is to take the gatehouse from behind and spring open the drawbridge and portcullis to break this siege open."

"You will still need magic to face those odds," Mona said.

"So be it," Thokar said. "Baradict, I want you to stay here and lead the frontal assault. Look for my sign in the sky, and make sure the men are armed."

"Aye, but I do so under protest. I don't like missing out on a sufficiently suicidal mission."

"I like this one," Zul said. "Perhaps we should make him our friend instead."

Zim flapped his wings. "No. He smells wretched." The ravens laughed.

*

They rode to the small stream beneath the most ancient walls of the city as quickly as they could in the dark. When they got there, they dismounted and handed the horses over to a soldier to look after them and take them back to camp after a few hours' time, assuming they did not exit the ancient passageway in failure. At the crossing of the river, they ascended the stone staircase. It was covered in over-growth and piles of ivy so as to be invisible from below, and it wound its way beneath a natural granite outcropping, hiding it from eyes above.

At the top of the staircase stood an open gate. Helga went first, but before she could enter, a familiar voice said, "Not a step closer. I have archers above you that you cannot see, and all of them are crack shots."

"Thorvald, we came as soon as we could," Helga said. "It's me, Helga."

"Yes... yes, *is* it Helga, though? What was your father's name?"

"Hrolfi. Easily forgotten, so don't feel bad that you did."

Thorvald stepped out of the darkness and pushed back the hood of his black cloak. He looked haggard beyond comprehension. His cheeks were hollow, and his eyes sunken above a wild, tangled beard. The veins in his wide hands stood out as he gripped his sword hilt. "I did not forget your father's name. I had to be sure it was you. I didn't recognize you. Come, all." He gestured for them to follow him into the darkened tunnel.

Their footsteps echoed softly on the wet stone as they entered in single file.

"I've been getting that lately," Helga said, walking closely behind Thorvald. The light was fading with each step.

"It's the ears," Thorvald said. "And the eyes. And other, more subtle things, I guess. You're the one who would know." Thorvald raised his voice. "Last one in shut the gate!"

Helga heard the gate shut with a loud, reverberating clang.

"I actually haven't looked into a glass in… Well, I don't remember the last time I did. Maybe close to a year ago, actually."

As they walked further into the catacombs, the darkness grew closer to total. The people surrounding Helga looked like vague shadows.

"Stay close to me," Thorvald said. "There are a few turns in here, and we don't want to get separated."

Thokar grumbled a soft word and held aloft his staff, which now gave off a soft green light, just enough to see by. In the rear of the column, Faralinda removed from a pouch at her hip a very small lamp, which was lit with its own magic fire, blue and flickering.

"Dreamer come again, I didn't realize you were mages," Thorvald said. "I'm trying to overthrow a wizard, not bring more into the city."

"Magic is powerful," Thokar said, "but not infinite. This wizard will have his breaking point, I am sure."

"I can only hope. We common folk are close to starving now. Magnus gives all his food to the soldiery; there's not a horse left in the city, and the granaries are being emptied. Even if we survive, we'll be eating bark come fall."

"It is not much better outside," Helga said. "But if we can break through, there is a chance to begin recovering."

"But under whose rule? Will your king of the north be gentler than Magnus?"

"He will have less power," Faralinda said. "And that is the beginning of caring for one's subjects."

"Aye," said Aarne, a massive man Thokar had chosen to go in with them. He had to stoop in the passageway. "When you fear having your head on a pike, it goes a long way toward sympathizing with the common man."

"I wish there was a way to restore King Ivar, but I suppose that possibility is long past. His mind is probably gone by now, beyond recovering," Thorvald said.

"I would hope not," Thokar said. "Even a vassal has value if he has wisdom and experience."

"Still not what I want for Thruddel."

"You may have to consider what you want among possible outcomes," Thokar said.

The air grew stale and heavy, thick and stifling, though it was also cold. It was still, and in the quiet between words, they could hear a disconcerting amount of detail in the passageways: breathing and the smacking of lips; the scraping of dust under boots; the soft jingle of mail links. The group ascended a staircase of slippery, worn stones and traveled through a tall passageway, vaulted like a temple or church. Ancient paintings covered the ceiling and walls, illuminated by Thokar's staff and Faralinda's lamp in a pale shimmering blue-green, like watching through water. What the paintings depicted was impossible to tell for sure, for age had caused the plaster to fall in many places and turn to dust. In some areas, whole sections of the roof had caved in, leaving odd scars of limestone in the great scenes.

What they could make out, at least consistently, were fair figures of warrior maidens and hard men, all with the lithe features of elves, and always there were depictions of dragons. Great serpents of green and gold, red and black, twisted around pillars and between heroic, defiant faces. Helga guessed they might tell of some ancient epic, but it was too hard to follow due to the damage.

"Have you ever seen such a thing?" Faralinda said.

"Yes," Helga said. "And even more impressive, in the sanctuary of Garamesh the dragon. These could have been painted by the same people, if not the same hand."

"The aesthetics are quite moving. Primal and yet more refined. Closer to... God, perhaps."

"Yes," Helga said. "That makes sense. They look different than the art of the dark elves, which-"

"Be quiet," Nit mumbled. He was a tall and lean half-orc, with hard grey eyes and a paler complexion than one of full blood. "Leave it to women to talk when a stray word could end them."

"Said by a man who has twice been challenged to a duel due to his own unruly words," Faralinda said.

"Didn't lose either one," Nit said.

"Quiet down," Thorvald said. "After this hallway is a passage that will lead out to the main street. I was careful not to be followed, but if day has broken, we may be exposed to curious eyes, and then we will never get a chance at my plan."

"Which is what?" Aarne said.

"You'll find out. Now quiet, all of you."

Helga shut her mouth, but found herself staring at the pictures as they rolled by, like watching history play forward in seconds, showing her things she could not possibly comprehend. When they reached the end of the gallery, they met a stone-framed door. Perched above this door was a statue of a Dragon, his eyes pale yellow gemstones. His claws were clutching the shut iron doors, and his wings were spread out above him, touching the ceiling with ribs of gilt.

Thorvald rapped softly on the door, making a rhythmic cadence of odd combinations. Quietly, the door opened to them, and they stepped through to find nobody on the other side.

"Almost there now," Thorvald said. "Have your weapons at the ready, in case I was followed."

Helga picked up her poleax and held the spear point forward. They walked upward through a winding stone tunnel until they reached a half-ruined room that was full of empty barrels. At one end of this room was a wooden staircase. Thorvald climbed this and opened a set of doors that were perpendicular to the ground. Soft moonlight streamed in, and they all followed Thorvald out into a modest garden. The moon had found an opening in the clouds above them and lit the snow-covered garden in a bright, pristine white below bare fruit trees.

"I will take us along an inconspicuous way to another sanctuary," Thorvald said quietly. "Shut the door behind you and try to keep up!"

They crossed the garden to a low wall. Thorvald stepped out of a break in the wall and looked around, then motioned the others to follow. They stayed close behind, crossing a narrow street before entering an alley that twisted and wound up and down over small paved hills. Helga could not keep track of which direction they were going, since it was very dark, and she could only occasionally see the moon peeking out between buildings. She thought this was likely by design to confuse the strangers, as much as it was for concealment.

After many turns, they reached a narrow space between two old stone buildings, one of which leaned slightly as its foundations had settled. Thorvald walked down a narrow flight of steps to a small alcove with a large wooden door set into old masonry.

Thorvald knocked again with an odd rhythm, and the door opened on its own. Thokar gave a hesitant look to Mona as if doubting they should follow the stranger underground again, but lacking any other course, he led the procession.

Inside was a low, long room lit only by a small fire in a hearth. Arms and armor sat around the room in heaps and racks. Several men stood facing the door with ready crossbows, and Thorvald was already busy pulling weapons out here and there. Thokar had to duck to enter.

"A bit of light, perhaps?" he said, setting his staff aglow. The men with crossbows lowered their weapons in surprise when they saw the face of the tall half-orc and his motley mix of companions.

"Orcs?" one of the men said. "Orcs? You said it was a woman."

"There is a woman," Thorvald said. "And her squad of warriors."

"And a mage," the other crossbowman said. "Dreamer, Thorvald, this is not what we expected."

"Well, it's what we've got," Thorvald replied.

"And there are four mages among us," Faralinda said. "A good match for your wizard, I shall wager."

"Torrey, go gather the others. We'll need all hands for this." Thorvald said.

"Aye," the first crossbowman said, and walked out of the room to the darkened spaces beyond.

Thorvald turned to the band. "Welcome to the fortress of the rebellion, my friends, such as it is. We've gained strength since last you were here, Helga, but most of the newcomers do not know of this refuge, since they joined hungry and not for the cause."

"Wise," Thokar said. "What is your plan?"

"Attack the castle."

"Out of the question," Thokar said. "We are not blind to the inner fortress, as many of the hamlet people informed us as to its nature. We are strong with magic, but not that strong. The castle will have to be breached with siege engines. We have already built these and prepared for this. I will help you defeat this wizard, but I will not have my men commit suicide for it. We ought to take the outer gatehouse."

"I wasn't finished," Thorvald said. "That will only give the wizard time to draw his men back into the keep, along with whatever city folk he deems worthy, and you will likely stall out the way you did before. No, we will attack the castle first and get him to shut the gates in desperation. That way, when the great gatehouse is broken, you will have an opportunity for real battle. The outer armies will drive the Thruddel soldiers against the keep, trapping them, because they won't realize that their own defenses have been put up against them."

"Interesting," Aarne said. "But how shall we accomplish this with so few?"

"I have more men available. The latecomers will be happy to finally do something. I'll set them to the castle. Mostly men with bows as I have few men with melee combat experience." Thorvald paused and scratched his scruffy beard hair. "Yes, we should have a few of your mages attack the keep, which will make the effort seem greater than it is."

"What about the outer gatehouse?" Thokar said.

"I have a few men on the inside," Thorvald said. "And a few more in the army that will abandon their posts if I can get word to them to do so. I can get the rear doors unbarred, which should make taking the gatehouse that much easier."

"My band is already readying a frontal assault," Thokar said. "Perhaps this will work."

"What if the wizard recognizes me?" Helga said.

"I barely recognized you," Thorvald said. "But it is a risk. Perhaps you ought to stay here."

"No, I intend to fight," Helga said. "I did not come here to be dead baggage for you again."

"Three mages ought to be frightening enough for your wizard," Faralinda said.

Thorvald gave Helga a strange stare. "Very well. You can attack the gatehouse."

"I will send Nit, Aarne, and Harpa with you," Thokar said. "They are worth at least five men apiece." He turned to Thorvald. "When do we strike?"

"Dawn. Eat well."

*

The sky was lightening to a pale pink-orange in the east below heavy clouds. The wind was pushing them ever closer, and Helga knew that it would be a cold and snowy day. She crouched among the stone of a forgotten watchtower, long crumbled save for a single wall and the remains of a parapet above. Once the city wall had adjoined the ruin, but had fallen away or been salvaged for other buildings once the great front gatehouse had been built.

It was this gatehouse that Helga watched, hunching beside Harpa, Nit, Aarne, and a small group of men Thorvald had attached to them. It was almost as well-defended from the back as from the front. The double iron portcullis was as strong, and the drawbridge, apparently enchanted to withstand fire and other manners of attack, would likely stand as well from the rear. Entrance to the great, round turrets that made up the gatehouse was accomplished through two ironbound doors, both raised above a stone staircase with a machicolation above each to repel possible attacks during a breach.

"Which door was supposed to be unbarred?" Helga whispered.

"Don't know. We'll have to guess," said Harpa, a wide-shouldered orc with dark grey skin. He smiled grimly as he spoke, as if excited about the possibility of death. He wore a coat of plates over mail, but they did little to hide his overgrown musculature.

They waited carefully for the sun to rise, as Thorvald had ordered. All of them held their breath as an armed man walked up the steps to the left-hand tower and knocked on the door. It opened and admitted him.

"It has to be the one on the right," Helga said.

"Why?" said Nit. His fingers danced anxiously on the hilt of his sword, and he adjusted his shield higher on his shoulder.

"Because the man at the door just let someone in at a knock. We're supposed to walk right in."

"He could let us walk right in now," Nit said.

"No, that soldier would have seen him leave the door unbarred. It has to be the one on the right."

"Let's go, then," Harpa said, and jumped over the wall, drawing his sword. Aarne was just as quick, shouldering his crossbow and aiming up, just behind Harpa. With a groan, Nit followed. He drew his longsword and motioned for the others to come. Helga ran across the empty courtyard, followed by Thorvald's men, who held bows and looked frantically at the parapet, as if anticipating some last failure.

Harpa jumped up the steps and hit the door, which swung open easily. The rest followed, into a small room with a table and ledgers, barrels of odd armaments and arrows, and one frightened-looking man holding his hands up.

"Help us or flee," Harpa said to the man, and then raced up a spiral staircase, leaving Helga and the others to follow as quickly as they could. At the top, there were two soldiers, caught unawares, holding crossbows. When Helga reached the landing, Harpa had already rushed forward, killing the first man with one blow that cut through his gambeson like grass. The other screamed and fired, but Harpa caught the bolt in his large, square shield. The man was already running away when he was hit in the back by a bolt from Aarne's crossbow.

The scream had alerted others, and into a narrow hallway ran three pikemen. Another man behind the new group fired a crossbow. The bolt bounced off the ceiling and struck Nit, sticking in the leather cover of his plate coat and doing nothing else. Harpa met the pikemen with his shield, turning points away and into his armor, which stood strong as the spears glanced off of him. Aarne had his own shield off his back and was swinging a flail, cracking the spears and knocking them from the hands of the defenders. Nit pushed up to the two-man shield wall and tried to reach over with his longsword, but the pikemen, who were retreating, still had too much reach.

Helga, not knowing what else to do, reached inward to find the wind and threw it at them. One fell at the burst of air, and the other two staggered back. Harpa and Aarne rushed forward. The flail flew wildly and crushed bones; Harpa's sword found gaps in mail and severed arteries. Blood poured out as they trampled the dying men, rushing forward to the first wench crank for the portcullis.

"We need to get the drawbridge down first!" Helga cried, trying to keep up with Harpa and Aarne. She stopped short as she entered a large open-windowed room above the portcullis. More bolts and arrows flew about them as the soldiery from the upper battlements came down a flight of stairs in the center of the room. Nit met the men, using his longsword as a deadly moving barrier.

Helga found in the room the great wenches that held up the drawbridge. A large iron lever held the gears of the wench taught. Helga kicked at the first one swiftly. It snapped off, and the chain flew off the spool. Half the bridge lurched forward a few feet, wrenching the chain on the other side with a terrible squealing, cracking noise.

"Quick, Helga, the signal!" Nit cried, holding back two soldiers with great sweeps of his sword.

Helga reached into her side pouch to retrieve the small clay cylinder that Thokar had given her. "Here goes nothing," she said. She slammed it down on the wall and threw it out the window. Seconds later, it exploded in a flurry of green flame and sparks, roaring as it fell to the moat below. Helga had a chance to look out the window and see movement from the Band's positions and a bright green firework in answer. A low covered siege engine with a battering ram on the front was already moving forward. Lines of archers moved behind

steel shields carried by armed men, along with a small cavalry detach-
ment.

Helga ran from the window to the second wench, which was
twisted badly on its mountings from the weight of only one side of the
bridge being released. Helga kicked the iron lever, but it did not
budge. She felt for the earth under her feet, and though she was on
stone, she felt again a firm strength in her limbs. She kicked with all
her force at the lever. It did not release the bridge; rather, it bent at a
square angle, and the chain remained where it was. Helga, still full of
exhilarating strength, brought the hammer of her poleax down on the
chain. Once, twice, thrice, and finally, the old iron shattered.

The drawbridge fell free, tumbling toward earth. The first spool
ripped from its mountings, sending mortar dust and small stones flying about the room. The bridge landed on an earth ramp (built by the
besiegers and mostly washed away by snow and rain) with a deafening
crash and a massive plume of dust. Helga leaned out the window,
suddenly afraid that the bridge had shattered from the fall. Below, the
dust cleared, and she could see it had not broken, at least not completely. Many of the wood planks were cracked or shattered, and the
lower hinges had ripped free of the gatehouse, but the iron bounds
still held, and the drawbridge still spanned the pit below. The band
was moving forward, and Helga could see the regular army was starting to assemble.

"Quickly!" one of Thorvald's men said. Helga turned to see him
struggling on the wench to the first portcullis.

"That's all we needed," Nit said. "They can knock down the rest
on their own."

"We can still make it easier," Helga said, and rushed to help Thorvald's man.

The wench was a large horizontal wheel with many wooden dow-
els to aid in its function. A chain came from each side to wrap around
part of the spool. Helga pushed, and the chains began to move. The
gate lifted into the upper house.

"Help!" Helga said, trying to reach the iron anchor-stop. Nit ducked under a sword swing and rolled to the wench to lock it open.

Men rushed around Harpa. Helga let go of the wench and grasped quickly for the magic in her mind. She threw out her hand, and, like an amplified campfire, she unleashed a torrent of blue flame on the attackers. They cried out, and the first in line panicked as they burned. Harpa, who still was sparring in the hallway, had been hit too, though lightly, and had dropped his shield to slap out a fire on his right elbow.

"Dreamer!" Harpa said. "You're as bad as Peridan." He extinguished the fire and found his shield again, but the soldiers were fleeing. He quickly turned back into the room to finish the few who remained alive and burning. He cried aloud, "Mercy!" as he thrust his sword into each of their necks.

Behind Helga, Nit and the others were already raising the rear portcullis. Helga ran to the arrow-slit to watch the covered battering ram moving onto the drawbridge. From the battlements above rained down a fury of arrows, rocks, dung, and refuse. A few of the arrows found their marks in the legs of the fighting men, but most stuck in the thick wooden roof of the battering ram.

More men came down a spiral stair in the far gate turret; Helga presumed it was to man the murder hole, and they were unaware that the room above the gates was held. Flanked by Nit and Harpa, Helga sent streams of fire from her hand again, but this time they were not as effective, and she realized her feeling of touching her magic sense was a little less than before. Nonetheless, it had an effect and stunned the men who were then driven back by Harpa and Nit.

"I have an idea!" Nit said. "Get that pitch."

Thorvald's men carried over a heavy bucket of black pitch. Nit grabbed it and threw it on the ground beneath a ladder leading to a higher level.

Helga, seeing what Nit intended, lit the pitch on fire. A few men above peeked down at the fire, then ducked away.

Helga turned as she heard footsteps from below, only to relax when a few men and orcs from the Band of the Badger bounded up, ready for action.

"Hel's fury, what happened here?" said the lead man.

"A bit of magic and a bit of fun," Harpa said.

"Where is Baradict?" Helga said. "I have urgent news for him."

The soldier pointed down the stairs. "Getting the fight on."

Helga nodded and ran down the stairs. She reached the landing door and opened it to find a full battle raging. The band had a full shield wall across the courtyard, and a milling unorganized infantry of Thruddel soldiers was crashing against it. Behind the infantry, Baradict rode his horse to and fro, barking orders. Arrows flew past him from the defenders of the ramparts, who were already abandoning the outer wall and taking potshots from the flanking parapets as the invaders poured in through the gates.

Regulars were milling their way into the gates behind the Band of the Badger, assembling into lines and trying to make some semblance of order to press the attack. Helga saw far along the lines of the wall, stretching all the way out to the end of sight, men were abandoning their posts and heading for the castle. As the last of the remaining men from the gatehouse and surrounding ramparts leapt down the stairs to disappear into the crowded houses, the Thruddel infantry turned to run, and the shield wall collapsed in pursuit of the rout.

"Baradict! Baradict!" Helga shouted. It was hard to press through the throng of soldiers, and her voice sounded thin and meager among the shouts of fighting men. By chance, Baradict noticed her and rode over.

"Where is Thokar?" he said.

"He is attacking the castle," Helga said. "The plan was to get them to shut the outer defenses against Thokar and the others, so that the Thruddel army would be trapped on their retreat."

"Hell of a plan," Baradict said. "Wish I'd thought of it. Well, that's what's going to happen regardless, but let's find the king or General Ragnur and tell them."

Baradict pulled Helga up onto his horse and rode her through the assembling men, back across the bridge to where a few garishly armored officers milled about on their horses.

"Well done," one of them said as they approached. Helga recognized him as the man who presided over the execution. "You've earned your keep and then some. I'll personally put up a hundred Aurals if you can do the same to the keep."

"Thanks, general," Baradict said. "We're running with some rebel elements from inside the city. The keep is already closed. If we press there with a firm set of lines, we can pin them against the other gates and slaughter them."

"Interesting," said Ragnur. "But also difficult. I'll have a hard time keeping men who've been pinned outside of a conquest for half a year from taking their owed pleasures. Might as well try to herd cats."

The other officers laughed.

"Well, you'd best learn how to herd cats, or you'll end up in a battle rather than a slaughter and be no better off than you were. Where is the king?"

"It takes time to put on one's armor," the general said. "Especially when the armor is as fine as Coladarn's." There was more laughter from the other officers.

"You'd best heed his advice, or the ravens will have your eyes," Helga said.

"Yes, we will!" It was Zim, who flitted down to sit on Helga's shoulder. "Perhaps the general forgets he is not king?"

"Egad, what is that?" the general said. "Get it away from me!"

"Heed my advice!" Baradict said, and heeled the horse to a gallop, heading back into the city.

315

XVIII. Awakening

HE RETREAT was long and bloody, for ultimately, the regular army did not attempt to rein in its soldiers, but let them loot at their own will and pleasure. The defenders lit houses and buildings on fire as they retreated, forcing the Band and the more disciplined regiments of the regular army to slog their way through wide city streets without protection and with constant arrow fire, at least until the afternoon when the enemy seemed to run out of arrows to shoot. The women and the children of the city fled before the onslaught, but there was nowhere to go, and many were killed or hurt deeply by the vengeful lust of Coladarn's hungry army.

Still, the commanders of the army found it remarkable how few they saw. They did not realize that in preparation for the attack, Thorvald had spread much word and had hidden away many families in secluded cellars and the underground haven that few in the city knew how to access or navigate. So it was that Thorvald's greatest heroism came not from fighting, but from the hiding of the innocent.

Helga rode with Baradict all the way to the gates of the castle. Zul and Zim were often aloft, watching the battle and giving information to Baradict. When they reached the castle, they found that the Thruddel army was already trying to mount a stand amongst the brawling mass of Coladarn's soldiers. The Band was there too, holding their shield wall and pressing the attack, then letting the cavalry flank and withdraw under a hail of arrows from the ramparts above. Each time, more of the enemy fell. It was there that they found Thokar, leading the assault and casting what magic he could up onto the defenders above. Like the great gate, the castle seemed very resistant to magic.

Every so often, a group of Thruddel soldiers would fall back, and the portcullis would open and let a few of them in before being shut again. The remaining men would curse their fellows for cowards and try to reform lines from the rout.

"Why don't they surrender?" Helga said.

"Helga, you are well," Thokar said, only then noticing she had arrived with Baradict, so focused was he on the battle. "That is good. I believe they fear death less than they fear being made a prisoner."

"It's got to be Magnus. Where are Mona and Faralinda?" Helga said. "Could they not assist you with what magic they have?"

"They are with Thorvald, resting and trying to treat a wound he received. We are all exhausted, Helga. Even I cannot find the will to continue casting much longer, but we have had the proper effect, I think."

"Where are they? Perhaps I can help."

"In a house down this street," Thokar said, pointing away from the castle. "It appeared to be abandoned."

Helga slid off Baradict's horse and trotted down the street with Zim flapping along beside her. She found the house easily enough by the small badger flag tied on a porch post. Inside, she found Faralinda and Mona sitting beside Thorvald, who lay out on a heap of bedding with his leg stuck straight out. On his thigh was a bloody bandage.

"Thorvald, are you alright?" Helga said, entering.

"Can't say I've had worse," Thorvald said. "Artery on my thigh got nicked a bit. Lucky we had a tourniquet handy."

"I have done what I can," Faralinda said, "but I am beyond my abilities now. I cannot find the words or touch the dream right now. I need rest."

"As do I," Mona said. "And I am weaker than Faralinda. Thorvald is healed, but not enough."

"Enough," said Thorvald. "I can feel the flesh knitting back together already. I'll be on my feet in an hour, I'm sure."

"No," Mona said. "Count yourself lucky to exit this battle when you did. Taking the inner keep will be brutally hard work, bloody, and not at all honorable. Rest easy while you can rest at all."

Helga sat down in a nearby chair and bowed her head. Sleep felt on edge suddenly, and she closed her eyes to it, losing track of the sounds of battle and slaughter outside. Images flashed behind her eyelids of bitter cold landscapes.

A rumbling brought her back from her wanderings. She got up and went outside to see a column of fire ripping through the men in front of the gate on both sides. The attack on the castle gate immediately fell back as another wave of magic was unleashed.

Through the lightly falling snow, Helga saw the wizard Magnus standing on the ramparts, his staff glowing. Magic surrounded him in what looked like a giant bubble. As arrows struck it, they rebounded, almost as if the bubble had turned them about and shot them back at the attackers. His face was a blur, but through the wind, she could hear his voice echoing across the city, shouting words that she did not know, but somehow could touch the meaning of, like a memory on the edge or recall but never fully realized. The words chilled her and made her stomach churn.

The lines of soldiers reformed only to be hit again. Bodies of fully armored men went flying like leaves in the wind. The wizard had been pressed and was now pressing back, more fully than any had anticipated.

"What is happening?" Faralinda said. She approached the doorway and froze as she saw the carnage. She turned away.

"Is there anything to be done?" Helga said.

"I do not know. This is power far beyond me, or even Thokar to repel."

Outside the gates, the Band of the Badger and the Northmarch regulars were falling back. The gates were opening, letting in the surviving soldiers of Thruddel. Helga saw Zul fly out of the snow, feathers ruffled.

"Quickly, Helga, we must get the men to retreat," she said.

"They have retreated already," Helga said.

"Further back. Past the walls of the city, if you can make it." Zul said. "The wizard has prepared something very terrible. Very terrible! I have seen it within the castle walls."

"Wait, I recognize him," Faralinda said, her eyes fixed on the wizard. "He was not always called Magnus. He was a friend of Peridan's many years ago. Many lifetimes ago, by human standards. Why? This seems so unlike him."

"He is not human, then," Helga said.

"Or more than human," Faralinda said. "He was a dedicated student of the arcane and the knowledge of the ancient world. He learned through Peridan much that was preserved in the libraries of Alfheim, where it is forbidden for a human to tread. He was powerful then, extremely talented, but not with such destructive potential, nor such lusty malice."

The wizard, seeing his enemies fall back, began to raise his hands and lift up great stones from the earth, which he tossed here and there, striking occasionally an armed man. Soon the armies had drawn back, leaving an empty space of dusty cobbles and ruined buildings between the castle and the lines, where the wizard could no longer ply his magic.

"What is his true name?" Helga said.

"Cato, or it was his name back then," Faralinda said.

"Perhaps you can reason with him, since he knows you," Helga said.

"Yes, perhaps, but how can I know who he is now? He was a good man when I knew him, but humans change."

"Silly elf," Zim said, hopping up beside Zul. "Zul said we must flee, and so flee we must! Do not wax on the past when your present is endangered."

"I shall try to talk to him," Faralinda said. "Maybe he has not changed totally."

Faralinda stepped out into the street and walked calmly toward the walls of the castle.

"Absolute fools!" Zim said. He took to the air, and Zul followed him.

"Farewell, Helga," Zul said, "I wish you had heeded me." She then disappeared with Zim over a building and was lost to sight.

Helga looked into the house to see Thorvald staring at her.

"I'm fine," he said.

Helga nodded and followed Faralinda down the street, keeping a distance and staying in the shadows of the houses in fear that the wizard might recognize her.

"Cato!" Faralinda cried, her voice amplified to a supernatural volume. The wizard stood up straighter and looked down from the rampart. "You were a good man, once."

Helga ducked down behind a pile of rubble. She stared at the wizard, whose face was just discernable. He was smiling slightly.

"Faralinda," the wizard said, his voice loud but not echoing. "It has been an age since last we met. Your beauty is no less than I remember."

"Then you *are* Cato."

"I am Magnus."

"Surely we can negotiate an end to this and come to terms without further bloodshed."

"I intend to end this, but not through negotiation. Already I am indeed ending it. As to whether blood must be shed, I shall leave that to you."

"What do you mean?"

Magnus nodded to someone on the ramparts, and across the edge of the castle, great cauldrons were brought up, steaming and reeking. The men carrying them wore cloth around their faces. Even as this was happening, a great, deep horn sounded, reverberating through the city.

"If you had continued to travel with Peridan, surely you would have avoided the fate into which you now fall," Magnus said.

"Peridan is fallen."

The wizard laughed. "Ironic that the man who taught me control over life and death, an immortal, would then die, only to allow a worse fate than death to his sister."

A memory tickled Helga's mind, of Peridan and the watchers, and thoughts of possibilities began to trace their way in and out of her memory. The Horn sounded again. She turned down the street to see dust rising, and the lines of the armies were moving, readying for something Helga could not see.

At that moment, Zim landed on a nearby rock, grumbling audibly and talking to himself. "Foolish Zim. Why do you return? Yes, Zald loved her. Bah!"

"Zim?"

"Helga, we came back to inform you. You cannot see it yet, but we have the advantage of wings, as you will agree is a superior-"

"Get on with it, you talkative crow."

Zim puffed his chest indignantly. "There is another army coming in from the outer walls and gates. Only some of them are human."

"What are the rest?"

Zim teetered on his legs. "Well, they are human too, only…"

"What?"

"They are dead."

"What?"

Zul landed on another nearby rock. "Yes, undead is a better word for it. Most unappetizing."

"Quickly," Helga said. "We must find the king and the general."

"As if they will listen," Zim said.

"They will have to."

Brazenly, Helga ran across the open space. Faralinda was running too, as if to intercept her.

"We have to find Thokar and the general!" Helga yelled to her.

"I know what is in those cauldrons!" Faralinda said.

Together they met and ran side by side. The wizard began conjuring magic again, hurling rocks that narrowly missed Faralinda and

Helga. The lines of the armies were still too far away for him to do any damage to them.

Thokar rode out with Baradict to meet them. Helga jumped behind Baradict, and Faralinda followed suit with Thokar.

"To the king, go!" Faralinda cried. Thokar immediately obeyed, and his destrier's hoofs pounded in a flat gallop to the regular army, ignoring magic and arrows from the wall above. The high officers and king were easy to identify, milling about at the back of the column. The infantry parted to let the horses through.

Helga screamed as an arrow flew through the air from behind the long line of the army and struck one of the officers in the arm, splitting the space between two armor plates and causing him to cry out in pain.

"What is this?" said the king, a middle-aged man in armor so heavily gilded it looked useless. He turned his horse about to catch an arrow on his breastplate, which repelled the missile easily.

"There is another army approaching from behind!" Helga cried as they reached the king. "Form lines facing backward, hurry!"

The captains of the army must have been listening, even if the general was not, for immediately the infantry moved through the archer corps in the rear to form a shield wall, while the front lines (or rather, those facing the castle) tightened up and remained steadfast.

"What *is* going on here?" The king asked again, blinking in surprise as a raven landed on the front of his saddle.

Thokar spoke. "Betrayal, or a plan better than ours. An army approaches from behind."

Already they could see a mass of milling men moving through the streets, strange in their loping gait.

"An undead army," Zim said. "Yes, indeed they are the dead from this morning, risen to fight again for the lord of the castle. Some are your dead, too."

"You must be joking," General Ragnur said. "The hills were clear just yesterday. We would have seen an army approach."

"Were you listening?" Helga said. "They are the men who fell in battle today. The army didn't exist yesterday!"

"Perhaps relief from the outer holds, sir," a captain said to the king.

"They could have been waiting for a time to strike," Ragnur said. "Remember, the freemen are warier of battle than regular soldiers."

As the king gazed out into the throng of disorganized men moving toward them, occasionally firing errant arrows, the reality of the undead was undeniable.

"No, they are right," he said, his jaw slack.

"Not the whole army," Zul said. "There are living men there too, on horses."

"We must go," Thokar said. "The band will need us. Send a raven if you have a desperate message."

"We are no messengers!" Zim said.

"You are now," Baradict said.

"You stay with the king," Zul said. "I will remain with Helga."

"I will not!"

Zul ignored him and hopped onto Helga's shoulder. Zim, displeased, did not fly away, but rather flapped over to the king's shoulder and rocked loudly.

"I suppose I've always wanted to learn just what a human king does," he said.

Thokar, Baradict, Helga, and Faralinda rode away with all speed, back to where the Band of the Badger was already engaged in a tight fight. Faralinda and Helga dismounted to find Mona already there, working some sort of conjuring in a small fire. Thorvald was there too, standing on his injured leg, a sword in his hand.

"There will be much blood," Mona kept saying to herself.

"Thorvald," Helga said. "Your day is done."

"Not yet," he said.

Helga ignored him and followed Faralinda to the front lines, where she began casting fire past the shield wall with reckless abandon. The attackers, Helga could see, were soldiers, bloodied and dismembered. Many had broken or severed limbs, a head that cracked open and still oozed congealed blood, or were missing parts of their face. Some even crawled along the ground, too damaged in body to walk.

The Band of the Badger fought with discipline despite the terror, each man covering the next as they stabbed with spears and slashed with swords. Over the top of the wall, more men drove pikes home into the attackers. None of the undead seemed willing to die a second time. A spear wound would not even bleed, save in small amounts, and always it was the heavy red clots of dead men. Only when the head was severed did the bodies cease to fight, or when it was so badly damaged that it would flail on the ground uselessly.

They kept coming, and the dead piled up, forcing the band backward simply to maintain their footing (and to avoid being grabbed at the feet by half a corpse, or bitten, which was worse). Near Helga, a man screamed, unwilling to fight as a corpse attacked that he clearly recognized. Helga dashed forward and crushed the dead man's head with an earth-empowered swing from her poleax, and then she put out a hand and lit the whole row of dead men into a wall of fire. They collapsed from the flames, but they were not wholly effective, and as soon as the flames died down, the corpses rose again.

Helga glanced over to see Faralinda doubled over with exhaustion, trying her best to attack the wall of the dead. Within minutes Helga too felt overwhelmingly tired, her limbs aching from the effort of slaying the undead and her spirit quavering from the exertion of her mind. She began to collapse, only to find Thorvald under her arm, supporting her and moving her behind the lines to catch her breath. He bled now in a dozen places, but looked oddly healthier than before, as if his spirit had healed his body for the battle.

Arrows began to fly too, fired by living men as wary of the undead as the band, hanging back behind the rolling waves of the risen.

"We cannot go on," Helga said. "They will chew all of us to pieces."

"Don't despair," Thorvald said.

"We can go on," Thokar said, riding up and casting a spell that knocked back a wave of undead. "The shield wall is stronger than the dead."

"These beings do not tire," Faralinda said. "It is only a matter of time, and with each minute, we retreat backward, toward the castle."

Thokar turned about and saw the men lining the ramparts. The great iron cauldrons were still there, sending up green, acrid smoke now rather than just steaming.

"You never said what those vats were for," Helga said.

"They are full of poison," Faralinda said. "A very potent one called *rychthavarin* that requires great sorcery to craft. A poison that touches your soul more than your body and will leave you an animated corpse."

"Like the dead that attack now?"

"Worse, for part of you will remain in the shell, like a lich but of lesser mind. Even its fumes can kill. It is powerfully dark magic, pre-served, now I shall say unwisely preserved, from the sunless years. I wonder how he came by it. Surely it did not come from Peridan… but then this man has lived a long time."

Helga remained silent, thinking of what Peridan had revealed about his knowledge of the undead. *Perhaps there will be a time to tell her all that, but not today,* Helga thought. *Today, let her fight and die loving her brother as a hero and scholar.*

"I will put a stop to this," Thorvald said. He started walking, still favoring his leg, through the Band and toward the castle. Helga jogged behind him.

"What are you doing?" she said.

"I am the one who orchestrated this, and I will end it." He turned and placed a hand on her shoulder. "Wait."

She obeyed, but wished she hadn't. Thorvald walked out into the clearing before the gates of the castle, shouting in the din and waving his arms.

Strangely, all went quiet in Helga's ears, not because the battle ceased, but because the wizard began to talk.

"Thorvald. Seeking a quick death? You will not get it."

"It is me that you want!" Thorvald shouted. His voice sounded tiny. "It is I who orchestrated this siege. Let us stop more loss of life, for both of us! Turn back the dead, and you can have me!"

"Thorvald," Magnus said, almost jovially. "You live because I have chosen you to live. You live because I enjoy watching you suffer, and because you are useful to my purposes. Or did you think I only watched you through others' eyes?"

Thorvald looked at his hands in sudden fear and realization. "How?"

"Through Freydis, of course, who did betray you, you should know, now that you are at the end. Yes, Freydis was mine, Thorvald." He laughed in a sickly, deep voice. "Your usefulness, I deem, is at an end."

With a flick of his wrist, the wizard caused a plume of fire to consume Thorvald, and he screamed as he collapsed.

"No!" Helga shouted out, and rushed forward. She wanted to put water on him… Water, the magic that she could almost feel but had never used, but it was too late. Thorvald died, leaving behind a charred and thankfully unrecognizable husk.

Helga stopped before the body, shocked.

"You," Magnus said, his voice filling her head. "It is you, is it not, Freydis? No, no… now that I gaze upon you again, you are not her; you are not like her at all. But you have returned…" The wizard leaned over the parapet, and his voice oozed anticipation. "Which means you have fulfilled your quest. The Water of Awakening."

"The well is dried," Helga said. Her voice sounded even smaller than Thorvald's in the empty loud street.

"You lie," Magnus said. "And you should not. I understand this precious relic, which only an ascended sorcerer would know the value of. Give it to me."

Helga hefted her poleax and felt with great effort for the place in her mind and body where she could grasp and unleash her magic.

"Give it to me, Helga, and I will cease this."

Helga had to pause at this offer. She didn't reach for it, but she could feel, or almost feel, the glowing vial tucked safely in her hip bag – that which she had fought so hard for. She looked around at the carnage on either side, the blood on the snow, and the waiting death of all at the castle walls. She felt smaller and weaker than she ever had before.

"So let it be traded," Helga said. "But you must be bound."

"I would not betray anyone in this," Magnus said. "But you can bind me if you find the magic. A gesture."

With the booming word, the undead suddenly stopped their attack and moved backward, their empty faces looking up at the heavy sky.

The wizard descended from the ramparts on an ethereal staircase, each step turning to solid stone under his foot before disappearing as he stepped off it. His red silk robes flapped about him, drawing all eyes in wonder.

Magnus stopped before Helga.

"The Water."

"Do you swear?" Helga said. Magnus extended a hand.

She reached to her spirit and wondered how she could make a bond for a man to tell the truth. She found nothing. Instead, she thought back to how she had first made the campfire: by imagining it. She tried, and after a moment of blankness, she imagined a liar, in its concept and with the form of Magnus. She imagined his heart stopping. Not knowing what else to do, she extended her hand.

"I swear," Magnus said. "So the bond is laid. And a powerful one." He shook her hand.

Helga reached into her pack and unrolled her leather satchel. There, glowing, was the glass vial of Garamesh's tears. She handed it to Magnus.

Around her, Helga heard the sounds of battle commence again.

"You swore!"

"My heart stopped beating long ago," Magnus said. "Now the last key is here, for true immortality, rather than this well-crafted lich."

He downed the vial of tears. Helga cried out. Magnus laughed at her, and then stopped with sudden silence. His face was fixed with shock, and he trembled. Everywhere, the dead paused, and the fighting stopped.

Magnus held up his hands to his face, and Helga could see through them, to his eyes, which were emptying of their life. He gave a whimpering scream, but it sounded only a little more present than a distant calling on the wind. Pieces of the wizard's clothes and body began to blow away, mixing with the snow swirling around them.

Helga saw him then for what he truly was, without the glamour to make him appear wise and healthy. His cheeks were a sallow grey, and his eyes were hazy. The flesh on his fingers was sunken to the bone, and his lips were rotted away, revealing bleached-white teeth. Everywhere on his body, his flesh was withered from centuries of preservation beneath his human exterior. His hair was ropes of grey, and then it was fading. He stared at his hands, growing translucent, with shock and wonder plastered on his ancient face.

Helga could clearly see the castle through him, and seconds later, the wizard was gone, leaving only footprints and rags where once he had stood. The vial lay in one of the footprints, upturned and empty.

Helga turned at a cheer from the armies. Beyond them, the dead lay still again. The humans who had attacked from behind were fleeing. The men on the ramparts stood dazed. Helga watched as the gaseous reek from the cauldrons began to subside and blow away on the wind. Helga felt frozen, and though she saw thousands of men breaking ranks to cheer one another, she felt defeated.

"That was brilliant," Faralinda said, running up to stand beside Helga. "He never understood the old powers, as much as he wished to."

"Where did he go?"

"Out of this world, and back into the Prim, I imagine," said Faralinda. "Once you carry something out of the Fay, it does not hold the same qualities as it does within. Within, the water awakes you to the World-That-Is, without... who knows? Clearly, it did not give Cato what he desired most, which was power and immortality." Faralinda paused, recognizing the muted and dark expression on Helga's face. "What is wrong?"

"My quest is failed," Helga said.

"Not yet," said Faralinda. "We can still brew a cure for your husband, but you may be delayed. The wizard is gone, but the castle still stands."

Faralinda guided Helga back across the trampled and bloody snowfields to where the Band of the Badger was resting and counting the dead. Mona was supervising triage, and Thokar sat on a rock nursing a cut on his neck. Baradict and Nit stood beside him, arms crossed and doing their best to not look totally exhausted.

"Is it bad?" Helga asked. She turned loose of Faralinda and collapsed into the shallow snow, feeling her sweat begin to burn cold.

"Could have been worse," Baradict said. "But now my heart misgives me for the women and children we have left outside."

"Zul agreed to check on them and the camp followers," Thokar said. "But I am confident. They can hold their own more than any human outsider would think, and it is clear this trap by the wizard was meant to catch us, not them."

"I wonder what there will be to plunder," Nit said, looking out over the ruined city. "Nothing more than scared children, I'll wager."

"We're not in the slave trade," Thokar said.

"I didn't mean it that way," Nit said. "But I have my doubts about these men from the Northmarch."

Thokar grunted and nodded. "That is the way of things in this part of the world, alas."

At that moment, Zim flew down and landed on the rock. "So, I see you are all still alive."

"You shall be having a feast today, eh?" Baradict said.

"I already have. But that is not why I am here. The king... How shall I put it? He is not so healthy at the moment."

"What happened?" Helga said.

"He got hit with an arrow," Zim said. "He's alive but doesn't look well. Ragnur is in charge now, yet I wouldn't trust him if I were you."

Thokar nodded silently. "A risk I didn't anticipate." He looked at Baradict. "Nevertheless, we will get paid, one way or another."

"The general seemed very impressed with you," Helga said.

Baradict laughed. "You always want to stoke morale in a battle, but I can tell you, Helga Ravenfriend, that if most of our employers had been able to choose, we would not be paid after the campaign."

Nit laughed and cast a devious look toward Baradict, who smiled grimly at him.

XIX. Debts

THE BAND of the Badger prepared hasty resting places in the burned-out houses and city buildings. Zul returned as they did so, reporting that their camp was secure. However, it had been attacked during the siege, not by enemy soldiers or the hordes of the undead, but by the camp followers and their hired men, who took the absence of the soldiers to be an opportunity for theft and debauchery. Zul happily reported that the women had slain these attackers and hung their bodies up outside of camp, and that she had personally eaten six pairs of eyes before abandoning the corpses to the crows.

The siege of the castle was a thing of little consequences for the remaining armies, whose infantry gained rest while the archers harried the defenders. Though Coladarn's regulars had been badly hurt by casualties and injuries, they had plenty of men to go over the walls with ladders and the siege engines that were brought up from the great city gate. Likewise, the Band of the Badger was able to re-use its own devices, as well as their magic, to break open the gate (which now seemed to have lost its enchantments). The men inside were disorganized and terrified without the wizard, and so had abandoned the outer walls quickly, falling back into the keep before the break of dawn. Within the courtyard, many withered corpses lay: undead men that had lost their enchantment with the passing of Magnus.

The next morning, Helga awoke to find the men reforming for the final breaking of the keep, with its massive tower capped with many (now broken) windows. She found Faralinda already there, watching the moving of the battering ram into place.

"Nearly there," Faralinda said.

"Yes," Helga said.

The soldiers hushed to a dead quiet when, before final preparations could take place, the doors of the keep opened, and a haggard captain staggered forward carrying a bedsheet as a white flag. He was followed by many more men, who laid down their arms and kneeled down.

Ragnur walked forward to accept the captain's sword. Thokar was already running out to meet him there.

"Come on," Faralinda said, and they too jogged to the center of the courtyard between the keep and the outer wall.

"I accept your surrender," Ragnur said to the kneeling captain. "And will grant mercy to you and your men with it." He took the sword and handed it to an attendant. He then looked at his captain and said. "Find your best officers so we may begin the collection of the treasure. I want the first choices to go to the eighth squad, after the officer corps, of course, for they were the most valiant."

"I trust you will not forget that, according to our contract, we were to be given first opportunity at loot," Thokar said.

"You have the city to loot at your leisure," Ragnur said dismissively. "The treasure is the reward for real soldiering."

"It is unwise to break oaths," Thokar said. "First choice of all treasure was our bargain, or we would have demanded salary."

Ragnur laughed. "Your agreement was with Coladarn. He is dead, and now I must rule this army in his stead. I declare your contract void. Now be gone from my sight, orc, before I have your band slaughtered."

"Orc, eh? As if you have the strength left." Thokar shouldered his staff. At that moment, an arrow flew, from where none could say for sure, and struck Ragnur in the eye. Immediately swords were drawn, and lines were formed.

"There are apparently still a few arrows remaining in the keep," Thokar said casually to the Northmarch captain. "Nothing we can't root out for you. You are in charge now, eh?"

"Yes," the captain said, his voice quavering. Regulars were moving about the courtyard, here and there with their shields up, trying to see where the arrow had come from.

Thokar smiled at the captain. "What's your name, son?"

"My name is Dagarn," the captain said hesitantly.

"Well, Dagarn, I trust you will act in good faith of our contract, created by your sovereign."

"Yes... oh, yes," the captain said. "By all means, take your share first."

Thokar smiled, showing his large, aged ivory teeth, and walked toward the keep, motioning the rest of the band to follow him.

Helga and Faralinda joined him, and as they walked into the shadows of the doorway, Helga noticed faintly glowing runes on the ground outside and a slight shimmering in the air near the dry pit surrounding the keep.

"The library should have what we need," Helga said.

"Good. Make that your first share," Thokar said.

"Where is the king?" Baradict said, joining them. "I thought Ivar was still on the throne."

"He was when I was here last, but that was months ago," Helga said. "He could have died since then. Of course, Thorvald thought he was being controlled by Magnus."

They found the king easily enough, and he was indeed still on the throne. At least, his desiccated corpse was. Faralinda and Helga approached the body, leaning sideways on the ornate gilded chair. Its flesh was withered and a dry grey-brown. Thokar looked curiously around the room.

"He turned into that yesterday." The voice belonged to a young and beautiful blonde woman who wore a crown on her head and a long, silvery dress. She stepped from a shadowed doorway behind the throne. Her head was bowed, and she hunched her shoulders as she walked up. "But he has not been himself for a long time."

"Indeed, he has not. It had to be the glamour of the wizard," Faralinda said. "This body is well-preserved, but I'm sure he died many months ago."

The woman seemed unperturbed.

"That's how Magnus – Cato – kept control over the guard," Helga said. "He murdered the king and made a slave of his body. I wonder how long it would have been before he could have named himself king."

"Did you know he never shared my bed?" the woman said.

"Leave this place," Thokar said. "This foul dream is ended." The woman bowed her head and walked out submissively, her hands folded.

Helga and Faralinda entered the library, the ultimate sanctuary of the wizard, to find it very untidy. Missiles from catapults and ballistae had crashed through the windows, and everything was covered in colorful, broken glass.

"This is the real treasure," Faralinda said, looking at the massive bookshelves filled with ancient texts. "Of course, it is nothing compared to the Great Library in Alfheim, but it is quite magnificent for a human collection."

"He was alive a long time to collect it," Helga said.

They had the library to themselves, for most of the Band found books to be uninteresting, and those that did enjoy books enjoyed mostly heroic tales, not catalogues of arcane leys or potion effects.

They found the wizard's collection of ingredients and talismans, and among these, Faralinda was able to find the remaining ingredients for Thokar's potion. Indeed, Thokar soon joined them, taking books, potions, ingredients, and trinkets for his and Mona's loot share. Faralinda chose books, rifling through the shelves with amazing speed, pulling out whatever she could find that remotely contained new information for her. She found also a focus alike to Helga's, made of a dragon claw gripping a crystal ball.

"A curiosity, but one that undoubtedly has some use, considering Cato kept it," she said, putting it in her pile. "What shall you take for yourself, Helga?"

"What?" Helga said.

Thokar chuckled. "You participated as a member of the Band, you deserve payment. More than that, you deserve double, for it was you who broke the siege."

"She deserves triple," Faralinda said.

"Aye," Thokar said, checking on books for himself.

"Well," Helga said. "Thank you, I suppose. I can't help but think a bit of gold would be nice to bring back home after all these days away."

"You should take books," Faralinda said. "Your powers are nascent, and you need a good education. I can select what you need."

"Take all that you can carry in a cart and horse, gold or otherwise," Thokar said. "I shall provide you a horse."

"But not a cart," Helga said. Thokar looked at her curiously. "Sorry, feeling a bit like a raven after all this."

Faralinda happily created a massive stack of books for Helga to take with her. It was, Helga realized, more books than the Jarl of Greenfeld had in his hall and more books than she had seen in one place outside the wizard's library. Once the three of them had thoroughly looted the library, they visited the treasury, which also had an armory in it. Helga selected two small chests and filled them with spendable gold, ignoring the jewels and other things in the king's horde. She did, however, select a very ornate crossbow to replace the one she had lost along the way.

These things the men of the band helped her take out of the castle and to a new camp the women had already created outside the castle walls. The defenders were lined up near the outer wall, under guard but not mistreated. A group of women and children from inside the keep were held as well, and fires were lit for their comfort in the cold, bright day.

That night there was much revelry, in both camps, for though the Band of the Badger had taken first loot (by rights and contract, all that each man could reasonably carry out by himself), there was so much of value remaining that even the Regulars received treasure and the promise of its value in their futures.

Helga, Thokar, and Faralinda, however, did not join. Thokar spent the night, assisted by Faralinda, brewing a potion to cure the sleeping Trindol's Mist Blight. He did it delicately, taking his time with each step to ensure it was made perfectly, for the Luminescent Russula was of very short supply. In the end, Thokar boiled down and distilled a clear potion that glowed slightly blue in the dark light of the tent.

He sighed when he was finished.

"That will cure my husband as well?" Helga said.

"Yes," Thokar said, his brow wrinkled. "But there is very little. One dose, I should think. I am sorry, but that was all that we had ingredients for." He handed a small, glowing vial to Helga. She stared at the light within. When she tore her eyes away, she saw Faralinda gazing at her. Though she was expressionless, Helga could see the disappointment in her clear eyes.

Helga stood up with the vial and headed to the opening of the tent. She pulled back a flap and watched as men and women danced around a nearby campfire, sending sparks flying up into the air to die amid the cold, bright stars. The stars, she saw, were familiar, but grew brighter as she gazed, bright even as they were in the Fay. She heard the music play: pipes and drums and zithers and hurdy-gurdies throttling forward in their jovial recklessness, and through the chaos, she could discern one common note, one tonic that bound all the melodies together. It bound the words, and the thrumming chords, giving purpose and meaning to the endless music.

That one note sang out clearly in her mind as the stars faded in her eyes, back to their normal brightness and hue. Helga turned back into the tent. She went to Trindol's side and watched Faralinda gaze at her husband and stroke his hair.

Peridan truly meant for him to survive, and he was right in that I could not understand the hardship of the elves, to be separated forever by this curse. She could not banish one more thought from her mind. *I have taken one part of Faralinda's eternal bliss. Shall I take another to keep one of my own, here in this changing and mortal realm? How can the loss of a few years compare to eternity?*

"Here," Helga said, and pressed the glowing vial into Faralinda's hand.

"I cannot take this," Faralinda said.

"I said I would deliver this cure to you."

"It is yours by right, and by your quest."

"And I give it to you so that Trindol can have life. It is what Peridan wanted to give you."

"What about Erling? What about your own husband and his life, and his desires?"

"My task was to retrieve the water of awakening, and I have abandoned that task for the mercy of many men. I gave an oath, and perhaps one day I will find forgiveness for breaking that oath."

"You made no oath to me."

"I want to do what I say I will do. I no longer want oaths to bind me." Helga sighed. "Besides. My husband is almost certainly dead by now."

"Do you truly believe that?" Faralinda said. "For your actions speak that you do hold hope."

"I still have hope," Helga said. Tears burst from her eyes and fell down her cheeks in great wet tracks. "But it matters not. I want Trindol to receive this. Give it to him quickly, I beg you."

Faralinda nodded. She removed the cap from the vial and opened Trindol's mouth. With his eyes closed, he moaned slightly. She poured it into his mouth, a drop at a time, so that he would not choke, until it was clear that he had consumed all of it.

Nothing happened for a tense few minutes, and Helga began to doubt that the potion could cure anything at all.

Then, Trindol opened his eyes. He looked around in surprise, but could not move his face to talk, nor could he find the strength to sit up. A slow, croaking vocalization escaped his lips.

"Trindol!" Faralinda said and threw her arms around her husband, who stared at her in disbelief and surprise, as if sight was something new to him. She began to sob loudly, and Helga smiled despite her own tears.

Helga stood up and withdrew from their tent, not wanting to intrude further on their reunion, and sat down beside a fire. She watched the dancers dance and listened to the tune a fiddler was pumping out, now all simplicity and joy. Harpa was there, and he handed her a mug full of mead, warm and sustaining. She drank it there and watched the men and women celebrate their sanguine rituals beside the bitter, pure snow.

She cried, but either nobody noticed, or nobody dared to mention it.

*

The sun was shining the next day, and the snow and ice on the roofs of buildings were melting, creating great long clear icicles on all the wooden eaves. Freezing water dripped down them, chilled by a harsh wind from the east. The soldiers were hard at work at dawn, doing the great tasks that always must be done after a battle, but which few historians care to mention: the burying or burning of the dead, the salvaging of equipment, the trying of deserters and disobedient officers, triage and healing for the injured, counting the deceased and preparing lists of who died, and the great work of managing payments and the distribution of treasure to a hungry and tired soldiery.

Helga watched this work on a field of red and white while she made her own preparations. A small wagon had been made available to her, with a sturdy horse to pull it. Into this wagon, she stacked her share of the treasure, including the horde of books Faralinda had insisted she take with her.

It was Faralinda who found her that morning, cheerful and yet sad.

340

"How is Trindol?" Helga asked.

"His speech is returned, but he is weak in the legs still. Thokar thinks it will take some time for all his strength to return, but Trindol thinks he will be ready to fight by nightfall. I have my doubts."

"Good, then, that the fighting is done."

"Indeed. I think it shall be done for some time, at least for us."

"Why is that? Are you leaving the Band of the Badger?"

"We are, even if Trindol does not know it yet." The two women chuckled softly. "This was always a fancy of Trindol and Peridan, and this campaign would have given my brother all he wanted to learn about men and also given him a store of hidden knowledge, his constant desire."

"What about you?"

"I think I prefer gardening to adventuring."

"I would have said the same thing last year," Helga said. "Now, I'm not really sure. I feel... like who I am is something more changeable than before."

"Well, you have changed," Faralinda said. She looked down at the ground. "Thank you for giving me the cure. But what shall we do about your husband?"

"I don't know," Helga said.

"Could we try to find the dragon again and get another vial of the water?"

"He is so secluded... I don't even know where his lair is, and it may be one can only get there by flying. There was a woman who healed me that knew Garamesh, but she lives far in the northeast, and even she did not anticipate the dragon's coming to her door. The only thing I could hope for is that I would see him again in the Fay wastes or mountains and that he would not think first of eating me. And meanwhile, Erling will be getting closer to death. I must return to him, even if it is to send him on his way."

Faralinda sighed. "I see. You are right, of course. Is there anything else to trade the volva? If she could indeed cure Erling."

"I have my armor and my weapons," Helga said. "Oh! And I do have a very small quantity of dragon's blood."

"Dragon's blood! How did you manage to prick the dragon?"

"He pricked himself. Does it have value? Perhaps I could trade it to the volva."

Faralinda shrugged. "Hard to say. I've never seen anyone use it or trade for it, probably because I've never seen anyone make a dragon bleed. In the stories, the really old ones of great heroes, when a dragon is slain, his blood turns to poison, and always the hero would die along with his foe."

"Garamesh called it 'poison and life,' but I don't know what that means."

"Dragons, when they speak, are known to speak in riddles. It might have something to do with the dual nature of things, here and in the Fay. Dragons are born of the Fay. Perhaps it gives life in the Fay but poisons here. Only Atalthal the Great was able to slay a dragon without suffering death himself, but he was a powerful sorcerer that could tap the Prim itself. He might have had a way to avoid the poison."

"He remains a powerful sorcerer," Helga said. She smiled at Faralinda. "If only we had more time to talk."

"We shall have more time," Faralinda said, tapping her mouth. "Yes. If you wish it, I shall accompany you to your home."

"That is not necessary," Helga said.

"I am in your debt now," Faralinda said.

"I was merely fulfilling Peridan's quest."

"That was not your place. I *am* in your debt. Let me come with you. Perhaps I can persuade the volva, or provide some comfort to your husband. I also desire, if you will consider, to train you in the ways of elvish magic. You have a rare, inborn talent, and though my own power is quite weak-"

"Quite weak?" Helga said. "You call what you did during the battle weak?"

Faralinda continued. "Though I am quite weak in my own talent, I am very well-learned. With these books and my own experience, I could give you a great deal of valuable instruction and help you develop into the powerful sorceress your talent hints at."

"I will help you learn to use that sword, too." It was Trindol, who had managed to sneak up on them. He was leaning on a staff for support and had his sword belted on (though he wore no armor). "It's an elvish blade. I can tell that from here, and you ought to learn to use it properly if you plan on keeping it."

Helga laughed. "I will have no need for sorcery or swordsmanship when I return home. I'm a farmwife."

Trindol chuckled. "That you most certainly are not, but to each is given the will to form his own life. I would still accompany you, if only because three on the road is better than two, even powerful as we are."

"As I am," Faralinda said with a smile cast to her husband. "You are still weak as a kitten."

"I'll be right as rain by nightfall, I'm sure." He looked at Helga. "But thank you, Helga. I live. What greater gift is there?"

"I don't know," Helga said. "I suppose you can come with me. I do not want to be alone on the road, after all."

*

That afternoon they bade farewell to Thokar and the rest of the Band of the Badger, who were disappointed at the departure of Faralinda and Trindol. Baradict seemed to be upset that Helga was leaving, deeming her "an asset too valuable to let go." However, in the end, the flattery did not win anyone over. Helga and the two elves left the city with the wind at their backs and the sun shining in the west.

"Where are the ravens, I wonder?" Faralinda said. She rode Trindol's horse alongside a small wagon, which was pulled by her own steed.

"My guess is still filling their bellies before the dead are burned or buried," Helga said.

"Valuable pets, I am told," Trindol said. He rode in the wagon, sitting tall but still looking far from fully healed.

"They have their own wills," Helga said, "and they will join us or not, according to their choice. I owe them a sort of debt, though they do not acknowledge it." *As I owed you a debt,* she thought. *Though maybe I have repaid it.*

They traveled into the night and camped well west of the city. On their way, Helga told them of her journey, of Garamesh, of the dunmen and the Watchers, and of her encounter with Atalthal in his strange realm, which was of particular interest to Trindol. She omitted the details of Peridan's betrayal, merely stating that he was killed as she attempted to escape the watchers, who wanted her soul.

Helga lit a magic fire, and she listened to Faralinda talk about her early days, which were ancient to the minds of men, training in magic and hoping to match her brother in power and majesty. She told other tales, too, of the mythical sunless days, when before the birth of men, elvenkind tamed a dark and twisted earth, and how the secrets of those times were forgotten when the age passed away, preserved in memory and history books, but not in method or practice.

Trindol equated Helga's tale of Atalthalda with a true expression of the dark elves' aesthetics and vowed he would journey there to meet them, whatever Helga warned. Wolves howled in the night as they hunkered down, but they were distant. Faralinda set a few wards around the camp as protection, and they slept easily.

*

They spent the next week and a half traveling up, over the mountains, and through sparsely farmed valleys before they reached the rolling hills that surrounded Greenfeld. On the third day, the ravens somehow found them again and decided to contentedly ride in the wagons, which perturbed Trindol, for they were not careful with their droppings. They were hampered severely by the snow and mud throughout the journey (annoying the ravens, though not enough for them to abandon the wagons), but Faralinda knew spells to quickly heat and dry the ground, easing their passage in particularly difficult areas. They lost two days climbing out of one valley in the foothills when they got caught in a sudden winter storm. They stayed warm easily with magic fire, but had to rely on the hunting skills of Helga and Trindol (who took a week to recover fully) to catch a few under-fed rabbits so that they could eat. The ravens, of course, had a tendency to begin eating the rabbits before they could be cooked, especially the eyes.

At last, they reached the rolling hills that surrounded the hold of Greenfeld. They were snow-covered white in most places, with a few rocks jutting up here and there. Farmhouses perched on hills stuck up obviously, creating what Trindol called "A most disturbed aesthetic." The first of these farmhouses they reached around nightfall, and at Helga's bidding, they worked their wagons up to the farmhouse to beg for shelter from another incoming snow shower.

The man who opened the door Helga recognized immediately. His name was Sathurn, and he had been a friend of her father for a long time. He, however, did not recognize her until she told him who she was, and then he became suspicious of the three travelers to whom he had lent the use of his barn and spare beds. Eventually, he admitted that she was who she was, but decided that he had not seen her in so long, he was remembering her as a child and not as a woman.

Passing by a looking glass, Helga was even more surprised over this reception, for when she looked at her reflection, she saw staring back the person she always had been. Her hair was longer and her face a bit leaner from the hard travel, but to her own eyes, she looked the same.

Two days later, they arrived in the town of Greenfeld proper. Approaching it, Helga was surprised to get both a rather cold reception and the odd stares she got on the outskirts. People shut themselves in their houses, and everywhere eyes peered out of frosted windows.

"They gaze at us oddly," Zim said. "I don't like it."

"It could be the talking ravens," Trindol said.

"Yes, of course," Zim said. "I forget how ignorant humans are."

"I'm sure we look nothing like what they are used to," Faralinda said. "More than a few people will stare at elves, and we three are all rather strangely armed and clothed. And we do travel with ravens in our wagons."

"Actually," Trindol said. "I'm surprised they aren't running for cover."

"They're a brave lot, for their part," Helga said. "But it's clear to me that they do not recognize me. I saw myself. I look the same, but people consistently say I look different."

"The same as how you were, or the same as how you remember yourself to be?" Trindol said.

"Are they not the same?"

"Of course they aren't," Trindol said. "Memory is imperfect, a product of the soul and the Fay and the Eternal Dream. To me, you do look different than I remember."

"I don't understand."

"Consider your ears," Faralinda said.

Helga reached up and touched her ears, which felt the same as they always had.

"Has it ever occurred to you that they are different than those a human usually has?"

"What do you mean?" Helga said.

"Your ears have points, my dear," Trindol said. "Does that not seem odd when you grew up in a village of mortal humans?"

"They've always been that way," Helga said, realizing she had never before considered the shape of her ears to be odd.

"No," Peridan said.

"Would you not remember that they are odd?" Faralinda said. "Would you not remember asking your mother about them, or the other children teasing you, as humans often do? Can you remember anyone ever mentioning them to you?"

"No," Helga said. She frowned and felt her ears again, contemplating that they were indeed out of the ordinary.

"The Fay has many powers that are difficult to understand," Faralinda said. "Rarely does any spirit return to the place of its birth, where all things are malleable."

"What else is different about me?" Helga said. "Do I truly look like an elf?"

"You look *very much* like an elf," Trindol said. "But there are other, more subtle things that make you look human. Just like how you can remember two faces, but not every detail between them. Your eyes have changed very drastically; that is definite as well."

"Perhaps a half-elf," Faralinda said.

"Yes, I think you could pass for a half-elf," Trindol said.

"You all look fairly close to the same to me," Zim said. "Tall. Two legs. Clothes. Hair."

Helga saw ahead of them Bjorn's shop, covered for the winter but lit up with lights. Smoke was coming from the chimney, and there was a smell of fresh food in the air. Helga smiled, though only for a moment, when she saw Bjorn step out into the road accompanied by his brother Sven. Her smile faded when she saw that they were armed with crossbows. Behind her, two of Bjorn's sons stepped into the road, holding longbows.

XX. Poison

"**D**ON'T COME any closer," Bjorn said. "We've been warned by the countess regarding strangers like you."

"Regarding me?" Helga said, stopping in her tracks. "I am no stranger. It's me, Helga, Erling's wife!"

"Not possible," Sven said, raising his crossbow. The ravens took flight and startled him. He fired off a bolt that went uselessly into a nearby tree.

Helga shook her head. "I know I've been away a long time, but-"

"That's not Helga," Sven said to Bjorn.

"Something is very wrong here," Faralinda said quietly.

"Don't you recognize me at all?" Helga said. "I *am* Helga!"

Bjorn shook his head and touched his temples, as if in pain. "I... don't know. You look a little like Helga."

"Those are elves, you fool," Sven said.

"Since when have you seen an elf?"

"I saw one in Thruddel."

Snorre spoke up from behind them, "No, that is Helga. Has to be her. It's the same voice."

Bjorn looked at his son and nodded. "Best get those horses out of the cold."

"I have stables at my home, if it has been looked after," Helga said.

Bjorn shook his head. "Just put them in mine for now. Sven! Go find my wife. She's at Runa's." He waved away his sons.

Sven grumbled. "Fine."

"I need to get to my husband," Helga said. "Does he still live?"

Bjorn locked his eyes with her. "You must come inside."

"What? Why?"

"All that can wait, please." He looked around, taking in especially the cluster of houses behind him, in the open court at the center of the town.

"But Bjorn-"

He touched a finger to his lips to silence her, and then pointed to the rear of his house, away from the town center.

They brought the wagons around to a warm hay-lined stable and unhitched their horses. Their wagons they left outside. The contents they covered with a canvas tarp, the assumption being that few would suspect simple wagons to be loaded down with gold and silver and just left in the snow.

They entered Bjorn's big house through the back door, which Bjorn barred behind them. His wife, Svanhild, was already there, heating up water on the stove. Bjorn brought them into a dim fire-lit dining room. His sons Snorre and Stein were already there teasing each other, but they shut their mouths as soon as they caught Bjorn's grim expression.

Sven came in too, looking warier of his brother than the travelers.

Bjorn motioned for them to sit as his wife brought out hot tea.

"Well, this welcome is warmer," Helga said, holding the tea. "Closer to what I expected, at least. But I must get to my husband."

Sven gave his brother a hard look.

"He is dead, then," Helga said.

Bjorn shook his head. "No, he is not. He is well... or was made well."

Helga stood up. "Then I have to see him! Thank the Dreamer; my failure isn't so bad."

"You can see him if you want, but I would not. I would leave here, Helga."

"What?"

"I would leave here and not return if I were you."

"Nonsense. This is my home."

They were interrupted by a loud clicking from the kitchen, and a slight cry of surprise from Svanhild, who said loudly, "There's a very large raven knocking at the window! Very large and very black!"

"Shoo it away!" Bjorn said.

"No!" Helga said. "Let it in." She found Bjorn staring at her in disbelief.

"Go on then," he said, not taking his eyes off Helga.

In flapped Zim and Zul, knocking over cups and plates as they hopped on the table and began pecking at dinner scraps.

"Do you always fly away at the first sign of trouble?" Trindol asked.

Zim cocked his head. "Of course. You don't grow as old as I am by letting people shoot you with arrows."

"That's also unfair," Zul said. "Did we not help you fight the dunmen? And the wizard?"

Trindol shrugged. "I suppose you did at that."

"In fact, I think we are owed a debt for those actions," Zim said.

"Consider your feast in Thruddel," Trindol said.

"What happened in Thruddel?" Sven asked.

"It fell to the combined armies of the Northmarch and Golice two weeks past," Helga said.

"See?" Sven said. "Just like the countess told us."

Bjorn shook his head. He fixed his eyes back on Helga. "Helga... I must believe that is you. There is much that has happened since you left." Bjorn took a deep breath. "After you left, the volva – Rafnhild – she left."

"Maybe a fortnight later, if that," said Snorre. "I'd barely been home a day..." Snorre's face became downcast, and he looked at the table. "I'm sorry I left you out there."

"I don't blame you," Helga said.

Stein spoke up, filling the awkward silence. "What a wretch she was upon leaving, too. Cursed us all for cowards and heretics."

"So what happened to Erling?" Helga asked.

"Well, your parents and his mother set about to tending to him," Bjorn continued. "But of course, Elof died the day after you departed."

"Erling's father is dead? He was the picture of health!" Helga said.

"Heart gave out," Sven said. "It was a good wake. That was actually the start of the problems with Rafnhild, because she demanded to tend the body."

"And all sorts of other stuff," Snorre said. "Foul old woman wanted his body to be put in a shrine."

"Anyway," Bjorn said. "We didn't let her do anything to him and sent him off the old way, which she was none too pleased about. Said you shouldn't be burning bodies in the winter as it angers the spirits. After that debacle, she took some insult from Snorre and left. So it was your parents and Frigga that looked after him till your folks got ill."

"They weren't the only ones," Sven said. "Half the village fell sick with some sort of plague. We still don't know what."

"I should tell you," Bjorn said. "That your parents both died. They weren't the only ones. Jarl Rolfagar died, too, as did both his sons. So did Bradley, the carl. We had a lot of grief. I'm sorry."

Helga sighed, but was too out of sorts to feel real sorrow for the loss of her parents. She knew it would come later, but what she felt now as an empty sick pit of fear rumbling beneath her stomach. That was a bad fate to reveal, but she knew it would get worse, for Bjorn would not be talking to her as such if it did not.

"We were almost too busy with the sickness to think about Erling, but into town came a priestess of Nostera named Eydis, who was also a noblewoman," Bjorn said.

"She says she was," Stein said. "But why should she never leave if she was? Doesn't she have some fief to see after?"

"Aye," Sven said. "This one."

"I don't understand," Helga said.

Bjorn continued. "The priestess cured the sickness and revived many who were near death. She even healed Erling, though it was a long ritual. When he came around, he was still weak and lamed, so she took to caring for him. With his relatives all gone, we didn't think much about it.

"Months went by, and the consensus was that you had died, just as everyone had warned. People felt it was poetic justice for your arrogance, not that they weren't also sad, but... there was a great amount of bitterness at that time." Bjorn paused and looked at Sven with raised eyebrows.

"Oh, I'll say it," Snorre said. "She married Erling, and everyone was damn happy about it. I never gave up hope of your return, just so you know."

"He's always had a mind for you," Stein said. Snorre punched him hard in the shoulder.

"That's enough," Bjorn said. "What Snorre said is true. Erling is married to the countess."

"Who is Jarl?" Helga said.

"Erling is," Sven said. "He was next in line after all the deaths, which hit the Jarl's house hard, and he had a knowledgeable countess and healer as a wife, so up he went with no objections."

"At least one objection," Bjorn said.

Sven shrugged. "Bjorn objected. And Snorre and Stein." A throat cleared from behind him, and he saw Svanhild with fresh tea. "And Svanhild. And me, but I'm ashamed to say I was pressured out of it."

"I never liked that woman or trusted her," Bjorn said. "Something not right about her. Not right at all."

"Clearly, she is very powerful to cure what you call the Moss Rot, or the Mist Blight," Faralinda said. "Even I lack such a power, and I am very well-learned, but I have never heard of a priest of Nostera being able to accomplish such a thing. It's a magical affliction, not a practical one."

"Well, he was cured," Bjorn said. "And convinced his wife was a fool who abandoned him."

Helga put her head in her hands. "What do I do?"

"Don't act hastily," Trindol said. "This Eydis should be approached with caution. I do suggest we consider leaving. Your husband is cured, which was your quest in total, but getting him back, if you so desire, might be dangerous, and worse, pointless."

"What do you mean, pointless?" Helga said. "I love Erling, and he loves me."

"He did, I'm sure," Trindol said. "But you had only a few months with him, and he's had more than a few months with this Eydis, and she saved his life and proved herself to him. Made him Jarl. Maybe he will not see your return as being welcome."

"No," Helga said. "What he did to prove his love would never make me doubt him, no matter the years." As she said it, in her heart, she trembled with uncertainty.

"And what was that?" Faralinda said. "You have never told me."

"He went to the underworld and retrieved my grandfather's true name from his ghost. It was a name he told only to me his whole life, as he was a foreigner to these parts. I also bid him retrieve a lotus of the dead as a gift, and he did. They grow only on the shore of corpses, far beyond the halls of Hel. Nobody would do all that and then not love me."

"Impressive," Trindol said. "But still, that is something he proved to you. What have you proved to him?"

"Be kind, Trindol," Faralinda said harshly.

"I am sorry," Trindol said.

Helga felt tears running down her cheeks. "I have traveled beyond the world's end to find life for Erling."

"He doesn't know that," Trindol said. "And therein lies my fear."

Helga nodded. "I see now. But regardless, I did not travel all this way, and fight through so many battles, to leave my husband to a usurper uncontested."

"Ah, so it is doomed," Zim said cheerfully.

"The entire hold may turn against you," Bjorn said.

"Let them," Helga said. "No offense, Bjorn, but I'm not so afraid of the men of this town. Where were they, after all, when Thruddel was falling?"

"The countess held us here," Sven said. "Which was wise, as Thruddel is now conquered."

"Wisdom and honor are not the same thing," Helga said.

"They're bewitched," Snorre said. "Whole lot of 'em."

"We don't know that," Bjorn said.

"What makes you think that?" Faralinda said.

"There are regular guards posted up at the Jarl's hall," Bjorn said. "We haven't had that in... ever, I think. Just a carl or two is all that the Jarl's ever held as retainers. Now we have townsmen, farmers from the outlands, coming in and working for the Jarl as guards and soldiers."

"Perhaps with the plague..." Helga said.

"No, it's something else," Bjorn said. "Maybe just gold."

"Maybe not," Faralinda said. "I think we are dealing with a powerful sorceress."

Helga rubbed her temples. "It's all so strange. Why? Why Erling?"

"He's a good man," Sven said. "Was a good man, anyway. Haven't seen him for some time."

Helga nodded. "Now, the real question. Do I confront them now or after my blood has cooled a bit?"

"Whichever makes you less afraid," Trindol said.

"Then now," Helga said. "They always jokingly called me Helga the Lion. Perhaps it's time I act like one."

"I prefer Helga Ravenfriend," Faralinda said.

Helga forced a smile. "I *am* that."

"I will be your second if needed," Trindol said.

"So it is doomed," Helga said.

"Let's eat on the way," Trindol said. "I hate the idea of dying on an empty stomach." Faralinda cast narrowed eyes at him. "Not that I intend to die, mind you."

*

Helga approached the fortified hall of the jarl on foot, with Trindol and Faralinda beside her. The ravens had flown ahead, as they preferred. The stars were shining brightly above, and Helga was reminded again of their beauty in the Fay and their colors. In her mind, she felt strong and confident. She felt right. She felt like herself in the best way, though mixed with that feeling was hot rage.

The gate of the hall, which was made of bound wood and iron, was closed, and a guard was sitting in a small turret overlooking it. He saw them and stood up, fumbling for a crossbow.

"It is I, Helga Ravenfriend," she called out to the guard. "I need to see the Jarl."

"Who is it?" the guard said.

"I just told you."

"Who are the others?"

"Faralinda and Trindol, elves of Alfheim traveling with me. We have much to discuss with the Jarl. Kindly open the gate," Helga said.

The guard narrowed his eyes and pushed up his helmet to scratch his head. Helga recognized him as Gunter, one of the townsmen who was a farmer when she left.

"Gunter, open this gate."

"How did you know my name?"

"I told you, I am Helga."

Gunter gave her a funny look. "No, you're not. I'm not opening this gate for you." He leaned out of the turret and shouted to somebody on the other side of the wall. "Best go tell the countess strangers are here."

"This is quite pointless," Faralinda said. She thrust her palm at the gate, and it burst into flame, then the iron crumbled. Helga ran forward and, feeling strength pour into her, she kicked the gate off its hinges. It went flying into the courtyard and stopped sliding in front of the steps to the hall, a useless burned husk.

"You have been warned!" Trindol shouted to the handful of men in the courtyard. "Remain at your peril."

There was a slight hesitation among the few would-be soldiers. One of them turned to run, and so they all did.

"Very effective," Zim said from a perch above the door of the hall.

"Most men are cowards when you give them the chance," Trindol said.

The birds flew down beside them as they ascended the steps to the great hall. Nobody stood at the door. Helga raised her hammer to smash the door, but Faralinda lifted a hand to stop her. With a push, the doors swung inward, revealing a small anteroom with stairs going up to either side. They pushed open the next set of doors, which were ornately carved with twisting serpents, and entered a wide and richly decorated hall. In the center stood an open hearth, and a great hood of a chimney allowed the smoke of a fire to escape. Meat was roasting on spits over the hot coals.

Revelers stood up from long tables full of food and drink. A few of them were lightly armored, but most were dressed in finery fitting the lower gentry. A few men went for the spears fitted on the walls, but did not attack, backing up to the pillars of the hall.

At the far end, seated behind a table, was Erling. Beside him was a young and incredibly beautiful woman, wearing a long, flowing white dress that accentuated her breasts and revealed a great amount of cleavage. Her hair was blonde, and her eyes burned a strange color of amber. She smiled darkly as Helga entered the hall. Erling stood.

"Who is this that dares enter my hall unbidden?" he called out. His voice was deep and powerful, and reverberated in the grand hall.

"I have been called Lion and Ravenfriend, but to you, I am Helga. I am your true wife."

"Eydis is my wife," Erling said. He moved around the table and drew a longsword from his hip.

"Do you really not remember or recognize me?" Helga said, suddenly soft and wondering.

She saw a cold uncertainty in Erling's eyes.

"Foolish girl," the woman at the table said. "Even at your end, you do not see. Erling is mine and always has been." She rose and walked around the table. The torches and fires in the room darkened, but her hair shone golden with its own light, and beneath that hair, her eyes burned like coals. "But of course, I am surprised to see you return. Impressed, really. I had you pegged as a foolish woman who would continue with any stupidity if she thought she would lose face by stopping."

The flames burned lower, almost extinguishing themselves so that the only clear light in the room was coming from Eydis.

"Careful," Faralinda said. "I can feel a conjuring in this dark." Faralinda cast a hand out at a nearby torch. Blue flames and sparks leapt from it, but it did not light. Helga tried the same thing only to find her magic fizzle. Zul, flying around the room, illuminated herself, but her light likewise was being swallowed up by darkness.

Helga, suddenly remembering another dark place, thrust her hand into her pocket and withdrew the star. It lit the room up brilliantly, and Erling cried aloud and covered his eyes against it. Faralinda shouted in fright as she realized snakes were slithering around their ankles, vomiting acrid venom upon the floor. Eydis did not move, but in that piercing light, Helga could see the woman differently. Her beautiful face was still there, glowering, but within it and without it was a larger, more wrinkled face, and deep beneath all of them was the amorphous skin of a grey, sallow creature.

"Rafnhild!" Helga said aloud. She felt for her magic and channeled it into her limbs, feeling burning strength infuse her.

"Arrogant brat," the volva said. "Did your beloved ever tell you the secret of his journey? I will take it that he did not, or surely you would not have tried what you tried."

Helga was suddenly speechless and weak.

"Oh yes, Erling was quite deceitful to you, I see. You tasked him, foolishly, with finding the true name of your grandfather and procuring a dead lotus without knowing what either of those means. Erling found his way to Hel, but it was much too frightening for him to get far. I found him there, quaking, and we made a deal. I gave him the true name of your grandfather, for the dead carry with them only their own names, and I am a master of the magic of the dead, and I gave him a dead lotus. The sealing of our deal was quite... Pleasurable for him."

"You lie," Helga said. She looked to Erling, whose face was cathartic and fixed in an open stare.

"I do, often, but not this time. He did not realize what bond I had made with him until I was already material in this world. The lotus was my sign to him of our bargain, which he thought I could not collect from Midgard. His lifeforce fed me – reinvigorated me."

Helga's head was spinning, and she could feel Faralinda's hand on her arm, holding her up. The light of the star seemed to dim a little.

"I tell you this only because I would give you the opportunity to leave here alive. I have grown strong. Despite what I have done to you, I do not hate you. You were never supposed to return, you understand. Nobody from this realm can find the Water of Awakening."

"I did," Helga said, her mind coming back into sharp focus as she finally understood. She drew her sword. "I found it, and I held it in my hands, and breathed it, and I ate it, and I drank it too within the endless dream. And I have become powerful too. I will take what is mine!"

Even as Helga sprinted forward, the world shifted and changed around them, going from a high hall of golden wood to a dark, dreary place of blues and purples. The lights were coming from nowhere and everywhere, except for the star, whose white light did not seem to land on the objects in the room, and Zul, who flew desperately around, clawing at phantoms and ghosts that swirled overhead.

The volva screamed an earsplitting scream and slid swiftly to Helga's right, avoiding her first sword swing and putting a table between herself and Trindol. The crone conjured up a ball of blue fire and hurled it at Helga, who split the fire with a quick slash from her sword. Helga drew forth her own heat, hurling it at the volva, who shrank back, then twisted and sprinted to the head of the darkened

359

hall, dodging more spells from Faralinda and a few fireballs spit from Zim. The raven had to fly high to assist his mate, and the room above them became a swirl of magic as the ravens fought against more shadow creatures conjured from the void.

The volva shouted a strange word, and purple flames began swirling around her, whipping out like a cyclone, trying to lash Helga and Trindol. Helga turned the flames aside with an unburned hand and leapt, empowered by her magic, high over a table to come flying at the volva. There was a burst of black-purple fire, and Trindol and Faralinda were knocked back. Helga felt strength flow into her body as she came down on the witch.

The creature turned to the side, and the stab missed, but Helga was able to fling out her right arm and strike with her sword. The tip cut into the volva with a bitter crunch, but the volva was not phased. She turned and lashed out with a spell that wrapped around Helga like black tendrils. Helga could feel them on her legs, but they recoiled from her arms and chest as if the armor pained them to touch. She slashed her sword down, and the ones wrapping around her legs disappeared.

A bolt of magic from Zim's mouth hit the volva in the back, and she screamed in rage. Her glamor of a beautiful blonde woman was flying away from her, like thin bark curling in a fire. The image of the crone was failing too, and Helga could catch more of the creature within, deformed and inhuman. From her hands, more magic flew, lacking form but having terrible substance. Helga felt it strike her armor and burn, and freeze, and create other less ordinary senses.

At the same time, Helga pushed back with her own magic, letting her mind grab at what was being fed to it through her extra sense. Images of worms became slithering bolts of fire. Thoughts of fire became coals flying at the volva, burning her. Memories of snow became biting ice. Faralinda was standing at her side, and Helga felt waves of flame fly out. Trindol was up and slashing at some phantom the volva had conjured. Helga was throwing rocks and steel from her hands, shredding the volva. She remembered Zald bitterly, and darkness shot from her to blind her enemy. With razor clarity, she remembered Erling, and magic flowed from her, stranger and darker than anything the volva had conjured. With a terrifying scream, louder than the loudest sound she could imagine, shaking the building and searing the minds of all, the volva was shattered, and a wave of light and dark, mingled and twisting, poured upon the ground like water. Layers of spellwork shot away and pelted Helga, who shielded her eyes.

The glamor was gone, and where the beautiful Eydis had been, Helga saw some twisted being she could not comprehend, like a watcher of the Fay and a corpse and a twisted dun-man all in one. Black bile was pouring from its mouth and nose as it collapsed.

Helga did not hesitate. She dashed forward and slashed downward, splitting open its chest, spilling amorphous organs and writhing worms, then she turned the blade and severed its head. A fountain of liquid shot up and burned the table that the being had fallen onto. Thick smoke billowed up and the body melted through the wood to burn the stone floor.

Helga stood there, panting, as the colors of the room slowly returned. She held up the star, and it pulsed with new life, showing to Helga, Faralinda, and Trindol, a withered being, already fading from the world, melting into the ground and flying away like paper in a fire. It was like the lifting of a bad dream. They all stared at the rapidly decaying body. Even the guests stood agape, backing up to the doors and far walls.

"It is finished, then," Helga said.

Trindol nodded. "I don't know what that was, but I am glad it is no longer in this world."

"Indeed," Zim said. "Even I can say it was ugly. And unappetizing."

"It was a volva of the dead," Faralinda said, kneeling by the fading remains and covering her nose and mouth. "A witch who lives in the nether-realms. I think it was once a fay creature, but like the dun-men, lust for life has twisted it."

361

Helga turned and saw Erling lying on the ground. She dropped her sword, ran over to him, and picked up his head. He did not move.

"Erling, wake up!" Helga said. Faralinda knelt beside her and put her hands on Erling's chest.

"He is very close to death," Faralinda said. "His spirit is departing. I am sorry. It seems his life truly was bound to the witch."

"Is there anything to do?" Helga said.

"I don't know," Faralinda said. "I can attempt healing magic."

"Try."

Faralinda nodded and laid her hands on Erling's chest again. She said some words softly. To Helga's ears, they sounded like a song, but the notes fell flat. A subtle glow infused Faralinda's hands, but Erling did not rise.

"It is nothing I can feel or cure," Faralinda said.

Helga collapsed down to her haunches. She felt tears coming again and willed them to stop.

"Is there nothing else?" Helga said.

"Nothing I know of," Faralinda said. "I know of nothing that can give life when the spirit leaves this world willingly."

Helga let tears fall upon Erling's face. She held her breath and then removed the pouch she held at her hip. She reached into it and unfurled Tisha's package. In it was the small, softly glowing vial of dragon's blood. She opened it and was assaulted by an acrid smell.

"What are you doing?" Trindol said. "That's poison!"

"Poison and life," Helga said. "It's all I have left." She held the blood up to Erling's lips and slowly dribbled it inside. Fumes escaped from his mouth and nostrils. He remained still.

"He's gone," Faralinda said. "I'm sorry, Helga. I'm so sorry."

Helga stood and looked down at her husband. She let the tears return and did not try to stop them. They fell heavy on his face, and as she watched them, she felt like she would never stop. Then, she did stop, and sniff, for she thought he had turned his head slightly.

She waited, and nearly jumped as his head moved to the side.

"Did you-"

Helga did not have time to complete her question, for with a sudden lurch, Erling sat up. His eyes opened wide, almost in terror. He turned, and he began vomiting. Up came what seemed like buckets of green poison, which fumed and burned the floor. He coughed and retched, and more came. Finally, he sat forward and wiped his face on his sleeve, burning away the material there.

"Erling," Helga said desperately. "Do you recognize me?"

"Helga?" His eyes blinked slowly. "I... had a dream. That you left me."

"I did, but only to get something very important."

"There was... Are we married?"

"Yes, Erling, I am your wife," Helga said.

"Of course. Then Eydis..."

"She's gone. Forget about that witch."

"I'm sorry, I don't feel well," Erling said, and vomited up a puddle of glowing dragon blood.

*

The sun was shining, but it was bitter cold in Greenfeld. Helga had brought Erling to an empty bedroom in the jarl's house, refusing to take him to the jarl's apartments and the unholy marriage bed there. Faralinda had tended to his superficial wounds and spent the better part of an hour probing him with her magic sense. He was awake but not well, still vomiting occasionally or losing track of where he was. When he finally fell back to sleep, they met outside his door.

"It's curious," Faralinda said. "Very curious."

"He's alive. That's curious?"

"Well... yes, frankly. But it's not just that. The dragon blood. It seems to have revived him, but it is clearly paining him greatly."

"I was out of ideas."

"It gives us some clues into the totality of dragons, and this Garamesh, who must be of the eldest of the race – the great dragons from the mythic ages. The blood of a dragon is life *and* poison. Life *and* death. As he lives, the blood sustains the dragon. As it is spilled, it brings death, so both death and life are within his being and are always linked together. I think perhaps, once Erling had died, the poison of the blood changed its purpose and brought him back, but what remains in him, now that he returns to the living, is killing him, I think. His body is rebelling against it, but I think the poison is still working within him."

"Is there any chance of him surviving?"

"Yes, I think so," Faralinda said. She frowned.

"What is it?" Helga said.

"Do we return from the other side as we were, or as something different?"

"I'll take him any way he comes."

*

Erling slowly recovered over the next few weeks, gaining enough strength to walk, but his thoughts were often confused. His memory seemed to be missing chunks, and not just from when he was under the influence of the witch. Here and there, he misremembered something from before, or forgot something about his life with Helga. Faralinda decided it was due to his being dead, or so close to death, and that some small part of himself was lost in the spirit severing.

In those first few weeks, Helga spent her free time restoring her homestead (she supposed she was married now to the jarl, but a woman's home is a special thing that even a great estate cannot replace) and studying magic with Faralinda, who was eager to teach. More eager to teach was Trindol, but Helga was not as keen on taking up the sword, seeing that as a bit useless when she was meant to go back to being a farmwife. Still, she studied what Trindol wanted to teach, for she found that by filling up her time with practice she spent less time crying. Many people had died since she left the previous year, including her parents, and their absence was more noticeable in the silences throughout the day.

One day Erling gained enough strength to go on a long walk, which Helga was very glad to take with him. As they were walking, Helga asked him, "Do you remember when you wanted to court me?"

"Yes."

"Do you remember the task I gave you, off-hand to win my favor?"

"Yes… you wanted me to find out your grandfather's name and find you a flower."

"How did you accomplish your task?"

"I asked your grandmother. She gave me the flower too since she had already picked some."

Helga sighed. "Can you tell me the truth, Erling?"

Erling frowned at her. "I am telling the truth. Or, I think I am. It's a jumble of images. Does your grandmother hate the light?"

Helga took a deep breath. "Yes."

*

One day Helga was serving lunch in her own kitchen with Faralinda and Trindol. A thought came into her mind as she was eating, and she got up and retrieved a book.

"Which book is that?" Faralinda said.

"Just a storybook from when I was a girl," Helga said. She opened it up and saw folded in the book by a drawing of a dragon, a single black flower, un-withered. "This was the witch's sign of the covenant." She pulled it out and threw it on the ground. With a snap of her fingers, it burst into flame and was gone.

"Good riddance," Trindol said.

Helga sat down and stared at her food.

"What is the matter?" Trindol said. "I think you've made a very good meal."

Helga shook her head. "I don't think I'm a farmwife."

They both laughed. "Just now realizing that?" Faralinda said.

"Yes," Helga said. "There are many things pressing on my mind. I have this power, and I feel that I ought to develop it and make use of it. That means leaving here and being something greater than I was."

"You are already something greater than you were," Faralinda said. "Or have you forgotten the past year?"

"It's not just that. I remember so clearly the heart of the Fay. It is dry and dying. Can it be saved? What shall I do with Erling? What about my family that is yet to be born?"

"You'll have to see what happens," Faralinda said. "I've had many adventures with my husband."

"But..." Helga hesitated. "What if the things the volva said are true? Erling has an incorrect memory of it. I think in my heart I believe her, and I'm not sure what I'm feeling about that. I'm not sure what it means for the idea I had in my head of him."

"The witch was very powerful, Helga," Faralinda said. "What he did in all likelihood he did not do with his own will, as you saw."

"I can't know that with certainty. Either way, I know that he is different than I thought, and I am also responsible for his plight, for being silly and making silly demands of a man who wished to marry me."

"You did a great deal for that man," Trindol said. "I think your actions may speak more to your heart than what your heart feels in itself right now."

Helga nodded. "The poison is still in him. I can feel it."

"You can?" Faralinda said. "I mean, you can. Of course." She sighed and folded her hands. "I do not think it will ever leave him, for that is part of the nature of that substance. It is eternal."

"How long? Garamesh said it takes years to make a drop of blood. Perhaps it gives as many in life."

"I wish I could know how many," Faralinda said, frowning. "For now, his body is stable and strong. Even a handful of years is better than none, is it not?"

"Too short a time to make the life we meant to make, then."

"What you do with those years is up to you," Faralinda said.

Helga smiled. "Then I shall not be idle."

Trindol laughed. "Nor shall any of us."

The End.

About the Author

DAVID VAN DYKE STEWART is an author, musician, YouTuber, and educator who currently lives in rural California with his wife and son. He received his musical education as a student of legendary flamenco guitarist Juan Serrano and spent the majority of his 20s as a performer and teacher in California and Nevada before turning his attention to writing fiction, an even older passion than music.

He is the author of *Needle Ash,* a military fantasy series set in the same world as *Water of Awakening, Muramasa: Blood Drinker,* a historical fiction novel set in feudal japan, and *Prophet of the Godseed,* a hard-scifi novel that focuses on the consequences of relativity in space travel, as well as novels, essays, and short stories.

You can find his YouTube channel at www.youtube.com/rpmfidel where he creates content on music education (including extensive guitar lessons), literary analysis, movie analysis, philosophy, and logic.

Sign up for his mailing list at dvspress.com/list for a free book and advance access to future projects. You can email any questions or concerns to stu@dvspress.com.

Be sure to check davidvstewart.com and dvspress.com for news, exclusive content, and free samples of all his books.